THE BANDAR-LOG:
A LABOR STORY OF THE 1950s

THE
BANDAR
LOG

A LABOR STORY OF THE 1950s

Alan Reid's previously unpublished novel

Edited by Ross Fitzgerald

connorcourt
PUBLISHING

Connor Court Publishing Pty Ltd

Copyright © Ross Fitzgerald 2015

PO Box 224W
Ballarat VIC 3350
sales@connorcourt.com
www.connorcourt.com

ISBN: 9781925138528 (pbk)

Cover design by Ian James

Alan Reid cartoon by Les Tanner, used with permission
thanks to the Tanner family, Judy, Mark and Michael Tanner

Printed in Australia

For the family of the late Alan Reid (1914-1987)

Foreword

by the Hon Tony Abbott MP

Alan Reid was the Paul Kelly of his day and the Labor Split in the 1950s was probably the most far-reaching convulsion in Australian politics.

It gave birth to the Democratic Labor Party and the National Civic Council and hastened the move of Catholics to the conservative side of Australian politics. Its repercussions are still felt even today, six decades later, in otherwise unlikely alliances across the party divide.

Reid was far too scrupulous a journalist to put two and two together to get five-and-a-half. For Reid, nothing that first hand witnesses hadn't verified could find its way into his reporting or his books—or, at least, that's what he told Greg Sheridan and me when, as wannabe journalists, we visited the largely retired Press Gallery legend in the late 1970s.

Still, it seems that the gossip and the conjecture that he'd accumulated demanded an outlet—hence this book, his fictionalised account of what he thought had been happening behind the scenes but couldn't quite substantiate.

In 1958, he turned the drama he'd been covering for the previous few years into *The Bandar-Log*, a phrase he borrowed from Rudyard Kipling's *The Jungle Book* that probably best translates as "vacuous chatterers".

Twice, legal action thwarted publication. The account that was too-close-to-the-bone to be tolerated, even with the names changed, could have been lost to our literature but for the efforts of another fine analyst of Australian politics, Professor Ross Fitzgerald, who uncovered the final 'galley proofs' of Reid's work in Sydney's Mitchell Library.

In some ways, the book illustrates how much has changed for the better since our grandparents' day. Many of Reid's characterisations could be questioned, including his rather florid depiction of my one-time political mentor, B.A. Santamaria, as "demure, smooth-cheeked, his face unlined and expressionless, like a Buddha slightly less than life-size, with the same air of calm, compelling benignity."

Still, the turbulence of times long past is full of instruction for all who would understand the turbulence of our own times. It's good that Ross Fitzgerald has rescued this important insight into events that have shaped our nation.

Tony Abbott, Prime Minister of Australia.

Introduction

by Professor Ross Fitzgerald and Dr Stephen Holt

Alan Reid's hitherto unpublished novel *The Bandar-Log: A Labor Story of the 1950s* was written in the late 1950s. A highly influential journalist, Reid was then working as Canberra correspondent for *The Daily Telegraph*.

The title 'The Bandar-Log' comes from Rudyard Kipling's *The Jungle Book*. In Hindi, 'Bandar' means "monkey" and 'log' means "people". The phrase "Bandar-log" means monkey people or, more generally, any group of vicious and irresponsible chatterers.

Originally called 'The Gathering', Reid's manuscript, which highlighted the Machiavellian nature of Australian and especially Labor politics in the 1950s, was submitted to Angus & Robertson in 1958. However Dr Colin Roderick, who worked at the time for A&R and later moved to Townsville to become Professor of English, claimed that Reid's novel was libellous. As a result, the publisher withdrew its initial support.

As we explain in our biography *Alan ("The Red Fox") Reid*, in 1960 another attempt at publishing the novel, this time by J.P. Atkins of Cleveland Publishing, also failed. The printer, Halstead Press, a subsidiary of A&R, was ordered to halt the print run by its owner-company.

A celebrated legal case followed the abandonment of the printing. Atkins (who was president of the Democratic Labor Party in NSW) sued Halstead for breach of contract. However, in September 1961

Judge W.B. Perrignon of the Sydney District Court found the novel to be libellous and the claim was dismissed.

Indeed in a legal first, Reid's novel had been judged to be defamatory without having been published!

Alan Reid's *The Bandar-Log: A Labor Story of the 1950s* is a document of considerable historical significance. A roman á clef, like Frank Hardy's 1950 novel *Power Without Glory*, its characters are thinly disguised versions of actual political players.

In particular, *The Bandar-Log: A Labor Story of the 1950s* is a fictionalised recreation of the great Labor split of the 1950s. This schism in Labor's ranks began in October 1954 when its erratic federal party leader Dr H.V. ("Doc") Evatt denounced the perceived influence wielded over the party by the anti-communist Catholic activist B.A. ("Bob") Santamaria. The resulting donnybrook involved personality clashes as well as ideological conflict. The messy saga featured a diverse array of participants including Catholic churchmen, trade union bosses, state premiers, state and federal Labor politicians and assorted commentators and journalists. The characters appearing in *The Bandar-Log* mirror, with varying degrees of faithfulness, these actual participants in the Labor split.

It is sixty years since the dizzying schism of the 1950s. By now, even expert political historians would be hard put to positively identify each and every one of the actual people on whom the thirty or so characters in *The Bandar-Log: A Labor Story of the 1950s* are based.

It is eminently possible though to list the real-life models for the key protagonists in Reid's novel.

Kaye Seborjar ("Cesare Borgia") is Dr Evatt, Australia's wartime Minister for External Affairs and Attorney General who led the federal ALP from 1951 to 1960. His disastrous denunciation of Bob Santamaria in 1954 was all the more spectacular because it followed a period when Evatt had been in a pragmatic alliance with Santamaria.

Bob Santamaria appears in *The Bandar-Log: A Labor Story of the 1950s* as Carr Domineco.

Evatt's chronically unhappy parliamentary deputy, Arthur Calwell, figures in the novel as Con Fortune. However this character at times bears some resemblance to Calwell's fellow Victorian (and Catholic co-religionist) Senator Patrick Kennelly who is still remembered, sometimes fondly, as Labor's ultimate numbers man.

Kent Kerstey is Dr John Burton, left-wing theorist and former head of the Department of External Affairs under Evatt. Burton became Evatt's principal ideological adviser when the federal ALP swung to the left after Evatt monstered Santamaria.

The fifth, sixth and seventh leading political players are the Sydney-based federal Labor firebrand Eddie Ward (Gilly Hoskin); a character resembling the young future Labor prime minister from 1972 to 1975, Gough Whitlam—who became an MP in 1952 (Tom Bannion); and hovering in the background the long-serving Liberal prime minister Robert Gordon Menzies (Alex Pope) who was in office from 1939 to 1941 and from 1949 to 1966.

The eighth and final essential character in *The Bandar-Log: A Labor Story of the 1950s* is the hard-bitten political insider Macker Kalley.

Alan Reid himself is the model for this character although the name clearly indicates a desire to pay homage to the author of that exemplary handbook for rulers, *The Prince*, Nicolo Machiavelli.

In real life Reid, a would-be Labor insider when Joseph Benedict ("Ben") Chifley led the party in the 1940s, resented the emergence of John Burton as Evatt's fierce anti-Santamaria conscience. Reid's anti-Burton animus coloured his day-to- day journalism in the 1950s and spilled over into the unfriendly depiction of Kent Kerstey in *The Bandar-Log: A Labor Story of the 1950s*.

The interplay between these eight main characters propels the narrative in Reid's novel.

The Bandar-Log: A Labor Story of the 1950s is very much a novel of its time: extremely male-centred and, with the exception of the Santamaria character, Carr Domineco, almost entirely Anglo-Celtic. As such, it reveals much about the nature of Australia, and in particular of the Labor Party in the 1950s.

It seems to us that it is well and truly time to publish Reid's hitherto suppressed novel. This is because Reid's depiction of the struggles between the federal Labor leader, Dr Evatt, and the tenacious Catholic activist, Bob Santamaria, is surprisingly relevant today. This is especially so given that Santamaria later became the first great political hero and mentor of a young and receptive Tony Abbott.

Professor Ross Fitzgerald and Dr Stephen Holt, May 2015

Ross Fitzgerald and Stephen Holt are co-authors of *Alan ("The Red Fox") Reid*, published by NewSouth Books, Sydney. It was shortlisted for the 2011 National Biography Award.

Acknowledgements

In bringing this book to fruition, I would like to thank my publisher Anthony Cappello and his excellent and extremely patient editor, Michael Gilchrist.

Thanks also to the diligent and helpful staff of the Mitchell Library at the State Library of New South Wales, Sydney—especially Jan-Amanda Harkin, May Ly and Craig Vail who provided access to the original manuscript and galley proofs of Alan Reid's unpublished work *The Bandar Log*.

I would very much like to acknowledge the assistance of Alan Reid Jr and the family of the late Alan Reid and also the family of the late Les Tanner—whose portrait of Alan Reid (which originally appeared on the front of *Quadrant* magazine) graces the cover of this book.

Anusha Rutnam digitally edited the old, complicated and arcane typeset manuscript into a readable format. Paige Hally then meticulously re-typed the manuscript from Alan Reid's original. Terry Moriarty's fact checking and proof reading was most helpful. Nathan Lentern painstakingly entered all the various corrections and edits into the new manuscript. Thanks also to Michael Wilding and Carl Harrison-Ford who have, for years, been encouragers of all my literary works, both fiction and non-fiction. Gerard Henderson of The Sydney Institute provided helpful advice on the structure and cover of the book. As always, Anne Henderson was very supportive.

I deeply appreciate that Prime Minister Tony Abbott found time in his extremely busy schedule to write a foreword about Alan

Reid, whom Abbott knew when he was a young journalist and Reid was toward the twilight of his long career. Thanks also to Murray Cranston in the Prime Minister's Office. Laurie Oakes, a colleague of the late Alan Reid, wrote an insightful postscript for which I am most grateful.

Most of all, I would like to thank my friend and fellow scribe, the Canberra-based historian and biographer Dr Stephen Holt who has been a source of great encouragement and wisdom in all matters concerning the late Alan Reid, including co-authoring our book *Alan "The Red Fox" Reid*.

The publisher has attempted to locate the holders of copyright for the material contained in this book. If anyone has been overlooked, they should contact the publisher.

Ross Fitzgerald
Redfern, Sydney,
May 2015

CHAPTER 1

Macker Kalley liked the pleasant, sensuous feeling of the sun on his back through the thinness of his shirt. He was relaxed and contented, as he always was when he worked in the open, in sunshine, with his mind moving in rhythm with the slow, sure tempo of his hands. He straightened himself, helped the calf to its feet, and watched while it staggered off, bawling, to the high rail fence that separated it from its fretting, bellowing mother.

Kalley was a slender, wiry man, with a hard, lined face, covered now with a stubble of beard. His hat was battered and shapeless, mottled dark around the brim and the edge of the crown with dust grained into grease. He took it off to wipe the sweat awkwardly, with his bent forearm, from round his eyes; the hair beneath, a faded, mousey brown, had receded in the front from a forehead that bulged slightly at the sides. His nose was thin and bony, curving in above a narrow, tight-lipped mouth. He was wearing heavy, broken working boots, coated with hardened mud. Drill trousers, wrinkled, were stained grey in spots with old, caked oil and dirt. The faded shirt had patches of sweat under the armpits, faded in colour where the sweat had dried, and inner patches dark with new wetness.

Kalley opened the gate of the yard and the calf went scrambling through. A man sat hunched on the top rail of the fence: "For a city man, Macker, you're a good hand with cattle."

"I ought to be, Lacey. I make my living from them."

Lacey Cottrell chuckled. White-haired, with washed out blue eyes, he had the heavy body of a man who had once been strong and nimble. "The politicians you work for wouldn't like hearing you say that, Macker."

"That line's always good for a laugh" said Kalley. "But they never apply it to themselves, only to their fellow politicians." Gathering the gear he had been using, he moved with an economy of effort, as though there was upon him a compulsion to reserve his energy.

"You won't stay a few days longer, Macker?" Cottrell asked from the top of the fence.

"Can't be done, I need to be back in the city tonight. The Party Leader is speaking."

"That Seborjar", said Cottrell. "The Party Leader. He must be an interesting fella." His voice was wistful. "You're lucky Macker. Knowing all those big shots. Seborjar and Con Fortune and Gilly Hoskin and the rest of them. You meet Presidents and Prime Ministers. To me, they're only names in the papers."

"I'd trade my cattle for yours, Lacey," said Kalley, lightly.

"I don't think you would." said Cottrell who squinted up at the sun. " I've a couple of jobs to do. I'll see you back at the house."

When Kalley reached the homestead, it was empty. He went through the kitchen, along the cool passageway to his room. It was tidy but anonymous, with the unlived-in appearance common to the bedrooms kept for guests on working farms. He took his razor and a change of clothing from his bag, and, barefooted, padded to the bathroom.

Would he trade his cattle for Lacey's? The face looking back at him from the mirror, craggy and lined, was secretive and withdrawn. He was forty. More than half his lifetime was behind him. "I still don't know the answer to that one," he thought.

Kalley had been sixteen when, years ago, Con Fortune had picked him up from the highway. He must have been an amusing, quaint sight to Fortune, as he got into the car out of the driving rain, which had plastered his long, uncut hair close to his skull. Hatless and without an overcoat, he had been standing there for over an hour, gesturing for a ride with patient stoicism, while under his breath he cursed the cars as they passed him, unheeding, until Fortune had offered him a ride.

When the lad had seated himself in the car, Fortune fumbled in the glovebox and produced a rag. "Here, get some of the water off you, boy," he had said.

Silently Young Kalley began to dry himself.

"Where're you going, boy?"

"Next town."

Fortune eyed him with an amiable but guarded uncertainty that was characteristic, in those workless days, of those in jobs against those out of them.

"What for?" asked Fortune.

"Looking for work." Outside the tyres hissed cheerfully on the wet highway while the windscreen wiper clicked to and fro.

Inside Fortune's car it was warm and dry.

"Got any folks, boy?"

"Yeah," said the boy. "Dead."

"Sorry." said Fortune softly.

"It was a long time ago. I've been living with an aunt. She died last year."

"What have you been doing since, boy?" asked Fortune.

"Keeping alive," said young Macker Kalley.

They had talked like this for miles, with Fortune doing the questioning, the boy replying with terse, laconic seriousness, as though he was struggling to be a man long before the years would permit him to be one. As they neared the next town, Fortune offered him a job. It was an impulse, based on sympathy and humanity. Sympathy and humanity, Kalley was to find later, were part of his boss. But as the years moved on, Fortune yielded less and less to impulses such as these. Without realising what he was doing, Fortune trained himself with rigour to forgo the humane impulse, and to weigh the value he was to receive against any possible kickbacks.

"It's not much of a job," Fortune had told the boy. "You'll be a kind of messenger for me. The money's small, but it'll keep you going. Until you find something else."

Young Macker was silent.

Fortune grinned. "Don't you want to know anything about what you'll be doing?"

"It's a job," the boy replied with the fatalism that he had acquired, even then, as his defence against a world that rarely had time or pity to spare for the weak and vulnerable.

The job had led by a long path to the bathroom where Kalley now shaved himself.

He stared at the stubbled face confronting him in the glass. The razor was pleasant on his skin, taking away the itch of the grey tufted beard, and replacing it with a smooth tightness of skin. It was hard for a man at forty to remember a boy at sixteen, even though the man had been the boy. The boy back there in the car with Fortune, his mind a confused jumble of half-formed thoughts and impressions, was as much a stranger to the person he had become as any other chance-met lad of sixteen would be to him now.

Fortune in those days had been a small-timer, on the fringe of politics; just breaking in. He had influence with a few minor union leaders who found his advice shrewd and profitable. He had a quick and ready compassion for misfortune, either self-produced or the outcome of harsh circumstance and hence undeserved. He found jobs for boys who had been released from reform school. When, as they often did, they quit those jobs to resume the life of a slum gangster or petty thief, he did not upbraid them. Fortune was not a reformer at heart. If men sought his help, he gave it. If they did not want it, he did not thrust it upon them. There was no harshness in his judgments. A man to Fortune was what he was. Provided a man's activities were outside politics and so offered no threat to his own ambitions, he was uniformly tolerant. The consequence was that he did not lose friends. Once he formed a friendship it usually lasted. He helped the old and the lonely, the sick, the maimed, the homeless and the timid. These became allies, mostly humble, ineffective allies, but loyal ones whose unquestioning adherence was not without value to him when he started to climb within the Party. As time went on he acquired other allies, more important ones. These were won to his side by harsher qualities. Fortune slowly discovered in himself a gift for organisation, and for exploiting the hates, grievances and jealousies of his fellows. And a capacity to talk impressively and to enjoy, like a drug, the impressiveness of his own words.

As Fortune moved up in the Party, Kalley went up with him. He had not been interested in politics at first. But watching and listening to Fortune he realised that politics was the study of deep, quick-changing currents in human societies that men, if they were clever, could divert to their own ends, and ride on, or drift with, to destinations that gave them the things they wanted—money, sometimes luxury, and the power that they all seemed to crave, but for differing reasons. "Politics—the study and manipulation of men—are the only hobby fit for a grown man," Fortune used to preach.

Gradually Kalley had been absorbed into the life that went on round him. He started to read voraciously, everything he could lay his hands on, sitting up far into the night in the cheap room that Fortune had found for him on the outskirts of the city. He began haunting the State Legislature, an old building, with an air of decayed, senile grandeur, seamy and shabby in its appointments, as though reflecting the shabbiness of the generations of humans who had inhabited it. He came to know many of the politicians, from carrying messages to them from Fortune. They accepted him as Fortune's emissary, and, flattered by his listening, enigmatical silences, they talked to him patronisingly but revealingly. They boasted to him of their qualities and shrewdness, using the shorthand of half hints, innuendoes and the occasional unguarded revelatory phrases that are the *lingua franca* of politics. He learned the stagecraft of public proceedings, and the management that was put into them behind the scenes.

"Look, Macker," Fortune said. "Don't get tied into this racket too early. It eats you up." He looked thoughtfully at the boy. "Go out and get drunk occasionally," he advised.

"I do," said Kalley.

"You're growing up, Macker. How old are you?"

"Twenty-two."

Fortune smiled good humouredly. "All right. You're old enough. Go out and get yourself a girl occasionally."

"I do."

Fortune's face softened. "But don't overdo it. I grew up the same way as you—alone and unsupervised, with a widowed mother who couldn't spare the time to look after her children properly because she was fighting, to the exclusion of everything else, to keep food in front of her kids and a roof over their heads."

His eyes clouded with the effort of memory. "The cheap little dames who'll climb into bed with you for the sake of a few kicks from a gin bottle and a laugh, and short minutes of hot forgetfulness. They're not all there is in the world, kid. If you're going to stay in this political racket, you've got to have an island. To escape to. To stay sane." He looked reflectively at Kalley. "I have a nice wife, Macker. She isn't interested in politics. I have kids, nice kids. They help me stay human. When I walk into my home, I'm on an island where nobody is trying to slip a knife into my back."

He laughed. "I'm talking a bit like a Dutch uncle. But there's sense in what I'm saying." He regarded Kalley with appraising eyes. "You've got a cold-blooded streak in you. I'd hate to have you for an enemy when you really find your feet in this racket. Stay human—and sane, kid. Get yourself a nice girl."

A smile twitched the boy's lips. "I'll try, Con," he promised.

"Try," scorned Fortune. "A good-looking kid like you ought to be able to pick from a dozen. If I was fifteen years younger, and not married, I'd collect 'em for you. Now get out of here and let me do some work."

As Kalley reached the door, Fortune's voice stopped him. "And don't forget, Macker, keep your private life separate from politics."

"I will, Con," the boy promised.

That talk had all been long ago.

Kalley finished shaving. He ran his square hand with the blunt-tipped fingers over his chin, feeling for roughnesses, and then padded across the bathroom to turn on the shower. That was one promise he had kept. He had married a nice girl and his personal life remained remote from the one he had in politics.

He had met Anne at a tennis club he had joined after he had been ill. The doctor had looked him over carefully and asked him his hobbies. "Reading?" the doctor said. "It's not enough. Take up some sport that'll keep you out of doors. There's nothing wrong with you that exercise and fresh air won't cure."

Kalley partnered Anne that first day at the tennis club. She was something new to him, a short, chunky girl, with wide shoulders like a boy, and cool, level grey eyes. She was always cheerful and kind. She liked people, trustingly, and when they hurt her, or disappointed her, she found brave excuses for them. When he met her family, he began to realise that the jungle he lived in was only one part of the world. Anne's father was a tall, slow-speaking man, an architect, who would never go far in his profession because he had a simplicity and easy generosity that made the chase for wealth and acclaim somehow pointless. But he had ability and talent and integrity, and he had given Anne and her mother a secure, poised background that Kalley had never known.

Kalley found the father and daughter puzzling in their unexpected candour. Anne's mother he understood better. She had once been ambitious for her talented husband, but had tired under the strain of trying to dissuade him from his habit of constantly stepping aside, uncomplainingly, to make room for less gifted but more determined rivals. She was without bitterness, but the material failure of her marriage had edged her temper with a polite impatience.

Neither parent had wanted Kalley for Anne. Kalley had worked hard to remove their intuitive suspicions, using the art and dexterity of the shrewd, calculating mind that he was now aware of as a powerful weapon. He impressed them. At times they liked him. But they could not forget that he belonged to a different environment, as alien from theirs as a foreign country, and they feared for their daughter and her future happiness. But when Anne had insisted on her love for Kalley, they were married.

"And it's worked," thought Kalley, standing under the shower with the pinpoints of water, cold and sharp, chilling his sun-warmed back. Anne and he had been married for fifteen years. Young Anne, short and chunky like her mother, and with something of her mother's directness, was twelve. "The two Annes—they're my island of sanity."

Kalley had accepted that part of Fortune's advice. His work and his private life were kept apart. Anne and he did not discuss politics in the real sense of that complex word. He chattered to her about the trivia—the humour, the pathos, the comedy in which politics abounded. But he did not attempt to put these isolated pictures together, so that she would see the pattern as he saw it—luxuriant, dangerous, lethal, shot through occasionally with an inexplicable streak of unselfishness and altruism, sometimes so big as to be incomprehensible, sometimes small but satisfying and warming, as it had been when Fortune, long ago, had offered a boy work out of kindness and compassion for his jobless loneliness.

Anne had met Con Fortune and a few of Kalley's associates. The meetings had been brief and casual. "She's a nice girl," had been Fortune's comment. "But keep her away from politics, Macker."

Only twice had politics intruded into the protected home. The first time came after Kalley had met Lacey Cottrell. Kalley had unexpectedly discovered the fascination of trout-fishing while he was delayed in a mountain town during a mission for Fortune. Lacey had come cantering his horse along the bank of the stream Kalley had been fishing. He reined up to talk with Kalley. The men had liked each other. Lacey invited him to his farm. The visits were repeated, and Kalley fell into the habit of staying with the old man at weekends and during vacations. He liked to work around the farm, and found that he had a talent for handling stock. A bad steer or horse that would put another man over the fence would stand quietly for Kalley, trembling and nervous, but tractable under his soothing hands.

The men had known each other for some years when Lacey suggested that Kalley should become his partner. The old man's washed-out eyes were without self-pity. "I'm getting old," he told Kalley in the cool of the evening, as they rocked, smoking in chairs on the wide verandah. "Too old to work the farm properly. My wife's dead. I've no kith or kin. You like this kind of work, Macker. How about it?"

"Thanks, Lacey," said Kalley. "But I'll have to ask Anne." He had motored back to the city the next day and told Anne about Lacey's offer.   Her strong small face was calm. "Darling," she said, "whatever you decide will be all right with me. I want only a happy husband."

"I'm always happy on the farm," said Kalley thoughtfully. "Doing that kind of work. There must be peasant blood in me somewhere. I suspect I'm just a hick at heart."

Anne's eyes were quizzically amused. "You suspect, darling. But are you sure?"

"Of course I'm sure," said Kalley uneasily. He had a feeling that Anne was secretly laughing at him.

Anne said gently, "Can you get politics out of your blood? They're a virus. I've heard you say that. You know they're in your blood."

Kalley rubbed his chin. "But other men have had the virus, too. They got out. Or were forced to leave. They were unhappy for a time. But they got over it. And lived."

"I know, darling," said Anne. She put her hand on his arm.

"I'm not trying to influence you. I'll go wherever you go. And if you're happy I'll be happy. But my feeling, Macker, is that you'll be happy only for a time. Then you'll start looking at the cattle. Dumb and heavy and stolid. You get a lift out of being in the swim. Knowing what's going on. Being part of history as it happens. Macker, you like the feeling of influencing events, even if you influence them only slightly."

"Maybe," responded Kalley. "I've seen the desire to influence events corrupt others, without them ever knowing that they were being corrupted. Maybe I'm corrupted, too?" Anne laughed. "That's a very big word to describe a very little failing, darling. A very human, understandable failing. But there's no hurry. Think over Lacey's offer for a week, then make up your mind."

A week later he told her he had decided against it. "You're right Anne. I don't think I would ever be happy away from politics." They had not discussed it again.

Lacey had accepted Macker's decision without argument. He found a partner, a silent, pleasant man, with a family who lived in a house Lacey had had built on his eastern boundary. Only occasionally did Kalley wonder whether he had made the wrong decision.

The second time politics entered their home was when the newspapers were gleefully forecasting the imminent fall from power within the Party of Con Fortune. For a time, Fortune had lost his grip. His elder son, a boy of seventeen, to whom Fortune was passionately devoted, had died of leukemia, unexpectedly and tragically, after a collapse from health into a hopeless sickness.

The only uncertainty was precisely when death would come. Fortune had become disinterested and apathetic. He had no deeply based foundations of unshakeable strength within the Party, upon which he could rest secure while he slowly recovered from his personal shock. He drew most of his power from his flair for constructing, out of a conflicting mass of prejudices, rivalries and cross-interests, alliances that endured until he had secured what he wanted, after which they sometimes disintegrated. His political empire was based almost wholly upon his energy, his personal drive and ingenuity, and his deft facility for intrigue. While those qualities were temporarily missing, his enemies within the Party set out to drag him down.

Anne had been reading the morning newspapers. She put down, thoughtfully, the last of them. "Macker, what happens to you if Con Fortune loses his job?" she asked.

Kalley shrugged. "Who knows?"

"But, darling," she persisted, "that's no answer. What happens to your job?"

"What will be must be." Kalley was watching the clock. He had arranged to meet Fortune at the State Legislature. Kalley looked at her. "Anne, this political racket . . ." He hesitated for a moment. "It's a strange life. It's not like any other. No-one can be sure when he gets up in the morning and faces his mirror that he can afford to nod his head. Metaphorically speaking, it might drop off. His political throat might have been cut in the night. From ear to ear. Possibly by someone he viewed as his best friend or his staunchest ally. It's a racket in which you have no friends, only acquaintances. And allies and enemies."

Anne said, "Are you serious, Macker?"

"I'm deadly serious. It is not like the life you knew before you married me."

Anne looked at the paper in her hands. The headline screamed: *"Fortune faces Party revolt—likely to go"*. In a small voice, Anne said, "Hardly a sure foundation for a family man to build his future on."

"There's no future in this racket. Only a present and a past." Macker smiled, and it was as though a light had been switched on behind his hard, lined face. He looked younger when he smiled, and the deep clefts running from his nose to the corner of his mouth smoothed away. "Don't worry, darling. I'd get another job. It mightn't be as good as this one. Certainly not as interesting, possibly better paid. It'd probably have to be outside politics. I've enough enemies in the Party to ensure that if Fortune falls I fall with him. But remember, darling, it was the way we decided to live when we turned down Lacey's offer. No regrets, sweetheart?"

"No regrets," said Anne uncertainly. She watched him as he picked up his hat. As he bent to kiss her, she flung an arm around his neck, pulling his face towards her. "No regrets, darling. But . . ."

"But what?"

"I hope Fortune wins," she said.

Fortune had won, and it had been largely Kalley's doing. Patiently he worked, hour after hour and day after day, seeing people; making promises of future political pay-offs. "Fortune's been only temporarily out of the ring—he's back fighting as he never fought before," was his theme. Kalley lied, cajoled, flattered, wheedled, blackmailed and threatened. He slyly revived old rivalries and promoted new ones. He set old allies at each other's throats with manufactured rumours that contained the grain of truth that Kalley knew was essential to their success. He stiffened the resistance of Fortune's wavering henchmen, whom he led to believe—wrongly—that Kalley's industry was merely the reflection of the reviving energy of the man he worked for.

Kalley's relationship with Fortune had changed subtly through the years. Fortune had grown used to turning to him for advice. Fortune had found that Kalley could shrewdly assess the trend of events. He was an able, discreet and persuasive negotiator. His judgment of the motives that drove men along the paths they followed were often sounder, as Fortune knew, than his own. Fortune was inclined to optimism; Kalley to pessimism. Fortune had expansive, generous moments when he expected the best of his fellow men and was disappointed when they produced their worst. Kalley expected the worst and was pleasantly but unenthusiastically surprised when individuals proved they had strengths and ideals that would endure under stress.

Fortune had wanted Kalley to go into national politics, thus moving out of the world in which he lived his political existence as the employee of a Party chieftain. "Just say the word, Macker and I'll see you get a good job. In the real big time. Giving the orders instead of taking them."

Even now, towelling himself years later in Lacey's big, draughty bathroom, Kalley could see the puzzlement in Fortune's face as he refused.

"No thanks, Con. Not for me. I'm one of the ruled, not a ruler.

That's the way I like it and that's the way it is going to be."

"What don't you like about the prospect of ruling? The responsibility?" Fortune had asked.

"It isn't that, Con," said Kalley. "I'm not afraid of responsibility. But I do fear corruption."

Fortune said sharply, "You know this racket as well as I do. A man does not have to be crooked. A lot are. You can't blame 'em. They've never had real dough in their lives. And here it is being presented to them on a plate. They take it. I don't like 'em taking it any more than you do. But there's nothing much you can do about it. It happens."

"I wasn't thinking of that kind of corruption," said Kalley. "There are other kinds."

"Such as?"

"Can't you see that when men become rulers—even would-be rulers—they start to change?"

"Sure," said Fortune. "But not all of 'em. I can show you some who have never touched a dishonest penny in their political lives."

Kalley smiled thinly. "You've a one-track mind, Con. You only think of dishonesty in financial terms. And your years of living in a political machine have blunted your sensitivity. To you, financial dishonesty is not a crime or the product of immorality. It is something that is inevitable. You accept it as in your everyday life you accept a common cold—as a nuisance, but an inescapable one."

"What other way is there to accept it?" asked Fortune good-humouredly. "Unless you are going to shut your eyes to the facts of life and pretend we can all be angels. But no-one has to be crooked unless he wants to be, Macker."

"I'm not so sure about that, Con," said Kalley, thoughtfully. "I don't think that in politics a man can be other than crooked. He can be financially honest, and still be dishonest."

"You're playing with words, Macker."

"There are more subtle forms of corruption than financial ones," Kalley said. "Forms that are beyond the mental vision of all but the rarest of rulers."

"And I'm not one of those rare characters?" challenged Fortune.

"No, Con. You're not."

"You're wrong," said Fortune. "To me they're always men."

"No," said Kalley. "Individually they are. But not in the mass. To you they're digits, units to be added up or subtracted at polling day. You've no feeling for the people who make up that mass. You use them scientifically. You're like an engineer at a dam. You control what goes through the sluice gate. You turn it off and on, almost at will. You're like the engineer, powerless against overwhelming floodwaters. Your floodwaters are the rare occasions when the masses go their own way crazy: when they temporarily smash through all your checks and controls."

"OK Macker. I have this blind spot. But you haven't. Therefore why not become one of the rulers? You can afford to become one."

Kalley said, "You're missing my point, Con. Deliberately, I suspect. What I am saying is this: I've seen big men, intellectually honest, high-principled men, corroded and eaten away by the lust to rule — to be a political boss. I don't want to go the same way. And always at the back of my mind is the fear that I would succumb to the corrosion as swiftly and completely as any of those at whom I've sneered for succumbing in the past. I'm afraid, Con. Afraid to expose myself to the temptations they face."

Having completed his toilet, Kalley now felt good. He dressed in his neat, dark suit, deliberately selected to give him protective anonymity. He wished that he could stay with Lacey a few days longer. The two Annes were enjoying themselves while he was away. They phoned him last night. They were having a mild shopping spree. But

Fortune had been insistent that he needed Kalley at tonight's meeting. "Seborjar has something on his mind; he wants to see me before the meeting," Fortune had said.

Kalley thought that his forecast, made when he fought Fortune's battle within the Party after Fortune's son had died and Fortune's spirit for a time seemed to have died with him, had proved correct. He had then told Fortune's wavering supporters that his boss would recover his grip, that his loss of interest was only temporary. Now Fortune was up there, right back on top. Only Seborjar, and possibly Carr Domineco, were more powerful in the Party.

Kalley opened the bathroom door and went down the corridor to his bedroom, his thin, lined face harder than it had looked with the masking stubble of beard. He packed his bag with the neatness of a man who had spent half a lifetime living out of a suitcase.

Lacey was waiting for him in the kitchen; "A drink before you go, Macker?"

Kalley said, with affection, "No thanks, old-timer. I'll get rolling."

Kalley's car was in the barn. It was a sleek job, low-slung and powerful. The old man patted it. "There's dough in your kind of cattle, Macker," he joked.

"It's a living," said Kalley who shook hands with the old man. The engine turned over smoothly, with a high-pitched whine. Kalley let in the clutch gently.

The track onto the main road was rough in patches. Kalley took it slowly. On the tarmac he opened out. The miles started to drop behind.

He thought, "It'll be good to get home with the Annes. They'll be glad to see me."

Kelley wondered what Seborjar, who hated Fortune, wanted to talk with him about.

Chapter 2

At sixty years of age, Con Fortune was thin, tall, with a keen, pleasantly ugly face, from which black wiry hair above the high forehead was brushed straight back. His hands were long, slender and shapely. He was conscious of them and their mildly mesmeric power, and used them, like a conductor, to emphasise what he was saying. He liked people to mistake him for a musician, though he could not play a note, and did not like music. For some reason, which he could not explain even to himself, it flattered his vanity that he was seldom identified by strangers for what he was, a professional politician. He dressed well, in expensive, beautifully-cut clothes, conservative, but somehow conveying a hint of bohemianism that was quite false. His manner was brusque and assured, with a surface of good humour, like the smoothness of paint over a hard, rock base.

Men's minds, and the complex ways in which they worked, fascinated Fortune. Men were the raw materials of his trade. He never tired of studying them, and he found the study rewarding. It enabled him to use their strengths and weaknesses to further his own ends. He believed that he was passionately devoted to the Party to which he belonged. He had told himself so often that the Party's policies and ideas were the only correct policies and ideas that he was no longer capable of questioning them. He never doubted the Party's teachings nor its value to the nation and to the voters. This gave him a single-mindedness that was a strength. But though he would have denied any such suggestion indignantly, his devotion to the Party was derived from habit and temperament rather than intellectual conviction. He could have given the same devotion to the Party's opponents. Basically, he was not interested in ideas—only in people.

His preoccupation with humans left him insensitive to his surroundings. He seldom noticed whether they were ugly or beautiful. He had grown used to the comfort that had entered his life increasingly as he grew older and acquired financial resources. He could not have reverted to the hard living of his youth without missing the ease of his present mode of life. But he would not have missed the refinements that came with comfort. His home reflected his indifference to anything but comfort. It had been furnished expensively under the supervision of an interior decorator with a nation-wide reputation. But the things that best expressed his personality had been added timidly by Lottie, his wife, or by himself.

The Christ in the entrance hall with the bared, bleeding heart, had been put there by his wife. It was a cheap, gaudy print. Under it a wax light, like the fat, chopped-off stump of a candle, burned night and day in a thick red glass bowl. Fortune never noticed that the print and the redly glowing light were out of place in the suave, fashionable hall. They were there, familiar. He accepted them.

Fortune considered himself a religious man. He was not particularly concerned with the moral teachings of his Church, but he was concerned about the religious symbols that were associated with it. These, by their material presence in his home, gave him the comforting reassurance that he was religious without the need for self-examination. They gave him a sense of purpose that strengthened him on the rare occasions when his confidence in his own ability to shape the outcome of events momentarily flagged. He was like a superstitious gambler who has faith in his judgment when he backs a horse, but likes his judgment reinforced by ownership of a lucky rabbit's foot.

Mostly he left to his wife the provision of the religious emblems in the house. But it had been he, not Lottie, who in the week after his son, Tony, died, had nailed the Crucifix to the wall in the dead boy's room, and lit beneath the impaled Christ the light in the red bowl that was the copy of the one in the hall below, and ordered and set up a *prie-dieu* under the Crucifix. Until then it had been a boy's room, furnished with a narrow bed cheerful under the striped blaze of a Navajo blanket cover, its shelves with the rows of battered-backed books, its photos, its bright easy chair, and its carelessness of comfortable arrangement. The religious trappings took away the boyishness. Michael, Fortune's surviving son, kept away from the room. To him, it was no longer Tony's room, but a stranger's. It gave Michael, who was normally healthily unimaginative, a feeling of distaste. Lottie went into the room occasionally to dust it, but she did not stay. Fortune went there to pray.

Father York, a gaunt, awkward, stooping man with a blunt, astringent tongue, who was Fortune's confessor, did not approve of the room's dedication to the dead boy. "It's unhealthy, Con," he protested. "Bring life back into it. Use it. Otherwise it's a cancer in the happiness of your home."

Fortune shook his head stubbornly. "I go there to pray, Father. For the soul of my dead boy."

"Rubbish," snapped the priest. "You go there to brood, man. Over the loss of your son, and over your own wrongs, and over the ruthlessness you encountered when his sickness and death made you vulnerable to your opponents." The priest's face softened. "Con, you're a good hater. You don't need an altar to keep your bitterness alive."

Fortune's face darkened. "It is easy for you to take that attitude. Tony wasn't your son. You did not sit hour after hour with him, day after day and night after night, knowing that he was going to die, and knowing that he knew he was going to die. Praying, humbly, for the miracle your mind tells you can't come, and yet your faith tells you is possible." His voice tightened. "And all the time men like Carr Domineco are working, coldly, without pity, to ruin you within the Party while you are distracted with personal grief. Why shouldn't I be bitter, Father?"

The priest said sharply, "Don't be a hypocrite, Con. Have you ever shown mercy to a political enemy?"

"Yes," said Fortune. And he believed himself, remembering generosities to defeated foes, and closed his mind to the knowledge that his creed was to be pitiless with any enemy who was still unbroken and unsubdued.

The priest watched Fortune's face. He said, sadly, "I repeat, Con. That shrine upstairs. It is not a shrine to your dead son. It is a shrine to your hate."

Fortune said, bleakly, "You wouldn't have me forgive and forget, would you?"

"Yes," said the priest.

"I'm not that good a Christian," admitted Fortune.

When the priest had gone, Fortune went slowly up the stairs, opened the door of the dead boy's room, and knelt at the *prie-dieu*. The Crucifix, with its hanging, brass Christ, was splayed blackly against the white-painted wall. Fortune tried to think of dead Tony, of the boy's nervous half-laugh, of his tense young face, of his affectionate ways and his odd shame that he could not duplicate at school the cleverness that his father was said to show in politics. But Tony was a shadow, hard to focus on. It was Carr Domineco who was real, who had substance, and was flesh and blood reality to Fortune as he knelt there. He remembered the night just before Tony fell ill that the two men had come to his home, Domineco and big, wedge-shaped Jasper Danke, of the loud, booming, confident voice. Danke was Domineco's bodyguard. Domineco, though fearless intellectually, was physically timid. He feared any suggestion of violence. He was frightened by the fierce anger that sometimes gripped arguing men. In the past, men who knew his weakness had used it against him shrewdly, storming at him in synthetic rage. Now he kept Danke with him always, as a shield against this fear. Danke was his mouthpiece in any discussions that might become heated.

Fortune had answered the ring at the front door, and had been surprised when he recognised his visitors. Domineco and he had been feuding politically within the Party for years. Fortune had ushered the men into the sitting room where Lottie had been sewing. He had introduced them and Lottie, fluttering, had gathered her sewing and left the room.

When the door closed behind her, Fortune dropped the thin pretence at urbanity he had maintained for the brief moments of his wife's presence. His eyes narrowed. He said, "What do you two vultures want?"

Danke smiled without humour. Large and dominating, he said in his truculent, assertive voice, "I take it you want us to come straight to the point, Con?" as though he were issuing a challenge.

"Why not?" Fortune asked curtly.

Fortune did not like Danke. He did not like his overbearing manner. He did not like the slavering, uncritical, adoring obedience with which Danke stooged for Domineco. Most politicians had obedient, unquestioning stooges. "But Domineco's are different from the usual stooges," thought Fortune. "There's something about him that brings out the groveller that's in every man. The rest of us have stooges, followers and supporters. They'll do anything for us while we're on top, or while they believe in us, or because they like us. But they want something back. A payoff. Or flattery. It's a two-way traffic. But with Domineco it's one way. He gives nothing, but takes all. He doesn't have supporters, he has devotees. To them he is without blemish, infallible: a Pope in a lounge suit, a modern saint with a God-sent mission." But despite his distaste for Danke, Fortune did not let the man anger him: he had long passed the stage at which he expended rancour needlessly on unimportant people, even when he disliked them. Danke was merely Domineco's faithful watchdog. If the dog was kicked, the master went unhurt.

Domineco was silent. He sat in his chair, demure, smooth- cheeked, his face unlined and expressionless, like a Buddha slightly less than life-size, with the same air of calm, compelling benignity. He was very small. But everything about him was exquisitely finished. The bones under the rounded plumpness of his flesh were light and delicate. His face, olive-tinted, was round and sleek, under a retreating, tight-fitting hairline. The mouth was unexpectedly prim, though full-lipped. His hands, which he held clasped in front of him, were sensitive and well-shaped, but tiny.

"Con," said Danke, with booming heartiness, "I'll put it to you straight. We"—he paused and nodded in the direction of the motionless Domineco—"Carr and me, we think that it is about time we—that is, you and us—had a pow-wow."

"What about?" said Fortune.

The big man made a conciliatory gesture. "About burying the hatchet, Con."

"Why?" said Fortune. "The only place I'd like to bury the hatchet is in your skull. Yours and Carr's."

Danke shrugged. "So you don't like us. So what? You're entitled to feel that way if you want to. But you've got to be realistic, Con. You know that."

"How realistic, Jasper?" asked Fortune.

The big man leaned forward in his chair and tapped Fortune on the knee confidentially. "I'll give you the picture as we see it, Con," he said. "You and us"—his thick thumb waved towards the silent Domineco—"we've been battling against each other for control of the Party for years. You are strong in the Party, but you haven't got control. Right at this moment we are even stronger, but we haven't got control. We've got a lot of power, but neither you nor we have the tight control that we want." He hitched his chair nearer to Fortune's. "But together, Con,"—his voice was persuasive—"we can own the Party."

Fortune tilted his chair back. He thought, "What's Domineco up to? What's coming? Where's the gimmick?" He was alert, like a ratting terrier, but he was outwardly relaxed, his eyes half-closed and reflective.

"So?" he asked calmly.

Danke was encouraged. He stabbed at Fortune with a blunt forefinger. "We're putting all our cards on the table, Con. Being completely frank." His eyes flickered to Domineco. "That's so, Carr, ain't it?" he appealed.

"That's so, Con," Domineco confirmed, the little man's voice was unexpectedly deep and musical, cultured and carefully modulated. He was said to be as fine and fluent a speaker as there was in the country.

"Look, Con." The big man leaned forward eagerly. "I'll tell you how it looks to us. There's a fight on now in the Party. The right wing—us—versus the left wing. We know you don't belong ideologically to either side. You're a middle-of-the-road man. You're in the position that you could join either side without losing face."

His tone changed subtly. Fortune felt the insinuated threat before Danke voiced it. "Better join us, Con. You've been in the Party a long time. You've not always been consistent. But you've been consistent in one thing. In Party fights, you've always ended up on the winning side. We're the winning side, Con." His voice had a triumphant note.

"We're winning now. You can't beat us, Con—nobody can. Better join us."

"You almost convince me," Fortune answered calmly. His mind was racing. He thought, "If you're winning, sport, why bother telling me? Why not go on and win?" He took a cigarette from the box on the small table beside him. "But I'm like the man from Missouri, Jasper. I have to be shown." He looked at Danke thoughtfully. "What makes you so positive yours is the winning side, Jasper? At the risk of being corny I point out there's many a slip 'twixt cup and lip."

"There'll be no slip, Con," said Danke. He struck a match, leaned across and held it for Fortune's cigarette. "We practically own the Party now." He sounded very confident, Fortune noted dispassionately. "The cup's at our lips. All we have to do is drink. We're the winners. Con."

"Thanks," said Fortune. He exhaled and held his cigarette, watching the ash grow. "But somebody might knock the cup from your hand, Jasper. Someone like me. Or Gilly Hoskin. Or half a dozen others. Perhaps the Leader—Seborjar himself."

"Seborjar?" Danke was scornful. "What's happening to your spy system, Con? Kalley on vacation? Seborjar is backing us. He's holding the cup steady for us."

Fortune ignored Danke. He turned to Domineco. "That right, Carr?"

"That's right, Con." The little man inclined his head gravely. "And you know me, Con. I don't lie."

Fortune felt his stomach muscles contracting. It was as though he had been punched. He believed Domineco. Domineco did not lie. The little man prided himself on his punctilious honesty in a world where lying was as natural as breathing. Fortune knew that he should say something, anything, to hide the shock of the news that Seborjar, who disliked him and had been trying secretly to undermine him within the Party for years, had joined his dedicated open enemies. "Hell, where does this put me?" he thought.

"Surprised, Con?" the little man asked gently.

Domineco was trying to gauge his reactions. Fortune knew that. It helped him recover his self-control. "Yeah," he said. "I admit it. I'm surprised. That's quite an alliance—you and Seborjar."

"We both want something," the little man explained unsmilingly.

"Yeah," said Fortune. "Seborjar wants to rule the country—and he doesn't care how he gets to do it. You want control of the Party—and you don't particularly care how you get control." There was tension in the room. The three men had the serene wariness—an air of being simultaneously fearless but cautious—that men who are expert in handling dangerous animals so often have. They were all three schooled in handling that most unpredictable of all animals, man. They appeared relaxed, yet at the same time they gave an impression of careful watchfulness. When Fortune rubbed his long forefinger horizontally across his top lip, and kept rubbing, Danke glanced at Domineco. Both men knew the gesture. They had seen it at Party rallies, at committee meetings, at Party functions, on innumerable occasions when Fortune was disturbed.

At last Fortune said, "You two have a boa constrictor by the tail, you know. Sooner or later, it'll writhe round and crush you." Danke said with loud confidence, "Seborjar?" He boomed his hearty, insincere laugh. "Don't worry about us, Con. We'll handle him."

Fortune said, his lips twisting wryly, "If you can handle Seborjar, you're the first in Party history who can."

He was trying to think out the implications in what Danke and Domineco had said. He did not like Seborjar, and Seborjar did not like him. So far Seborjar had not been sufficiently strong to break Fortune's power within the Party, but an alliance between Seborjar and Domineco would change the balance of power in the Party. Hitherto

Seborjar had been hostile to Domineco, and Domineco had been working for Seborjar's overthrow as Party Leader. Together they were probably stronger than any combination Fortune might be able to build up against them. What attitude should he take? How frank were Domineco and Danke prepared to be? How frank should he himself be? Should he speak his mind? Or stall for time to think around the new development? Or should he react as his instincts told him to react, and tell them to go to hell and to take Seborjar with them?

Domineco said, politely, as though aware of the thoughts racing through Fortune's mind and making time for him to sort them out, "I can understand your doubts, Con. Seborjar is not a man to be trusted."

Fortune said, with exaggerated, angry sarcasm that he did not try to hide, "Brother, that is a masterpiece of understatement." Seborjar's record over recent years was common knowledge among the Party Leaders. Seborjar had been for a time the great progressive—allied closely with the authoritarians of the Party's extreme left wing, almost but never quite Marxist, against everything in the present system, the champion of the underdog and the oppressed. Then he had found that that line was getting him nowhere, so he had crossed to the Party's moderate right wing, outwardly linking up with such as Fortune, and verbally flaying his former allies. Now he was moving across to the authoritarians of the Party's extreme right wing.

Seborjar was versatile, Fortune thought sardonically. And Seborjar had more than versatility. He had the knack of survival. He had the gift for making himself the nation-wide symbol of things about which large numbers of people felt deeply—sufficiently deeply for even the more sophisticated of them to shut their eyes, in some cases deliberately, to his obvious duplicity in a mass orgy of wishful thinking.

Seborjar was a symbol of radicalism and the universal brotherhood of man when he was running with the Party's extreme left wing. Civil liberties, and the freedom of the individual, when he was with the moderate right wing. "Probably selfless patriotism and 'My-country-'tis-of-thee' now he is with the authoritarian extreme right wing," thought Fortune.

The silence lengthened without awkwardness. "Domineco's clever," thought Fortune. "He's not trying to panic me into a hasty decision that I might repudiate on reconsideration. He genuinely wants me with them." Aloud, Fortune said, "You've got Seborjar. Or you think you have." He could not resist the gibe at Seborjar's untrustworthiness. "Why do you want me?" Knowing the answer to his query, and knowing that they knew that he knew the answer, but determined to satisfy himself beyond question.

Danke said, with heavy humour, "We like you, Con. That's why we want you. We like you."

Domineco intervened. His eyes, impersonal, speculative, black, fringed with long, silken eyelashes, fixed on Fortune gravely. "We think we can take over control of the Party without you, Con. That's our judgment. We can muster considerable support. Seborjar can whip up mass support. He can appeal over the heads of the Party Leaders, who distrust him, to the mass of Party members who don't really know him, and who, because they don't, will rally to him because to them he stands for something. But you carry some big guns, too, Con. You're liked. You're trusted. You're an old-timer. You've lots of friends within the Party, particularly among the old guard who are always influential in a crisis. You're a fighter."

Fortune said, tonelessly, "Thanks for the build-up." Domineco smiled briefly. "Spare me coyness, Con," he said. "It's not a build-up. It's accurate. You know that." He tugged at the lobe of his small, well-shaped ear. "I'm being quite honest with you, Con. I'd sooner see you stripped of any influence or strength you have within the

Party. Frankly, I don't like you. I don't trust you. And I don't like what you stand for, politically. You are too tolerant of left wing influences within the Party. You have a horror of the tight discipline that a modern State demands. I'd like to forget about you, Con, and push ahead without including you in our plans." His voice was calm and dispassionate. "But I can't ignore you, much as I'd like to. You're too big, too well entrenched in the Party. Without you, and over your opposition, we can probably win. With you, we can certainly win."

Fortune said, reluctant admiration in his tone, "Fair enough, Carr. That's putting it right on the line. But what about Gilly Hoskin? He's not going to like this."

"Hoskin?" Domineco's round, childlike face, with its Buddha-like, blandly knowing innocence, was impassive. "Hoskin does not worry us, Con. Hoskin can lead a fraction but not a faction. His power within the Party is too narrowly based. He lives off out-dated prejudices. A class-consciousness that has no real appeal nowadays, except to a few disgruntled individuals and an odd intellectual or two. And off the loyalties and greed of the gangster element, with which Hoskin, ironically—for I believe he is scrupulously honest personally—has got himself inextricably involved. Hoskin is an inferior Jack London in an age that has forgotten London because his undisciplined, unorganised emotionalism is an anachronism in a modern society."

He clasped his hands across his neat little paunch. "No, Con. Hoskin can be a nuisance. An almost indestructible nuisance, but a nuisance, not a danger."

Fortune nodded slow agreement. It was a workmanlike assessment with which he could agree. At moments like this Fortune realised why Domineco retained his almost hypnotic sway over his followers. The little man thought on a bold scale. And his Party record showed that he was prepared to act as boldly. Danke interrupted, unable to check his impatience. He growled, "Well, Con. What do you say?"

Fortune said, with contempt, "Take it easy, Jasper. I'm thinking."

Danke was irritating, but he was small-time, the organising muscle for Domineco's planning brain. Domineco was the man who counted. Fortune found himself admiring the little man, in a detached way, for the quality of his mind. He disliked the man and what he stood for. But Domineco was not to be brushed aside. He believed in things genuinely, with conviction and without humility. He had a moral basis. Within the context of his mind twisted with fears and forebodings for the future spiritual welfare of man, he was rigidly honest. He had no self doubts, only a sombre certainty in the rightness of the courses he so implacably and devotedly pursued. He was a back room Hitler, with Fascist sympathies superimposed on deep religious feelings, and the surface mildness of an Oriental sage.

Domineco said, casually, as though it were an afterthought, though Fortune knew that the timing was calculated, "We are, of course, Con, prepared to pay a price for your support. A high price."

Fortune said, bluntly, "What price?"

Domineco placed his fingertips together. His eyes, black and compelling, fixed on Fortune. "We believe—and Seborjar believes: that, we know, is why he is with us—that within a reasonable period, probably by the next elections, we can put him in this country's Number One job. We have the organisation to do it. It's good, efficient, and growing."

In the street outside a motor-car horn sounded and kept on blaring. Young voices were raised gaily. Fortune heard a girl's name called. Danke glanced up annoyed, but Domineco continued without seeming to notice.

"Only the voters' suspicion of Seborjar's radicalism—his possible sympathy with Marxism and Marxists—has kept the Party out of power. Alex Pope, who leads the rival Party and who now governs the country, is an impressive figurehead. I don't underestimate his appeal to the voters. But his first-class tongue conceals a second-class mind. The voters are beginning to realise his considerable limitations. They're uneasy. They'd like a change. Once we tie in with Seborjar it will be a guarantee to the voters of his anti-Marxism. He should get to the top."

The little man paused. Taking a handkerchief from his breast pocket he dabbed at his lips tidily. His movements had the same smooth delicacy as his tiny physique.

"You still haven't stated the price, Carr," Fortune reminded him.

Domineco looked at him without expression. "You can go up right to the top with Seborjar, Con. If we can get him there—and we think we can—the Number Two job is yours."

Fortune fought to keep control of his excitement. This was really big-time. How he would like it. Con Fortune up there, with the biggest. The boy from a poor, underprivileged home controlling what a nation should do, think, and say. It had always been a possibility, he knew as he made his tortuous way up in the Party. Lincoln had gone from a log cabin to the White House. Con Fortune had had his beginnings in a dilapidated, broken-down shack, in a grimy working-class district that was the urban equivalent of Lincoln's backwoods cabin. Even now, high as he had climbed within the Party, there was something unreal about the position. Yet what was being offered him was not a pipe-dream. It was possible. He knew that. Domineco knew it. There were no limits to what he, Domineco, and Seborjar could do in partnership.

He could no longer sit quietly. He got up from his chair and prowled restlessly round the room. The two men followed him with their eyes. Fortune's forefinger was rubbing continuously against the smoothness of his upper lip.

He could do so much up at the top, for the ordinary, decent people, who got pushed around and were trampled and were vulnerable, easily hurt, in the rat race that was modern life. They did not want much—just peace, security, jobs, and some trust in the future for themselves and their children. He would be able to help to get them those things.

There would be others up there with him at the top. Domineco, with his streak of mysticism, his fanaticism, his determination, at whatever cost in effort and tireless energy, to save mankind from the abyss of Godless Communism which, to his mind, ever yawned before it.

And there was Seborjar, brilliantly mad, pursued by a sense of historic destiny, driven on by the atheism which he intellectually accepted but subconsciously rejected, into striving to find history books which were men's recorded memories of the immortality that his religion denied him. Untrustworthy and eccentric. Once his immediate comforts were met, attractively disinterested in money or those whose only qualification was that they possessed it. Gifted. Fearless. A fighter who in pursuit of his aims never flagged in courage or enduring, dogged tenacity. Subtle, a self-deceiver, who could with equal honesty identify his views with any group who at any given moment were in a position to advance significantly his limitless ambitions. Forever making clumsy mistakes that damaged him in the voters' eyes, and so debarred him from power. Yet possessed of enormous recuperative powers, able to pluck some advantage from the very clumsiness of his errors; and to use them to become a living, tangible symbol of things in which people believed deeply. Freedom of speech. Freedom of the individual. The rule of law. Mouthing tirelessly old, but valuable, catch-cries. Haunted by the lust for earthly power and a desire for immortality in the memory of man, as though he needed these compensations for his lost belief in a God whom he had rejected.

Fortune leaned against the window, and gazed out into the darkened street. There was little traffic. It was a quiet street—a quiet neighbourhood. The people in it lived family lives. They were mostly in their houses now, reading, listening to the radio, watching television, or just talking, while the youngsters, heads bent under a circle of lamplight, were doing their homework or were already in bed.

Fortune swung round. The two men were watching him expectantly.

He said, quietly, "Sorry. But I can't be with you."

Domineco's smooth, round face was unmoved. "That final, Con?"

"That's final."

Domineco did not argue. He stood up, a plump little man, who should have been comical but was not, and whose tiny stature should have lacked dignity, but had it. But Danke snorted and demanded, truculently, "Why, Con? Why?"

"Domineco knows why, Jasper," Fortune said. "I don't like you or your faction. The ruthlessness of your tactics. The way you demand uncritical obedience. Your intolerance. Your dedication. I don't like what you stand for. In particular, your authoritarianism."

Domineco said, quietly, "You know what this means, Con?"

Fortune shrugged. "I can guess," he said.

Without emphasis, Domineco said, "We shall destroy you, Con."

Fortune laughed. In a voice in which there was good humour he said, "If you can, Carr. You've been trying to do it for years. And I still live."

Domineco said, "But this time, Con, we shall have Seborjar helping us."

After the men had gone, Fortune put out the lights and went upstairs. He undressed and stood at the open window, looking out into the night, thoughtfully smoking a cigarette. From behind him in the darkened room, Lottie's voice asked sleepily, "What did those men want, Con? Was it anything important?"

Fortune said, "Only some business they wanted to talk over with me, Mother. Go to sleep."

He heard the bedclothes rustle and Lottie's soft, "Goodnight, Con."

His mind was still working. He tossed his half-smoked cigarette down on to the lawn. "Young Tony will be angry," he thought, unaware of what was shortly and tragically ahead for the boy. Tony had the job of mowing and keeping tidy the front lawn. He hated to find butts of cigarettes and burned-out matches on the grass.

Con felt no resentment against either Domineco or Danke for the bluntness with which they had made their offer of an alliance. He had himself been involved in dozens of such deals, sometimes successfully, sometimes as Domineco and Danke had been tonight, without producing the results he wanted. It was rather flattering that Domineco had to come to him. Domineco would not have wanted to. He did not like Fortune's politics. Domineco's approach was a tribute to Fortune's strength in the Party. Well, he was going to need all of that strength, with Seborjar and Domineco's forces ranged against him.

He moved to his bed and slipped between the sheets. From the single bed alongside him he could hear Lottie's light, regular breathing. She was asleep. It was a long time before he, too, fell asleep.

The following day Tony was sick. Fortune was not alarmed. Boys had their ups and downs. He ran his hand over the curly, tousled hair black against the whiteness of the pillow, and said affectionately, "Be careful of yourself, kid," and left for his office. There was a Party conference coming up. Ballots were to be held for several important Party positions. He was worried. It was a challenge to his ingenuity and skill in manipulation.

Seborjar and Domineco were a formidable combination, but

not unduly so. Not to Con Fortune, he thought. He enjoyed such challenges, he told himself.

So things went on for a week. Then Tony suddenly worsened. There were consultations between the doctors. Other doctors were summoned. They stood grave-faced around the bed of the boy, who had gone waxen coloured and still, so that to look at him tore at Fortune's heartstrings and a lump came to his throat, and his eyes misted.

Carter, Fortune's family doctor, told him the diagnosis, his voice heavy with sympathy and helplessness. "How long?" asked Fortune, incredulously. His hands were trembling. He could not master the twitch at the corner of his mouth.

"Three months, Con," said Carter. He raised his hand in a tired gesture. "Perhaps a little longer. Perhaps a little less. We don't really know."

"That's impossible," Fortune said flatly. His eyes were wild and glistening. "Look, Doc. You doctors. You don't know everything. Maybe there are other doctors. Get 'em. Wherever they are. I've got friends. They'll see they get here. Cost doesn't matter. I've got money."

Carter said, with sad finality, "To pretend to you would be cruelty, Con. No doctor can do anything. He can try. But he can't do anything. Your boy's in God's hands."

"I don't want him in God's hands," said Fortune, excitedly. "I want him here. Alive and well, not sick and dying."

From then on the weeks had been a nightmare to Con Fortune. Strange doctors came while he and Lottie had huddled together in the living room downstairs. The room was no longer friendly and home-like, but an unfamiliar purgatory. The doctors had gone upstairs with Carter, assured and masterful, only to come downstairs with sympathy that was half professional, half genuine, replacing their assurance.

And as they went through the door, Fortune cursed them silently for their helplessness, knowing how irrationally he was behaving, even as he did so.

The nights were torture. The boy liked to have his father with him in the room, talking, as though his father could repel what was waiting out there in the darkness. Fortune would reel out of the sick room in the dawn when the boy was either asleep or in the torpor of exhaustion, unshaven, red-eyed, with the tears streaming down his face, and his mind shrieking, "Why, God, why?" Lottie, grey-faced, grey-haired, shapeless in her plain pale blue wrap, would be waiting for him, swaying in her chair with exhaustion and grief. They would huddle briefly together, as though trying to find some solace against their sorrow in the humanity of their closeness. Then Lottie would go into the sick room to take over Fortune's vigil while Fortune threw himself on a bed to stare, sleepless, at the ceiling, his mind a bewildered, racing, aching thing, until he was called back to the sick room when the boy awoke.

Then the boy died. Domineco sent a wreath. It had not penetrated Fortune's dulled mind that while he had been obsessed with Tony, Domineco had tried to destroy him politically in the Party. He had held the card that accompanied Domineco's wreath in his fingers; across it was written in a sharp, clear hand, "May God bring you, your wife and family solace in your tragic bereavement—Carr Domineco." Fortune felt imprecisely, without putting it into words or conscious thought, that a death like Tony's left little room for the violent emotions of hate and enmity.

Only gradually, as he recovered from the shock, did it start to penetrate into his mind that while he had been preoccupied he had been nearly destroyed within the Party. Only Kalley, cold, withdrawn, outwardly controlled and insensible to the normal emotions that swayed other men, had at one stage stood between Fortune and political obliteration. But once realisation started to penetrate Fortune's mind, it penetrated swiftly.

Previously Domineco had been a man he did not like, following policies he did not like. Fortune's emotional approach to the man now changed. He could appreciate the wisdom in what Kalley said when Kalley told him with the air of tired detachment that Kalley affected, "Look, Con. You can have your dislikes in this racket. Dislike is a cold thing. You can dislike someone and think at the same time. But you can't hate and think simultaneously. Hate is violent. It warps judgment, and it destroys the man who yields to it."

On his knees before the Crucifix in dead Tony's room, Fortune knew that Kalley was right. But he could no more prevent himself wallowing in the consoling luxury of his hate for Domineco than an addict could leave alone the drug that he knew was harming him, but which gave him ineffable pleasure. Fortune had not told Kalley. His hate was a secret vice. But it was there, enriching him, he felt, in a sense that mere dislike could never do. Domineco had become an obsession. He could hide the obsession, and pretend to Kalley that politically he was the old Con Fortune, impersonal, capable of standing aside from his own emotions, critical and objective. But the hate was there all the time. Even now it was crowding the memory of Tony from the room, consolingly filling the vacuum created by his death with its living, vital quality, so that the image of Domineco was clearer in Fortune's mind than Tony's.

Fortune crossed himself and got to his feet. Even now Domineco did not know the intensity of his hatred. Fortune had concealed it, with the practice of years, from Domineco, as he had from Kalley.

Seborjar was no longer important to Con Fortune. Domineco was. He had met Seborjar shortly after the funeral. Seborjar had said, "A terrible blow, Con." He seemed moved. "If I had known." He shook his head sadly, "I would not have joined your enemies at the Congress."

Fortune's eyes glistened wetly. He had not yet recovered his self-control. He said, thickly, "Thanks, Kaye. But it didn't matter. I survived."

"Yes," Seborjar said. "As it happened, Con, you survived."

With his voice gruff, as though consciously trying to cover his feeling, he added, "But it wasn't my fault you survived, Con. It was despite my efforts. I repeat my regrets." He walked away a few strides, then returned. "Give my condolences to your poor wife, Con," he said. Con noticed there were unshed tears in the Leader's eyes.

He had not told Kalley what had taken place between the Leader and himself. Kalley was too cynical, too unfeeling about such things for Fortune's taste. Kalley would have cast round for an ulterior motive; he would have praised, in his cold, grating voice, the quality of Seborjar's histrionic ability. Perhaps Seborjar had an ulterior motive, and was acting a role. Fortune preferred to think that Seborjar had been sincere. He felt warmer towards the man, and his new tolerance for Seborjar deepened the hate he held against Domineco.

He glanced round Tony's room, bowed towards the Crucifix, and went out, closing the door behind him.

Downstairs, Lottie was waiting for him, patiently, her face anxious as it often was nowadays.

She said, gently, "You look tired. Con. White and drawn. Why don't you rest for a while?"

He said, "I think I shall, Mother. But if I drop off to sleep, wake me early. In plenty of time for dinner."

She complained, "You don't have to go out tonight, do you, Con?"

"Yes, Mother," he said absently. "There's a meeting. Seborjar's speaking."

Seborjar had asked to see him before the meeting.

What did Seborjar want to see him about, he wondered.

CHAPTER 3

The music was fast and brassy. The spotlight picked out the entertainer on the dance floor. Her feet were motionless, her shoulders still, and with her head flung back, her face was contorted with artificial abandon. Her belly writhed rhythmically in time to the music, as though it had a sensuous life of its own. The darkened room was packed, thick—with the smell of closely-jammed rich and the sickly perfume of cosmetics and powder warmed with wine and humidity. There was prolonged rattle from the drums. Then silence. The dancer's writhing's ceased. She stood for a moment, her spangle-covered pelvis thrust forward, her legs, strong, rounded, wire-muscled, apart and gaping, her face smiling, young and avid beneath her make-up. The lights went up.

"Jaysus," said Brock Medway. "She's got tits on her like pumpkins."

He was a young-old man, prematurely grey-haired. His shoulders pushed against the unpadded cloth of his cheap suit. His hands were soft, but big and square-tipped. He had thick wrists of exceptional muscular strength. He had taken off the blue-tinted rimless glasses that usually gave him an air of scholarly seriousness. In his unlined face, his lips were full. Mark Payten noticed that was as though he schooled his mouth consciously to tight severity. But since he had been drinking, the force of his features had disintegrated, like a crumpled mask without the backing of firm flesh and bone.

As the evening progressed, Medway had become more excitable. He grinned continuously, his mouth loose and moist. His behaviour grew coarser and louder. His expression alternated between vacancy and a cunning that Payten found rat-like in its shifty furtiveness, at once fearful and aggressive

During the day, Payten had listened unenthusiastically to Medway declaiming against the evils existing within the Party, the immorality, the drunkenness, the dishonesty and the laziness of a section of the Party's hierarchy. He thought, with tolerant disgust, "Another phoney. Just like me." He consoled himself that he, at least had the humility to acknowledge his own frailties and to wish occasionally that he could shed them.

Aloud, Payten, relishing his own malice, said, "Brock, your slip's showing."

"Whose slip? What slip's showing?" Medway demanded.

"The same slips as mine—hard liquor and soft women," said Payten.

Across the table from them the loose jelly of Joe Lilley, whose buttocks dripped off his chair and hung pendulously, in obese suspension, shook with laughter.

"Mark," he said appreciatively, "you'll be the death of me yet." His voice had an ingratiating quality that contrasted with the authority of his manner.

Lilley represented himself as belonging to the "earthy" wing of the Party. He had a hog-like love of food and wine. Years of indulgence had bloated his once strongly built body without, as yet, weakening the animal-like healthiness of his powerful constitution. He had a flair for organisation and a willingness to accept, within the Party, tedious jobs, unwanted because of their lack of glamour. He had a gift for building these jobs with patient doggedness into positions of influence. To get such jobs he was prepared to humiliate himself to an extent to which other men, with more pride, would not go. As a result he had been insulted and derided, even by his close political associates, for so long that to treat him in this manner had become a fashion. It came as a surprise to his intimates when they found out, as they sometimes did, that gross and pig-like, Lilley had an intellectual background. His father had been a professor. His mother was a minor poet, a bitter woman, with a tongue barbed with fishhooks and a taste for radicalism. When young, Lilley had shown aptitude for academic work. But only rarely did anything he said reveal his heritage of culture and the scholarly training of his youth. At Party conferences he was a slick, showy, intelligent and convincing speaker, with a demagogic touch. He spoke in a slangy, racy style that the lower ranks of the Party members admired as democratic. Most Party Leaders sneered at him and his ambitions, and were contemptuous of his abilities. But over the years he had wormed his way tenaciously into their ranks. Unmarried, he had a contempt for women, whom he viewed as chattels. He was a man of two environments—the Party and money-making—and they were so inextricably mixed as to appear as one to the casual eye. He preached the doctrine of justice for the workers, and mistreated his own employees. He had a moon face, with heavy dewlaps. His eyes were as expressionless as tiny, black pebbles stuck in suet. Payten looked at his bulk across the table and thought, "You'll die in an uglier fashion than from laughter, my friend."

Payten was dark and alert, with aquiline features that had an actor's mobility. A lawyer turned politician, he had a reckless, gibing tongue that brought him a reputation for sardonic, wisecracking unreliability. He could seldom resist the temptation to mock, even at himself and his pretensions. Aloud he said, "Why should I do the hangman out of a job, Joe?"

Before Lilley could retort, Medway said, thickly, "I'm a married man. With kids. I'm no womaniser."

Payten felt faint amusement. He was not used to men who worried about justifying or excusing themselves outside politics; "Relax, sport. You're among friends, you're not trying to impress your church-going voters."

Medway had graduated to politics from the waterfront. The nightclub atmosphere was new to him. He liked it. But he knew he should not be attracted by it. The tougher, harsher conditions of the waterfront district which he represented were his bread and butter. His drunken mind struggled for some means to express this. Apart from themselves, the diners were dinner jacketed, the women in expensive evening gowns. "Puffs" said Medway, belligerently. "Cream puffs. That's what they are." Though he spoke loudly his words recoiled from the hum of conversation and the soft music of the band, which had started playing again.

"Look at that one." Medway pointed derisively at a woman dancing on the floor. She was tall and slim, with a quiet, tired, grave face. "Naked to the navel. And as flat-chested as a boy." He made a smacking-noise with his tongue. "But that other one. Tits on her like pumpkins." His hands waved excitedly.

Lilley chuckled. "Take it easy, Brock. Don't get too loud." He winked at Payten, his eyelid flickering across the flatness of his eye as fast as the strike of a lizard's fly-hunting tongue, so that all Payten received was an impression of blurred speed. "Would you like to meet her, Brock?" His jowls trembled with the kindly, fat man's jollity that left untouched the calculation of his eyes. He nodded waggishly towards the curtains through which the dancer had disappeared. "The titty one—the dancer."

Medway's face was eager. "Can you fix that, Joe?" His mouth was slack and wet.

"Sure," said Payten before Lilley could reply. "Joe's a fixer. From way back. He fixes for all the visiting out-of-town firemen. First he fixes them with unlimited liquor. As much as they want. Free. Then if they display any interest, he fixes them with women. Free." He laughed. "But it isn't really free, Brock. Sooner or later you pay for it."

The smile still on his face, but resentment edging his voice, Lilley said, "You make me sound like a brothel keeper. Is that kind, Mark?"

"No, it isn't kind," said Payten cheerfully. "But it's damn accurate." He was enjoying himself. He knew that he was violating the fundamental political rule never to offend needlessly. But what the hell? Being offensive to Lilley was a pastime in which he could indulge light-heartedly.

Lilley was a realist. He was not a sensitive man. Unlike Seborjar who never forgave anything, who cherished grievances over some slight, real or fancied, for years. But Lilley was too shrewd to bestow upon himself the unrewarding luxury of resenting a verbal insult. How was it somebody had described him. The perfect politician—all hide and no conscience. Payten chuckled to himself. That was a clever definition, he thought.

Medway said reproachfully, "That's no way to talk to Joe, Mark." He wagged his head solemnly. "Joe's okay, Mark. A good Joe."

"You'll learn, son," said Payten, with offensive patronage. "Christ," he thought, "I feel good." Liquor did strange things to him. He went up and down like a yo-yo. At the moment he felt on top of the world. He was savouring his own cleverness, rolling it round his mind, like someone rolling a liqueur round his palate. Lilley was a trader in men's weaknesses who knew that all were weak, and that drink, women and soft living—particularly soft living—were the most common of those weaknesses.

A trader who knew that these commodities could be dealt in profitably.

Payten raised his glass with a flourish. "We ought to drink a toast,

Brock. You and me. To Joe. To Joe, the perfect seducer. Any mug can seduce a woman, but Joe specialises in seducing men."

Lilley said peevishly, "Lay off, for Christ's sake, Mark. All I'm trying to do is give Brock a good time."

"Sure," said Payten. "Like you try to give a good time to anyone who someday might be able to do you some good." The drink tasted sour in Payten's mouth. His mood changed. Suddenly he found himself thinking of Eileen, his wife, the woman he lived with but hated. It was years since Eileen had walked into his office, carelessly left unlocked, one night when he had excused his absence from home with the plea that he was working late. She had surprised him with his secretary, flushed, tousled, half-drunken and half-naked. It was the culmination of a series of affairs which Eileen had either suspected or actually discovered and forgiven. The girl, young and defenceless, had cried as she dressed, her fingers fumbling with nervousness, shame and shock, while his wife had watched, her eyes blue, hard and contemptuous. When the girl had gone, Eileen had said, "This is the end, Mark." He said, torn between hate and regret, "You're leaving me, Eileen?" The woman was big and heavy, her youthful shapeliness buried under the thickened hips and fleshy thighs. But she was still possessed of the keen, hard mind that had first attracted Payten to her years ago, when they had both been law students. She regarded him with a coolness under which he smarted.

"No, Mark, she said. "We've grown daughters. They'll be finding husbands soon and having children of their own." She regarded him thoughtfully. "You're a weakling. A glib, slick-talking weakling—an ageing goat who'd like to think himself insatiable. You possess ideals that you're incapable of ever shedding, but which you haven't the strength to try to live up to. No, I'm not leaving you. I'm too old to start a new life. Particularly when it could mean wrecking my daughters' lives. I'll stay, Mark. But from here on, our lives are separate. You're crow-bait, Mark. Rotten meat off which your carrion friends—Lilley and his kind—get their living."

Payten looked across the table at Lilley. Already the fat man had forgotten his irritation in the delights of the meal. He was forking food into his mouth steadily, relishing it. His earlier exhilaration gone, Payten thought, "Eileen was right. I'm crow-bait." He wished she had been wrong or he had the toughness to prove her wrong. Lilley, if he had not bought him, had at least made the down payments. Payten could not live within his income. Nowadays he relied increasingly on Lilley's racetrack tips or on his advice as to how to pick up a quick profit through stock exchange investments. Even on the occasional cash loan, sometimes repaid, sometimes not, when funds were low and he was hard-pressed.

Tonight Lilley would pick up the bill when they were leaving. Lilley invariably picked up the bill. In a strange way he was honest. He wanted future favours. He bought them. Payten could—and had—done him favours both within the Party, and in his money-making, through contacts in Federal and State administrations. Medway, on the other hand, could do nothing for Lilley, as yet. But some day he would be able to. In his own home territory, Medway was climbing the Party ladder. He was looked upon as a promising man. Unless he slipped in that long climb upwards, he would, in years to come, be in a position of power and influence. He had already formed connections and contacts, small but growing. It was upon their growth that Lilley counted. He cast his bread of small-time pandering to his fellows' weaknesses upon the political waters, knowing that some, at least, would come back more than tenfold.

Medway said, slurring his words, "Look, Joe. Can you fix it? For me to meet her? The dancer?" The room seemed hotter. The waiters threaded their way between the tables with the smooth, gliding speed of practice. Across the room, Payten saw a man's face he knew vaguely, and acknowledged the smiling nod with a wave. Medway's expression was vacuous, wet-lipped and empty. Payten wondered whether there was anything to him. He had lost confidence in his ability to base judgments upon a human exterior.

Earlier Medway had appeared impressive, grave-faced, judicial, balanced. Payten wondered which the real Medway was. Medway drunk, or Medway sober? Drunk Medway seemed to Payten almost weak-witted. Yet in his own State the man was acquiring a solid Party reputation for his foxy cleverness, his guile, his drive and his successes, modest as yet, but promising. Payten realised wryly that there was no contradiction in this. Morons and madmen could go far in politics. Hitler was only one among many. A public manner could hide mental deficiencies. In the final analysis, energy, tenacity, ambition, and above all, luck, were more rewarding political attributes than integrity, ability or originality of mind.

Lilley put down his fork. Grease shone at the corners of his mouth. He wiped it with his napkin. He looked pleased. "He's a born fixer" thought Payten with grudging admiration. "Some people fix for money. Others for power. Others to curry favour. Lilley likes fixing for all these things, particularly money. But over and above that, he likes fixing just for the hell of it." Lilley snapped his fingers at a passing waiter. "Tell Joseph I want him," he ordered.

Medway said, defensively, "No harm in a bit of innocent fun, is there? Because a man's married and has kids there's no reason, why he shouldn't know a girl. Innocent-like, I mean. No hanky panky." The cunning was back in his face.

Payten said maliciously, "Look, sport, I wouldn't care if you went to bed with every woman in the room. But for Christ's sake don't give me that drivel about innocence. I'm not interested in whether you're going to sleep with this dame or conduct a prayer meeting. But she isn't the type for prayer."

Medway banged the table with his big fist. He said, with angry, drunken insistence, "I'm married."

Payten said, "Probably more than your parents were."

Lilley said, quickly, "What's the matter with you, Mark? Get off the man's back. He's away from home. In a strange State. All he wants is a bit of fun." He winked at Payten, his eyelid shuttering at high speed. "You enjoy your fun, Mark. Politics are tough. There's nothing in 'em but hard work and headaches. Why begrudge a man his pleasure."

Medway said, "I don't like that last crack of yours, Payten." Red patches of anger flushed his cheeks.

Joseph materialised at the table. He was tall, thin, swarthy, with a world-weary face. His dinner jacket was that of a headwaiter. Lilley greeted him enthusiastically. "Joseph," he said, "this is Mr Medway. Look after him. He's a friend of mine from out of State." He was fulsome and fast talking. "This boy's going to be big in politics, Joseph. Be nice to him." He grew suggestive. "It'll be worth your while some day." To Medway he said, "Joseph owns this place. He's okay. He was in trouble with the police recently. Over one of his other joints. For selling liquor without a licence. I fixed that, didn't I, Joseph?"

"Sure, Mr Lilley," said Joseph, without expression. To Medway he said tonelessly, "Mr Lilley can fix most things in this State."

"Sure, I can fix most things," chuckled Lilley. Payten wondered what that bit of fixing had cost Joseph. Not money, he guessed. Lilley's habits had changed with his growth of stature within the Party. He did not worry about chicken-feed these days. His operations nowadays were so close to being legal that a high-class lawyer could make them appear so. In politics it was the small stuff that was dangerous. It left a trail behind. A cancelled cheque or an entry in a bank account that was awkward to explain. But Lilley would see that Joseph paid for the fixing in some way. By giving him a special service, perhaps, that he could impress with his importance men like Medway, hard-bitten in politics, but unsophisticated away from them. Or by acting as procurer for Lilley's friends.

Medway said abruptly, "What about this dame, Joe?" He was still angry, but the flush was going from his face.

To Joseph Lilley said, "Mr Medway wants to meet Annette. Ask her to come to the table, would you?"

Joseph's expression did not change. "Of course, Mr Lilley." He went off with the smooth waiter's glide that he had carried with him into the ownership.

The men sat in silence, with Medway glowering at Payten who elaborately pretended innocent unawareness of the younger man's hostility.

Lilley was relieved when Annette arrived. She was younger than she had looked on the dance floor. She had changed into a low-cut evening dress that barely covered her big, young breasts. Men's eyes followed her as she picked her way between the close jammed tables. Her face was thin, with dark, unexpectedly soft eyes. She slipped into a chair as the men stood for her, Medway swaying slightly. She said, "Hello, Mr Lilley. Hello, Mark."

Lilley said, "My dear, I want you to meet a friend of mine—Brock Medway."

She regarded Medway critically. "A politician?" she asked. "All Mr Lilley's friends seem to be politicians." Medway had sat down and was pouring out a drink for himself and the girl. She put her head on one side. "But you're younger than most of them." She made a grimace of distaste. "They're mostly old fat men with big stomachs and wandering hands."

Payten said, "Brock hasn't a big stomach—yet. But he's got wandering hands, Annette."

When Medway asked the girl to dance, Lilley said jovially, "Keep the big ape off your toes, Annette." Payten said, "Keep him off his face, Annette. He's going to fall on it very soon." The girl looked puzzled, apprehensive. As they moved away, she put her hand lightly under the large man's elbow, guiding him. He was staggering slightly.

When they were out of earshot Lilley said, "Stop needling him, Mark."

Payten responded lightly, "I don't like sanctimonious drunks."

"You don't have to like him, pal. But he could be useful."

"He's a drunken bum."

"You're wrong," Lilley insisted. "I've checked. He seldom drinks. He can't take liquor. So he usually leaves it alone. Don't underrate him, Mark. He's got something."

"Yeah," said Payten. "Hot pants."

Lilley glanced round warily. He shifted his chair closer to Payten. In a low, confidential tone, Lilley said, "He's got more than that, Mark. This boy's a natural born blackmailer. He's going places."

Annette and Medway were moving slowly round the crowded dance floor, locked together. The big man was leaning heavily on the girl. The other dancers politely ignored them, though Payten saw the occasional amused glance and lifted eyebrow.

Medway was talking into the girl's ear. Payten said, "I know where he should go. On to a psycho-analyst's couch."

Lilley said tolerantly, "So should most of us in this racket." He was studying Medway. He said, without looking at Payten, "You know what gives with me and Seborjar?"

Payten said, "Yeah."

"Seborjar wants me as Party Chairman." Lilley waved a pudgy hand deprecatingly. "There are thirty votes on the committee that makes the decision. You know the split up. Domineco controls eight of them." His face contorted with a sudden spasm of hate. Normally Lilley kept his feelings under tight control. Payten wondered what quality Domineco had that unleashed passion. Men either worshipped him with a fanatical devotion or hated him intensely. There was no half way, ever.

"That priest-loving bastard wouldn't throw me a vote under any circumstances. He'll plump for Tom Bannion, even though he doesn't like him. Domineco has eight votes. Bannion's got four votes he can count on. Three votes are Hoskin's men. They'll do what he says. Hoskin won't vote for Bannion. He'll back Seborjar against Domineco. So he'll have to back me whether he wants to or not. Six of the committee are Fortune's boys. They will vote whichever way Fortune tells them to. Seborjar controls two votes. There are seven floaters. Nobody knows what they'll do." He paused. "This vote'll be decided by Fortune and the seven floaters." He lowered his voice. "Seborjar reckons he can tie up Fortune. Maybe he can. But that still leaves the seven floaters. I want some of them to feel safe."

"What's that got to do with Lover Boy?" asked Payten who stabbed a thumb over his shoulder in the direction of Medway on the dance floor. He thought, "Politicians are the same the world over. No wonder a mediocrity like Stalin could beat a near genius like Trotsky. We can't resist the temptation to spill our guts about what's in our mind. Surely Lilley knows that I'll hare off to Seborjar to tell him what he's telling me now. Maybe that's why Lilley's spilling his guts. Perhaps he wants to get something to Seborjar that he does not want to take direct himself. But why? What he's up to could anger Seborjar. And he's completely dependent on Seborjar's support for the chairmanship. Is he mug enough to trust me? Does he imagine that my interests are so closely bound up with his advancement that I give him greater loyalty than I give Seborjar?"

For the first time that evening Payten felt clear-headed and alive. Politics were the great delusion. To the man who lived in them, they were the unseen strings that jerked every human puppet. These people surrounding him, they were not there because they were hungry and wanted to eat, thirsty and wanted to drink, or because they were rutting or liked dancing, or were seeking the escape of an evening's entertainment. They were there because he and others who pulled the strings ordained that they should be there, eating, drinking and exchanging amorous glances across the table, laughing or relaxing. That was what gave politics their fascination—this mad belief that nothing outside politics had reality. He knew it was fantasy. But he accepted the fantasy as reality. It bolstered his ego. God must feel like that, he decided, and grinned at the arrogance of his imagery.

"What's so funny?" Lilley demanded. "That Lover Boy should be important in this set-up? Don't judge him at his drunken worst, Mark. That boy's got something."

"What?" said Payten.

Lilley waved away impatiently the waiter who was refilling his glass. "Why do you think this young feller's an up and coming man in the Party? Why? Go on. Tell me. Why?"

"The usual combination of factors, I suppose. Luck. A quick, lively tongue. Ruthlessness. Ambition. A few connections. Not too many scruples and a good line of bull. Possibly, to start with, a few beliefs that he's lost somewhere along the line."

Lilley was starting to sweat in the hot atmosphere. Little beads of moisture were forming under the dark bags below his eyes. He pulled out a handkerchief and wiped his face. "Medway has or had all those things. But he's got something else as well. Perry Nova's backing him."

"Perry?" Payten swivelled in his chair to stare with quickened interest at Medway on the dance floor. Annette caught his eye. She waved, uncertainly. "Perry's a member of the committee that'll decide the Party chairmanship."

Lilley said, "You aren't telling me anything, Mark." He was watching Annette and Medway. He grimaced and waved, like a gargoyle, as they danced past on a level with the table. Medway's steps were uncertain.

"What's Perry pushing him along for?" asked Payten. "This boy's strictly small-time. Slick perhaps, but definitely small-time. He'll always be small-time. He might get somewhere if he was from an important State. But he's from a small, hick State. He can't do Perry much good."

Lilley said, "Remember when Perry got involved in the steelworkers' national wage deal?"

"Sure," said Payten. "Somebody sold the steelworkers down the river."

"Who sold 'em?" Lilley asked.

Payten sipped at his drink. His restless, mobile face was thoughtful. "Rumour has it that it was Nova." He put down his glass. "But you can't make that horse gallop, Joe. You can't prove it."

"I can't prove it. But Medway can, Mark." There was an odd note of resentment in the fat man's voice. "Medway was sent by the steelworkers of his State to assist Perry on that deal. He's got a nose like a fox for smelly fish. He smelt the fish and I'm told he dug 'em up. Apparently he plays the game the hard way. Perry has been pushing him along in the Party ever since, yet Perry doesn't like him. Adds up, don't it, Mark?"

"Seborjar know this?"

The fat man smirked. "That's why I can afford to tell you, Mark. It's not that I trust you, pal. I know you're Seborjar's jackal. But Seborjar can't afford to touch this one. It's too close to the knuckle. He's doing a Pontius Pilate. Washing his hands. Pretending he knows nothing about it. But we—you and me—we can do something about it, Mark, and I'm sure Seborjar would like us to."

"He's an evil bastard." At that moment Payten hated Seborjar for demeaning him. The contemptuous arrogance with which the man took it for granted that he, Payten, would do his dirty-work, as though he was honoured by being permitted to do it. Seborjar must not touch pitch; he could not be defiled, but nothing was too vile to be undertaken on his behalf, provided he could pretend, as much to himself as to others, that his hands were clean. But he did not care who else was defiled by doing his dirty work, so long as what came out of the filth and dirt helped Seborjar. And yet the man was not crooked in himself, though he expected, almost demanded, the faithful among his followers to work crookedly on his behalf. He was bigger than any of them. In serving Seborjar his adherents wanted to achieve some gain either for themselves or for the man they served. They had small objectives. But somewhere ahead of Seborjar was the confused, unexpressed but glittering end that he was striving for— a place in history.

And he would not let what to him were the trifles of normal standards of morality and the little decencies of human existence stand between him and the end he was pursuing. Self-interest bound Payten to Seborjar. But Payten knew other, larger things, also bound him to Seborjar as compellingly as self-interest, the lure of stature— for politically Seborjar was big. The power of Seborjar's shifty, moody personality, sombre and morose, yet with facets that gave him at unexpected moments a homely, fascinating charm. A perverse admiration—Payten ruefully acknowledged his perversity—for the often costly loyalty that Seborjar gave to the weaklings, neurotics, eccentrics and sycophants who were the inevitable retainers at his political court. Payten knew how Seborjar operated. He would never say directly that he wanted some dirty trick pulled. He would weave and shuffle and talk round in circles until somebody like Lilley would come to understand what he wanted done. And after it was done Seborjar would pretend to himself even more convincingly than to others that he had no part in it, and he would be shocked and upset when it was drawn to his attention. "He's an evil bastard," Payten repeated.

With a fat man's playfulness that left untouched his inner

bleakness, Lilley said "That's no way to speak of our venerated Leader, Mark. The man we support. Seborjar. The great friend of the common people. "Nevertheless he had been startled by the violence of Payten's reaction. He said, soothingly, "Not turning moralist in your old age, are you Mark?"

Payten shook his head. He downed his drink in a gulp. His small face had a monkey's hurt melancholy. "It's too late for that." He ran his hand over his thick, black hair, with the grey streaks that gave him an air of distinction. He said, "Forget it. Mostly I can take Kaye Seborjar in my stride. But sometimes he makes me want to spew."

"Sure, Mark." The fat man's eyes were expressionless. "But don't let it get you down. There are no heroes in our racket." He made a gesture that embraced the crowded, noisy room. "These mugs have their heroes, Mark. Some of them think of Alex Pope as a hero. Some of them feel the same way about Seborjar. But we know better, Mark. Or we should. We live with these heroes. We launder their underclothes and get the sour smell off 'em. We know that they're just ordinary men, mostly miserable bastards who'd send their own mothers to a political knackery if the price was right. Kaye Seborjar in many ways is a prize louse. But that isn't important to you or me, Mark. What is important is that he is our horse. We're backing him. You partly because you believe in him. Me because it suits my book to do so. But the point is that we are backing him to be in the prize money. And in this game you've got to ride to win."

Payten said abruptly, "What does the prize money mean to you, Joe? Why do you want more dough? You must be lousy with it already."

Surprise was in Lilley's voice. "You don't think it's just dough I'm interested in, do you, Mark? I thought you had more intelligence. I've got more dough than I'll spend in my lifetime. But I want other things. If I have just dough, what am I? Another rich man. They're a dime a dozen, Mark."

"Money talks," said Payten, doggedly.

"Sure," said Lilley. "Money's strong language. But there are other tongues. I don't want to be just a rich man, Mark. All kinds of mugs who can't do anything else can make money. You know 'em and I know 'em. And outside their ability to make dough they're nothing. Poorer men take off their hats to 'em that's true. But I want rich men to take 'em off, when I walk past. You've got to have more than money for that to happen. You've got to have power, prestige, pull."

"You've thought it all out, haven't you, Joe?" Payten derided. "Yeah, Mark, I'm not just a rich man. I'm more than that. That's the difference between characters like you and me and these mugs." His pudgy hand dismissed the people in the crowded room. "We think it out, sport. And we know what we want. We're a separate breed—you and me. We're the same breed as Alex Pope, Seborjar, Carr Domineco, Fortune and Gilly Hoskin. We might hate each other. We try to destroy each other. But under the skin we're brothers."

"We walk with dead Caesar." Payten was surprised at the seriousness with which the fat man received his remark.

"Not only with dead Caesar, Mark. With Nero, Hitler. Alexander, Mussolini and the meanest, most unsuccessful revolutionary who ever tossed an ineffective bomb or incited an abortive revolt. We are the men who rule or want to rule."

"So to get to rule we use a lousy blackmailer like Medway?"

The fat man shrugged. "Nero used thumbscrews, Hitler the concentration camp, Caesar secret police, and Mussolini the castor oil bottle. We have to accept—reluctantly in some cases that Domineco would not hesitate to revive the thumbscrew nor Hoskin the concentration camp. But our breed never changes. We're just a bit more civilised, only because we have to be. So we use a blackmailer in place of an assassin, financial pressure in place of the castor oil bottle, deceit in place of the thumbscrew."

Despite himself, Payten was impressed. "That isn't a very pretty picture, Joe."

"Ours isn't a pretty business, Mark. Fascinating, absorbing. Exciting. Rewarding, if you're good at it. But not pretty."

"Okay," said Payten. "So you've provided an ethical justification for dealing with a blackmailer. So you deal. As you would have done whether you could justify it or not. What kind of proof has Medway got on Perry? Documentary?"

"So I'm told." The fat man's voice was uncertain. "But he's cagey. I've been feeling round for an opening for days, but he jumps right away whenever I switch on to Perry."

A passing man bumped into the back of Payten's chair. He apologised. He was youngish, with a soft, round face and a stammer. Payten flashed at him his warm, practised politician's smile. It made his face look open, friendly and likeable. "It's okay," Payten told the young man who headed towards his table, lifted by the intimacy of the contact, thinking what an attractive man was the stranger with whom he had had the momentary meeting.

"Medway won't give anything away for nothing, Joe"

"I know. I'm a bit jammed. What's his price? I get the impression he's hungry for money. He's never owned anything that amounted to a damn. There's a greedy look about him. But I can't offer him dough. I'm getting too big to be tied up in deals like that. I've hinted Seborjar's interested in him—that in certain circumstances I can arrange for the Big Man to give him patronage."

"What did he say?"

The fat man laughed, "He doesn't only want a bird in the hand. He wants its life insured. The cheeky young pup." He blew out his cheeks. "He asked me how long Seborjar was going to last as Leader. Could I give any guarantee?"

Payten said, with genuine appreciation, "I can see his point. Better a good safe goldmine like Perry, who is not a particularly controversial figure, and will be there to be worked for a lifetime, than Seborjar's richer lode that might pinch out tomorrow. He's a shrewder young man than I've been giving him credit for being."

Lilley said, "He's shrewd enough—sober. I'm jammed, Mark. I need Perry's vote. And whichever way Perry goes Max Steiner'll follow. Steiner's just a faithful echo of Perry. Steiner's union job depends on Perry's goodwill. Those two votes. They could be decisive. I can't be sure of either of them without Medway. You can bet both Fortune and Domineco are pouring the pressure on Perry. I need Medway."

"But Medway doesn't need you," said Payten. The music had stopped. The dancers were leaving the floor. He could see Annette moving towards them with her lithe, dancer's smoothness, Medway behind her. Payten stood up. But the girl paused before she took the chair he pulled back for her. She said hesitantly, watching Lilley, "I should be getting back, now. I'm on again soon." Her smile was troubled. Payten got the impression that she disliked Medway but did not want to offend Lilley. She said, "Thanks for the dance, Brock." Medway said, "It's nothing." He patted Lilley playfully on his balding head. "Joe, here, can fix things. Can't you, Joe?" Lilley said, cautiously, "Fix what, Brock?"

Medway slumped into his chair. "Joe, I want a little favour. I want to show this little girl here the town. Don't I, honey?" He had a drunken air of cunning; "You said you could fix things, Joey boy. Well, fix this one. Fix it with Joseph she doesn't have to go on again." His hand clamped over the dancer's bare rounded shoulder. "You fix it, Joey. Like you said you could." Annette said, uncertainly, "I don't think I can make it tonight, honey."

"Of course you can make it." Medway leered. "Joe'll fix it. Won't you, Joe?"

"Sure," said Lilley. "I'll fix it." His eyes were calculating. "A nice little party. At my place, eh? You haven't seen my place, Brock. Just out of town. It's big and very, very private. We'll rustle up a couple more women." He chuckled. "I'm a bachelor. Mark, for all practical purposes, is also a bachelor. We'll make a night of it."

"Nothing doing," said Medway, "This dancer and I are going to be on our own, see? We've got an understanding, haven't we, honey?" His voice was getting ugly. Payten thought, "Unless Joe does something quickly there'll be a scene." He did not like scenes. They were all politicians. Public scenes never did any politician any good. He said, "For Christ's sake, Brock, pipe down." To Lilley he said, "Let's get out of this joint."

Medway angrily half rose from the table and said, "Not without the girl." The diners at the neighbouring table were starting to watch them. The girl looked frightened. Medway's waving arm swept a glass from the table.

"Careful, Brock, careful." Lilley glanced round. He heaved his bulk up from his chair. Lilley said, "I'll fix it with Joseph. Leave it to me." He gestured at Payten. "Come on, Mark. We'll see Joseph."

Annette, her thin young face anxious, got up to follow them. Lilley said, "No, my dear. You stay with Brock." He patted her with seeming kindliness on her bare shoulder. The girl sat down reluctantly. "Don't worry," he told her. "I'll fix things with Joseph."

Lilley waddled purposefully towards the door leading to the entrance foyer. He seemed to know everyone. He clapped men on the back as he passed, calling them by name.

But outside in the deserted foyer, he showed his irritation. "What a lousy break." He looked across at the yawning hat-check girl behind her counter, and lowered his voice. "It's taken me a week to persuade that suspicious hillbilly to let down his hair." His voice rose in a squeak of mimicry. "'I don't drink, Joe,' he kept telling me. So I get him drunk and what happens? He sees a big-bosomed dancing girl and he wants to be alone." He clapped Payten on the shoulder. "I was planning for you and me to do some heavy work on him tonight." "Tell the girl to scram," suggested Payten. "She'll do what you tell her to do."

"No," said Lilley. "You saw what he was like with you. Surly and quarrelsome. If I send the girl away, he'll sulk. Let him have her. He'll have to keep." He sighed. "I'll fix things with Joseph." He started up the staircase at the back of the foyer. He paused. "Don't go back to the table without me, Mark. You and he are likely to quarrel. He's one of those bastards who get cross-grained in liquor."

Payten lit a cigarette. Out here, muted by distance, the music was pleasant and soft. He caught the eye of the tired girl behind the hat-check counter. She smiled impersonally. Behind him he heard the sharp tap-tap of a woman's high heels. It was Annette.

She slipped her arm through his. She looked across at the hat check girl. She kept her voice low. She said, "Mark, do I have to go with Brock?"

"You do what you like, Annette."

She nibbled at her lip. Her big soft eyes looked over-strained. He had a feeling that she was close to tears. She said, "I don't like him, Mark. Brock, I mean. He frightens me. He talks as though he's crazy."

Payten felt sorry for the girl. The dual nature of his reaction irritated him. On one hand, he felt paternal. His eldest daughter was about her age. Annette was about twenty-two, he figured. Yet he was conscious of her big, young breasts and of the curve of her thighs under the tightness of her dress. He said, "He's not crazy, Annette. Not that I know of. But he's not used to drinking." Annette said, her voice tremulous, "He acts like a type that wants to hurt you. They get you on their own and want you to do things. Filthy things. And then they want to hurt you. They enjoy hurting."

Payten realised with a sense of shock that she was speaking from an experience that went far beyond her age. "You don't have to do anything you don't want to do. It's a free country. Tell Medway to go to hell."

People streamed out into the foyer, chattering and laughing. Annette waited until they had collected their things from the hat-check girl. "Will Mr Lilley like that?"

"Tell Lilley to go to hell, too," said Payten. He wished she did not look so youthfully forlorn. He could smell the heaviness of her scent and feel the closeness of her hard, muscular body.

The girl said bitterly, "I've got to eat, Mark."

"We all have to." said Payten.

"Mr Lilley's important in this town. If he blacklists you with the agents, you can't get a job. Not one that pays you anything worthwhile. But if you help him out—you know—what I mean—with some out-of-town big shot, like Brock, he'll see that you get the breaks. He's good that way. He got me this break with Joseph."

"Did he now?" said Payten. He had known Lilley had a finger in many pies. But the theatrical world was one he had not known about.

"I don't really mind. Helping him, I mean. I don't pretend, Mark. I am not the virginal kind. I like men and a bit of fun. And Mr Lilley's friends, they're mostly a bit old for me, but some of them are pets. But this Medway man. I'm frightened of him, Mark!"

Lilley came into sight at the top of the stairs. They watched him come down heavily, wheezing as he said with fat man's bonhomie, "Haven't run out on the boyfriend, Annette?"

Payten said, abruptly, "The girl's frightened of Medway, Joe."

Lilley was breezy. "Nonsense, Brock's a nice boy, I've just fixed with Joseph that you don't have to go on again, Annette. You can leave with Brock when you like."

"He wants me to go back to his hotel with him. Do I have to, Mr Lilley?"

Lilley said sharply, "You don't have to do anything, Annette." Payten said, his voice rising in irritation, "For Christ's sake, Joe. The kid's frightened of the gorilla."

Lilley said, "Keep your voice down. You're not addressing a public meeting." He glanced across at the hat-check girl. She was reading a paper spread on the counter. She was not paying any attention. He said, his tone kindly, "You're nervy, Annette. Imagining things. Brock's okay. Just happy. But it's quite all right, my dear. I understand. You run along home. I'll explain things to Brock. It'll be a bit embarrassing, but I'll explain." The girl's eyes were miserable. She looked very young and vulnerable. She hesitated. She said, "You're sure he's all right, Mr Lilley. Not crazy or anything?"

The fat man was smoothly reassuring. "Of course I'm sure, my dear. I know Brock. He's a nice fellow."

She wavered. "If you're sure he's all-right, Mr Lilley." She was pathetically anxious to please the fat man. "Well, okay then. Forget it. I guess I'm just imagining things." She smiled. The smile was unsure. "I'll go get Brock. I told him I was going to get a wrap."

"You're doing me a favour, Annette," said Lilley, softly. "I never forget a favour. I shan't forget this one."

"Thanks, Mr Lilley." She hesitated. Then with a boldness that Payten had not expected she said, "About the favour, Mr Lilley. They're auditioning at the Globe. For an understudy for Maria Montes."

Lilley smiled. He took out a notebook. He scribbled in it. "You'll get your audition, my dear. It wouldn't surprise me if you got the job."

The men watched the girl sway along the foyer. Her back was straight and supple—a dancer's back.

Suddenly Payten said, "Will she get the job?"

"Sure," said Lilley. He slipped the notebook back into his pocket. "I always pay off." He looked at Payten. His eyes were expressionless. "This girl'll tell others she did a favour for Joe Lilley. She won't say what the favour was. But she'll hint that it was kind of important. And it paid off. Those she tells'll be anxious to do me a favour. In the hope of a pay-off. It's a form of advertisement, Mark."

Payten said, "How's it feel to be a procurer, Joe?"

"You ought to know," said the fat man, coolly. "You didn't lift a finger to stop it." He took a cigar from an inner pocket, stripped off the cellophane with careful, pudgy fingers, and bit off the end. "I was only the accessory after the fact," Payten retorted. "Sure," said Lilley. "Coming home?" He lit the cigar. He puffed at it, and rolled it wetly round his lips.

They retrieved their hats. Outside the night was warm and calm. It was after midnight. Taxis were still taking home the late theatre crowd. The doorman saluted Lilley. Lilley, who said, "How are you, Karl?"

"Fine, thanks, Mr Lilley," said the doorman. "A taxi?"

"Share one with me, Mark?" Lilley asked.

"No," said Payten. "I don't want to be at close quarters even with myself tonight."

Lilley chuckled without resentment. "I'll walk with Mr Payten for a few blocks, thanks, Karl." He slipped something into the man's hand. "Night, Karl."

"Night, Mr Lilley. Night, Mr Payten."

The men walked slowly. Cars passed them constantly. But there were few pedestrians. Lilley said quietly, "You'll get over it, Mark. We're playing for big stakes."

"Sure," said Payten. "That's what Seborjar tells me."

"He's right, you know, Mark." Lilley drew at his cigar. The end glowed redly.

"Sure," said Payten. "But at the moment I don't feel so good about it."

"You'll recover, Mark," he said in the semi-darkness. "You're upset now. You're a bit of a romanticist. You read too many good books when you were young. About the gallant knight, without fear and without reproach. And the lady, beautiful, fair and virtuous." His chuckle was deep-throated, without malice. "So you play-act. You're the knight who's let his golden spurs get dirty. And Annette's the lady, beautiful, fair and virtuous, whom you failed to protect."

"Sure," said Patten. "It's all a hallucination. Neither of us to curry favour with a drunken, hypocritical bum, who is also probably an astute blackmailer, fixed it so that a girl who is frightened is practically forced into bed with him. I didn't hold her legs and you her arms. We weren't quite that brutal. But it's about the only thing we didn't do." He stopped and thrust his face close to Lilley's. "Look, Joe. I know I'm in the political racket. I'm prepared to play it tough. But surely there are limits."

"Nobody's ever reached 'em," said Lilley. A pedestrian passed the men. Lilley pulled at Payten's arm. "Ours is the only profession in the world in which the horizons are limitless." He drew at his cigar. It was out. He said, "Damn this cigar. Got a match?"

Payten passed across a matchbox. Lilley relighted his cigar. "It's like this, in our game you have to work with the tools that are to hand. Okay. Maybe a tool like Medway shouldn't be in it. Maybe I shouldn't be in it. Maybe you shouldn't. But we are. That's politics. It doesn't matter how idealistic the ideology is. That can only ever be a part of politics. Politics aren't what the long-haired professors say they are. Politics are a way of living that attracts more villains than altruists, madmen as often as balanced men, crackpots as well as visionaries. Our good fortune—the good fortune of those who adopt this way of living—is that ordinary men don't see that. They're not close enough. If you're at any distance you can't pick out the cracks in the Pyramids."

"What's that got to do with Medway?" asked Payten. "Or Annette?"

"It's got this to do with it," said Lilley. "Medway's a tool we can use. But we can use him only if he's willing to be used, or we've got the power to use him. He's not willing. So we've got to get power from somewhere. Or persuade him into willingness. Meanwhile we've got to handle him carefully. So we study him. Find out he drinks. But we also find out that when he's drinking he's woman-hungry. He's bad-tempered and unbalanced. If he doesn't get a woman he'll almost certainly hold a grudge against us. So we give him a woman. So what? I can understand a man wanting a woman. But I can't understand a man wanting or getting so involved with a woman that it interferes with his politics. One's emotional. The other's reasoned. Medway lets his emotions over-ride his reason. He gets no sympathy from me for that."

"And Annette?" asked Payten sharply.

The fat man tossed his cigar butt away. "She doesn't sell herself for money. She sells herself for advancement in her career. Sex is a weapon you can't use often in our game. Most politicians are too shrewd—too unemotional when they are away from a speaker's platform—to allow it to interfere with them politically. But you find a politician silly enough to be snared, and a dame silly enough to be used as a political pawn, it's part of the game."

"Jesus, you make me sick to the stomach," said Payten.

An empty taxi pulled into the kerb. "You'd better make a swift recovery."

"Why?" asked Payten.

The fat man paused with his hand on the taxi door, "Have you forgotten? Seborjar's speaking tomorrow. His cohorts among whom you and I are numbered, are expected to be present. Night, Mark."

"Night, Joe," said Payten absent-mindedly. He stood on the kerb, a lonely figure as the taxi drew away.

CHAPTER 4

Mark Payten, his lively face, intelligent, small and engagingly monkey-like under the dignity of dark, well-brushed hair, frosted with silver, blasphemously claimed that having Tom Bannion in the Party was uncomfortably like having Christ at a meeting of Christians.

"Fellow should be hanging between two thieves instead of consorting with hundreds," he complained with mock seriousness.

Payten's wisecrack went the rounds of the Party, was laughed at, and forgotten. But it expressed pithily the feelings of many of the Party veterans about Bannion. He made them uneasy. He was humourless and very earnest.

In a different type of man, these qualities would have been endured with patient, stoical forbearance. The Party was the haunt of eccentrics and cranks, from religious ones with a mission to food faddists who found a symbolical connection between a vegetarian diet and their political theories. If Bannion had remained the harmless political dilettante which the Party originally considered him, he would have been accorded tolerance. But Bannion was not harmless. In some ways he was naive and unworldly. But he also had tough, worldly qualities. He had a strain of ruthlessness, a determination not to be switched from his purposes and aims by obstacles that would have daunted a less tenacious, more experienced man, a capacity for tireless, driving effort, and the sustaining arrogance of conviction.

Among the major Party Leaders, only Fortune had regard for Bannion. Kalley suspected that Fortune saw in Bannion virtues that he would have liked to possess himself. Seborjar was suspicious of the man, as he was of anyone who had an independent mind. Domineco detested him, because he had a moral basis, like Domineco himself, but was nevertheless opposed to Domineco's dedicated narrowness. Gilly Hoskin hated him. To Hoskin he represented an infiltration of the Party by the wealthy, privileged classes that Hoskin had disliked all his life. Others found him merely irritating. Some of this irritation stemmed from the fact that his values were mostly old-fashioned.

They were values that it was fashionable in the Party to sneer at in private. But in public they had support because of tradition and the touchiness of the voters. Bannion believed in honesty, the family as a basis of society and civic rights. Seborjar professed the same beliefs, but enunciated them differently. The older man had the stature and guile to give them a new slant. He fitted them into a world instead of a national context. It was a slant that somehow gave them an aura of novelty, even in the Party. Bannion went on consciously applying them to the people around him.

The Party Leaders could understand Seborjar, even when they despised him. They knew that Seborjar exploited these themes to further his own complex ends. To them this was an old, familiar and permissible political technique. But Bannion puzzled them. He acted as though he believed in the threadbare clichés. They could not reconcile his apparent sincerity with their disillusioned knowledge of themselves and their fellow men—particularly themselves. Despite antagonism to him in the Party hierarchy, an antagonism which grew as he became more deeply involved in Party affairs and so better known, Bannion had over some years slowly acquired a following, small but influential, among the Party's rank and file. He even had a tiny group of supporters in the hierarchy itself. Among this group were men who found that supporting him was advantageous to their private interests.

But among the group were also those who had preserved standards of conduct despite the amorality of a political environment. They believed that Bannion provided a useful counterweight for corrupting influences. It was from this belief that their original support stemmed, though their loyalty later tended to become a habit and to rest as much upon their respect for Bannion's personality. But Bannion as yet owed the standing he had in the Party to Fortune. Bannion knew this. So did the clique that had grown up around him.

It had been Con Fortune who first selected Bannion and thereafter fostered his rise within the Party. Fortune, with the unobtrusive Kalley at his shoulder, had been attending a minor Party rally in a rather rundown, ill-lit hall in a working-class district near the waterfront. Fortune had not been very interested. The business was dull and so were the speeches.

Then Bannion rose to speak. He was a dark man, with intense, unhappy eyes. His skin was yellowish, the colour of thin mud. He was tall, over six feet, very straight-backed, with wide shoulders and a lean waist. He was then in his early thirties. His left hand was deformed. He held it in front of him, bent across his chest, with the fingers withered and twisted, like a talon. Mostly he kept it unnaturally still as though he did not want to draw attention to its unsightliness. But sometimes he forgot. When he did, and lifted it in straining to emphasise a point, the gesture gave his words a touch of controlled passion. Fortune listened to Bannion thoughtfully. The man spoke slowly and deliberately. He gave an impression of having considerable strength. His voice was firm, cultured, rather thin, but compelling. He did not have much to say. But what he had to say was expressed precisely and with conviction.

"Who's that character?" Fortune asked Kalley as Bannion sat down amid a rustle of approbation.

Kalley said, "Tom Bannion."

"He's got something," commented Fortune.

"Money. And a social conscience."

"He's got something else, too," said Fortune. "Where's the dough come from?"

"Inherited," said Kalley. "Hence, probably, the conscience. No need to work. But he does. He's a consulting engineer. Good."

"How come you know about him, Macker?" Kalley lit a cigarette: "He's been round in the Party for a while. Joined up after the war. I've heard him talk at a few rallies. Like you, I thought he had something." "Ex-serviceman, Macker?"

"Ex-officer type," said Kalley. "With his engineering qualifications could have sat out the war in a nice office. But joined the Air Force. Wound up commanding a bomber squadron. Got a Jap bullet through the heel of his hand. Came out his elbow. Smashed a few things on the way. Crippled his left hand. You probably noticed."

"What's his gimmick?"

Kalley shrugged. "I dunno. Doesn't seem to have one. Just seems to have a bug for politics. Got it during the war. A lot of 'em got the bug then. To come home and do politics over. Make 'em honest and the world fit for ordinary little guys to live in. Most of 'em came home and forgot it. Bannion didn't."

Pulling thoughtfully at his long upper lip, Fortune said "I'm looking for someone to fill Matt Obley's job, Macker. I haven't anyone in mind. We'll have to do something soon, or it'll be smelling right in our laps. I was quite impressed with Bannion. We could do with picking up some new talent. What do you think?"

Kalley's eyes moved slowly over the room. He could just see the top of Bannion's dark head where he was sitting. Down at the front, a man was declaiming passionately. He was short and fat and bald. Sweat was pouring off him. He knew Fortune was present. It was important for a man who had political ambitions to impress a Party Leader. Back in the shadows at the rear of the hall neither Fortune nor Kalley was aware that he was speaking, though their practised ears would have picked up automatically any worthwhile statement if it had been made, and their conversation would then have been immediately deferred.

Kalley said, "He could be a nuisance. He's starry-eyed. The starry-eyed boys argue back. They've got minds of their own." "Sure," said Fortune. "They're hard to handle, but they can be handled. And properly handled, they're good value. My off-the-cuff reaction was that this character has something. You've been studying him for some time. You think he has something. We've got to dump Matt—fast. If we put in one of our boys and things go sour we're no better off. We still take the rap. If we put in someone who's had no previous connection with us and things go wrong we can disown him and it's no skin off our noses. What d'you say? It's not as though Matt's job is really big-time. If we toss it to this character and he rats on us, he'll still be small potatoes and we can axe him any time we want."

Over the years Kalley had become so much part of Fortune's political empire that Fortune now viewed him more as a junior partner in its management than as a paid employee. Without ever consciously acknowledging it to himself, he assumed that his own interests and Kalley's were inextricably bound together.

Kalley said impassively, "Suit yourself, Con. I've given you the picture. He's starry-eyed. The starry-eyed boys in my book are unpredictable. You can't bet on 'em without risk. Mostly the stars go from their eyes, but sometimes they don't. And when they don't they see visions. And follow 'em. But as you say Obley's job is small-time. If you should decide to give it to this fellow and he rats, it's only a minor nuisance. Not important. And you could be picking up a good boy. A useful boy. He might prove hard to handle. But my judgment is that he has brains." Fortune thought for a while. He said, "We'll look him over, Macker. Fix it for him to see me as soon as this show's over."

It had taken some time for Fortune to get away when the meeting ended. He was surrounded by a swarm of men who wanted to impress him. The patronage of a Party Leader was the surest way to advancement. Fortune held court in the emptying hall, exchanging a few words and a jest with those he spoke to. He recognised the little, fat, bald man who had tried so obviously to impress him with his speech. "Yours was a very fine contribution, sir—very fine," Fortune said smoothly. "Given me a lot to think over." Kalley, on the outskirts of the crowd, smiled thinly. He was positive that Fortune had not registered a word the man had said. He squeezed his way through to Fortune, with Bannion behind him. The others reluctantly gave way. Kalley introduced the men.

"I'd like a few words with you, Mr Bannion," said Fortune. "Is there somewhere we can talk?"

"Why, yes," said Bannion. His manner was quiet but confident. It had an authority that had also been there while he was speaking. Kalley wondered how Fortune would react to it. Fortune did not like authority in others. Bannion considered for a moment. "Would you care to come home with me? For a cup of coffee. I live across town, but I have a car outside."

"That would be very pleasant," said Fortune, politely. He explained that they also had a car. He and Kalley would follow him. Fortune made his adieux. He and Kalley were escorted to their car. Those escorting them were obsequious but thrusting, trying to combine just the right note of joviality and nonchalant intimacy with reverence. "Men don't change much," thought Kalley. "In politics, at any rate. They're feudal to their backbones. The Party chieftain takes the place of the mediaeval baron. But the retainers behave in the same fashion."

Behind the wheel, following a sedately-travelling red tail light that was Bannion, Kalley asked, "Well? What do you think?" He nodded at the big, luxurious car ahead.

Fortune said, "Perhaps not so impressive at closer quarters." He was thoughtfully silent, rolling a cigarette from corner to corner of his firm, humorous mouth. "But still impressive," he added tolerantly.

When they slowed to turn into a wide driveway behind Bannion, they had crossed from the factory area and were in a well-to-do residential section. The houses were big and imposing, set in extensive gardens. Fortune said, "You were right about the dough, Macker." They pulled up behind Bannion on smooth, well-kept gravel.

A light burned on the big porch. Bannion opened the door with his latchkey and ushered them in. They were in a large, spacious entrance hall, white painted. A bowl of roses glowed redly on a dark, highly polished table beneath a big, square mirror. Kalley got an impression of homely luxury. The house had a careful, lived-in feel.

Bannion called, "Janice, are you there?"

A door opened on their left. A tall stately woman came through it. At first sight Kalley thought she was a young girl. She was thin, dark-haired, with a heart-shaped face. She said, "Darling" and lifted her face unselfconsciously. Her eyes were big and brown and warm, "Like a spaniel," thought Kalley. Bannion leant to kiss her. He said, "Janice, we have visitors." He introduced Fortune and Kalley. "They're important men in the Party," he said with ponderous, unsmiling gravity. Kalley saw that she was older than a first glimpse suggested. Like Bannion, she was probably in her early thirties.

She said gravely, "This is indeed a pleasure. I have heard a great deal of you, Mr Fortune, of course." She shook hands with them solemnly, carrying out a rite. Kalley thought, his face a mask but amusement stirring in him, " This family takes itself—very seriously." She led them into the room she had come from.

It was large, pleasant, graceful. The furniture was comfortable, gay and bright. There was a grand piano at the end of the room; on it stood a big bowl of flowers, warm with colour. She gave the men cigarettes and poured them drinks.

Fortune told her that she had a very beautiful home. Kalley knew that Fortune did not know whether it was beautiful or not. He was assessing it in terms of money. With a touch of malice, Kalley noticed that Fortune was awkward and shy, as he usually was with women he encountered away from the familiar environment of a political meeting. The Party was a man's world. Some women participated in its workings. But Party politics, unlike those of the salon or a King's boudoir, seemed to unsex women. They grew hard-faced, bleak-eyed and thin-lipped. Kalley had found that women who made their living from horses and dogs tended to take on many of the characteristics, including the physical ones, of their charges. It was the same in the Party. Women who made a profession of Party politics usually looked like Party politicians. Their sex had to be deduced from the accident of their skirts. Fortune was at home with such women. He probably never realised that they were women. They were votes of one kind or another, of neuter gender and indeterminate sex. Wives were different again. Fortune met them only seldom and then fleetingly.

Outside his home, he had no feminine contacts, only political ones. Most Party politicians were similarly placed. Some provided opportunities for extra-marital sexual activities, but they were usually with tarts, or some little typist attached to politics in some way and prone to be impressed by a politician's importance. Those high in the Party seldom became involved with women except on a purely physical plane. Their passions were conserved for politics. It was not that they were cold-blooded. Some were highly sexed, powerful animals who had to have an outlet for their physical urges. But they had not sufficient emotion left over from their profession to view women as other than minor factors in their lives, "We're either low-lifers or exemplary husbands," thought Kalley, amused.

Mrs Bannion said, "I was about to make coffee when you men arrived. You'll have some with me? Tom will, I know. He is an inveterate coffee drinker." Fortune murmured that they did not want to cause any inconvenience. He was enjoying his drink. But he did not sound enthusiastic. He was a sparing drinker. He liked to keep his head clear always.

"It is no trouble, Mr Fortune," the woman said in her light, serious voice. She was on her feet. At the door, she paused. "And Tom. Pour another drink."

Kalley noted with amusement that, with the woman gone from the room, Fortune's assurance was immediately re-established. He glanced at his surroundings with bold, quick eyes, and whistled quietly. "A nice layout you have here, Mr Bannion," he said. "I'm surprised that a man of your obvious wealth is in the Party. We are—or we are supposed to be, but then theory very seldom matches practice—the champions of the underdog and underprivileged. Your interests would appear to be on the other side of the fence. With our opponents."

"The extent of a man's wealth does not necessarily decide his politics, Mr Fortune." Bannion had tucked his crippled hand inside his coat, in the Napoleonic fashion. Kalley thought, "The poor devil's sensitive about its ugliness." Bannion looked at the tip of his cigarette. "You have other wealthy men in the Party, you know, Mr Fortune. Seborjar, for example."

"Sure," said Fortune. "But the wealthy men in our ranks are seldom with us from conviction. They usually want something. Something specific. Seborjar's a quite typical case. Seborjar wants to get to the top. He has money. But he didn't come out of the top drawer. It's much harder for a man who didn't come out of the top drawer to get to the top with our opponents than it is with us. So Seborjar's with us."

"Hardly a flattering picture of the Leader,"

"It was intended to be accurate, Mr Bannion, not flattering."

Kalley was interested in the struggle that was taking place in Bannion's mind. It showed in his face. The man obviously wanted to continue the discussion on Seborjar. But he was intrigued by the suggestion at the back of Fortune's words involving himself. Finally he said, "How do you know that I'm not like Seborjar, Mr Fortune? That I don't want to get to the top?"

"I don't know," said Fortune. "I'm just trying to find out."

Bannion said slowly, "I've never actually thought about getting to the top. I don't think I want to. And certainly not enough to want to get there in any group other than the Party, I don't like what your opponents stand for, Mr Fortune." He paused reflectively for a moment. "You ever been a soldier, Mr Fortune?"

"No," said Fortune. His face was expressionless. "I've been a politician ever since, as a boy, I talked my way out of a job at the steelworks into a job as a union organiser. Every politician knows his hide is too valuable to be exposed to shot and shell. Particularly when those tossing the shot and shell are playing for keeps. A politician is not a man who risks his hide. He exhorts others to go and risk their hides. There have been exceptions to this rule. But surprisingly few, Mr Bannion, surprisingly few."

Kalley saw an expression of distaste on Bannion's face. He thought, "Con's baiting him hard. First an open attack on Seborjar. Now he wants to find out if he's uniform-crazy." Still, it was a good tactic with a political novice like Bannion. Such men were not trained to hide their inner thoughts like the old timers were. Through such baiting it was often possible to find out what made a man tick politically. Bannion said, "I've been a soldier, Mr Fortune. In the air-force." His mouth was a thin, tight line.

"So what, son? So you think I should have been one, when I had the chance in the First World War? Maybe you're right. Maybe I should have gone. What would you have me do? Say I'm sorry? Bit late for that, isn't it? And across that interval of time even I couldn't tell you now whether my regret would be real or simulated."

Bannion said, "No, I suppose not." He brooded for a moment, his dark eyes thoughtful. He said, "I'm sorry, Mr Fortune. I did not intend to be offensive."

"You weren't," said Fortune. "Make your point."

"It was just this," said Bannion. "While I was away I used to think a lot. The war brought me into contact with men I'd never known before. Decent men. Good men. They'd known nothing but slums, poverty, unemployment. They'd gone hungry in the midst of plenty. They'd been homeless while homes stood empty, rotting wastefully, for want of a tenant." He got up, a tall, impressive man, with an unhappy, purposeless air. He started prowling round the room. "The inequality with which the wealth of this country is distributed got me. When I got home I found that things had improved quite a lot. But still not enough, I felt. The inequalities were too great. That's why I joined the Party, Mr Fortune. It has aspects I don't like. The racketeering, the petty grafting, and the shabby opportunism of those controlling it. But its basic ideas are right."

Fortune said, dryly, "I'm one of the controllers, son." Bannion said slowly, "I wasn't really thinking of you, Mr Fortune. I was thinking of Seborjar."

Fortune said, with mock relief, "Well, we share one distaste in common." Kalley could see that Fortune was enjoying himself. Over the years, he had learned to know when Fortune was attracted to someone. Bannion obviously attracted him.

Bannion said quietly, "Seborjar, in my judgment, is authoritarian-minded. I don't know whether his authoritarianism inclines towards

Communism or Fascism. If there is any difference between those creeds, it is too subtle for me. Have you ever seen the end products of authoritarianism, Mr Fortune? Real authoritarianism?"

Bannion reminisced, "I was in Europe after the war. I inspected some of the concentration camps. I watched the refugees come over the border. Small, frightened people, leaving behind them everything they owned and sometimes the people they loved. Not very politically minded, most of them. The type of people that in a democracy would go through life without getting into trouble with anyone." His face darkened. "It was terrifying, Mr Fortune."

Fortune said, "Don't get a phobia about Seborjar, son. About him being authoritarian. It's Domineco who's authoritarian-minded. Seborjar's just on the make. He's a phenomenon you'll often find in politics. A man with limitless ambitions. He'd sell his mother if it helped his ambitions. He wants to get to the top, and stay there. It's as simple as that."

But Bannion's hostility to Seborjar had helped, Kalley saw, to make up Fortune's mind. Abruptly he said, "Forget Seborjar, Mr Bannion. Sooner or later he'll collect what's coming to him. It's a miracle he's survived this long as Leader. Miracles don't keep on happening. But I've a proposition you may be interested in."

Bannion said, politely, "What is it, Mr Fortune?"

"Do you know Matt Obley?"

Bannion nodded. "I've never met him. I know of him, of course. He's financial secretary to the Central Funds Committee, isn't he?"

"Yes, Matt's a god boy," said Fortune. "Reliable, faithful, loyal. His politics are sound, too." Kalley grinned into the drink Bannion had handed him. As far as he knew, Obley had no politics. What Fortune meant was that whenever Obley had to cast a vote, in the committee or in any Party ballot, he had always voted the way Fortune had told him to.

Fortune pulled at his long top lip. "Matt's got one weakness. He has sticky fingers. He can't keep 'em out of the cash register. Lately he's been overdoing it. I've warned him repeatedly. But this time he's gone too far. I can't cover for him. I've got to get rid of him. I need somebody to fill the job. It's not a big job. But it's a step up on the Party ladder. Do you want it?"

Bannion said incredulously, "Do you mean to say you've known this has been going on for a long time, Mr Fortune? And you've covered up for him?"

Fortune said, "Don't turn censorious on me, son." He smiled. His face lighted with sudden, disarming charm. "During the war when you had a good, loyal man, and he landed in some minor scrape, what did you do? Hit him with the book? Or try to get him out of it?"

Bannion said, stiffly, "I tried to get him out of it."

Fortune said, "Politics are a kind of war, son. Only the armies aren't government. They're private. Matt's part of my army. He's had his faults. But he's fought for and with me. I don't like making him a casualty, but he has to be expended. If he isn't, the safety of my entire army is threatened. That's the only reason I'm dumping him, boy. I wouldn't like you to be under any illusion about my motives."

Bannion said, "That's a strange attitude, Mr Fortune. I gather that if I accepted the job—and found evidence of his dishonesty—you wouldn't want him jailed, or anything like that." Fortune said, patiently, "I'm being honest with you." He paused. "I'll call you Tom," he said suddenly. "This mister business has whiskers on it. My name's Con." He gestured at the silent Kalley. "And that's Macker."

Bannion said, "This is a new world for me, Mr Fortune." He shook his head distractedly. "Sorry. Con, I mean. I know the Party only at its lower levels."

Kalley said, bleakly, "The higher you get the lower you'll get."

Fortune chuckled. "You'll find Macker's a cynic, Tom. But mostly he's worth listening to. He's grown up in this racket." He turned back to Bannion. "As I was saying, Tom, I'm being honest with you. I ask in return that you be honest with me. If you feel you can't take the job without trying to jail weak, stupid Matt, say so. I'll find someone who can. And I'll hold no grudge. What do you say? Matt, I point out, will be heavily punished. He's not been stealing taxpayers' money. Only funds from the Party which has grossly underpaid him for years. He'll lose his job. He has no qualifications. He never had any, for this job, or any other. He's been in the job so long that I forget who put him there. Probably he was somebody's friend. He's soft. The minor jobs in politics—unless you are using them as stepping stones to bigger things—make you soft. He won't get another job, in politics or out of them. He's finished. Why jail him?"

The door opened. Bannion's equally tall wife entered. She was carrying a laden tray. She was flustered. "Probably has a maid to do the serving but wants to demonstrate that she's democratic," surmised Kalley. "I'm sorry I was so long," Mrs Bannion fussed. Constraint showed in Fortune again. He sat on the edge of his chair, lean and angular, his long legs folded awkwardly. Kalley had noticed years before that Fortune never looked a woman in the eyes. His glance would go from one side of a woman's face to the other without pausing. Yet women generally liked him.

As Mrs Bannion poured the coffee, she recovered her poise. She chattered amiably. She had three children. All daughters. Was that not bad arranging on Tom's part? She smiled at Bannion, her heart-shaped face alive and gentle. Did Mr Fortune have any children? "Yes," said Fortune. Some of his self-consciousness went. He had two boys. He told her their age and where they went to school. Michael, the younger, was clever. But Tony. He shook his head in mock despair. But Tony had other things. He was kind and considerate and had a quiet humour and a laugh that made you glad you were alive. "You know how it is, Mrs Bannion," he said. "He has the gift for happiness and

making other people happy." Mrs Bannion nodded sagely. She knew
how it was. Her youngest was exactly the same. Sweet and lovable. She
made everyone happy just by being around.

The woman turned to Kalley. Was Mr Kalley married? Did he have
any children? Kalley told her tersely that he had a wife and small
daughter. She waited politely. But Kalley said nothing more. There
was an hiatus, chill and uncomfortable. Then she turned back to
Fortune. Kalley smiled to himself. He knew she did not like him.
His lack of warmth, so different from Fortune's while Fortune had
been talking about his family. Kalley thought sardonically, "You'll
learn, sister. If your husband stays in politics." He saw no reason
why he should share, even fleetingly, his intimacy with the two Annes
with this stranger. She was not part of his private life, but of politics.
The Annes were his private preserve. He guarded them jealously. He
watched the woman obliquely. She obviously adored her big, intense
husband. She kept throwing him little smiles. If she had any interest in
politics it was because he was interested. Kalley judged that whatever
her husband did or said, she would back loyally. She would encourage
him to hold to what he thought was right.

Bannion abruptly put down his coffee cup. "Janice, Mr Fortune
has just offered me a Party job."

She said, "That's wonderful, darling." To Fortune she said, "Tom's
a fine man, Mr Fortune. Anything he does he does with all his heart.
The Party is lucky to have him."

Bannion said ruefully. "The Party doesn't know its luck, Janice. So
far I haven't made an impact."

"I'm sure the Party is lucky to have him, Mrs Bannion," Fortune
said. He sounded apologetic. "The Party's like the mills of God. It
works slowly. We are supposed to be a radical Party, but there's no
Party as conservative as a radical Party. It doesn't like changes, in
either personnel or ideas. The job I've offered Tom. It's not a big job.

It's been full time for the man who has been doing it. But Tom can probably handle it in a couple of hours' work a week. It would not interfere greatly with his private business. However, it could be a start. These jobs often lead to bigger things in the Party."

"You want that, don't you, dear?" she said to her husband. To Fortune she explained, "Tom's been restless. Frustrated. He feels that an individual cannot do much, alone, without a position in the Party. And he feels there's so much to be done. So many things crying for attention. Let go by default." She smiled fondly across at her husband. "When he comes home from Party meetings he tells me about these things. They distress him. He's been used to doing things, in the Air Force, and in his profession, quickly and efficiently. This dreadful waiting for people to take any notice of what you're saying or advocating. It's angered Tom. Tom's a man of action, Mr Fortune."

Bannion protested, "Janice, you sound like a salesman, trying to put me across to Mr Fortune. You'll embarrass him. Not to mention me." To Fortune he said, "Janice is an enthusiast, Con."

Mrs Bannion said, "Darling, you're an enthusiast, too. Anything you decide to do you do with all your energies."

Fortune said, "That's not a bad way to do things, Mrs Bannion. My offer is open. It's up to your husband." He stood up. "Well, Macker and I will have to be getting along. Thanks for the coffee, Mrs Bannion. And the drinks."

On the porch, Fortune repeated his good-byes. He added, "Tom, I'll have to fill that job within the next forty-eight hours. If you decide to take it, phone me. If you don't phone I'll assume you don't want it. If you can't get hold of me, let Macker know your decision."

Bannion said, "A difficulty occurs to me. The job's elective, isn't it? The committee votes on who is to fill it. I don't know anyone on the committee that I'm aware of. They don't know me. What happens?"

Fortune said, "That's the least of your worries, Tom. Leave that to Macker and me. We own this particular committee. If you decide on the job, the job's yours."

Mrs Bannion said, puzzlement in her light, pleasant voice, "That sounds rather undemocratic, Mr Fortune."

Fortune smiled, "It's the way a Democratic Party works."

Bannion and his wife waved to them from the porch. As the car turned out of the driveway, Kalley said quietly, "What's your judgment, Con?"

Fortune slumped in his seat, his long, bony legs extended. "Nice fella," he said judiciously. "Bit intense. But the mob likes 'em intense. The kind of burning-eyed character who'd give a mass Party rally a big lift. Remember old Stack Certise. Big black eyes blazing out of his white face. God, he could lift 'em out of their seats. Mad, of course. But what a mob orator!

This fella's got something of Stack about him. Not so flamboyant. Probably not so crazy. The same intensity. Apart from the value he may have to us as a speaker, he's inexperienced. He's still a small boy lost in a big world. But nobody's fool. A few ideas. Anti-Fascist and anti-Communist. Capable of learning his way around fast." He folded his long legs closer and said, "Damn these carseats—they're too short." He readjusted himself. "Whether he'll be any good to us, of course, depends on whether he can get over his first hurdle."

"What's the hurdle? Matt Obley?"

"Yes," said Fortune. "Bannion's apparently got the reformer's itch. His thinking is still simple. He sees things in black and white. Either you're honest or you're not. If you're dishonest you should be in jail. If you're honest you shouldn't be. It's either this or that. It is his bourgeois upbringing. He can't see that a man can be dishonest in one percent of his dealings and honest in the rest. For Bannion there are no intermediate shadings. It's black or white. Maybe he'll learn differently. Maybe not."

Kalley braked for a stop light. He threw the car into neutral. As the engine gently ticked over he said, "You're a wily old fox, Con."

"I know," said Fortune. "But what particular piece of foxiness are you referring to?"

The light changed to green. Kalley put the car into gear and they moved slowly forward. "That guff about private armies." He tried unsuccessfully to mimic Fortune's intonation. "Loyalty to the boys." He looked at Fortune. "Good stuff that, Con. The kind of stuff that would appeal to a man with Bannion's background."

"I know," said Fortune, placidly. "That's why I used it."

"I know there's that element in it, Con. You're a loyalist, one of your more attractive qualities. You'll stick yourself out for your boys. So long as it's not too risky. But there's more to it than that."

"How do you see it, Macker?" Fortune asked, calmly. He liked talking this way with Kalley. Such conversations were part of their relationship, so close in politics, so distant as far as their private lives were concerned. Kalley, he knew, said what he thought when they were talking together.

"I see it this way, Con. You don't want to jail Obley. You like him despite his weaknesses. But not jailing him pays off politically, too. If you jailed him you'd get some of the backwash. He's one of your boys. He's been one for years. You wouldn't be too popular with the respectable section of the Party for involving the Party in a public scandal. This way you get rid of him. That demonstrates your honesty to the respectable section of the Party. You clean up the mess discreetly. They'll applaud that. Your own boys will know it's got to be done, in their interests as well as yours. But the fact that all you do is get rid of him will help you. 'Con isn't vindictive,' they'll tell each other. 'Matt let him down badly, but he let Matt off as easily as possible.' They'll be reinforced in their belief that you are loyal to those who serve you."

They were getting near Kalley's home. Fortune said, "That's about it, Macker." He sounded amused. "Anything wrong with my reasoning?"

"No," said Kalley. "It's sound, Con." He pulled the car up at the pavement and got out. Fortune slid across to the seat he had vacated.

"Night, Con," said Kalley.

"Night, Macker," said Fortune. Absently he added, "Give my best to the wife."

Kalley knew the words had no meaning. He knew that Fortune had no interest in Anne, except as an appendage to Kalley. He did not expect Fortune to have any interest. She was outside politics, and hence outside the range of his association with Fortune. He stood on the sidewalk for a moment, watching the tail light of Fortune's car disappearing. Then he turned and entered the house. As he crossed the threshold he deliberately closed his mind on Fortune and Bannion and the Party. Inside the two Annes were waiting for him. Little Anne would be asleep. But big Anne, wide-shouldered, chunky, refreshingly direct, would be awake. "I'm on my island," he thought, happily. "With the drawbridge up."

Bannion did not phone. He came personally. Fortune was out. He had been summoned urgently to a meeting of Party managers at the Legislature. Daryl Kandur, a lean, cadaverous man with bad teeth and a flattened nose, who acted as Fortune's runner to his waterfront associates, was with Kalley. They were in the tiny office Kalley occupied next to Fortune's bigger but only slightly less dingy office, when Mrs Belasco knocked and came in. Mrs Belasco was a neat, middle-aged woman, with a blunt, competent manner. She was the widow of a man who had been associated with Fortune in his early political days. When he died, Fortune offered the woman, left penniless and with an infant, the post as his private secretary. She was capable, loyal and secretive but tactless. She adored Fortune, tolerated Kalley, but disapproved of most of Fortune's hangers-on. She glared at Kandur, who self-consciously brushed at the greasy dandruff embedded on the shoulders of his wrinkled, dirty suit. Kandur said, hastily, "I'm off, Macker. Nothing Con wanted?"

"No," said Kalley. When the door shut behind Kandur, the woman made a grimace of distaste. "I can never understand why Con surrounds himself with drunken deadbeats like Kandur," she said, angrily.

"He has to, Aggie," said Kalley, quietly. "They're part of his strength. Kandur's been a cog in Con's machine since they were boys. Once he was a spruce, energetic young fella. Going places. Then the drink got him. And women and horses. But he never ever ratted on Con. And Con doesn't dump old pals—unnecessarily. It's part of his stock in trade." He raised an eyebrow. "Besides, Kandur's useful. Don't ask me why, but he still has considerable drag on the waterfront. He knows everyone. Everyone knows him. If there's a string down there that can be pulled, he can pull it. And when Con's interests are involved he pulls 'em. The whole lot."

The woman sniffed. "Well, I won't have him in my office. He smells. I don't think he has had a bath in weeks." She remembered her errand. "There's a man in my office. Wants to see Con. Name's Bannion. Interesting looking type. Dark wavy hair. A tall man. Attractive in a life-is-real, life-is-earnest kind of way."

"I know him," said Kalley. "Send him in, will you, Aggie."

Bannion entered slowly; his crippled hand was inside his coat.

He had not been attracted to Kalley at their last night's meeting.

His wife had summed up his feelings. She had said, "I like Mr Fortune, Tom. He's nice. He seems so awfully . . ." She groped for a word. "Trustworthy. That's what he is. Trustworthy. But that awful little man with the cold eyes." She had shuddered. "There's something reptilian about him. He's dangerous. Like a snake." She had repeated her shudder. "I'm sorry for his wife, there's something inhuman about him."

Bannion said, "I was hoping to see Mr Fortune."

"Con's out. Won't be back today. Grab a chair. What's on your mind?"

Bannion felt uncertain. He took a chair. Should he tell his decision to this neat, colourless man with the fingers heavily stained with nicotine and a mouth like a rat-trap?

Kalley sensed his uncertainty. He said, without expression, "It's okay. Con has authorised me to act in this matter. If you're round here much you'll find I often act for Con." He smiled thinly. "I understand that unofficially I'm described as Con's tomahawk man."

Bannion thought, "What the hell?" If he was going to get into the inner workings of the Party he would have to get used to dealing with men he instinctively disliked in dingy offices that somehow seemed appropriate to dingy dealings. He said, "As there was a proviso I had to undertake to fulfil, I thought a conversation with Con would be more satisfactory than phoning."

Kalley said, "You mean Matt? Well, what's the verdict?"

Bannion said, slowly, "I thought over what Con said about Obley. I think I see his point. It would be unnecessary cruelty to jail Obley."

Kalley said, quietly, "Apart from the fact it's good politics, it's quite a good point, really." Bannion glanced at him sharply. He wondered whether the hard-faced little man was being sarcastic. He could not be sure. His handling of a wide variety of men during the war years had given him sensitivity on how men were feeling. But Kalley was something new, outside the range of his experience.

Bannion said, "I'm prepared to forget about Obley after he's out of the job. I would be delighted to take the job. You can tell Mr Fortune—Con—that I'll clean up the mess to the best of my ability. And there won't be future messes. He can rely on that."

"Okay," said Kalley. "Then it's a firm deal."

Bannion went to get to his feet, but Kalley waved him back into his chair.

"We'll package it on the spot," said Kalley. He took a cheap, black-backed notebook from his pocket and opened it. He found the page, picked up the phone, and dialled.

Bannion heard him say, "Pony? Kalley here." There was a second's silence. Then Kalley said, "Con knows about that. I phoned you on something different. Con wants the committee to meet tonight and fire Matt. Don't give any reasons. Matt knows what they are. Just fire him. Matt won't protest." There was a pause. Then Kalley's voice continued, "Con's sorry, too. But it's got to be done. Then you nominate a man named Tom Bannion. Keech can second his nomination."

Again there was a pause. Kalley was gazing straight ahead, blankly. Then he smiled bleakly into the instrument. He said. "Pony, you may have kinda promised to get the job for Billy Condon. It doesn't surprise me. You're into Billy for a nice piece of change. We know that. But you'll have to get out of your gambling debts another way than working your bookie pal into a Party job."

He put his hand over the receiver and said across the desk to Bannion, "The trouble these characters can get themselves into!" He resumed speaking into the receiver. "Yeah. Tom Bannion." He spelled the name. "And no funny business, Pony. Con wouldn't like it. Our majority on that committee is eleven to four. That's the vote we want for Bannion. Neither more nor less. Okay, Pony. Watch it." He cradled the phone.

Bannion said, "So that's how these things are arranged." There was a sour downturn to his lips. Kalley thought, "He'd like to pull out. He doesn't approve of the deal, me, or the way it's done. But he wants the job. He thinks it's a move in the right direction and he's not going to let squeamishness come between him and opportunity." Not every man had his price. But those who wanted to rule mostly had theirs. Bannion obviously could not be bought for money. He could probably never be bought completely. But a large part of him could. With the down payment of a piddling little job that presented a chance to move on to bigger things.

Kalley nodded. "Normally that would be sufficient to wrap it up neatly." He took his little cheap notebook out again. "But there's a complication in this one. A loose string to tie up." He ran his finger down a page and found the entry he wanted.

"I gather from your phone conversation I have a rival," said Bannion. "A bookie." There was a trace of distaste in his voice.

Kalley picked up the receiver. "That's right, friend," he said tonelessly.

"Could be rather humiliating if things went wrong," said Bannion.

Kalley replaced the receiver carefully. " Look, mister, there are a few things you'll have to learn if you're going to work with Con. The Party isn't a kindergarten. Nor a gathering of Knights of the Round Table. It is a big, loose organisation that deals in a lot of commodities. The most important commodity it handles is power." He shook out a cigarette, his yellow-stained fingers precise in their movement." With power—even a little power—you can do lots of things. A lot of men besides political idealists know that. That's why no political movement in history, aristocratic or mass, has been able to exist without a fringe of racketeers attaching themselves to it. In the wealthier parties—like our opponents—or the more puritanical parties, like the Communists, the racketeers disguise themselves. In the wealthier parties they hide behind the front of near legality and slick company lawyers. In the

Communists they mask themselves behind political slogans and the pretence that their particular line of banditry has an ideological justification."

He lit his cigarette, blew out the match and placed it in the ashtray without taking his eyes from Bannion. "We're a mass party," he said. "We are democratic to the extent that we still maintain the fiction that the rank and file have the final decision on Party matters. We're nothing of the sort, of course. But fiction is more acceptable than truth. The illusion is more real than the actuality. Being a mass democratic party we are vulgar. Even our racketeers are vulgar, obvious racketeers. Like this bookie who's your rival. He probably has no interest in the Party. He couldn't care less. But if he can get himself made financial secretary of the Central Funds Committee it's dough in his pocket. As a bookie he's at the mercy of any cop who wants to put the squeeze on him. He can wind up in the hoosegow or be bled dry. But as a bookie who is also a Party official, however small, he's got power. It mightn't be a great deal. But it's sufficient to take the cops off his back and to give him an immunity that other bookies haven't got."

"Why the lecture?"

"I just wanted to point out to you that there's nothing humiliating in being opposed by a bookie," said Kalley. "It's a fact of life in this Party. Before you hit the top, you'll be opposed by a lot of queer people. Don't let it upset you. If you do, you're no good to Con."

"A friendly warning?" said Bannion.

"A warning," said Kalley. He picked up the phone and dialled. He waited for a moment, scrawling idly on the pad in front of him. Then Bannion heard him say, "Keechy? Kalley here." A pause. "Yes, I know. There'll be no smell. We're fixing it tonight. Pony's calling the committee together. Now get this. Con wants a character named Bannion—Tom Bannion—put in." He spelled out the name again, patiently. "Pony's been told. You're to second Bannion's nomination.

There could be a slip up. I don't think Pony'll try to double-cross us. But he's into Billy Condon for a piece of change. Billy wants the job. If Pony tosses in Billy's name, you take over. Nominate Bannion yourself. I'll fix a seconder. I'll be in touch with the rest of the boys today. They'll know to take their lead from you if Pony tries to pull something. You got the name? Bannion." He spelt it again. "Okay, Keechy. Look after yourself, fella." He replaced the receiver.

"That packages it?" asked Bannion.

"That packages it," said Kalley.

"What does Con want in return?" asked Bannion. "Apart from my undertaking about Obley, all he'll get will be the knowledge that the finances the committee administers will be handled honestly."

"That's all Con wants," said Kalley. He thought of the complex, tenuous bonds that were already starting to tie Bannion to Fortune. Bannion's discovery that he shared with Fortune a dislike of Seborjar. Bannion's knowledge that Fortune had secured the job for him. The flattery of knowing that Fortune had thought sufficiently highly of him to get him the job. And these ties would become stronger in the future. Going on the committee as Fortune's nominee, he would be identified by the Party as a Fortune man. Relying on Fortune both to keep the job and for future advancement. Turning to Fortune for advice. Getting used to fighting his own and Fortune's political battles so that fighting on Fortune's side came ultimately from habit rather than deliberate choice. Failing some Party crisis that would involve a question of principle in which they would take opposing sides, or a deliberate defection by Bannion for a higher price to some enemy of Fortune, Bannion from here on could be relied upon as a Fortune supporter. Not until he became a Party Leader in his own right, if he ever did, would he again be in a position to make completely independent decisions. And Kalley, basing his judgment upon his assessment of Bannion's personality, believed that if the man ever did achieve the status of Leader he would line up in the ranks of Fortune's enemies reluctantly and under the compulsion of circumstance that left him no alternative.

Bannion would have an old-time concept of loyalty. He would not sell out lightly the man who gave him his start in the Party. "That's all Con wants," Kalley repeated, his lined, hard face impassive. "No sticky fingers in the money, and the committee's affairs run honestly."

As Bannion walked down the broad, shallow steps to the sidewalk from the old, drab building that was State Party headquarters and in which Fortune and Kalley had their offices, he felt a sense of achievement for the first time since he had joined the Party shortly after the war. He stood on the sidewalk, looking up. The building was grey and shabby. It was located in an older part of the city, hidden away, grudgingly, behind giant shopping blocks that faced away from it as though the modern shiny buildings wanted to turn their backs on the decaying area. On the other side of Party headquarters, the city sloped away, downwards, growing ever seamier and more depressing until it reached the soiled griminess of the waterfront.

Bannion thought. "Well, I'm on my way. But where?" He had the same expectant feeling he had when he joined the Air Force way back there when both the world and Bannion were simpler and somehow less uncertain. It was a feeling that he had dedicated himself to service, mixed with a doubt and fearfulness about what that service would entail. He could not work out why he had this feeling. When he joined the Air Force he had been a young man surrounded by young men, keen, a little nervous, anxious to do something, zestful, but mostly pretending a hard- boiled, tough cynicism about why they were where they were, a wisecracking manner that failed to conceal their exposed and vulnerable youth. But the men he was now associated with were not pretending, Bannion thought. They were genuinely hardboiled and tough. Kalley, that cold little man in the grimy, ill-furnished office with the window that looked across the city's drabness towards the waterfront. "A repellent man," Bannion thought, remembering friends who had fought and died for the democracy that Kalley stripped naked with the pitiless efficiency of a morgue attendant preparing a corpse for dissection. Fortune was a better kind of man. He seemed kinder, more human, without Kalley's unemotional callousness. Probably other parties were, as Kalley said, not much different, except that their adherents more often pretended, even to themselves, that their motives were pure and disinterested. They protested that they were working for human welfare—the wealthier parties by sending their highly paid lawyers into the courts to cloak their banditry with legalisms, the Communists and the Fascists by mowing down with machine guns the unarmed and uncomprehending masses in the name of the brotherhood of man.

Maybe living the way they did, the way they had to, as the rulers of a raw, democratically based party, making few pretences away from the hypnotising make-believe of the public rostrum, the Party Leaders were more honest than their opponents. Their dishonesty lay in their refusal to educate their fellow men—the ruled—to knowledge of the universal sinfulness of Man which the leaders accepted among themselves openly—in many cases tacitly, and in some as naturally as breathing.

Bannion thought sombrely, "There's a flaw in that thinking somewhere. There must be. If there isn't it makes Kalley, detached, mordant, bitter, as honest a man as I've met." He did not like the thought. With an effort he switched his mind back to what the future held in store for him politically.

As he walked away from Party headquarters along the shabby blocks towards where the shopping centres were located, he felt that he was at last really making progress. A tall, striking figure, with his withered hand out of sight under his coat, he felt happy. He had ideas. He knew that. He was well educated in a Party in which educational qualifications still gave a cachet. He could speak. Already he had experienced the exhilarating lift of galvanising a dull, heavy meeting into life and emotion. He was sincere. He was sure of that. Unlike these others, he would not sacrifice principle for advancement. Fortune had been curious about whether he wanted to climb to the top. Bannion himself had never thought of it. But if Fortune was inquisitive about it, apparently Fortune thought he had qualities that could take him there. "Maybe," he thought. "Maybe. We'll see." Kalley's hard, lined face floated up out of his subconscious mind. He was conscious of a slight irritation.

In the years that followed, Bannion justified Fortune's selection of him as a man who had something. He became a familiar figure at Party rallies. His wealth enabled him to give the attention to Party duties from which others were debarred by outside interests, and the necessity to earn a living. Big, with dark eyes smouldering in the muddy brown of his long, serious face, a powerful dogmatic speaker with radical views, he acquired his own small following within the rank and file, many of whom felt the man's intense sincerity. His alliance with Fortune was loose, though Fortune consistently backed him and expected—and received—in return Bannion's support. This was particularly valuable when, as sometimes happened, a Party manoeuvre caused the fight to be waged from public platforms before massed audiences. There Bannion was at his best. But Bannion was too painfully earnest for Fortune to make him a close henchman. Bannion became too agitated about minor peccadilloes for Fortune's taste. He had a gift for transforming a minor tactical move into a full-scale crusade. Fortune told him once, "If you can win on a narrow front, never extend the battle. You could lose."

Bannion looked at him with resentful eyes. He was with Fortune and Kalley in Fortune's office. He said, "If a thing's right, Con, you've got to fight—against everyone, if necessary." He had recognised the axiom Fortune had quoted. It was one of Kalley's. "It's a matter of conscience, Con," he added. Fortune said, "You want to watch that conscience of yours, Tom. It's like halitosis, socially. It could ruin you politically." "Better ruin than rottenness," said Bannion.

Kalley recognised the danger signal in Fortune's flush. He interposed with smooth coldness, "It's a matter of degree."

Bannion said, "What's a matter of degree?"

Kalley smiled without humour. "Both ruin and rottenness."

Bannion, his anger diverted from Fortune, said, "I'd like to know what your basic political philosophy is, Macker. You seem to hold the entire human race in contempt."

"No," said Kalley. "Only politicians."

"What do you really think of them, Macker?" asked Bannion.

"Of them?" the little man's voice was quietly derisive. "Of you, you mean, Tom. You're one of them. You mightn't acknowledge it to yourself. But the years have made you so."

"All right." The big man was impatient. "What do you think of us, Macker? Really?"

The little man's face was a frozen mask. "All politicians are bastards, Tom," he said. "But some are bigger bastards than others. They can't help being bastards. They're born that way."

Bannion said disgustedly, "You make democracy sound hopeless." Kalley said, "I like a democracy. In a democracy you get a selection between a variety of bastards. You can always—if you've got any sense—select the least evil bastard as your ruler. But in Fascism or Communism you don't get a selection. You just get a bastard over the top of you. And usually he's the biggest bastard of the lot. When the bastards are left to inbreed instead of, as happens in a democracy, being culled out a bit by the voters, it's almost invariably the most unscrupulous, the most ruthless, the most vindictive, and the most ambitious bastard that gets to the top. That's the way politics work, in the Kremlin or in the Party. Politics are cosmopolitan. Only the techniques vary. The bastardry is constant. You know that."

"I know nothing of the sort," Bannion fumed. "If I thought that I'd go out and cut my throat."

Fortune had recovered his good humour. He said, "Don't cut it before Friday, Tom. The Management Committee meets then. And we need you there. It'll be a line-ball vote." Kalley said, poker-faced, "No need to cut it at all, Tom. You're by no means the biggest bastard round this town. And if you cut your throat it's more than likely that a bigger bastard'd move into your shoes."

Fortune said, his wide, humorous mouth creasing with sudden charm, "That's the highest compliment I've heard you pay anyone in years, Macker."

Bannion said, "No wonder the Party's rotten. People like you two help to make it so." He stormed angrily out of the room, slamming the door behind him.

The looseness of the alliance between Fortune and Bannion, which arose largely from Bannion's inability to see politics through Fortune's more tolerant eyes, worked to Bannion's advantage. He was able to build up around himself a group, closer in spirit and outlook than Fortune could ever be, without interference. Though this group functioned as an auxiliary of Fortune's political faction, it was semi-autonomous.

On the morning of Seborjar's rally, Bannion held a meeting in his office of the group in the Party hierarchy with which he was associated and of which he was now the *de facto* leader. His office was not in Party headquarters, but down town in the high-priced business section. It was a hangover from the days before he gave all his time to the Party, and was part of a suite that he maintained from his own pocket. He had furnished it when he was active as a consulting engineer. The office was large, well-lighted, and airy. He sat behind his wide desk. The rest draped themselves on the modern, metal furniture. There were four of them.

Louis Vittor was a professor of political science at the State University. He was something over forty, a thin, lively man, with a brisk manner and an intense face which lit charmingly when he smiled. He was a mass of contradictions, liberal in his opinions, a belligerent atheist, and prudishly narrow in his habits. He was a bachelor, fearful of women, a fussy, tidy man with an enduring, enthusiastic faith that an enlightened economic policy was the cure-all for social evils, and that Man had within him the potential for perfection.

Sarly Longac was a huge, ponderous man of immense strength. He was very quiet, calm and just. He ran a small union with paternal authority, and was respected by both his members and the employers with whom he had dealings. His reputation was that no agreement with him need be in writing. His word was his bond. He had started life as a watchmaker. Though his thick, sausage-like fingers looked clumsy, they were deft. He was completely fearless. Two of his three sons had been killed in action during the war. He had not reproached them when they disagreed with his pacifism and enlisted. He lived with his white-haired wife and his surviving son, almost as immense as himself, in a tiny home in the inner suburbs. Father, mother and son were a tightly knit group, all devoted church-goers, who belonged to a little non-conformist sect, and were addicted to hymn singing. They spent their surplus income on various charities to which they also gave the use of their leisure. Longac had worked his way up in the Party almost solely on the personal respect accorded him.

Franky Canover had been a butcher before he was elected to the State Legislature. He was a pleasant, fattish man, with a round, plump, rather stupid face. He parted his hair in the centre, and had a sickly, unsure smile. In the war he had been decorated three times for outstanding bravery. He wanted vaguely, to help other people, but was not quite sure how. He owed his rise in the Party to Joe Lilley, who had fascinated him with words. It was in the immediate post-war period. Lilley thought he could possibly exploit Canover's three decorations to organise him on to the Party's Management Committee, where he would be a vote in Lilley's pocket. Lilley had succeeded. Canover had an engaging modesty. Once on the committee he sat there unsure, guided from outside the committee by Lilley's directions. He felt there was something wrong in the set-up. Lilley and the conservatism of the Party which caused the job of the nonentity to be safer that of the man who engaged in controversy, kept him on the committee year after year. But when Bannion was finally voted onto the committee Canover switched his allegiance from Lilley to Bannion with a relief which, at the time, he could not explain even to himself. It was his rebellion against the corruption with which he had unknowingly been surrounded. Bannion's influence, backed by Fortune and Party habit, had kept him on the committee since.

Maury Fines held no Party position. A garage mechanic, he was a thin, scrawny man, with heavily bowed shoulders and long, nervous fingers that he twisted and pulled at continuously. He had been a Japanese prisoner-of-war. His experiences had left their mark. He could forgive being beaten and ill-treated by the Japanese. That was part of the risk of war. But he had spent months in a camp terrorised by a gang of racketeers among the prisoners. They had fleeced their fellow countrymen, extorted from them and his best friend, who had defied them, had been found dead with a razor-like fragment of a knife blade driven into his back. He hated the racketeers who hung at the outskirts of the Party. He acted as Bannion's executive officer. Usually Bannion enjoyed these meetings. They reminded him of the briefings he held during the war before he led his squadron, with its multiple bellies stuffed with the explosive materials of death, off the ground. He was no longer, as he had been then, the autocratic ruler within the confines of his command. Here he was merely the first among equals. Yet he experienced a greater sense of power than ever he had felt back in those nearly forgotten days. Then his freedom of choice had been limited. As a politician, he felt himself unfettered, circumscribed only by his own abilities, political circumstance and the strength of his pertinacity. But today had been different. Vittor had been difficult. The professor had moments of stubbornness when he refused petulantly for hours to budge from a viewpoint. He thought that the group should not attend Seborjar's rally that night. They all disliked and distrusted Seborjar. Why be hypocrites? Besides, their presence, indicating to the voter's unbroken Party support for Seborjar, was bad politics. It helped to build Seborjar up, which was the last thing they wanted to do.

"We've got to be there," insisted Bannion. "Our absence would cause comment. The Party tradition is that even if you don't like the Leader you back him—while he is the Leader. We'd lose some of our rank and file support if we showed hostility publicly."

"Somebody must take a stand publicly against this man sooner or later," said Vittor. "I'm sick of working against him behind the scenes and dutifully applauding him when we're on a platform with him in public. It is not only dishonest, it's bad politics. It suits Seborjar not to have the fight in the open. He can play off one enemy against the other. Let's drag the fight out from the Party's back room into the public arena."

Sarly Longac nodded his big head with slow approval. "Something in that, Tom," he approved. "Louis could be talking good sense. If we believe Seborjar should be replaced for the Party's good—as we do—let's say so. It's a risk. We mightn't be able to carry the Party with us. But it's a risk we've got to take sooner or later. We've got to stand to what we believe. Unless we are prepared to let Seborjar carry on as Leader indefinitely. And I, for one, am not prepared."

"Let's not be premature," said Bannion quickly. "We know that there's an excellent chance that I'll be Party Chairman within the next six weeks." Kalley's face, hard, mocking and tough for a moment came to his mind's eye. Irritably he erased it. "As Chairman I'll wield considerable power. With the backing of that power we can afford an open, public breach with Seborjar."

He extended his crippled hand. With his good hand he started to count off on the withered twisted fingers the points he made. "The competition for Chairman is fining down to two—Joe Lilley and myself. There are four votes in this room, Louis, Sarly's, Franky's and mine. Domineco hates me, but if he has to choose between me and Joe Lilley he'll throw his votes my way. He has eight. Con Fortune has six. He'll back me. Eighteen votes, out of a total of thirty. Enough to win. Why create a situation now that could react against us?" His hands were trembling as he strove to impress the others. "Let's create the situation — after we've won."

Fines said harshly, "By God, that's good sense. We've got Lilley— and Seborjar, licked right now. Eighteen to twelve. And we might do even better. Pick up a couple of swinging votes on the committee. I'm with you, Tom. I say play it quietly until we can afford to play it tough. It's not long to wait—six weeks. I've waited years to get at some of these crook bastards in the Party. Why take any risks now?"

Longac had not been hard to convince. Despite his attachment to principle, his training in union politics had given him a flexibility that Vittor on occasions lacked. Vittor had been harder to budge, but finally he succumbed. When they left, Bannion leaned against the window, staring down into the street, far below.

"Damn Vittor and his narrow nonconformist background," he thought. Vittor professed to be an atheist, but he had been raised as a Lutheran. This early training gave him an intellectual prudery that Bannion was finding increasingly irritating. "Vittor's an awkward ally," Bannion thought. "There's nothing much I can do about him at the moment, though. Maybe later, I can replace him with someone more reliable."

His mind went on to consider Seborjar's rally. He would be there on the platform, with the rest of the Management Committee.

He had already decided his attitude. He would sit behind Seborjar, expressionless. His applause would be only perfunctory. The rank and file would see that he was going through the right motions. But the more knowing ones among the Party leaders would detect that he was prepared to let things move towards a showdown. It would not do him any harm. Almost to a man they disliked Seborjar, anyway, though, unlike Fortune, they kept their dislike carefully concealed.

Tonight could be a turning point, he thought. He wondered if it would be, or whether it would be as unproductive as scores of such meetings he had attended in the past. "I'll find out," he thought, philosophically, "tonight."

CHAPTER 5

Elsa, Gilly Hoskin's wife, was a small, neat woman. She had a tight face in which the mouth was peevish and discontented. There was no crispness about her. Her features blurred into each other to produce a nondescript effect. In contrast her voice was sharp and decisive.

She said, "You'll have to move soon, Gilly. Otherwise Seborjar'll outlast you."

She and Hoskin were at the breakfast table. They lived in the decaying, grimy working-class district that Hoskin represented in the Legislature and refused to leave. Outside the house was a replica of those among which it stood—squat, dreary, depressing. The neighbouring dwellings pressed around like a dirty corset, cramping and constricting. Inside, the front room where Hoskin saw his electors had the same dinginess. But once that room had been traversed the house became transformed. Though tasteless and tiny, the rear rooms had comfort, even luxury. They were expensively furnished. The minute kitchen had every convenience. The dining room in which Hoskin and his wife were finishing their breakfast was bright and well equipped.

Hoskin knitted his brows. He said, "Elsa, you can't rush these things. If you do you wreck them. Everything becomes ungummed. You have to be patient."

Hoskin was a short, square-shouldered man, as flat-bellied now as he had been when in the harsh days of his youth and early manhood he had made his living prize fighting. He had a scarred, flat face which when he was angry was a ferocious, frozen mask, intimidating and ugly. His flashes of anger had once been genuine. Nowadays they were mostly synthetic, his scowl a weapon to be used consciously and with deliberation. Apart from manufactured wrath which, as he grew older, he used more sparingly so as not to cheapen its effectiveness, his offensive weapons were a forceful wit and a bellowing laugh that cut arrogantly across the feelings of his victim. He did not drink or smoke, but he did not parade his abstention as a virtue. He liked his trim, muscular body, and wanted to keep it that way. He was personally honest and politically unscrupulous, fearless morally and possessed of unlimited ambition.

"You can't afford to wait much longer—you're not getting any younger, Gilly," said Elsa.

"I'm only fifty-six," said Hoskin, defensively. "Fifty-six isn't old in politics. I'm younger than Seborjar."

"Seborjar's within reach of the summit," said Elsa. She was poised and detached. Hoskin had the sense of impatient inadequacy that he so often felt in her presence. "While he remains Party Leader he'll continue within reach of the summit. It only needs the Party to regain popularity. Or for the government to disintegrate. Some lucky turn of the political wheel. And Seborjar'll have Alex Pope's job. It won't be you who'll have it, Gilly. You've further to climb than Seborjar. Sooner or later you have to climb to where Seborjar stands now—to the Party leadership. But even when you get there you have no chance of getting to the top—into Alex Pope's shoes—in less than two legislative terms. That's six years, Gilly. At the best—if you replace Seborjar as Leader this year—you'll be sixty-two. That's about your limit. After that you'll be struggling. Against something you can't beat, Gilly. Time. The politician's worst enemy."

Hoskin got to his feet. He was not angry—he was thoughtful. But habit put the semblance of anger into his voice. He said, "I'll get there. We've come a long way from Colton, Elsa. People said I'd never get as far as I have. But I'm here."

"Yes," said Elsa. "But time was on your side when Benny Deakin picked you up out of Colton's shanty town and gave you your start. You were only a baby then."

Hoskin laughed. He said, "You came from the same shanty town, my dear. And I wasn't such a baby. I'd had twenty-two professional fights when I met Deakin. And I won twenty of them."

Elsa said, calmly, "And hated every fight, Gilly. Even the winning ones."

"Sure," said Hoskin. "I was frightened. It wasn't bad when I was having the best of it. I got a boost out of my superiority. But I was always frightened, even when I was winning. Frightened of being hurt. But I never showed my fear, Elsa. Sometimes, even now, I have nightmares. A glove's coming towards me. It gets larger and larger until it blocks out everything else. And then something explodes in my head and I wake up sweating."

"You're still frightened, aren't you, Gilly? Of people like Seborjar?" Elsa's voice was gentler. "Men who can hit back? Men with the good education that you never had? What they'll do to you? What could happen to you because of the things they do to you? The fear of being beaten. You hide it well, Gilly. But it's always with you. Yet you've a better brain than Seborjar, for all his learning. You've more ability in your little finger than Fortune has in his whole length. You're good, Gilly. You were born to get to the top. But you're frightened."

Hoskin said defensively, "You've got it wrong, honey. I've tried to explain to you before. They can't frighten me with their words and what they might do to me. They're not hitting at my body. It's pain, physical pain that scares me. Nothing else. I'm not frightened of the other things that might happen. I know that I'm better than any of them — good enough and tough enough to beat them all."

"Perhaps," said Elsa, noncommittally. She stood up with a gesture of finality and started collecting dishes. She said, "Better get going, Gilly. They'll be waiting for you at the office."

She went with him to the front door. As he kissed her he put his arm roughly round her shoulder and squeezed her. "Don't worry, honey," he said, "Things'll work out. I'll make 'em work out." Elsa gazed at him. Neat and nondescript and middle-aged, she still possessed reservoirs of passion that had chained Hoskin to her for over thirty years, and that she drew upon in the secrecy of their bedroom after the lights had been put out. It was as though she needed darkness to come alive and to shed the cold, withdrawn surface that she presented even to Hoskin other than in the warm, fumbling blackness. She said, "You'll have to start making them work out soon, Gilly—the years are running out on us."

Hoskin often walked to the office. It was part of his gospel of fitness. He walked quickly, his arms swinging, his torso slightly forward so that his weight was thrown on to the balls of his feet. A vigorous, compact man, bareheaded, his brown, thick, straight hair brushed back from his wide forehead, only slightly tinged with grey. Normally as he walked he did his thinking about the problems that would confront him during the day. But Elsa had shaken him, with her insistence that for him time was running out.

He wanted the Party leadership that Seborjar held. The leadership would put him within striking distance of the greater prize that was his aim and that Elsa coveted for him—Alex Pope's job as ruler of the nation. But even if Elsa was right and time was running out for him, there was nothing much he could do about it. These things could not be rushed. If they were, they receded like mirages, mockingly, to a greater distance. Timing was as important as any other factor in politics.

Two years earlier he had coldly worked out his tactics. None of the Party's hierarchy, himself included, liked or trusted Seborjar. Completely without conscience, able to bend circumstance through sheer force to meet his need of the moment, and sincere in that he deceived himself before he deceived others, Seborjar held on to the leadership because of these qualities. But he also held on because his enemies seemed incapable of combining against him.

Hoskin knew that if he combined with Seborjar's enemies they collectively had prospects of dragging down their hated Leader. But there was no certainty that Hoskin would be Seborjar's replacement. Too many men held too many grudges against Hoskin. Men he had used and thrown aside. Men who did not like his violent class-conscious politics, with their undertone of Marxism. Men who shared his ambition to replace Seborjar, but with themselves, not Hoskin.

Before he could destroy Seborjar with the certain knowledge that he would replace him, Hoskin had to create a vacuum around Seborjar by destroying those Party Leaders who were his rivals or who had sufficient power in the Party to put up their nominees against him as rivals. "That's not fear as Elsa hints, but good sense," he thought.

Domineco had to be destroyed, the delicately plump little man with the Messianic mission and the dedicated, narrow vision of a sinful, heedless world plunging into the abyss of Godless Communism. Domineco himself was not a rival. He would not appear on stage. He was the master puppeteer who, remote and screened from the audience, operated the directing strings. He would have a puppet to set up in opposition to Hoskin, and such was the little man's dexterity and power within the Party that his puppet could become the Party Leader.

Fortune's power within the Party also had to be destroyed, or at least broken. Fortune, like Domineco, would not want the leadership for himself. But Fortune was a machine man, a mechanic, not an artist like Domineco, who not only operated the puppets, but also wrote the script. Fortune liked to pull a lever here that exerted a known and calculated power there. Fortune had no deep-rooted political convictions. What he liked was smooth-running things, and himself running them. Bannion, the muddy-faced, cripple-handed idealist, to whom inherited, unearned wealth had brought not worldly ease but a troubled conscience, would probably be Fortune's nominee as Seborjar's successor.

He had had other rivals once, thought Hoskin. There had been, two years earlier, the grimly capable Deputy Leader Carmont, who in his belief that Seborjar must quickly fall, had yielded to a sudden upsurge of reckless ambition and had lost his prestige and influence within the Party in his desperate, shameless determination to be all things to all men. There had been, alas, the sensitive, serious minded Mastey, who was not unlike Bannion in his type of idealism but who lacked Bannion's toughness. Carmont and Mastey had been rivals then. But they were so no longer.

Seborjar and himself in concert had broken their influence in the Party. Hoskin had helped Seborjar to do this deliberately as part of his policy of trying to create a vacuum around Seborjar in which only he would exist when ultimately Seborjar fell. Seborjar did it because it suited him in the case of Carmont to have as his Deputy somebody discredited, and ineffectual, who did not represent an alternative Leader in the Party's eyes. In the case of Mastey it was hate. Mastey had the genuine convictions that Seborjar would have liked to have and which he tolerated only while those holding them were obscure. Seborjar had the intelligence to fear the idealist, which he could not be, more than the schemer, which he was.

Hoskin had crossed from the grimy residential section where he lived. The streets he went along were pleasant and wide and shaded with trees. The houses each had their own individual gardens. They were bright and clean in the morning sunshine.

He had no feeling about Carmont. Carmont, lean, bent, his curved nose protruding savagely, giving him a hawk's cold ferocity, had once been his friend and closest political ally. They had worked together in political partnership for years. Their political outlook was similar. Both believed that they had an infinite compassion for the harsh lot of the underprivileged, whereas really this compassion was resentment against the privileges others were born to, and that they had to struggle to obtain. But he had aided Seborjar to destroy Carmont without a qualm. Carmont was in his way. Carmont had to be removed.

Only once had he been napped by sentiment, thought Hoskin. As Elsa had said, Benny Deakin had picked him up out of his Colton backwater. But for Deakin he would probably never have gone into politics. But while it was Deakin who picked him out of his Colton obscurity in the first place, it was Deakin who had so nearly put him back in it. Through sentiment.

"Christ," he thought. "I've come a long way since Colton!"

He had been born in Colton, a dreary, sprawling, coalmining town, squalid and remote, at the end of a railway spur line up north, on the State border. His father was a drunken old tramp, who worked as infrequently as he could. His mother was a shiftless whore who had drifted from one construction camp to another, behind her wandering man until he finally discarded completely any pretence at the habit of work and had settled down in a deserted shanty on Colton's shabby fringe where the town ended and the griminess of the coal mine workings began. The woman was as unconcerned about conventional niceties as her husband, and had been readily available for any male passerby with a supply of cheap liquor.

The home environment of his early childhood had had little effect on Hoskin. In later years he had only contempt for those whose neuroses were traced to father or mother complexes. From his earliest boyhood he had known that he was different from his parents. He was self contained. He had a passion for neatness and cleanliness. When he was fourteen he got himself a job in the mines. It was inevitable that he would drift away from the shanty where his parents boozed and lived in depressing, animal-like sordidness. He found himself a place in a miners' boarding house, rough but clean, and went to live there. When two years later, after heavy rains, the Coroner sent for him to identify his parents who had been drowned in the flooded creek which ran behind the shanty, he experienced no emotion at the sight of their muddily grey bodies, naked and obscenely indecent when the covering canvas was twitched back to expose them.

"Probably drunk and got into trouble trying to cross the creek," guessed one of the policemen standing around.

"Probably," said Hoskin. He went away and forgot them. It was as though they had never existed.

Then when he was eighteen he became involved in a fight outside the mine. His opponent was a massive, bull-necked man, with a blustering, overbearing manner, who had a bad reputation, particularly when drunk. Hoskin was short, but wide-shouldered, muscular but light. Some of the older miners wanted to interfere. They thought Hoskin would be butchered. But Hoskin cut his opponent to pieces. Among the onlookers was a thin, scrawny man named Tomson, who had managed a few minor fighters for a while in the city, but who had been unsuccessful in this field and had returned to Colton. Tomson walked home with the boy. He said, "Ever thought of trying the fight game, kid?"

Tomson stopped and looked him up and down, measuring him with half-closed eyes. He said, "It could be worth your while, Gilly. You're light and strong. You're not going to grow much bigger, but you'll get stronger. You're fast. You showed that back there. You pack a punch in both hands."

"I don't like fighting," said Hoskin.

"There's dough in it," said Tomson. "You'll get more dough beating someone's brains in with your knuckles than you'll ever get out of a mine with a pick and shovel."

It was the mention of money that had lured Hoskin. He could never get enough. Ever since he was a child he had been saving and frugal. When occasionally he got money for running errands for the miners' wives, or doing odd jobs, he held on to it carefully. He was never tempted to get it other than honestly, though he was never sure whether this stemmed from fear, caution, or inborn morality. He stayed away from the group of youngsters who would pilfer and rob.

The evening after the fight at the mine he went to the dilapidated gym Tomson ran on his reputation that he had once managed city fighters. Over the next few years Tomson got fights for Hoskin, mostly on the coalfields, but now and again in the city. Hoskin never really found out how good he was. He never fought anyone who had real class. He built up a string of wins. But he was always frightened, and from the moment he climbed into the ring until he was back in the comparative quiet of the crowded dressing room, his stomach knotted in a terror that his flat savage face did not betray.

It was through fighting that he met Benny Deakin.

The Party was down on its uppers, like the times. Throughout the country, thousands were jobless. Men walked hopelessly from town to town, seeking work, or sneaked aboard train freight cars to be bludgeoned off by railway detectives. Benny Deakin was State Party Chairman, a thin little man, with a bland, child-like face with bright and piercing eyes. He affected dark, sombre clothing and a precise, finicky, sneering manner. Off the orator platform he was insignificant. He would have gone unnoticed in a crowd. But on the platform he was transformed. Words intoxicated him. He had a voice deep and rich as an organ, and as inflammable as petrol. He had started life as a school-teacher, but had switched to become one of the country's most fiery and truculent union leaders. But he had lost his grip upon his union when his eloquence had plunged it, unprepared, into a series of open clashes with police and law officers—clashes from which he was discreetly absent. Even then the magic of Deakin's tongue and his capacity to blend fact with fiction so skilfully that even he could not disentangle them accurately, would probably have preserved his union empire. But he fell sick at a vital moment, and in his absence the facts proved superior to the fictions he and his supporters had conjured up to excuse the fear with which he had fled from the troubles that his words had started. In the Party, events, his own eloquence and a talent for exploiting the circumstances of the moment—and the leftward drift of a Party confronted with a world-wide depression that revealed the poverty of ideas among the Party's bewildered and uneasy leaders—all these things had forced him to the top.

Colton had been selected by the Party as a starting point for the long march back to power. The Party was out of office in the State. It had been voted out shortly after the depression had started. But its opponents had proved as ineffective in providing work for the jobless. Colton had been particularly hard hit. One by one the mines had closed. The streets were crowded with men out of work, hungry, miserable, and hopeless.

On the day that Deakin arrived to address the mass meeting out on Slag Hill, where the miners had for years held their meetings, the town was excited and jittery. As unemployment had spread across the State, bringing in its train a fatalistic recklessness and lawlessness on the part of jobless, desperate workers, there had been a reaction. The more prosperous, who were possessed of property, had banded together. The outcome was a defensive organisation known as the Patriots' League. It was run by men who had had military experience in World War I, or had a yearning for military organisation. The Patriots' League had fascist overtones. It was recruited mainly from bank clerks and ex-college men whose muscles had been developed on the playing fields, not in the workshops or mines. Several union leaders had been bashed in night swoops upon their homes by League flying squads. Meetings of the workless had been broken up with violence. There was a rumour that the League was bringing men into Colton to make Deakin's meeting a trial of strength.

Deakin had asked for a squad of musclemen to be present at the meeting. Tomson had provided the squad from the men who trained at his gymnasium. Hoskin would have attended the meeting, anyway. He had been married for twelve months. Elsa, his wife, was the daughter of a man who had been killed in the mines. She wanted to get her husband away from the mines. Hoskin would have left, but he was trapped. He did not get enough fights to live on. For a while they had provided a useful supplement to his miner's pay, but the mine at which he worked had closed down from lack of orders, six months before the meeting. Now he and Elsa were living meagrely on his fight earnings, and these were not enough. He wanted a job.

Even now, years later, he walked towards his office, a well dressed and prosperous man, well-fed and self-assured. Hoskin could remember every detail of that meeting. Deakin had been late. A chill wind was blowing across Slag Hill. Beneath the raised dais around which was grouped Tomson's squad, the huge crowd was passively quiet, the torches held by the men flickering and then flaring, the flames almost horizontal as they were caught by the wind. It was miserably cold. Hoskin shivered in his thin jacket.

Old Tawney, the Colton miners' leader, who was organising the meeting, came down off the dais to where Tomson and Hoskin were stationed at the rear. The old man was angry. He said, "We're running out of speakers, Tommo. Deakin's over two hours late." He rubbed his big knotted hands together. "Jesus, it's cold. I want a stopgap speaker. One of the younger men. This crowd'll get fed up soon if we don't give 'em Deakin. I want a good, young spruiker. In a hurry, Tommo."

Tomson, his face in the shadows, announced, "Gilly here can talk like a conveyor belt once he gets going."

The old man thrust his face close to Hoskin's. His eyes gleamed in the gloom. He said, "It's you, is it, young Hoskin?" He paused and then said, slowly, "I've heard you speak at union meetings, haven't I?"

"Yes," said Hoskin.

"You weren't bad," said the old man thoughtfully. "You weren't half bad." There was a murmur from the crowd. "They're getting restless. Damn Deakin. What's your politics, boy?"

"I don't like fat men," said Hoskin. "Fat men with moneybags. Fat men who sit on their moneybags and get fatter while we starve. Fat men with their fat greasy women who get fatter on our sweat."

The old man said fiercely, "That's my breed of politics, boy. You think you could talk 'em to the crowd?"

"I could try," said Hoskin.

"Well, try," said the old man. Grabbing Hoskin by the arm, he led him on to the dais. There was a murmur again from the crowd. The old man gestured the speaker away from the microphone. Still gripping Hoskin's arm, he announced "Now while we are waiting for the main speaker we are going to hear from one of our own." The old man's voice boomed through the microphone. "Not old and tired like me. But a young man, strong and willing. A young man who's entitled to something from this country of ours. Who's entitled to the work that he's willing and anxious to do. A man who is a fighter. A young man but who has already been thrown on the industrial scrap-heap." The old man had a sense of theatre. He raised his clenched fist above his head. His shadow was black and restless in the torchlight, his silver hair streaming in the biting wind. "Friends, I bring you Gilly Hoskin, born and bred in this district and denied his manhood's right—the right to work."

Hoskin swayed on the edge of the platform. Below him the blobs of upturned faces floated in the darkness as though disembodied. It was the first time he had spoken from an elevated position. He had a strange sense of familiarity. Suddenly he realised what it was. It was like being in the ring and watching an opponent lift himself groggily from the canvas. There was the same hallucination that the pale face waiting hopelessly to be smashed was floating in air, without attachment to a physical body. But now that pale face was multiplied into the thousand and more pale faces of the waiting crowd. A sense of power that he was never to lose again in such circumstances gripped him. His knuckles tightened on the throat of the microphone. "Friends," he shouted, "I have a message."

The wind tore the words from his lips. But the microphone picked them up and the loudspeakers in the surrounding trees passed them on as echoes and lashed them at the crowd. Its murmur died away.

"My message is this . . ." Hoskin could feel the unseen eyes out there in the darkness fixed upon him. He was the focal point upon which everything centred. Again he had the sensation of being in the ring. But there was a difference. He was alone. No opponent could hurt him. He was showing his ability as a dancer would, solitary in a circle of light, knowing that outside the ring of radiance, eyes were watching him.

He threw out his chest. He stabbed a threatening finger dramatically and savagely over the heads of the crowd to the right in the direction of the mines. "My message is this." His voice rose threateningly. "While there is a pinched and starving belly in Colton not a penny"— he sucked his breath back noisily into straining lungs—"not a penny to the bloated financiers who suck the lifeblood of this rich State." Hoskin felt a sense of surprise. He had not known what he intended to say. The words had come to his mouth as naturally as breathing. He realised, with a sense of excitement, that he had heard them before. From one of the old miners talking low-voiced during a meal-break in the pit when the elderly men discussed ideas and the books they had read and the young ones listened with downcast eyes.

The crowd was still roaring, when a thin voice shrieked out of the mass below him, "That's revolution, Gilly." The surge of power rose higher in him. He flung up a hand arrogantly and the crowd quietened. "No," he said. "That ain't revolution. That's plain human decency." Again the crowd roared.

"We don't want the moneybags' rotten and resented charity," he shouted. "We want jobs. A fair day's pay for a fair day's work." Out of the corner of his eye he sensed movement. Men were crowding on the platform behind him. Deakin had arrived, he guessed.

He decided to wind it up. "We can't fight 'em—these greedy, leeching moneybags—with our bare hands," he yelled. "They own the guns, the police, the soldiers and these fancy boys who swagger round in black shirts to act as pimps and bashers for them. But we can fight 'em with our votes." He paused. "For the sake of our children, for the sake of our wives, for our own sakes"—his voice rose to a shriek—"let's do it."

Even now, thirty years later, walking through the placid, well-ordered streets of the city warm in the morning sunlight, Hoskin could remember how he stepped back dramatically into the darkness with the crowd howling its approval. And the sweat running down his back to chill him as his excitement receded and the cold, blustering wind cut through his thin jacket.

Deakin had sent for him the following day and congratulated him. Deakin had arrived on the outskirts of the crowd just as Hoskin had started speaking. He had been impressed. He then used Hoskin as a speaker in the campaign that saw Colton return the Party candidate with an overwhelming majority and start the Party on the movement that ended only when it regained control of the State.

During the campaign, Hoskin realised that he was a gifted speaker.

He spoke rapidly, firing his words with machine-gun speed but still selecting instinctively the telling and striking ones. He had a tenacious memory. He had done little serious reading. But he had listened for hours to the older miners talking, the men who had the old mine workers' tradition of self-education, and who read Marx and Lenin and the great socialists as well as the Bible and Tom Paine and Winwood Reade's 'The Martyrdom of Man'. Hoskin too, started to read avidly but he found that already tucked away in his mind were the phrases and quotations from the older men that he could use as though they were the product of his own research. He loved standing up there high above the crowd, playing on its collective emotions, enjoying the way in which he could stimulate them.

After the campaign, Deakin sent for him. Deakin was in his cheap hotel room, packing, to return to the city from which he had been absent while he had master-minded the Colton campaign. He snapped his bag shut and said in a rich, musical voice, "Look, Gilly. You're wasting your time in this town. I've been watching you during this campaign. You've got something, feller." He dragged the bag off the bed and dropped it on the floor. "You can talk. You've got ideas. You've got all the energy in the world. Why don't you get out of this backwater? Into the big world?"

Hoskin said, "It ain't that easy, Mr Deakin. I'm a miner. That's the only trade I have. Except fighting. Tomson tried to get me a break in the fight game in the city. He got me a couple of fights, but I couldn't keep going. They didn't want me." Deakin said "The fight game's no good, Gilly. That's strictly for suckers." He strolled to the window and stood looking down at the street. "Look, Gilly. I like you. I've listened to you and seen what you can do with a crowd. Politics is your game." He gestured down at the street below. "You can hang round here. You might get a break in local politics. But you might have to wait for years. And sooner or later you'll have to go to the city if you're going to do any good. Make the break now, Gilly."

Hoskin said, unhappily, "I would if I could, Mr Deakin. But I'm broke. Flat broke. I'd have to pass the hat round to raise even my train fare."

Deakin considered, his chubby face with the dark, sparkling eyes calculating: "You and I talk the same political language, Gilly. The Party's got to go left. The country's ripe for it. Mass unemployment. Poverty. Hunger. Desperate want. Houses tenantless while penniless families sleep under bridges. Farmers who can't afford a load of coke producing foodstuffs that coalminers can't buy. Starving coalminers out of work because farmers haven't the means to buy the coal lying uselessly at the pit-tops." His face darkened. "All the classical requisites for a mass revolution. With only one thing lacking. A war. That'll put arms into the hands of the workers. And still you only have to brand a man as a Bolshevik, and every weak sister in the Party starts flinching like a nun who's heard a dirty word. It's a word that doesn't frighten me, Gilly."

"It doesn't frighten me, Mr Deakin," said Hoskin.

Deakin picked up his bag. "So long, Gilly. As soon as I can make a place for you in the Party I'll send for you."

He kept his word. Two months later he sent for Hoskin to come to the city. Hoskin became a Party organiser.

Looking back now, Hoskin realised that he had had a good political training. The Party paid his salary, but he worked exclusively for Deakin. Deakin taught him everything he knew—and Deakin knew plenty. Hoskin got to know not only how to sway a Party rally, but how to do the back room organising. He learned how to manipulate votes and, what was as important, how to hold them at Party rallies where men were likely to change their minds as opposing factions brought pressure and the bribery of promises to bear. He learned that all votes, venal or idealistic, informed or uninformed, had an equal value, and that it was good to have right on your side, but to win it was better to have the numbers. He finished up helping to run as Deakin's lieutenant the machine that Deakin operated within the Party itself. As a reward, Deakin got him into the State Legislature. He was the youngest member of that body—with a fast-talking, lucid tongue that marked him out as a man of promise, with a big future.

Hoskin escaped the disaster that overtook most of Deakin's personal followers when Deakin lost his power in the Party. He had known that the vote on the Party's Management Committee was going to be close. But he had expected Deakin to survive. He had told Deakin that he would be waiting for him in his room at the Legislature building when the meeting, at which Deakin lost the Party's chairmanship, ended.

A friend on the committee had phoned him to tell him that the vote had gone against Deakin. When Deakin, white-faced but composed, arrived, Hoskin said,

"Bad news, Benny. I'm sorry."

The little man slumped in a chair. He said bitterly, "Yeah. The bastards. They got me, Gilly. It was that horse-faced bastard Fortune who did the engineering. He's sly and slimy. I should have cut his throat when I had the chance. I never liked the bastard. Grover's the new Chairman. But Fortune's the rising power in the Party. Watch him, Gilly. He's clever. And determined."

Hoskin said, "What are you going to do, Benny?"

The little man said, "I'm going to have a drink." He slipped a flask from his hip pocket. "I brought my own, Gilly. I know you don't stock any." He took the inverted glass off the neck of the carafe on the table and up-ended the flask into it. He waited until the glass was half filled before he raised it to Hoskin. "To the end of an era." he said.

"What era?" asked Hoskin.

"Mine," said Deakin.

"What happens in the new era, Benny?"

"Plenty," said Deakin. "I'm going to come back, Gilly. In a big way. Remember what I've always preached. That this country is ripe for leftism." He took a gulp from his glass. "That position still obtains. This pause that is enabling Fortune to climb towards the top of the Party—it's only a pause. The swing to the left must go on. I know that, Gilly. You know that."

"Sure," said Hoskin. "But it could take a long time, Benny. What are you going to do in the interval?"

Deakin said, slowly, "I made a mistake—an understandable mistake. I thought a bloke could do anything with words, particularly if you could use them as I use them to intoxicate and thrill. But I was wrong, Gilly. Words help a man win power. But they are not power in themselves. A man in this racket has to have his power firmly based. Otherwise he's got no grip on the ground. Any storm can shift him if it blows hard enough. I lost my base when I lost the union. I'm going to get it back, Gilly."

Despite himself, Hoskin was impressed. "Can you, Benny? Get it back? "

"Yep," said Deakin. "For the present I'm pulling out of Party activity."

"What do you want me to do?" asked Hoskin. "I've still got a lot of connections."

"I don't want you to do anything," said Deakin. "Sit tight. Just go on as though nothing has happened. And if you tangle with Fortune, watch yourself in the clinches. He fights dirty." He paused at the door. "So long, Gilly."

"So long, Benny. Good luck."

Now, years later, Hoskin remembered with resentment the lump that had been in his throat. The downtown traffic was thickening around him. He paused at a corner and waited, jammed in a crowd, until the traffic lights changed and he could cross.

"Deakin taught me a lot," he thought bitterly. "But he forgot to teach me that there are no friends in politics, and that you can't trust anyone — that everyone's frightened and that men get old and lose their nerve."

Deakin had drifted away from the Party and from Hoskin.

Hoskin heard about and from him occasionally. For a time it looked as though he had a slender prospect of regaining control of the union that he once owned. But he missed out. He occupied himself for a while in organising a left-wing group in the Party. But it never became a worthwhile force. Nothing he touched politically was a success. He dropped out of sight. Hoskin had not heard from him for over two years.

Then Hoskin made his first real political advance. He resigned from the Legislature to run as the Party's nominee for Mayor of the City. Neither Grover, the then Party Chairman, nor Fortune, thought he could win. That was why they backed Hoskin in his ambition. Fortune particularly wanted to get rid of Hoskin. Hoskin's offence in Fortune's eyes was that they belonged roughly in the same age group. At some stage their ambitions would clash. Hoskin had a Party following, not big enough to be menacing, but sufficient to be irritating. Fortune preferred him not to win. But he also calculated that if Hoskin did win there was no kudos in City Hall for him.

City Hall was a corruption spot as far as the Party was concerned. Various Party Leaders had tried to clean it up and had lost their administrative reputations in their attempts. Fortune had no particular desire to reform it. His main interest was in national power. Nationally City Hall had neither significance nor power. The mayoralty itself was a Party stepping stone. But apart from the mayoralty, City Hall was merely a gangrenous sore which attracted the less ambitious and most venal of the Party's blowflies and maggots. Fortune felt that if Hoskin wished to risk his mounting reputation upon cleansing it that was no skin off his prominent Fortune nose.

When Hoskin had his surprise win at the City polls that made him the City's Mayor, his phone went continuously with people ringing to congratulate him. Deakin was among those who phoned. He said, "Congratulations, son." His voice had the rich throatiness to which Hoskin had responded in those earlier Colton days.

Hoskin said, "How are you, Benny? It's good to hear you after all this time."

"Never better, boy. Never better." Deakin's voice had not lost the old confidence, Hoskin thought. "You've come a long way, Gilly. You'll go a lot further. But watch yourself with those tough boys at City Hall." The chuckle at the other end of the phone held a note of genuine mirth. "They've been round a long time. They know the Party machine backwards. Don't step on their toes too heavily. Otherwise they'll cut your throat. Just for laughs and to see the blood run."

"They're going to get their toes stepped on," said Hoskin. "I was elected on a clean-up-the-city platform. That's how it is going to be, Benny. And I don't care whether they're Party members or against the Party. The racketeers and chisellers are on the way out."

The voice at the other end of the wire held a note of amusement. "Good for you," it said. "Then you're going to need me more than ever, Gilly. Those boys down at City Hall'll kick in your political teeth if you don't have some help that you can trust and that knows its way round. I'm that help, Gilly. I can handle those monkeys. You know that."

"What do you mean, Benny?" Hoskin asked uncertainly.

"I want in, boy. An appointment to your personal staff. You'll be handling a budget that's bigger than that of most States. You can't clean up the place alone. It's too big, Gilly. The grafters and the hustlers are too well entrenched. They've got connections. Fortune and the others won't be out to help you. It'll be their friends that you'll be liquidating. You've got to be clever as well as tough to beat this line-up, Gilly. I want in, boy."

Hoskin hesitated. He spoke into the phone politely, "Well, I don't know that I can do that."

"Of course you can." The rich voice was amusedly assured. "You owe it to me, boy. Who got you your first break? Who taught you all you know about politics? Me. You're still young. With lots to learn. What you need is an old dog who knows all the tricks. Who knows 'em? Me, Gilly." Hoskin paused . "Maybe you've got something there, Benny. But you're bad medicine politically. The word is that you've been running with the Communists while you've been operating that left-wing splinter group of yours. What's the angle? Decided to revert to political respectability, Benny?"

"I'm making a comeback, boy." The voice at the other end of the phone was mildly derisive. "Not a big comeback—I'm past that. But a small one. It's mighty cold out there on the extreme left wing. There's no future in it, Benny. I've found that out. I'm not the stuff of which martyrs are made. I'm getting old. I've got to get in out of the rain. Or finish up on the scrap-heap. No-one else'll take me. They're scared of my left-wing associations. But you shouldn't be. You were always a good left-winger. I need you, boy. You can't wipe me off like a piece of snot at the end of a dirty nose. You owe me. We've been through too much together in the early days. Good days they were, Gilly. Good days."

Despite the words, there was no pleading in the voice. It had the same note of confidence that it had held years ago when Hoskin first listened to it, and Deakin had been Party Chairman. Hoskin said, "I'll have to think it over. Give me time."

"Sure," said Benny. "Twenty-four hours. I'll phone this

time tomorrow." There was a click. Hoskin cradled the phone, thoughtfully.

Elsa had been against him renewing his association with Deakin. But Elsa had no depth to her political thinking, she had no political ideology. Her ambition was purely personal. She was a wife. She had a husband. . She wanted him to get to a peak that she had no desire to reach herself. The fact that Hoskin's career was in politics was not important. She would have goaded him on to reach the top if he had been a clerk or a gangster. The field in which he worked had no meaning—only the goal. Unable to have the children that she never missed and never wanted, she subordinated everything to pushing Hoskin upwards. She was prepared to sacrifice her own happiness and welfare to the advancement of her husband's career. Despite her lack of political depth, Hoskin listened to her on political matters. She had intuition.

When he told her of Deakin's approach, she said in her harsh, prim manner, "Don't have anything to do with Deakin, Gilly. You've outgrown him politically. He can now only do you harm."

"I dunno," said Hoskin, slowly. "Benny's clever. Brilliantly so. He knows the back alleys of the Party like nobody else. I'm going to be a bit isolated at City Hall."

Elsa said, "You have plenty of friends, Gilly. Men you've helped. Who rely upon you for advancement. Use them. They're your creations. You were Deakin's. He will always resent you for having outstripped him. Forget him."

"I can't wipe off the man who gave me my start."

"I could," said Elsa, simply.

Hoskin turned off the crowded street. He crossed the narrow strip of lawn in front of the Legislature building and went up the broad shallow steps to the entrance. The guard on the door said cheerfully, "Good Morning, Mr Hoskin." Hoskin nodded and went on through the dark, high corridors with their atmosphere of decaying grandeur; past the dim, oppressive, massive oil paintings of bygone, forgotten legislators with which they were lined. He let himself into his office through his private door. He sat down behind the desk. His mail, opened for him, was waiting on the pad. He started to go through it. But he only half comprehended what he was reading. His thoughts were back there with Deakin.

Hoskin had found at their first meeting after he had been elected as Mayor that the years had dealt harshly with Deakin since he had lost the Party chairmanship. He had a faint air of physical decay. His skin was unhealthily tight over the sagging looseness of his flesh. It exuded a moisture compounded of body oils and alcohol. The eyes were small, bloodshot and rheumy in the ruins of his once round, child-like face, now bloated and soft. But the voice was the same— deep and persuasive. He said, "The old partnership, Gilly, eh? Like old times."

"Yes," Hoskin said. "Like old times."

Deakin said, with a note of obsequiousness, "Bit different, Gilly. I was the boss then. Now you give the orders. What's my role?"

Hoskin said, "You know what this job is to me, Benny?" "Sure," said Deakin. "A springboard. To bigger and better things."

"Yeah," said Hoskin. "I can come out of this with two things. A top flight reputation as an administrator. And a top flight reputation as a reformer. They're worth votes, Benny. Not just Party votes. But votes outside the Party. Votes I'll need someday to get to the high places. This city has been run like a broken-down brothel. Higgledy, piggledy and anything goes. Inefficiently and dubiously. I'm going to change that."

"Sure," said Deakin.

"That'll be my side of the show, Benny. The administrative side. I'll look after that. You won't come into it."

"Sure," said Deakin.

"But we've got to look after the political side, too, Benny. Every cheap, chiselling bastard in the Party seems to have been able to get his fingers into the City till. Mostly the civic fathers — those bastards who are in the Party only to dabble in minor graft. But quite a few of their friends in the Party machine get a cut, too. I'm going to clean 'em out, Benny. That's where you'll come in. On the political side. I'll need an extra pair of eyes and ears. You'll be 'em."

"It won't be easy, Gilly," said Deakin.

"I know," said Hoskin, grimly.

Deakin shifted his eyes reflectively from the ceiling to Hoskin's face. "What happens if they're Fortune's boys? Or Grover's? Or any other of the big boys of the Party?"

"We nail 'em," said Hoskin. "Ruthlessly. Openly. And with the maximum of publicity."

Deakin looked sly: "What happens if they're your boys, Gilly? Or tied up with someone in the Party who's running with you?"

"We still nail 'em," said Hoskin. "But more discreetly. As quietly as we can. And with a minimum of publicity. But we still nail 'em, Benny."

"Is that what you want?"

"Yes," said Hoskin. "It's what I want."

"You're sure that's what you want, Gilly?"

"Sure I'm sure."

"Okay," said Deakin. "That is what you'll get."

Deakin had appeared to give him what he wanted, thought Hoskin, seated at his desk in his empty office, staring at the pile of mail in front of him.

Backed by Hoskin's authority, Deakin had declared war on the old racketeering element in the Party that had used City Hall as a citadel from which it made freebooting forays upon the City, as though it were a rich, defenceless empire to be looted and plundered at will by marauders emboldened by years of impunity. Deakin had pursued this element mercilessly. Those caught had in some cases been expelled from the Party. At Hoskin's insistence. Deakin did the policing of City morality. And in eliminating the old-time racketeers who had believed themselves impregnably entrenched, Deakin had kept Hoskin's trust. He had not sought to replace the men ousted from City Hall with men who owed loyalty primarily to him, and not to Hoskin. Those he brought in were Hoskin men.

It had been the Casimar documents which had first aroused Hoskin's suspicion. Deakin was not usually persistent or impatient. But he kept bringing the Casimar documents to Hoskin for signature, and Hoskin sensed strain.

"I'm in no hurry, Benny," Hoskin told Deakin. "If we let this thirteen acres go as a factory area, I can't see much prospect of ever putting in a recreational centre over on that southern side."

"You can always resume," argued Deakin. "It's an opportunity to pull down some of those slums on the outer ring and replace 'em with a recreational park."

"I could if the housing project over that side were going better," agreed Hoskin. "But it'll be a long time before that's completed. And I don't know whether I'm ready to wait that long for a recreational centre. There's now no hurry. I've time to think round it."

"Tolman's getting a bit impatient—and desperate."

"Tolman?" Hoskin's face was blank. Then he remembered. "He's the character who wants it as a factory area."

"Yes," said Deakin. "And he's getting a bit steamed up."

"So what?" said Hoskin sharply. "Some small-time business man is getting steamed up. So what?"

"Tolman isn't small-time," persisted Deakin, "and he contributes fairly lavishly to Party funds. He thinks he's entitled to a decision fairly soon." Watching the older man's ruined face, Hoskin could not decide whether the beads forming on the pouches beneath the bloodshot, small eyes were sweat or the moisture that his flabby, alcohol-soaked body continually exuded.

"I'll decide when he's entitled to a decision. He'll get it when I'm ready. Not before. " said Hoskin.

When Deakin had gone, Hoskin was uneasy. He rang for his official secretary. When the man came in Hoskin said, "Storey, what do you know about the Casimar project—that south-side block that I've been considering earmarking for recreational purposes?"

For a second the man's face was frightened. Then it went smooth and expressionless. "Very little, I'm afraid, sir," he said.

"What do you mean, very little?" said Hoskin. "You don't normally know very little about some project the City's got on hand."

"This is a matter that Mr Deakin is handling," said Storey. "I don't interfere in matters Mr Deakin is looking after. None of us do."

"I see," said Hoskin. He was playing with his paper knife. "Why is this rather unusual course followed on matters that Mr Deakin is handling?"

The secretary's face was suddenly troubled. He said, uneasily, "Well, I—that is to say we—the permanent officials at City Hall—we understood—or maybe rather we felt—with justification I hope— that that was the way you wanted things." He gestured, worriedly. "That's been the system for some considerable time now, sir. Ever since you've been Mayor. Administratively we—the permanent officials—are the channel through which most everything passes to you. But occasionally Mr Deakin tells us that he is looking after some particular matter for you. We bow out. He takes over." There was anxiety in his eyes. "Nothing wrong, is there, sir?"

"No," said Hoskin. "Nothing wrong." He thought for a moment.

"Get Mr Tolman — the bloke who's involved in the Casimar matter— for me on the phone, will you, Storey?"

"Yes sir," said the secretary. The door closed behind him. Hoskin had the impression that he was relieved to get out of the office.

Even now, years later, Hoskin could remember the humiliation of the telephone conversation. Tolman had a hectoring, unpleasant voice. When Hoskin announced himself Tolman said, "It's about time I heard from you, Mr Mayor."

"Why?" asked Hoskin.

"Why?" snorted Tolman. "Christ, you political bastards aren't even honest in your bloody dishonesty. Look, mister, I've paid for the goods. I want delivery. I want the goods I've paid for." He threatened Hoskin. Unless he obtained "delivery" soon he would spill. He did not give a damn for bad publicity. "But it'll bloody well ruin you, Mr Mayor," he blustered.

"You'll hear from me—soon," said Hoskin. He hung up, furious. Then he phoned Grover.

"I want to see you, Frank," he said. "In your capacity as Party Chairman."

"Sure," said Grover. "Will I come to City Hall? Or do you want to come down here?"

"I'll come down there," said Hoskin.

Fortune, who was then the Party's State Executive officer, was with Grover who said, "You told me that you were seeing me as the Party Chairman. So I thought we'd better have Con with us. Okay with you?"

"Okay," said Hoskin. He sat down. Grover was behind his desk, with Fortune flanking him, seemingly studying his nails.

Hoskin said, "Frank, I want an immediate State inquiry into charges of corruption against Benny Deakin and a south-side industrialist named Tolman."

"Christ," said Grover. His face paled. He was a neat, little plump man with a cap of tight-fitting close-curled hair. "Who's making the charges, Gilly?"

"I am," said Hoskin.

"You are!" There was incredulity in Grover's voice. His eyes flickered towards Fortune.

"Yeah," said Hoskin. "I am."

"Jesus," said Grover. His small shrewd eyes were anxious. "Hasn't the Party enough trouble in this State without you making more?"

"I'm making it," said Hoskin.

Grover's eyes flickered in Fortune's direction. He said, uncertainly, "What's happened, Gilly? You and Benny busted up?"

"As from today," said Hoskin, grimly. "He's been grafting. I only found out this afternoon."

"Balls," said Fortune. He did not look up. He was still examining his nails.

"Tolman admitted it," said Hoskin. "Over the phone to me, this afternoon."

"That isn't what I said balls to," said Fortune. His long, high-beaked face was calm.

"What did you say it to?" demanded Hoskin.

"To you playing the injured innocent," said Fortune, coolly. Hoskin half rose, his face black with anger. He said, dangerously, "I ought to put your teeth down your throat for a crack like that, Fortune."

Fortune's face creased in a smile without mirth. "Don't pull that strong-arm stuff on me, Gilly," he said. "I don't like it."

"Break it up, the pair of you." Grover said sharply.

Hoskin said, "Well, get him off my back, Frank. Or I'll break his."

Fortune said, derisively, "Me? On your back, Gilly? That's rich." He chuckled.

"How do you see it?" asked Hoskin savagely.

"You've been on my back ever since you've been at City Hall," said Fortune. "One by one you've ridden every one of my boys out of the Hall. Some on the end of a pretty dirty stick. You've yelled 'Copper' every time a boy belonging to somebody other than yourself has looked sideways at a bit of loose change. And as you got rid of them you've filled the Hall up with your own boys." He lit a cigarette. "It wouldn't have been so bad if you'd been on the level, Gilly. If you hadn't been quite so hypocritical about it. If you hadn't been bringing in your own boys through the back door as fast as you emptied ours out through the front. If you hadn't been streamlining the graft so that all the small, dangerous hit-and- miss stuff was cut out and the big safe stuff channelled through Benny." He loosed a stream of smoke offensively in Hoskin's direction. "That's how I see it, Gilly."

"You see it the same way, Frank?"

Grover shrugged. "Every shrewd operator in town knows where to go to if he wants something done—within reason—and if he has the price. To Deakin. The Mayor's right-hand man. The charges are high. But the service is good."

Hoskin had a sense of panic. He said sharply, "You bastards ain't ganging up on me?"

Grover spread expostulating hands. "Why should we, Gilly? We've both a vested interest in keeping the Party out of trouble. Bust the lid off the City scandals and what happens? It's all over the country tomorrow. Every paper screaming at us. Yelling that we're a gang of cheap chisellers not fit to be trusted with the administration of a city, never mind the State or the nation." He glanced at Fortune. "Con probably agrees with me that you've done a good job as Mayor. Did we squeal when you emptied our boys out of City Hall? We knew that they were hip deep in petty rackets. So you cleaned up the petty rackets. And in doing so you did the Party a lot of good. We aren't kicking because Benny's been taking off a bit of cream. That's his business. And yours. The way it has been handled the Hall's comparatively respectable. Compared with the old days."

Hoskin said, more calmly, "In other words, you birds'd sooner see things continue as they are now. Is that it?"

Grover nodded. "Yeah," he said. "For the sake of the Party, Gilly."

Hoskin said quietly, "How about Tolman? He's threatening to blow his top. Claims that he's paid his money. And has nothing back for it."

Grover said, "What's Tolman asking for? Is it unreasonable? Can it be justified?"

"It could be reasonable," said Hoskin. "And justified quite easily."

Grover said, "Well, give it to him. That'll shut him up. And, after all, he's paid for it." He chuckled, his eyes creasing at the corners. "Benny's kind of committed you to it, Gilly."

The room was very quiet. Hoskin heard the sigh of Fortune's breath as he exhaled cigarette smoke from his lungs. At last he said, "No. I want an inquiry. By the State. And Benny sent to jail."

Fortune said, softly, "Suppose we tell the boys at the State Legislature no inquiry. What then, Gilly?"

"You'd be seen as acting in your own interests," said Hoskin. "You don't want the kind of trouble that'll make it harder for you to get votes for the machine at the next elections, State or Federal." He stared at Fortune aggressively. "Well, I'm going to protect my interests. I'm going to have an inquiry. If the Party doesn't give me one through the state Legislature I'll force one by publicly demanding it. Clean or dirty. The Party can have it either way. But there's going to be an inquiry."

Fortune shrugged. "That's putting us over a barrel, Gilly. But the Party won't be the only loser from an inquiry. You'll lose, too, Gilly."

"My hands are clean." said Hoskin, fiercely. "Any court in this country can comb my bank account. It's honest money. I earned it the hard way. I was duped as badly by Deakin as any of his victims."

"Sure," said Fortune. "But you've been building up a reputation as an administrator."

"Yes," said Hoskin. "And I'm proud of it."

"But how are you going to keep it?" asked Fortune. "The best you can hope for from an inquiry is a complete exoneration. But, heads or tail, you must lose, Gilly. You preserve a reputation for honesty. And what happens? You're left without a feather to fly with as an administrator. For your exoneration is an admission to the world that you are a mug, so big a mug that when a stinking mess was brewed up in Benny's office—less than ten yards away from your own—the smell didn't even reach your nostrils. Where's your administrative reputation then?"

At the time, Hoskin had thought Fortune was using merely a debating point to dissuade him from an inquiry; but looking back across the years, Hoskin was aware that Fortune's judgment had been vindicated. The inquiry was held. Hoskin was exonerated from any suggestion of implication in Deakin's unofficial financial transactions.

Deakin went to jail. There was a section of the Party that did not like that. This section was indifferent to Deakin, but not to the implacable hatred with which Hoskin had pursued his former benefactor and later henchman. "Gilly oughtn't to have turned copper—things shouldn't be handled like that in politics," was a sentiment largely unvoiced.

But, Fortune thought Hoskin had been right about the damage that the inquiry did his reputation as an administrator. He sat automatically turning over letters that his mind did not register. It had taken him a long time to live down the Casimar scandal—and Deakin. If he ever had. It was like the Ancient Mariner's albatross, hanging round his neck. He would get rid of it for a while, and then something would happen to recall the old crime. And the Albatross was still around his neck, with its plumage draggled like his administrative reputation and dead eyes that were like Deakin's as they led him out of the courtroom to the sentence which he knew, at his age, he had slender hopes of surviving.

Hoskin stabbed at his bell. His confidential secretary was tall and slender with a narrow waist and a big bust. She dressed well and smartly. It was suspected in the Party—wrongly—that Hoskin's interest in her extended outside the office.

Hoskin said, "Any calls, Mavis?"

"Sorry, Mr Hoskin. I didn't realise you had come in." He seldom used his private door, but entered through the outer office. "Mr Kerstey's office has been on the phone several times. Mr Kerstey wants you to see him as early as possible."

"Damn Kerstey," Hoskin said. "If he wants to see me, let him come here. I'm not an office boy!"

"I'll let him know," said Mavis.

"Do," said Hoskin. He picked up the letters again. "Damn Elsa," he thought. "She's made me jittery, made me see old ghosts." He started to go through the letters more carefully, while waiting for Kerstey.

Kent Kerstey was Seborjar's closest associate in the Party. Kerstey was a scientist for whom a brilliant future had been forecast before he turned to politics. He was over forty. But he was always spoken of in the Party as though he were young. There was something immature about him—the immaturity of unfulfilled youthful promise. He had regular handsome features, prominent dark eyes, a fine head, a loose, moist mouth, and an insolent, supercilious manner. He had his brilliant academic record, little balance, and less discretion. At times he exercised an almost Svengali-like influence over Seborjar. At other times they fought in the dubious privacy of Seborjar's office suite, vicious verbal battles, unrestrained in their exchanges.

The relationship between Seborjar and Kerstey intrigued the Party's inner circle. Hoskin had heard Mark Payten, impish and reckless, describe it as "incipient homosexualism" and had listened to Payten drunkenly argue that this sexual bent, of which Seborjar himself was unaware, accounted for Seborjar's penchant for surrounding himself with a group of odd, eccentric and sometimes unreliable young men, to whose views and outpourings he listened more intently than he did to the more prosaic, earthier advice of the recognised Party Leaders. Hoskin, however, whose straight-forward masculinity predisposed him to be sceptical of this exotic explanation, was inclined to accept the theory that Fortune had once told him had been advanced by Macker Kalley. Kalley's view was that there was nothing sexual in Seborjar's instinct to surround himself with men of Kerstey's type. Seborjar wanted about him only men who fed his ego. He did not want those with minds of their own, who would supply him with independent, objective advice or who would leave him when he insulted and belittled them. He wanted those who would tell him, "Mr Seborjar, you're wonderful—only you would have the genius to think of that," and who, if they fought with him, would inevitably come crawling back as Kerstey had so often done, declaring their allegiance because no-one else would have them when they craved like drug-takers the stimulant that only politics and being at the centre of things, as Seborjar was, could give them.

Hoskin had almost finished his letters when Mavis knocked on the door. "Mr Kerstey's arrived."

"Send him in," said Hoskin.

Kerstey had an association with Hoskin that was concealed from the Party. The association had been formed largely because Hoskin had a trait that was valuable to him politically, and which he was uneasily aware he possessed. He was attracted by informers. Most politicians maintained a network of informers whom they protected, encouraged, used and for whom they had contempt. Hoskin's network was unusually extensive, possibly because in him the contempt was lacking. He had an affection, which occasionally he felt was unclean, for the informer. The closer the relationships between the informer and the man informed on, the more despicable the betrayal of trust and confidence, the deeper was Hoskin's affection for the informer. Kerstey was closer to Seborjar than anyone. Seborjar was morbidly suspicious, a man to whom the most simple act on the part of some acquaintance was capable of a dozen devious explanations. He trusted few. Kerstey was one he trusted. But whenever the older man followed his own line on some particular issue on which his ideas were opposed to Kerstey's, Kerstey betrayed him. But Kerstey had cunning. He betrayed him only to those whom he knew would not, in turn, reveal his duplicity to Seborjar. Hoskin was the main recipient of these betrayals. Kerstey sensed the perverse loyalty Hoskin afforded his informers.

Hoskin could never fathom why Kerstey betrayed Seborjar. Kerstey was an influence in the Party only because he had Seborjar's ear. He had no standing in his own right. Despite his brilliant academic background, he was naive, without subtlety or ability, and could be outmanoeuvred and out-generalled in Party affairs with contemptuous ease by men who had no intellectual capacity, but who had learned to survive on instinct, like animals, as they battled to exist in the Party. When Seborjar fell, Kerstey would fall with him. It was inevitable. Yet Kerstey continued to betray Seborjar as though his Party future was not irretrievably bound up with Seborjar's. "Maybe he's like Judas— born to betray," thought Hoskin. "Or maybe his ego is such that he cannot understand that he is a force in the Party only because of his hold on Seborjar."

When the door closed behind Mavis, Kerstey said, insolently, "I sent a message over an hour ago that I wanted to see you, Gilly. What happened?"

Hoskin said, "If you want to see me, Kent, you know where my office is. I'm not the hired help around here."

Kerstey retreated, as he always did, before a frontal attack. "No need to go high hat on me, Gilly," he complained. His face was sulky. He said, "I've news for you."

Hoskin said nothing. His flat face was impassive. Kerstey said, "Don't you want to hear it?"

"Sure," said Hoskin, who leaned back in his chair.

"You don't seem very enthusiastic," said Kerstey, impatiently.

"Any reason I should be, Kent?"

Kerstey was radical—much further to the left than Hoskin. Some Party Leaders suspected that he was a secret Communist. Hoskin did not believe this. His judgment was that Kerstey was too inept politically to play such a subtle role. Kerstey, Hoskin considered, was guided politically not by what he believed in, but what he was against. He was fanatically anti-Catholic. He could trace every shortcoming in the modern world back to the same malign source—the machinations of the Roman Catholic Church. He had other phobias, but this was his strongest. Because the Communists were against most of the things that the Catholic Church was for, he tended to run with the Communists. Hoskin believed that the explanation for many of Kerstey's political postures was as simple as that.

Kerstey brooded for a second: "You should be enthusiastic, Gilly. You're a leftist. It could be that the Party is at last going to assume what should be its correct task—the task of leading this country to the left, instead of compromising with its conscience, as it has been doing now for years. Condemning monopoly capitalism, but buttressing it with a reformist programme. Talking about pie in the sky and the establishment of the millennium, and dissipating its energies and strengths on piddling trifles like a few social welfare gains."

"Jesus," said Hoskin. "You sound like a bloody professor."

"I'm describing the current set-up in the Party, Gilly," said Kerstey resentfully.

"What's going to alter that set-up?" Hoskin asked. His eyes were intent under heavy scarred brows. "It's what the Party has been doing for years."

"Seborjar could alter it," said Kerstey. "If he suddenly threw his weight in the right—or left-direction. And received backing from the right people. He's capable of achieving anything, Gilly. Of giving the leadership that's needed."

"Cock!" said Hoskin. "Seborjar couldn't lead a flock of homing pigeons. Where's he led the Party to so far? To Domineco. To the dead end of Fascist-mindedness and fanaticism. Domineco's the big noise in the Party, sport. Seborjar's only his mouthpiece."

"You're wrong, Gilly." There was a note of triumph in Kerstey's voice. "Seborjar's through with Domineco. That's my news. He's breaking with that priest-ridden bastard—permanently. He told me so himself."

"And you believe him?" .

"Look, Gilly," said Kerstey. He hitched his chair closer to Hoskin's desk. "You don't know the Big Man like I do. You think he's mad. All right. Maybe he is. But he's mad in a sane way." Kerstey's voice was confidential. "He thought Domineco's influence and Domineco's machine could take him to the top. So he and Domineco became allies. He doesn't like Domineco or what Domineco stands for. The authoritarianism. The fanaticism. The frenetic anti-Communism. For deep down in the Big Man is a streak of genuine belief. Sometimes it's hard to find, but it's there. But that doesn't matter. He wants to be boss of this country. So he ties in with Domineco."

"Portrait of an opportunist," gibed Hoskin.

"Okay, Gilly. So it's a portrait of an opportunist. But because he's an opportunist—or realist—Seborjar's restless. He has been tied up with Domineco for a long time now. Long enough to get to the top. But he still isn't there. Alex Pope is still running the country. It is not Domineco's fault that Seborjar hasn't made the grade. It was Seborjar's blunders, not Domineco's, that have kept him where he is. But Seborjar doesn't see it that way. He thought Domineco could take him to the top. Domineco hasn't. Therefore he looks round for someone who will. He's looking now, Gilly."

"How sure are you of your facts, Kent?" asked Hoskin. "As sure as I'm sitting here," said Kerstey triumphantly. "Seborjar told me himself. Not in so many words. He's incapable of doing that. But in the hints and half hints that he always uses. I know Seborjar. Like I know myself. This is the straight goods, Gilly."

Hoskin brooded; "What's in it for me, Kent?"

Kerstey's face lightened. His smile was young, boyish and mischievous. When the surliness vanished, he had charm. "That's your problem, Gilly, not mine," he said, winningly.

"Yes," thought Hoskin. "You would take that attitude, you irresponsible, treacherous, good-looking young bastard. Politics aren't to you a way of life, as they are with me and most of the Party Leaders. To you they're an excitement, an outlet for your recklessness and destructive instincts. Like speed-car racing is an outlet to other men with different interests." Aloud he said, "Seborjar'll need a new ally, Kent. Who'll he team up with? Me? Fortune? Who?" He had no respect for Kerstey's political judgment. But he knew Kerstey had a flair for forecasting accurately the lines along which Seborjar's devious mind would work.

"I dunno." Kerstey's face was thoughtful. "I tried to pump him. But you know what he's like when anyone starts asking questions. He became suspicious. Paranoid. Shut up like a book. Wouldn't tell me anything."

"Try guessing," invited Hoskin.

"Well, he wouldn't tie in with you," said Kerstey, "Knowing the way his mind works, I'd say he figures you're already in his bag. You're against Domineco. You've always been against him. You've hated his guts for years. If Seborjar comes out against Domineco, you automatically line up on his side. You're Seborjar's natural ally. He never looks for natural allies. He picks 'em up, anyway. He wants unnatural ones."

"Who's unnatural enough to line up with Seborjar?" Hoskin said, with grim humour.

"Fortune, maybe," said Kerstey. "Even Tom Bannion. Joe Lilley, certainly, if the price is sufficiently high."

"Not Fortune," said Hoskin. "He hates Seborjar's guts."

"He hates Domineco's, too," said Kerstey. "Which does he hate worse?"

But Hoskin was not listening. He was following his own thoughts.

"I couldn't see Seborjar winning Bannion over," said Hoskin. "Bannion doesn't like Domineco's politics. But he likes Seborjar's less. I don't think Bannion'd sell out his beliefs for Seborjar."

Kerstey smirked. "Bannion's an ambitious man, Gilly. He pretends he isn't. That he's the great idealist. That's crap. Pure crap. I think he's like Seborjar. He wants to get to the top. He's dedicated to that objective, like Seborjar. But he conceals his dedication. I think he is for sale. And that if Seborjar decides to make an offer, he'll sell."

Hoskin drummed on the desk with his thick, strong fingers. "When do you think Seborjar'll make his first open move, Kent? Against Domineco, I mean?"

Kerstey shrugged. "I dunno, Gilly. The Big Man vacillates over making a decision. But once he decides anything he usually moves fast. Maybe he'll show his hand at tonight's meeting. You're going, of course?"

"Sure am," said Hoskin. He came from behind the desk, to accompany Kerstey to the door. "This is one meeting I wouldn't miss for a fortune," he said. There was no expression in his ugly, scarred face, and flat, deep-set eyes.

CHAPTER 6

K aye Seborjar usually spoke with angry assertiveness, even when the audience was friendly. The citizens now being lashed by his tongue sat in rapt attention, their eyes glued on him.

To an impartial observer, Seborjar was ordinary enough to look at. He was not big, yet like some actors who are small of stature, he created an illusion of size, and with it a quality of domination. At close quarters he had a well shaped head with heavy-lidded eyes that were restless and hard and, to many of his rank and file, he held an almost hypnotic power. The head tended to dominate his unimpressive physique, so that the mental image of him in his absence was that of a man with a big, powerful frame. He kept his hair close-cropped, which gave a suggestion of bristle—like the mane of an old black bear. He had the unhealthy pallor which was the result of living continuously indoors. His clothes, expensive, tailored were worn with an exasperating carelessness that was somehow attractive given his forceful personality. Seborjar had few orator's tricks. The Party did not regard him highly as a vote-winner from the platform, though it respected his ability to project a more attractive image of himself upon the public consciousness through his actions rather than his speech. Wealthy himself, he had a wealthy wife, willpower, and a tough wiliness. But he had few friends, and seemed unaware that he lacked them.

He had the capacity to betray or double-cross allies without it penetrating his consciousness that he was doing so. He was jealous of anyone whose intellectual pretensions matched his own, and contemptuous of those who were intellectually his inferiors. Circumstance, lack of scruples, and his own doggedness, had made him the Party's National Leader. A ruthless determination and conscienceless ability to fit his flexible political beliefs to the needs of the moment had kept him there.

Mark Payten slipped into a vacant seat beside Macker Kalley. The hall was crowded. Kalley liked the dark, alert man's cynical flippancy, even though Payten was a Seborjar henchman, and, as such, in opposition to Fortune within the Party. Kalley believed that somewhere, deep down, Payten had a basis of political principle. Payten had originally joined Seborjar under the pressure of necessity. He had been on the losing side in one of the feuds that periodically racked the Party. He had to join Seborjar to preserve himself from political oblivion.

But Kalley believed that Payten had become a Seborjar camp follower for more than reasons of self-preservation. Kalley had the impression that Payten had a real regard—which he attempted to conceal with smart witticisms—for the older man's strength and sense of historical destiny. From his seat alongside Kalley, Payten listened to Seborjar for a moment, winced ostentatiously with an actor's enjoyment at the exaggeration of his shudder; "God, the votes that man costs me." He nudged Kalley. "Your boss wants you, Macker."

In the semi-darkness he pushed past people in the row until he reached the centre aisle. He tiptoed down it quietly. There was a crowd around the door. Forcing his way through, he noticed the faces; attentive, rapt, listening to Seborjar. Outside in the lighted corridor he paused to light a cigarette then went down the stairs to the room below the hall that Fortune was using as an office; "How's it going, Macker?" Fortune said.

Kalley said, "The usual."

"It beats me," Fortune said. "Seborjar always gets a big hand. Yet nobody is ever quite sure what he is talking about. He has no platform manner. His voice is harsh."

"He's got something, Con," said Kalley.

Fortune sighed, "I'd like to know what it is, Macker. Nobody who knows him trusts him. And those who don't know him either idolise him or think he is anti-Christ. But somehow—God knows how, Seborjar's the Party Leader. He wants to rule this country, and yet he's done more, through his own stupidity to prevent that ever coming about." He shrugged. "Well, that's politics for you, Macker! Crazy, ain't they?"

Kalley noncommittally drew at his cigarette. The distant applause came as a subdued rumble. Fortune said, "But that's beside the point, Macker. I just wanted to tell you. I'm backing Joe Lilley for Party Chairman." There was silence for a second. Kalley exhaled a lungful of smoke. He held his cigarette out in front of him. Then, tonelessly said, "Is that wise, Con?"

Fortune lifted his shoulders in a deprecating gesture. "I've made a deal with Seborjar."

Kalley said, thoughtfully, "Lilley is a cheap, grafting, fat chiseller, Con. He'll go chasing the dollars, while Seborjar chases the power. That suits Seborjar—makes Lilley his creature. While Seborjar stays on top, Lilley'll always be his creature. You don't like Seborjar, Con. You reckon he's bad for the Party and if he gets to the top'll be bad for the country. Why deal with him?"

Fortune said calmly, "Politics make strange bedfellows, Macker. Seborjar can't last forever."

Kalley said, "Famous last words, Con. If you make a mistake, he'll outlast you. The dogs have been yapping and biting at the heels of the old bull for years. And he has been big and strong enough to blunder on, taking the dogs with him. You've been one of them. Always tagging along behind, hoping that some day you'll get your teeth into him and drag him down. And all the time the old bull is getting nearer his destination."

Fortune's face lost its imperturbability. The carefully schooled nonchalance went from his voice. He was eager, suddenly alive: "What is it, Macker? What is his destination politically? How high can he climb? Who's he going to climb with—or on?"

Kalley said, slowly, "With whoever'll take him to the top."

Fortune said, "It won't be me, Macker. This alliance is only temporary. My enemies in the Party—Domineco and his organisation—are bitter. They know I loathe the things they stand for. Their ruthlessness. Their suicidal craving for a Holy Crusade against the Communist heretics. If, in this atomic age, they have to decide between a war that will destroy mankind or a compromise with Communism, they will elect eagerly for destruction. They hate what they call indiscipline and I call individual freedom. They want to restore peasantry, this time in an urban as well as a rural setting. Their ideal man is bovinely content, stupidly docile and subservient to the divinely inspired, crazy guidance of leaders whose minds half the time are preoccupied unrealistically—and intolerantly—with the problems of life after death."

Kalley said, without expression, "Thought it all out, haven't you, Con?"

"I've had plenty of opportunity," said Fortune, defensively. "Domineco has been operating in the Party for years."

"You're just quoting," Kalley said. "You might feel such things. But you don't think 'em or talk 'em, Con. You don't have to justify yourself with high-falutin' stuff. Like Seborjar." "Okay," said Fortune. "So I'm quoting. So I'm quoting Seborjar."

Kalley said, softly, "Took him a long time to wake up to Domineco, didn't it? Maybe he was deceived. Maybe he thought these angles out just recently. Over the past few weeks. After running with Domineco for years. Do you believe that, Con?"

"Okay," said Fortune. "So Seborjar's a liar. And a hypocrite. But that doesn't change anything. Domineco and his organisation are still out to get me. They can't forgive because I won't be with them. They've nearly got control of the Party now. Sooner or later, unless I do something, they'll get me. So I'll knock over Domineco and his crew. Then when we've knocked them over . . ."—he drew a long forefinger significantly across his throat—"then I'll knock off Seborjar."

"You? And who else, Con?" There was mockery in Kalley's voice.

"You and me, Macker," said Fortune. "We'll knock him over. Just as we've knocked over bigger and better in the past."

Kalley's face, craggy and lined, with hard eyes like stones under heavy brows, was expressionless. "Not bigger, Con. Nor better. Seborjar's different. You think you're tough and ruthless. You are. You wouldn't have climbed as high in the Party if you weren't. But sooner or later, Con, you run up against your conscience. Because it would wreck the Party in which you believe, you pull your punches. Or the things you should do are going to hurt someone who is your friend or has helped you. And sometimes, when that happens, you hold off. You don't do the things you should."

Fortune said, "You wouldn't want me to be completely ruthless, would you, Macker? A bloke has to live with himself."

Kalley said, "I don't want you to be anything, Con. I'm just telling you what you are. Mostly you ride roughshod over the lot of 'em, friend and foe alike. But every so often you start looking at yourself in the mirror when you shave. You start wondering whether that feller in there is really Con Fortune—who dragged himself out of the gutter because he had a mission. A mission to help his fellow man, particularly those who stayed back there in the gutter because they were weak, or sick, or helpless, or pushed round."

Carefully, Kalley picked up a dead matchstick from the ashtray. "You get sentimental, Con. Your heart, not your head, rules you. It doesn't happen often. But it does." He broke the matchstick into halves and put the two pieces back into the ashtray. "You couldn't stay alive alone in the arena with Seborjar, Con."

Fortune said, slowly, "Sooner or later I've got to get in the arena with him, Macker. It's like death. Inevitable."

"Sure," said Kalley. "But climb in before you're isolated, Con. You can't possibly win against Seborjar and his organisation or any of the others that are fighting inside your weight division."

"You think Seborjar overmatches me?" There was no irritation in Fortune's voice.

"Yeah," said Kalley. He watched the smoke curl up thinly from the end of his cigarette. "Seborjar is big stuff—really big. You only see his like once in a generation. He's the stuff of which world figures are made, Con. A man who believes that he was born to rule. But he can be toppled. In fact Domineco and his gang are ready to sell him out. It is only a matter of time before they do. When they do he'll be isolated. Vulnerable. Friendless. Gilly Hoskin might try to prop him up. But only until it suits Gilly to pull away the props. A lot of others in the Party who have no tie-up with Domineco are worrying at his heels."

Kalley's eyes, thoughtful, calm, hard, switched to Fortune, who was massaging his chin ruminatively. "Why do you think he's turned to you, Con? Because he likes you? Because he trusts you? Because politically you share the same ideas?" He shook his head slowly. "You know he hates your guts, Con. He has for years. You've been a consistent opponent—one of the few he has never been able to bulldoze or hypnotise into at least outward submission. But now he must break the lineup of his enemies within the Party. The line-up's getting too formidable. If he doesn't break it, he's through as Leader. That's why he wants your backing, Con."

Fortune said reflectively, "He claims he's on the level, Macker. He might be, this time. He's desperate enough to be. He's promised to listen to me. To accept my advice."

Kalley was gently derisive. "He's made such promises before. Where are the men he made them to? Forgotten, Con. Out of politics, or discredited. He made the same promise to Domineco when he thought Domineco could get him to the top. You know that. I know that. Now he's buying you over with the same promise. To help cut Domineco's throat. Just as he'll buy someone over later, to help cut your throat. You're only welcome in his camp on his terms, Con. As a complete stooge. And you haven't the temperament to stooge indefinitely."

"You're too pessimistic, Macker." Fortune said, without irritation, "A man must take risks in this racket."

"Okay," said Kalley. "It'll be your throat that'll be cut. Not mine."

Fortune chuckled. "We'll be the ones doing the cutting, Macker,"

"The way I see it Seborjar's hopeless as the Party Leader. But we're stuck with him. For a while. Until we dispose of Domineco."

"And then?"

"We dispose of Seborjar," said Fortune. "There's not much chance that he'll grow stronger while we're dealing with Domineco. If ever he got to the top he would be—I admit—the worst menace to this country in our history. To stay at the top, he'd sell out everything I've ever believed in. But the risk is slight. The voters won't have him. They've shown that. He'll never rule this country."

Kalley said quietly, "This is a democracy, Con. With a two party system. Under that system a Party does not win power. The Party that has power loses it. And while Seborjar remains Party Leader there is always a chance that the turn of the wheel will put him in the top job.

"Sure," said Fortune. There was a trace of impatience in his voice. "I know that. Normally that's the way things work. But there's an exception to every rule, Macker. This is the exception. Seborjar's too discredited. He's done too many wrong things. He has too many strange notions. He's suspect."

"Suspect with whom, Con?" asked Kalley. "How many know what an unreliable, unbalanced character he is? A handful of politicians. Whose personal well-being is so closely bound up with his while he remains Party Leader that they have to support him and praise him and build him up. The Party chiefs like yourself. Whose organisational loyalty demands that they should hold him up to the public as a paragon even though privately they loathe him."

Kalley stubbed out another cigarette. "The ordinary rank and file members don't know him. The voters don't know him. All they know about him is what men like you have told 'em. If they disregard what his political opponents and the newspapers say about him—as voters often do—they have only your version to work on. And you've told them he is a grossly maligned man. You've explained away his every mistake. You and your kind helped create the legend. Now you're stuck with it—while he remains in charge."

Puzzlement showed in Fortune's face: "You're out of character, Macker. You're losing your detachment."

"Not me," said Kalley. The smile on his hard, lined face was guarded. "You know me, Con. The onlooker. Not involved. The spectator at Vanity Fair."

Fortune said, dubiously, "Yes. Mostly, Macker. But I suspect you on this one. You must occasionally get your feelings tangled up with your politics. How do you really feel about Seborjar? Personally, I mean."

"Personally? I rather like him. He's mad, of course. Like Hitler, Mussolini, Stalin, Cromwell, Robespierre and a host of others. Who weren't in the racket just for a living, or a bit of easy graft, but for something bigger. A place in history. Or just because they were addicts where power was concerned."

Overhead there was a round of applause. Kalley's face lifted to the ceiling. "Seborjar's mad, too. But in an interesting way. He's unpredictable, unscrupulous, and uninhibited by the decencies that bother others like the claims of friendship, or loyalty to old beliefs, or a feeling for his own countrymen."

Kalley's smile was bleak. "Seborjar's even abnormal for a politician, Con. He likes applause. The applause that the mob are giving him now. It adds to his sense of power. He's like all politicians in that. But he's indifferent to what people think about him. He doesn't really care. Seborjar's not the usual democratic politician, who, thank God, fears the voters. He fears nothing—except missing out on a place in history. He knows that history has a habit of immortalising those who lack the normal little decencies, whose name will be remembered long after his victims are forgotten."

Fortune said, "Christ, Macker. You paint a black picture. Yet you say you like him."

Kalley shrugged. "Only as an individual, Con. I like freakish individuals. Seborjar's a freak. I don't like him as a ruler. Men like you, Con, haven't the ruthlessness to filch the few liberties that the ruled still have in a democracy. Your consciences grow tender. You wonder occasionally before you go to sleep at night whether you're doing the right thing. But not Seborjar. He'd sleep like a healthy child, untroubled, whatever he did. He'd take liberty away in the name of liberty and if necessary convince himself that liberty was what he was conferring. Don't help him to the top, Con. You'll live to regret it. If you do."

Fortune said, "You're way over my head, boy. I'm a practical politician. Not a theorist. But you're safe. The feeling against Seborjar is too strong. It must have worked its way down to the voters. These things usually do. They must know him. Maybe not as the sinister figure you make him out to be. But as untrustworthy. I'm sure they distrust him too much ever to take him on."

Kalley shrugged. "Have it your own way, Con. But with Alex Pope running the country you're taking a risk. Pope is capable of making a dozen mistakes before his term is up, any one of which could put Seborjar right into the top job. Seborjar knows that. Why do you think he is hanging on so grimly? Making deals with men like you, who loathe him? Just to be a Party Leader who is out of office? No, sir. Seborjar is fighting to survive so that when the wheel turns it'll take him to the top."

Fortune said, "You've got a mind like a sewer."

"I've spent a lifetime working in a sewer. In politics. In them but not of them," said Kalley.

Fortune responded without resentment, "Maybe I'm not seeing the picture accurately. One of us has it out of focus, Macker. But I've made up my mind. I'm throwing in with Seborjar—temporarily. He's broken with Domineco—permanently. Together we'll get rid of those threatening us within the Party." He repeated the gesture of drawing his forefinger across his throat. "Then I'll get rid of Seborjar. Once that's done, the Party can really go hunting for national power. Okay?"

"No, it's not okay," said Kalley. "Not as I see it. But you're the boss."

From the hall above came the muted rumble of applause. Fortune grimaced at the ceiling. "Seborjar ought to be pleased," he said. "The crowd up there is really giving his ego a boost."

Fortune got up from his chair and, tall and angular, started pacing the room. Without looking at Kalley he said, "When we back Joe Lilley for Party Chairman, you know what that means, Macker?"

"Conscience worrying you, Con?"

Fortune looked at Kalley and smiled. "Yes," he said.

"So it should," said Kalley. "If we are backing Lilley for Party Chairman, Tom Bannion has to be destroyed. That is, if he persists in running for the chairmanship."

Fortune looked at the floor, his fingers interlacing nervously. "That's your job, Macker. To dissuade him from running. Or to destroy him if he insists."

"Okay," said Kalley.

Fortune said uncomfortably, "Doesn't it worry you, Macker?" Kalley smiled. "Why should it, Con? Bannion's your friend—not mine. He's honest, and Lilley isn't. Bannion believes in such airy-fairy things like the Party and human dignity. Lilley believes in the weight of his wallet and the skill of his lawyer. But then as the Party's Lord High Executioner, Bannion'd try to treat your enemies with justice, even if you had helped to put him in the post. Whereas Lilley'll do what Seborjar and you tell him, so long as you're both in the saddle and until Seborjar tells him to cut your throat. But these are factors you have to consider, Con. Not me."

Fortune mocked, "The perfect mercenary, aren't you, Macker? No moral or ethical questions for you. You do what you're told because you're paid to do it."

"You're wrong, Con," said Kalley. "It's just that my kind of ethic is old-fashioned. I work for whoever pays me. You pay me. When you ask for advice I give it. Honestly. You choose to disregard that advice. All right. That's no skin off my nose. You tell me to do a job. I do it. Mine not to reason why."

"No problems, eh, Macker?" said Fortune.

"No problems. Just a few simple values. And no ambitions. That's why you can trust me, Con. While you can't trust anyone else."

There was a knock on the door. "Who is it?" Payten entered.

"How are the conspirators?"

"Plotting," said Fortune, lightly.

Mark Payten's thick, black eyebrows shot up almost to his dark hair. His smile was sudden, soft, warm and impish. He had a gaiety that was infectious. Wearing a red carnation in his buttonhole, a foppish grey waistcoat that gave his short slim figure a rakish air, and a mischievous expression, he said, "They're winding it up upstairs. You should see the Big Man. He's standing like the Statue of Liberty; you'd think every word he spoke was Holy Writ. The crowd won't leave until he stops talking. He won't stop talking while he's got a crowd. It's a deadlock."

Fortune said, "He'll go all night at that rate."

Payten said, "One side'll weaken soon. Though it won't be Seborjar. But once they start moving off, he'll give it away. He objects to his words of wisdom being drowned out by the shuffle of departing feet." He yawned. "I don't blame him. I object myself. He's coming down when it's all over. Complete with retinue. For a drink."

Fortune said, casually, "Did he say anything worth a pinch?"

"The usual drivel, said Payten. "We're living in the atomic age. One boom and it's doom. Alex Pope wants civilisation to commit suicide. These are parlous times. Only one man in the world has brains enough to know what should be done. No giveaway prizes for identifying who that man is. Everyone knows. Seborjar. Cheers. A few hoots—surprisingly few. The same old line."

"You make it sound unutterably dreary," said Fortune.

"It was," said Payten. "On stage, at least." He grinned impishly.

"But they tell me it's been interesting back stage. Where the scene shifters operate. It is even said that we're in the same camp, Con."

"Could be," said Fortune, noncommittally. "How does that prospect appeal to you, Mark?"

"Christ," said Payten. "Anything is an improvement on Domineco. I've never been comfortable while Seborjar's been running with him." His face went solemn. "Domineco's like a mole. Always working underground. Pushing one of his boys in here. Another in there. And what boys. Faithful, narrow, dedicated. Pimps and informers. Ruthless. I never knew when he'd decide to knife me in the back. I need a drink."

Fortune opened a cupboard in the corner of the office and started taking out bottles. "There are glasses on that table behind the desk, Mark. Help yourself." Feet trampled on the stairs facing the open door. Payten, gulping his drink, said "Meeting's over, Con."

Seborjar had put on his hat. It seemed too small and perched on top of his head. He strode into the room, head thrust forward, arms swinging. He brought with him an aura of strength and self-assurance, which his ill-fitting headgear seemed only to emphasise. He was listening intently to something Gilly Hoskin was saying into his ear. Hoskin seemed angry. His hands were waving. His face was scowling. He broke off what he was saying when they approached Fortune.

There was animosity between Hoskin and Fortune. Their strengths were similar. Neither had the faculty for mustering support for the cause they espoused. But both had the capacity to play on the hates, jealousies, fears and weaknesses of their fellow politicians so that they would combine against persons or policies they opposed. But Fortune, a man who boasted that he had never read a book but had acquired his education from life, was more subtle, devious and painstaking than Hoskin, who, though self-educated, had been an earnest student in his years in politics. They had clashed several times within the Party. Each time Fortune had outmanoeuvred with intuitive, even-tempered guile his fiercer, more intemperate opponent.

Hoskin said, without warmth, "How are you, Con?" He didn't wait for an answer but walked across the room to Kalley.

Kalley said, "How are you, Gilly?" The room was crowding. The men were pouring drinks and talking animatedly.

Hoskin turned his scowl on Kalley. His mouth was tight, with the corners drooping downwards like deep scars. "What gives?" He pointed towards where Seborjar and Fortune were talking. Seborjar was nodding slowly, as though he was agreeing with everything Fortune said.

"Who knows?" said Kalley.

Hoskin looked down at him bleakly. "I've never had a shot at you, Macker. But it's only because you've never moved into my gunsights. Don't tempt me, brother."

Kalley said, "You're terrifying me, Gilly."

The noise was mounting. Under its protection, Hoskin said quietly, "So Seborjar's broken with Domineco, Macker. At long last." His small, deep-set eyes were watching Kalley intently.

"I wouldn't know, Gilly," said Kalley. "I only work here. For Fortune. Remember?"

"Sure," said Hoskin. "I remember. Some day it mightn't be convenient for you to have me remember. But remember, I will."

"They're the chances a man has to take in this racket," said Kalley.

Luke Coles crossed the room to join them. He was long, angular and conceited, with sloping shoulders shaped like a longnecked bottle, a tiny head and an intellect to match. He always listened to Seborjar with reverence but without much comprehension. He had no ambition but to survive in the easy political living into which he had found his way almost by accident, through a Party split when candidates had been hard to find for hopeless seats. He had been prevailed upon to stand for election and to the consternation of wiser men who could see no chance of him winning, had received a comfortable majority. A bachelor who lived with his widowed, ageing mother to whom he was devoted, his compassion for the underprivileged or sick or aged was quick and warm. Hoskin used him as a tool; Seborjar as a court jester. He had a high voice and a low humour. Women were his passion and his hobby. He said loudly, "You fellows the pallbearers? Where's the coffin?"

Hoskin said, "I'm trying to find where the body's buried." He nodded across at Seborjar and Fortune. Coles peered at them through the smoke haze that was beginning to fill the room. With a shrewdness Kalley did not expect he said, "Maybe this is a wake—Domineco's." He drifted off.

Payten joined them. Hoskin was uneasy with the mocking little man, as he always was. He swallowed his soft drink in a gulp and moved away. Kalley watched him moving restlessly from group to group, exchanging a word here and there then moving on.

"Hoskin's working hard," chortled Payten. "Trying to catch up with what's happening."

Kalley said, gently, "He knows, Mark."

"How about the act he put on for Luke Coles?"

"It was an act, Mark," said Kalley. "Gilly's an old dog. He can smell these things in the air. He doesn't need much to go on. A sniff here. A sniff there. Then he puts two and two together. He knows the set-up. If I'm any judge, that was what he was brawling about with Seborjar when he came in. About Seborjar throwing in with Con. Everyone in the Party'll know the score tomorrow."

Payten said, his eyes curious, "How'll Bannion react, Macker?" He glanced round the room. "By the way, he's not here." He sounded faintly surprised.

"Bannion?" Kalley's face was expressionless. "He's not as hypocritical as some of us, Mark. He limits his dealings with Seborjar to official occasions. I didn't expect to see him."

Across the room Hoskin was in deep conversation with his closest henchman, Jeb Marney. Marney represented a Federal district. He was old but sprightly, fattish, with a few straggling hairs dragged across his near naked head. He had a face that from a distance was pleasant, but up close cunning and furtive. The lids of his hard eyes drooped tiredly, but he had the energy of a young man. He was vindictive and spiteful and feared.

Payten nodded at them. "I wonder what devilry is being cooked up there. Between Hoskin and his ageing henchman."

A politician they both knew from the State Legislature wandered over to them. He gossiped for a while. He was trying to find out more about the Seborjar-Fortune alliance about which he had heard. Kalley listened to Payten fence with him. The man finally abandoned the contest good-humouredly. "You're a pair of tight-mouthed bastards," he said. "I'll get my news elsewhere." He glanced at his watch. "I'm off home, I've a wife and family waiting for me."

"Politicians shouldn't have wives and families," Payten said. "It doesn't seem proper, somehow, to think of them with private lives." His dark, mobile face was serious. "He's a volatile bastard," thought Kalley. "On top of the world one moment. Gloomy the next." Aloud he said idly, "How come, Mark?"

Payten said, "A politician is like something hanging in space. Living in a strange, cut-off world. No beginning and no end." He looked at Kalley from the corner of his eyes. "You ever get that feeling, Macker?"

"Sure," said Kalley. "We all do at some time or another."

"Jesus," said Payten. "Wouldn't you like to live a normal life sometimes? Not trying all the time to work yourself into a position from which you can play God?"

"Sure, I'd like a normal life." He thought of the two Annes. "Part of me lives one," he thought.

"Speaking of a normal life, Macker," Payten said, suddenly casual and relaxed, "What were you before Fortune got hold of you?"

"Nothing," said Kalley. His lined face was expressionless.

"You must have been something," protested Payten. "I was a lawyer. A man has to be something."

Kalley said, "Why the quiz session, Mark? Most anyone in the room can give you my biographical details. Just as I can give you theirs."

"Just curious," said Payten. "You were in this racket before I entered."

Kalley shrugged. "Okay, I was a kid. Couldn't get work. Fortune gave me a job. Running his errands. Found I had a talent for politics. Exploited it."

"That why you stick to him, Macker?"

"Yeah," said Kalley.

"You've never thought of switching—working for someone else?"

"Seborjar tell you to ask me that, Mark?"

"No." The little man flushed suddenly and angrily. "Well, all right. He did. Nothing wrong with that, is there, Macker? Fortune can't last forever. Some day you'll have to look for another job."

"Yeah," said Kalley. "Some day. Tell Seborjar I'll wait for that day, Mark."

There was a sudden silence. Both men glanced up. A woman was standing at the door. She was middle-aged and plain, with a comfortable, heavy figure. She stood, hesitating.

Kalley was watching Seborjar. Seborjar looked around and saw the woman at the door. His face softened and grew eager like a boy's. His politician's self-consciousness—the knowledge that eyes were always on him and that he must play in public the role of the great man—vanished.

Seborjar strode across the room to her with both hands out. "Martha." There was a joyous lilt in his voice. He put his hand carefully and solicitously under her elbow and drew her into the room. He said, "Gentlemen, I think most of you know my wife."

Kalley said, softly, "So the Big Man's human."

"Yeah," said Payten, "But only just."

CHAPTER 7

Kalley opened the door of Bannion's outer office. The girl behind the desk alongside the inner door, smiled at him impersonally, "Good morning, Mr Kalley. Go right in. They're waiting for you."

Kalley paused with his hand reaching for the door handle. "They?" His thin, lined face was expressionless.

"When you phoned you were coming over, Mr Bannion had Mr Longac, Mr Vittor, Mr Canover and Mr Fines come across. They're inside."

"Thanks," said Kalley. He went in and shut the door quietly behind him. He nodded at Bannion, who was seated behind a big desk, his long, muddily yellow face moody. His eyes went from Bannion to the others who were seated in a ring round Bannion's desk.

"I see the gang's all here, Tom."

Bannion said, "They're as interested as I am in what you have to say, Macker."

Kalley shrugged. He sat in the chair across the desk from Bannion. He turned it sideways so that he brought the faces of Vittor and Canover, who otherwise would have been slightly behind him, into his view. "I'm just the messenger, Tom. It's up to you to decide who hears the message. Con doesn't mind."

"Why didn't Con come himself?" asked Bannion, mouth tight and pursed. The others sat silent and watchful.

"Con didn't want an argument." Kalley took out a packet of cigarettes, shook one loose, and lit it with nicotine-stained fingers.

"So he sent his tomahawk man," snapped Fines, who looked sick. The whites of his eyes were yellowish.

"So he sent his tomahawk man," said Kalley. He inhaled deeply. "Con reckoned that this was something that should be dealt with without heat. The way he saw it, you fellers might feel bitter about what he's doing."

"Bitter!" said Fines. His long fingers were twitching. "Con's selling us down the river, and he thinks we might feel bitter!" He laughed without amusement. "Any reason we shouldn't?"

Kalley said, "Feel as bitter as you like. That's your privilege. But Con says you should play it shrewd. Don't cut off your noses to spite your faces."

"That's nice of Con," mocked Fines. "Play it shrewd. Your heads are going to go on the chopping block, anyway. Seborjar is arranging the axeman. But don't disfigure yourselves, boys. Con wants you to look nice as corpses."

Longac said, quietly, "Easy, Maury. Maybe Con was wise not to come himself. Let's hear what Macker has to say."

"Fair enough," said Kalley who pushed his chair further back from the desk. "I suppose you know Con is backing Lilley for the Party chairmanship?"

"We know, Macker," said Bannion, angrily. "Everyone in the Party knows. It went the rounds last night after the meeting. How Con was selling us out. The fact that he and Seborjar were teamed up. How they were both backing Lilley."

"Okay," said Kalley, coolly. "But that was just rumour. Now I make it official. Con is backing Lilley."

"Why?" asked Longac in his booming voice, unruffled.

"Con's reasons are his own business," said Kalley bleakly.

"And what does he want us to do?" asked Vittor. His shortsighted eyes blinked truculently behind his gold-rimmed spectacles. "Acknowledge that the great Con Fortune has spoken? Do nothing? Not lift a finger while the Party is placed under the control of a cheap, nasty racketeer devoid of principle or morals?"

"That's what Con wants you to do," said Kalley. "He wants you to do nothing. To withdraw Tom's nomination for the chairmanship. To sit tight. To hold your forces together. To wait."

When Longac said, "Con's asking a lot, Macker," Kalley shrugged. "You've no alternative. Without Con's backing, Tom has no more chance of becoming chairman than a snowball has of staying unmelted in hell." His eyes went from Longac, calm and thoughtful, to Vittor, nervously tugging at his hair, to Canover, whose eyes in his heavy, fat face were puzzled, to Fines, restlessly plucking at his fingers. Then Bannion.

Bannion said, sharply, "You seem sure of yourself, Macker."

Longac said, without heat, "We could fight, you know, Macker. There are other people in the Party than Seborjar or Fortune. What happens if we fight, Macker?"

"Domineco'll probably throw in with you. But how will you like being tied in with that bunch? My hunch is that you wouldn't like them as running companions."

"You're putting the case, Macker," said Vittor irritably, "Not cross-examining us."

Kalley smiled. "Okay. You fight. But you can't beat numbers. You fellers know that. You've five votes. Yours, Tom's, Louis', Franky's. And Sarly's. Five out of thirty. If Domineco throws in with you, as I'd expect him to do, there's another eight. That gives you twelve. At the most there are seven votes uncommitted. Seborjar and Fortune are in a better position than you to sew up most of those."

"Con doesn't want you destroyed. But if you oppose Lilley, it gives Seborjar a chance to go after the lot of you. And Con won't be able to protect you without coming into conflict with Seborjar. Which he doesn't want to do just yet."

Longac said slowly, "And if Tom does pull out and doesn't contest the chairmanship against Lilley? What then?"

Kalley's voice was level. "You sit back for three years. The three years during which Lilley is chairman. I don't promise anything. But circumstances change. At the end of three years . . ."

He shrugged. "Lilley." He drew his forefinger across his throat. "Seborjar." He repeated the gesture.

"Balls," said Fines, who waved his finger at Kalley. "We can't sit back for three years, Macker. And you know it." He looked around angrily. "We aren't popular with the racketeering element. Any of us. They want our blood. Yet you suggest that if they are allowed unchallenged to take over running the Party for three years they'll leave us undisturbed. That's balls, Macker. Once they're in control we're gone. Seborjar'll be after our scalps. He'll use Lilley and the racketeers as his instruments. Whatever power we have now in the Party will go. You know that. Con knows that." He turned to Bannion. "What Con wants us to do, Tom, is commit political suicide. So that he'll be spared the inconvenience of executing us."

Kalley said, calmly, "That's not right. Con doesn't want you eliminated. It suits him to see your group survive. Apart from the fact that he likes each of you personally, it helps to offset Seborjar's power. And Hoskin's. If Tom'll go quietly, there's a good chance you'll survive. If Tom insists on contesting the leadership it's a declaration of war. Con wants you all to be sensible."

Longac said, "What do you think, Tom?"

Bannion walked over to the window and stood for a moment staring down into the street. He leaned his back against the window and sombrely said, "I think that if there's something you believe in, it's worth fighting for."

He looked at Kalley and there was a sour downturn to his lips. "You've influenced me Macker. Once I wouldn't have accepted it, but now I believe that it is impossible to have a political party completely clear of corruption. But there is a difference between having corruption existing on the fringes of the Party and that same corruption eating its way into the vitals of the Party. If Lilley goes in as Chairman, the corruption shifts from the fringe to the heart. I won't be a party to that."

Kalley said, "You can't stop it, Tom. It's the numbers that count in this racket. Not words. And Seborjar and Con between them have the numbers."

"Maybe," said Bannion. "But at least I can try to stop it."

Kalley said, calmly, "Con's not going to like this, Tom. He's not going to like it the least little bit. Nor is Seborjar."

"Con can go to hell," said Bannion. "And so can Seborjar. I'll be running for the chairmanship if I only get one vote—my own."

Kalley's face was expressionless. He said to Longac, "How about you?"

Longac's ponderous body was relaxed. He said, "I'm with Tom, Macker."

Kalley said, "You're taking a big risk, Sarly. Tom's an amateur. He has dough. He can afford ideals. You can't. You're a professional."

Longac said, placidly, "You forget, Macker. I've a citadel to retreat into if things go wrong. My union."

"We can blast you out of that," Kalley said.

Longac chuckled. "Who are you trying to kid, Macker? Seborjar has had his stooges trying to blast me out for years. But they've got nowhere. Maybe they would if Con joined forces with them. But I know Con as well as you do, Macker. Con isn't like Seborjar. He isn't vindictive. He'll run me out of politics if it suits him to do so. But he won't pursue me in the union."

Kalley said, "Maybe you're right, Sarly. Maybe Con won't pursue you into your union. But you'll be dead as far as politics are concerned."

The big man smiled gently. "We've all got to leave sooner or later the things we love, Macker. Even the world we live in. And while living, boy, we've got to live with ourselves. If I have to pay with my political existence for an easy conscience, I'll pay. If Lilley and his kind are the ones who are going to own the Party I'm not sure that I want any part of it."

Kalley turned to Vittor. "What's your play, Louis?"

Vittor's thin, serious faces was intense. "I don't like evil, Macker. Lilley is evil, Seborjar even more evil. One will steal your purse. The other your beliefs. I don't wish to be associated with them. My vote will go to Tom."

"Even though it means you're running with Domineco?" Kalley said. "Domineco, who stands for everything that you two loathe?"

Vittor's face darkened. "Bad people often ride on good bandwagons, Macker."

Kalley's eyes fixed on Canover. He saw the misery in his eyes. Canover was a member of the Legislature. If he chose the wrong side and it was defeated, he could lose his comfortable seat in parliament. Kalley thought, 'He used to be a butcher. He hasn't worked at his trade for years. He's soft. He won't like going back to hard work. Not after having it easy so long in politics.'

"So where do you stand, Franky?"

"Christ, Macker. Can't Con be talked out of this crazy idea? Of backing Lilley? Jesus, I used to stooge for him on the Management

Committee. Before I met Tom and Tom woke me up to what was going on. Can't you talk Con out of it, Macker? Con listens to you."

Kalley's face was impassive. "Con's determined. He's made his deal with Seborjar. And you know Con, he doesn't go back on a deal."

"Not much," snorted Fines. "How about us? He's thrown us to the wolves."

"Rubbish. Con never promised to support Tom for the chairmanship. You fellers simply assumed he would." Kalley shrugged. "And normally he would. But things aren't normal."

"What makes them abnormal?" snapped Bannion, still leaning against the window, his eyes angry.

Kalley said, quietly, "Don't bump your head against a stone wall, Tom. Con's made up his mind. He doesn't unmake it easily. That's why he is where he is today. Look at what is, rather than what might have been."

Vittor said irritably, "You're the perfect tomahawk man Macker, The boss decides something. It doesn't matter whether it is right or wrong, good or bad. You're with him. But you could try and talk him out of it. Just try. It can't do any harm."

"I've tried, Franky." Kalley liked the fat, slow-thinking ex-butcher. "I did no good. Con's determined. He wants to do the best he can for you fellers. He doesn't want to see you crucified. Which is what'll happen if Tom contests the chairmanship against Lilley. That's why I'm here today. To let you know what Con intends to do. And to give you a chance to declare yourselves. Con likes you. But don't get in his way. If you do, he'll have to trample over the top of you. He won't like it. But he'll do it." He stubbed his cigarette into an ashtray. "How about it, Franky? Where do you stand?"

The fat man's eyes went slowly round the room. The others were watching him. "He's the weak link," thought Kalley, who felt a surge of compassion for him being so exposed, so confused.

Canover sighed. "I don't want any trouble, Macker. But I've gotta stick to my friends. Tom's been a friend for years. Ever since he's been on the Management Committee. I've gotta stick. I'll vote for Tom."

A small, neat figure, bleak and forbidding, Kalley said, "Okay. So we know where we stand. I'll let Con know. There'll be no hard feelings on his part. Personally, I mean. Politically it'll be a different matter."

Fines said, "They're hard feelings on my part, Macker. Tell Con that. I don't like traitors."

"What does Con owe you fellers? He made you. He'll break you," Kalley said.

Longac said quietly, "Queer things happen in politics, Macker. Tell Con not to get too cocky too early. Maybe Tom'll have the numbers when it comes to a showdown."

Kalley said, "If Tom wins, it'll strengthen Carr Domineco in the Party. An engaging prospect I don't think. The five of you are anti-Domineco. But Tom, if he becomes Chairman, will be Domineco's captive. Domineco'll be the senior partner in your alliance."

"We'll cross that bridge when we come to it, Macker," Bannion said harshly.

Kalley lit another cigarette. His eyes narrowed; "Ambitious men often have strange bedfellows, Tom."

"Tell that to Con, Macker," said Bannion angrily. "It was he who climbed into bed with Seborjar. Not me with Domineco. I have no ambitions. Beyond wanting to see that the Party doesn't fall into the hands of rapacious opportunists like Lilley."

"Okay," said Kalley. "So you have no ambitions, Tom. But you'll be standing for the chairmanship. That's what I'm to tell Con, isn't it?"

"Yes," said Bannion.

Kalley walked to the door. "I'll be seeing you," he said. Vittor got to his feet. "I'll have to be getting back," he said. "I can't waste all day. I'm a working man. I have students to lecture. Where you heading, Macker?"

Kalley said, "I'm meeting Con at the Legislature."

Vittor said, "I'll walk that way with you." He looked at Bannion. "Nothing further Tom?"

"No," said Bannion.

The two men went through the outer office, nodding their goodbyes. They stood silently in the crowded lift, each alone with his thoughts.

As they left the building, the sky was clouded. A cooling wind was blowing. Vittor walked with quick strides. Kalley fell in alongside him. Vittor said irritably, "What's wrong with Con, Macker? Why's he doing this?"

"He wants something. He's going out to get it."

Vittor responded, "But what does he want? Domineco's head on a platter? Surely he could have that without allying himself with Seborjar."

"How?" asked Kalley, who found it difficult to keep his place alongside the quick-striding Vittor.

"Somehow." Vittor's face was troubled. "Something could have been worked out. And this way, it only strengthens Domineco if we win. And Seborjar if we lose. God, Macker, what a dreadful duo. Domineco and Seborjar."

"Which do you like least?" asked Kalley.

"That's like asking me which I'd prefer to go swimming with—a shark or a crocodile. I don't know, Macker. I frankly don't know," said Vittor who stopped suddenly on the pavement. "Tom's straight. And honest. He has ideals. He has beliefs. I don't agree with all of them. But I admire the way he sticks to them."

Kalley said, "You're describing Tom as he was, Louis. Not as he is. Tom's been a fair while in politics now. Some of the gilt has worn off his angel's wings."

"You're a cynic, Macker. A disbeliever. Is there anything you believe in?"

Kalley smiled. "Not much, Louis. Except the imperfection of man." He glanced at his companion. "Tom has things lined up to dump you, you know, Louis."

Vittor laughed. "Macker, you're getting crude. That one's too obvious."

"Okay," said Kalley, good-humouredly. "But you're not a comfortable character to have around in politics. You're long on conscience. Short on flexibility."

Vittor's thin, intense face suddenly creased in thought. "Do you know something, Macker?" he asked. He had occasionally an almost boyish directness. "Or are you only guessing?"

"I know something," said Kalley. "You've been arguing recently with Bannion. On tactics and other things. Tom was in last week. He told Con. He sounded irritated. He didn't say anything positive. But I got the impression that if he had the chance, he'd dump you. Hard."

"Your imagination is working overtime, Macker," said Vittor, without conviction.

"Suit yourself, Louis. You're entitled to believe what you like. But watch yourself, feller. Ambitious men don't like to have as colleagues men whose sensitivity about what is the proper thing to be done gets in their way."

Opposite the Legislature, Kalley stopped. "See you, Louis. Don't leave off your mail shirt." Kalley crossed the road without glancing back. Vittor stood watching him. Macker went up the broad stone steps into the Legislature building. He nodded at the attendant.

Fortune was in the office of one of the Party's members. Kalley waited outside, smoking thoughtfully. He was surrounded with butts stubbed out under his heel when Fortune came through the door.

Fortune looked keen, pleasant-faced, relaxed. "Sorry, Macker. Been waiting long?"

"A while." Kalley fell in beside Fortune, his head at the level of Fortune's shoulder. As they left the building's wide steps, Fortune said casually, "See the boys, Macker?"

Kalley paused to light another cigarette. "Yes, indeed. Where we heading, Con?"

"Back to the office." They walked for a while in silence. Then Fortune said, "What's the answer, Macker?"

"No dice, Con. Tom insists that he's going to run. The others are backing him."

"Well, I expected that. Any weak sisters, Macker?"

"One. Maybe two. Franky Canover declared himself for Tom. But he didn't like it."

Fortune said, "Did you expect him to? He's got a wife and family. No dough. He used to be a butcher. This could cost him that sweet cop." He nodded back over his shoulder towards the Legislature building. "Butchering'll come hard after what he's been doing. Curious, isn't it? That it should be Franky? With more decorations for physical courage than a normal man would collect in three lifetimes. And no moral stamina." He shrugged. "Well, that's the way it goes. I've seen it before. Heroes on a battlefield but frightened men when the issue is moral."

His eyes were on Kalley. "Who's the second, Macker?"

"Louis Vittor."

Fortune whistled. "Well, what do you know?"

"I don't think he's frightened. What's he to be frightened of? Politics aren't his living. He's an amateur. Not a professional. But he's worried about Domineco."

"So he should be!" said Fortune.

Kalley laughed . "Where can he turn to get rid of that worry, Con? To Seborjar and Lilley? And to do that he has to dump Bannion. Not much of an alternative."

Fortune said, "Which would you choose, Macker?"

"I'm the hired hand, Con. You do the picking. I back whichever you tell me to back."

"Okay," said Fortune. "Which'll Vittor back? Seborjar or Domineco?"

Kalley considered. "At the moment, Domineco. But he can be swung. His loyalty to Bannion's holding him. That can be undermined. But he's got to be handled right. Very delicately."

Fortune said, slowly, "He'll have to be handled, Macker. Things aren't as easy as they look."

Outside the Party headquarters, Fortune nodded to a functionary they both knew. "Good day, comrade. Warm enough for you?" As they rode up in the lift, the lift man gossiped with Fortune. He had a son who had won his way on scholarships to become a nuclear scientist. He joked, "I'm telling the young feller that he'd better stop making those atom bombs, Mr Fortune. Otherwise we'll be atoms."

Waiting with a list of phone calls, Mrs Belasco followed them into the inner office. She started to tell Fortune what they were. Fortune smiled at her. "Later, Aggie. Keep everyone out. I don't want to be disturbed." As she went out, he shut the door.

Kalley said, "Some of your boys don't like it, Con?"

Fortune rubbed his forefinger across his long upper lip. "I didn't like the way they took the news."

"Any open defiance?" asked Kalley. He sat down opposite Fortune who slumped loosely in the chair behind his desk.

"No," said Fortune, quietly. "I would have preferred that. I could have threatened them and make them too frightened to vote other than the way I told 'em to. But they just heard me out. And said nothing. But I didn't like the way they looked at me. We're going to lose a couple of votes, Macker. Not openly. But under the lap. They'll go to Bannion."

"Nothing much we can do about it, Con," said Kalley. "Unless you fix for the vote for the Chairman to be taken on a show of hands instead of by secret ballot."

"Makes it too obvious," said Fortune.

"Who cares? Provided you win. And a show of hands is not like a secret ballot. A lot of men who are courageous in secret get chicken livered when their vote's public. They won't dare to cross you openly, Con."

"I dunno," said Fortune. His forefinger kept rubbing across his lip. "They might still defy me. Even in an open vote. There is going to be plenty of blood-letting out of this caper. I don't want too many of my boys wiped out."

"Not so good, Con," said Kalley.

"Not so good," Fortune agreed. "What's happening, Macker? Usually I can trust my fellers to do what I tell 'em to."

"Your boys are mostly old-timers," said Kalley, slowly. "They put on a front. They're hardboiled. They'll do a bit of grafting. They'll look after their own interests all the time. But most of 'em have some regard for the Party. It's meant something to them. They don't like seeing it handed over to Seborjar and Lilley. Seborjar frightens them. And Lilley. They'll tolerate him, deal with him, while he's on the fringe of the Party. But there's something indecent about him running the show. They feel it, Con. In their bones if not with their heads. It's as I told you last night. You're asking for trouble."

"We talked it out last night, Macker," Fortune said. "I've made my decision. I'm sticking to it."

Kalley shrugged. "Okay, Con. You're the boss. But if you're scared of a drift among your own boys it isn't going to be easy. How about Hoskin's votes?"

Fortune said, "They're right. They're a different type from mine. Less independent. They can't exist without Hoskin. And they know it. My boys existed before I came on the scene. They could exist without me. No. Hoskin's votes are all right. So are Seborjar's."

"So we can balance out, Con. You lose a couple of your votes to Bannion. We can pick up Canover's with a bit of pressure. Possibly Vittor's. If we do, we're back to where we started from. With the vote being decided by the seven floaters."

"That's how I see it, Macker," Fortune passed a pencilled list across the desk to Kalley. "There are the seven. For some reason Seborjar doesn't want you to do anything about Perry Nova and Max Steiner. He's an idea that Lilley can work on 'em—successfully. I don't know the angle—yet. But I will. When I do, we'll decide whether to leave them to Lilley, or whether we'll work over 'em ourselves. Okay?"

"Okay, I reckon I'll go round the traps, Con. See if there's any rabbits in 'em," said Kalley who sometimes used a phrase from his rural childhood. He went through the door into the outer office. He shut the door behind him quietly. Fortune was leaning back in his chair with his feet up on the desk. His face was thoughtful. Kalley told Mrs Belasco, "I won't be in again today, Aggie. Keep the home fires burning."

"I'll try," said the woman. Her small, intelligent eyes were curious.

"What's in the bazaar gossip, Macker? Rumour has it that we have new allies."

"Rumour has it correctly," replied Kalley. "Seborjar and Lilley. How d'you like it?"

The woman said, "Truly, Macker?"

Kalley said, "Truly, Aggie."

The woman said, "I don't like it at all, Macker. He smells that dirty old waterfront rat. Daryl Kandur smells, too. But I prefer his smell. It's healthier."

"What's your beef, Aggie?" said Kalley. "Seborjar or Lilley."

"Mostly Seborjar," said the woman. "Lilley's just an ordinary crook. But Seborjar's a hypocrite." She paused. "I went to Seborjar for help after my husband died. You knew that, didn't you, Macker?"

"I didn't know it, Aggie."

"Yes, I went. Seborjar wasn't then the Leader. He was just a Party big shot. I couldn't get in to Seborjar. So I saw Kent Kerstey first. I told Kerstey who I was. I didn't need to tell Kerstey that my husband had worked for the party all his life. He knew that. But he didn't know that he was a generous, open-handed man who couldn't keep his hand away from his pocket when he listened to a hard-luck story, and who died leaving me flat broke, with a baby." Her voice was hard. "So I told Kerstey that and that I needed a job and that I wanted to see Seborjar to see if he could help me get one."

"So, what, Aggie?" Kalley prompted gently.

"So Kerstey went in and told my story to Seborjar. He came back and told me that Seborjar was busy. He was preparing a speech for that night. Couldn't see me. Didn't know when he would be able to." Her eyes were glittering. "I heard Seborjar speak that night. Do you know what his subject was, Macker? The status of women. He wasn't leader yet. So he could afford then to advocate equal pay for men and women. He wanted women given improved status. To be in no way inferior to men before the law. To be protected against the economic blast. They were the mothers of the nation. They—and their children —had to be protected by society. They cheered him and clapped him. All the feminists—and there were plenty there—thought he was wonderful."

"And you?" said Kalley.

"Me, Macker?" The woman smiled. "I didn't want equal pay. I just wanted a job. Otherwise I would have gone hungry. And so would my kid. So I buttonholed Con in the hall foyer. He had been at the meeting. I'd never met Con before. I told him who I was and that I wanted a job. He didn't say anything about equal pay or the status of women. He said 'Your old man was a good man. He was my friend.' He told me to start work the next day." The woman's eyes were moist. "So here I am. Still working for Con. Knowing that if I hadn't been up to the job Con would have helped me find another one before he fired me."

"Con know about your experience with Seborjar?" asked Kalley.

"Yes," said the woman.

"He's a strange man, Aggie."

"Who?" said the woman. "Seborjar or Con?"

"Maybe they both are, Aggie," said Kalley, who went out whistling softly through his teeth.

CHAPTER 8

Kalley had met Lanny Bellin soon after he started to work for Con Fortune. Bellin then was in his mid-forties, comparatively young by political standards. But he was already a Party legend. He was the brains and directing genius of one of the largest and wealthiest unions in the country. He used the union's organisation and its resources as the base on which he built his political power. He owned and operated, as personal possessions, the Party's political machine in three States where the Labor Party was almost impregnably entrenched in office. The elected administrators carried out Bellin's orders. He also had considerable power in other States, through his union's influence upon the local Party machines. Though Bellin himself seldom occupied a Party post, he made and unmade many of those who did. In the Federal structure he also had influence. But Bellin was a rare phenomenon in politics—a man who simultaneously enjoyed the exercise of power and yet recognised when circumstance dictated cautious restraint. He did not overreach himself. He would have liked to rule on a national scale. But he knew that in a democratic tradition—however fictional that might be—he could endanger the power he already possessed. So he used his immense influence with moderation.

Among his many Party alliances Bellin had a loose working arrangement with Fortune, whose shrewdness and boldness attracted him.

Kalley early found that Bellin had an odd weakness that stemmed from his physique. A thin wisp of a man, with a weak, delicate body, Bellin resented his physical deficiencies. So he surrounded himself with a bodyguard of huge, strong men. Nominally they were union officials, they were on the union payroll. Actually they were his personal strongarm squad. In a bar, Bellin enjoyed singling out someone large and muscular, picking an argument, lashing his victim with his clever, biting tongue. Usually his insults were accepted meekly. He was widely known in the cheap, rough bars patronised by the manual workers from among whom his union found its recruits. When his victim did not retaliate he persuaded himself that it was he who was feared, not the formidable thugs surrounding him.

When occasionally the butts of his verbal aggression rebelled, he stood aside, a smirk on his face, while his bodyguards took care of him.

Bellin had bouts of heavy drinking. But even when drunk he was wary and foxy, finding Kalley tight-lipped and secretive. The age gap between them was such that he could not visualise the boy ever becoming a danger to him. When drunk and feeling loquacious he often sent on his goons looking for Kalley. Bellin enjoyed the intent, deferential attention with which Kalley listened to him. It flattered him. Once, talkative, after he had had Kalley summoned to the bar where for hours he had been drinking morosely, he had advised the younger man in his harsh, twanging voice, "Never select lieutenants on the width of their foreheads, Macker. Pick 'em on the size of their shoulders. Or the breadth of their arses. A big man usually has a small brain."

Kalley said, "That how you pick your lieutenants, Mr Bellin?" "Yes," said Bellin. His hand was unsteady as he lifted his glass to his lips. Some of the liquor slopped over. "You know what they call me, Kalley? Pope Lanny. I'm not even Catholic, and they made me a pope." He gestured with his glass at two of his bodyguards leaning against the bar out of earshot; "You know what they call those mugs? My college of cardinals. None of this crap about democratic control in my union, Macker. I'm Pope. I own the show. I run it. The cardinals carry out my orders. The way elections are fixed in my union the rank and file can't get at me even if they want to. They can't without inside leadership. Leadership that has to come from one of the cardinals. I can lose control of the union only through a palace revolution." He chuckled, without mirth. "So I've made certain that there is no-one in the palace capable of leading a coup. They're all wide in the shoulders, broad in the arse, and short in the brain."

"But you seem to worry about your rank and file, Mr Bellin," protested Kalley.

"I do the best I can for them, boy. That's my justification for existence. And it's also good sense. But I don't worry about rank and file revolts. Don't fall for this line about democratic control. When an organisation gets as big as my union, or as big as the Party, rank and file control doesn't work. Nor does the rank and file revolt on their own accord. Not provided you fight to look after them honestly as I do. To get them the things you feel they're entitled to. But you have to safeguard yourself too, boy. By making sure that they don't get leadership." He waved contemptuously in the direction of his bodyguards. "I've made sure of that."

"But what happens when you decide to pull out, Mr Bellin? You've built a political empire. Without an heir, one of your gorillas will have all your power. And none of your ability."

Bellin said, "I haven't bred my own heir, boy. I've no kids. Why should I care what happens when I'm gone? I'll die with my political boots on." His lips curled. "There was some French woman. I've forgotten her name. She played it high, wide and handsome. She didn't care what happened when she snuffed it. When people asked her what would happen she said, 'After me the deluge.'" There was a node of admiration in Bellin's voice. "That's my philosophy, boy. After me the deluge." With a sardonic edge to his voice, Bellin added, "You're young enough to see the deluge. It'll be interesting for you to recall what I've just said."

"But why, Mr Bellin?" Kalley persisted. "Why do you want a deluge? They say in the Party that you've always exercised the power you've had responsibly. Why should you want a deluge when you move out?"

Bellin said, absently, "You ask awkward questions. Why do I want a deluge? I dunno. Maybe I've a grotesque sense of humour. Maybe it's my vanity. To ensure that my successor isn't as good as I am. Perhaps then I'll be remembered a little longer. Maybe I don't even want a deluge. Maybe I'm just providing myself with a justification for surrounding myself with lieutenants so lame-brained that they will never threaten my overlordship."

"Chris Tion isn't lame-brained. I keep my eyes open, Mr Bellin."

"Yes," said Bellin. "And they're good eyes, boy. You're quite right, Macker. Chris Tion isn't lame-brained. He's the exception that proves the rule. A big man, but he has brains."

Bellin lifted his glass carefully. "I make a prophecy, Macker. If he outlives me, Chris Tion'll be my successor. And should be. He's fifteen years younger. I don't think he'll make a move against me while I'm alive. He'd like to, but he's too cunning. He has patience. The prize is worth the waiting. A strong union and the best political machine in the country. If he reaches for the prize during my lifetime it may elude him. It won't if he holds his hand. And I make another prophecy. When he takes over the union, he'll canonise me. Saying it was the last wish of Saint Lanny." He lifted his voice. "Hey, Chris, here. I want you."

The man who walked towards them was tall, wide-shouldered,

beautifully dressed with a hard, controlled face. He looked like a boxer, so skilful that his trade had not left its mark upon him.

Bellin said, curtly, "Sit down, Chris." He studied him for a moment. "Drink?"

"No, thanks, Lanny. You know I don't drink." There was a note of rebuke in the voice.

"I'd forgotten," said Bellin. "Your weakness is women. It's a weakness that'll get you into trouble some day, Chris. Politics and women don't mix."

"They do if you're careful." Tion added with a tinge of mockery in his voice, "Wouldn't care to give it a try, boss?"

"Woman isn't my meat." Bellin's eyes were bleary. Kalley was always amazed how he managed to remain both lucid and intelligent when drink-sodden. Alcohol didn't affect his tongue or brain. Only his body. He said, "The boy and I have been talking politics, Chris. We want a third opinion. Pretend you're Lanny Bellin, Chris. Try and put yourself in my shoes."

"That's one thing I would not care to try, boss. Those who try to put themselves in your shoes usually find themselves with their future all behind them."

"That's right," said Bellin. "Never forget that, Chris. The boy thinks you have brains. I'm inclined to agree with him."

Tion looked hard at Kalley. "Thanks for the good opinion, Macker. But it wont go to my head"

Bellin said, "Keep it that way. Chris. Then one day when I've pulled out you could own both the union and my political machine. Okay. Let's assume I've pulled out. You're in the saddle. You're running the show. What would you do, Chris? Operate things as they are? Or make a few changes?" He ordered another drink but his eyes did not leave Tion's face.

Tion's wet lips had suddenly gone dry. "What's the idea, Lanny? You don't think I've been up to something?"

Bellin sneered, "Conscience twitching, Chris?"

"Nothing like that Lanny," said Tion, who twitched nervously. "You know me better than that, Lanny. I'm one hundred per cent loyal."

The older man said with cold menace, "You'd better be, Chris, if you know what's good for you. But I don't want a mouthful of slaver about loyalty. I asked a question."

Tion glanced at Kalley. "How about sending the kid away?"

"The kid's all right," said Bellin. "He can't hurt you, Chris. And he can't hurt me. Besides, he's tight-mouthed. And we're dealing with something hypothetical." Although he was quite drunk, his enunciation was perfect.

Tion waved a deprecating hand. "Look, boss, I don't pretend. I want to fill your shoes. When you're ready to vacate 'em. But not while you're there to fill 'em. You're a superb organiser. As good as this country has seen. Or is likely to. The political machines you operate are run in a first-class manner. You've got your union sewn up from top to bottom. It's tight-knit, efficient, effective, strong. Your members are satisfied. When you speak the heads of this country listen to you and give you what you want."

"There's something working in that Neanderthal skull of yours," said Bellin impatiently.

"You can get almost anything you want off anyone in this country," said Tion. "They'd crawl—most of 'em—on their bellies to give it to you, Lanny. From fear. Or for a pat on the head, and your support for something they want. Or because between your union and political power you can push virtually any individual or company, however wealthy, up against a wall and kick 'em to death. You've accumulated more political power, probably, than any other individual in this country. But you don't demand things. You ask for 'em. And you're always careful to see that what you ask for is not excessive. I can't understand. Asking. Careful. You. That, Lanny, I just don't get. If ever I have the power you have, Lanny, I'll use it. That's what it is there for."

"You're a fool Chris." Bellin said contemptuously. "A cunning one. But a fool." Bellin jerked an arrogant thumb over his shoulder. "Now beat it."

Tion rose resentfully. He said, "No need to turn nasty. I was only trying to answer your question."

"You did," Bellin said, curtly. He ordered another drink from a waiter. Tion's retreating back was stiff and hostile.

Kalley said, softly, "After you the deluge, Mr Bellin."

Bellin said, "You still here, boy? I'd forgotten you."

"I'm still here, Mr Bellin. Why is Chris a fool? Cunning, but a fool."

The older man looked at him with hard-worn eyes that the bleariness of drink did not soften. He said, irritably, "I'm not running a school of political education for ambitious juveniles. Work it out yourself."

"1 think I have," said Kalley.

"What's your conclusion, boy?"

"The voters don't like people who flaunt their power openly. That's why you have the power you have. Because you don't swagger round thrusting it down the throat of the public. Only down the throats of selected individuals, like Tion, who can't resent anything you do, because you own 'em, body and soul. Or because they are powerless to do anything against you. But Tion'll swagger around indiscriminately. That's why he won't have the power you have, Mr Bellin. Because he won't be able to use power shrewdly."

"Don't ever ask me for a job, boy. You won't get one."

Kalley said pokerfaced; "Not wide enough in the shoulders, Mr Bellin?"

He had thought to restore the older man's good humour with his sally. But Bellin was still hostile "You're too wide in the forehead, boy. You'll go a long way in this racket."

Kalley said, gently. "Not me, Mr Bellin. It's Tion who is going places. Remember? After you the deluge."

"That's right, boy." Bellin's eyes swivelled to the three men at the bar. "After me the deluge."

Bellin's prophecy that Tion would succeed him proved correct. Bellin died on his fifty-eighth birthday. His union gave him a funeral as magnificent as a feudal baron's. Tion announced that, on his deathbed, Bellin had expressed the wish that Tion would be his successor as the union's leader. Tion made the announcement with emotion deepening his voice. During Bellin's last illness, which had been a protracted one, Tion had acted for the ageing, ailing chieftain. With a brutal, efficient ruthlessness worthy of Bellin himself, he had weeded out potential rivals within the union's ranks. He took complete control of the union machinery for the election of the new leader.

In falling heir to Bellin's union empire, Tion also fell heir to the Party machines that Bellin had built up in the various States. But while successful as a union leader, Tion lacked Bellin's touch in politics. Setting out to use massive power, he lacked Bellin's cold political mind and Bellin's finesse. He was crude and arrogant, continually antagonising people—powerful people. He had no fixed policies. He was swayed by whims, hates and prejudices, one moment backing one group in the Party, and the next their opponents. He quarrelled with Con Fortune. He opposed Kaye Seborjar for a while, and then supported him. He formed an alliance with Carr Domineco and then, over a minor and largely imagined affront, fought with him. One by one he broke off the loose but effective alliances that Bellin had maintained with formidable groups within the Party. He did not lose all Bellin's former power—while he maintained his grip upon his union, and that continued as tight as ever, to lose all was impossible. But gradually the political empire he had inherited became a shadow of what it had been under Bellin. Tion's name did not appear among Fortune's list of the seven uncommitted voters on the Party's thirty-strong Management Committee that would decide between Lilley and Bannion for the Party Chairman. But the names Bart Collon and Marty Efton did. They were Tion's creatures. Kalley did not bother about them. He knew that they would vote as Tion instructed them to vote. Kalley did two days' work, exploring Tion's most recent moves in case he had made any of which Fortune was ignorant. Then he told Fortune, "I'm seeing Chris Tion today, Con."

They were in Fortune's dingy, gloomy office at Party headquarters.

"Good, Macker. We need Collon and Efton."

"What do we offer for 'em, Con?"

"We offer nothing, Macker. Absolutely nothing."

Kalley said, "Chris'll want some quid pro quo."

Fortune said, with good-humoured contempt, "He won't get it off me."

Kalley said dispassionately, "He's an irrational bastard, Con. He mightn't like that. Why not throw him a bone?"

Fortune responded, "Let Seborjar throw him a bone. We've no loose bones lying round, Macker. We want 'em for our own boys."

"He mightn't play, Con," Kalley warned. Fortune was confident. "He'll play." He stabbed at the pad on his desk with the point of his pencil. "Tion is strictly small-time. He's in the big time but only because Lanny Bellin had a pathological fear of able lieutenants. He doesn't make his political decisions on what's to his advantage. He's governed by his hates."

Kalley said, "He hates you, Con."

"I know," said Fortune. His wide, firm mouth was smiling, "But nowadays he hates Domineco worse. I don't spill over into the union field as much as Domineco does. Tion's obstinate, but he's not stupid. He knows that without his union he's a nobody. I couldn't take his union off him. But perhaps Domineco could. So he hates Domineco more than me."

"He doesn't like Bannion, either," said Kalley.

"Why should he?" Fortune shrugged. "Bannion's gone a long way. He's getting close to the top. Further than Chris has been able to go in the Party. Chris can't see why. Bannion hasn't a union. He hasn't the power base that Chris has. Yet he's outstripped him. Chris can't forgive him for that. He's jealous of Bannion."

Kalley pursued his lips thoughtfully. "Maybe it'd be wiser if I didn't go near him, Con. Just took it for granted that he'll throw his votes to Lilley."

"No," said Fortune, firmly. "He's such an unpredictable bastard that we can't ignore him. If we do he's just as likely to take it as an affront. Turn sulky. And out of small-boy pique throw his votes to Bannion. See him. But promise him nothing."

Kalley sighed. "I don't think he's going to like it, Con."

"He'll get over it. And he's not without cunning. He knows Seborjar's desperate. He'll go running to Seborjar for a pay-off. Seborjar'll toss him a bone. It won't need to be much of a bone. Seborjar can have him made chairman of some minor committee—give him some job from which he'll get a bit of prestige but no power. Seborjar'll be delighted to. Firstly, to assure himself of Chris's votes for Lilley on the committee. And secondly, because the Big Man'll feel that he's putting something over me. He loves to play both ends against the middle."

"Nice friends you have, Con."

Fortune laughed. "They aren't friends, Macker. You know that. I'd sooner be friendly with snakes."

"Well, wish me luck, Con." Kalley went out of the office, down in the dingy lift, outside into the sunshine. Told the taxi driver where to go and leaned back, relaxed, against the cushions.

Tion had a luxurious suite of offices in a tall building in the smart downtown section. Kalley went along a thickly carpeted corridor and through the door on which was engraved in gold the union's title. The air-conditioned office was cool. It was more like the headquarters of a wealthy company than a union premises. A smartly-dressed young woman swung her chair round from the switchboard she was operating.

"My name's Kalley. I have an appointment with Mr Tion."

"You're expected, Mr Kalley. If you just follow Miss Wilson, she'll show you to Mr Tion's office,'"

Tion was seated behind a huge desk. He was in his shirt sleeves. He looked hard and muscular and fit. Abe Lomas was with him, leaning against a filing cabinet. He was old, with heavy stooped shoulders, a bald shiny head and opaque tired eyes. He was shabbily dressed and untidy. He looked out of place in the lavish, spacious room. Kalley knew Lomas. He acted as a political adviser to Tion. His judgments and advice were reasonably shrewd. But he could not control Tion.

Tion said abruptly, "What do you want?"

Kalley sat down. Tion repeated, "What do you want?" He paused "There's the door. If you don't like my manner, you can walk out through it any time you want."

"I will, Chris. When I want." Kalley shook a cigarette out from the packet he had taken from his pocket. He lit it slowly and puffed out the smoke. "But what I want—or would like—right now. Chris, is a bit of information."

"What kind of information?" said Tion.

Kalley shrugged. "The kind about the Management Committee. The kind that'll tell me whether you're backing Lilley or Bannion."

"What's it to you?" Tion asked.

Kalley smiled without mirth. "You know that Con's backing Lilley. Everyone in the Party knows that by now. So where you throw your votes has become important to us."

Tion said, "Jesus, what do I owe Con Fortune? Why should I throw 'em to anyone he's supporting?"

Kalley said, "Self-interest, Chris. Self-interest."

"I'll decide where my self-interest lies. Neither Con Fortune nor anyone else is going to make up my mind for me." His manner suddenly changed. "How about a drink, Macker?" He nodded at the silent Lomas. "Abe'll have one with you."

Kalley said, "No, thanks, Chris. Bit early for me yet."

Tion said, "Maybe we could make a deal."

Kalley said, cautiously, "What kind of a deal?"

Tion said, "You want my votes. I want other things."

Kalley said, "What kind of things, Chris?"

Tion nodded at the silent, watchful Lomas. The old man was still leaning against the filing cabinet. "Abe and I have been talking things over, Macker." He leaned back in his chair, a large, strong man with a hard, confident face. "I don't particularly care who wins this fight, Macker. I've nothing against either Domineco or Bannion."

"Don't give me that crap, Chris," Kalley said, calmly. "Domineco's already tried once to take your union off you. He'll try again."

Tion's mouth pouted angrily. "You and Con are a pair of smooth, self-satisfied bastards. You worry about looking after yourselves. I'll worry about looking after myself and after Domineco."

"Be realistic, Chris," said Kalley, his manner faintly amused.

"Don't pull that line of bull that you've nothing against Domineco. You've plenty."

Lomas intervened, "Look, Kalley, do you want Chris's votes or don't you?"

"We want 'em. But we don't want a line of sales talk that wouldn't deceive a babe."

Tion said, his face ugly, "Don't get too loud-mouthed, Kalley. Or I'll arrange for that blabbermouth of yours to be closed. Forcibly."

"You're scaring me to death, Chris. But then I scare easily."

Lomas said, "Christ, Macker, have some sense. There's no need to turn nasty."

"Tell your boss that, Abe. Not me."

Tion stood up. "I'm not in Fortune's pocket, Macker. If he wants those votes there's a price to be met."

"What's the price?" asked Kalley.

Tion made his points on his thick strong fingers. "Firstly, the penal clauses against unions have to be withdrawn."

Kalley said, "That's a Federal matter, Chris. We can't do anything about it until we get Seborjar elected to the top job. And that won't be tomorrow. And Con couldn't promise you that, anyway. It's outside the range of his influence. You know that. You'd have to ask Seborjar for it."

"I won't ask," said Tion. "I'll tell Seborjar I want it. But I also want Con's promise that he'll support the move in the Party."

"Don't you trust Seborjar?"

Tion guffawed. He had recovered his good temper. "Do you?" he challenged.

"He's our friend," said Kalley. There was no flicker of expression on his face. "How do you know you can trust Con's promise of support?"

"I don't," said Tion. "But Abe has a touching faith that I haven't. He believes that when Con gives his word he seldom goes back on it."

"I think Con'd give that pledge. After all, it's Party policy to wipe out the penal clauses. What else?"

"The next two are in Con's orbit, not Seborjar's." Tion's eyes narrowed calculatingly. "I want Con to fix it so that the State Legislature lays it down that no state or civic contracts are issued until the contractor produces a certificate that he operates a one hundred per cent closed shop as far as this union is concerned."

Kalley whistled. "That's an awful lot of power to give any one man, Chris. You'll be the boy who'll be issuing the certificates. It gives you a power of veto on any contract."

Tion said, his eyes sly, "Domineco'd give me that. For my votes."

Kalley said, "Domineco still has to win, Chris. Personally I don't think he can. Even with your two votes."

Tion said, "That's Con's risk. Not mine. I've little to lose. If I back Domineco he'll leave me alone in the union. And even if he didn't it wouldn't matter. I can handle that monkey. If he doesn't win I'm no worse off. But if he does, Seborjar and Con'll both have had it. And I'll get what I want."

Kalley said, thoughtfully, "We couldn't give you control over contracts as nakedly as that, Chris. The newspapers'd kick us to death."

Tion said harshly, "I don't care whether it's naked or disguised. So long as it's real."

Lomas said quietly from his vantage point of the filing cabinet, "And one hundred per cent unionism is Party policy in this State, Macker."

Tion sneered, "These political monkeys are always prepared to forget Party policy. Until policy changes to suit 'em. What about it, Macker?"

Kalley puffed at his cigarette. "You mightn't get it in the form you want it, Chris. The Party'd have to provide some kind of an appeal against your certificate. Otherwise we'd run into serious trouble with the electors." His face was expressionless. "You know what they're like, Chris. Suspicious. They might figure you were taking a rake-off." He sighed. "But Con'll probably fake a deal. To give you at least part of what you want. What else is on your mind?"

Tion said, "I want greater representation on the Management Committee. I want Abe put on."

Kalley said, sharply, "Con won't deal on that, Chris."

Tion said, "Somebody's going to, Macker."

"It won't be Con." Kalley was definite. "Con's got his own boys to look after. He's not putting any of your boys in."

"I want Abe on, said Tion stubbornly. "In addition to Collon and Efton. I've only two votes on that committee. That's not enough, Macker. I want more."

Kalley said, looking across at Lomas, "Con's got nothing against Abe, personally. But he's not trading away any votes on that committee. You can forget that, Chris. Why don't you see Seborjar. Maybe he'll agree to put Abe on in place of one of his own stooges."

Tion said, "You might have something there."

Kalley said, "If I haven't, you still won't get Abe on in place of one of Con's boys. That's final, Chris."

Tion pondered, his heavy brows knitted. At last he said slowly, "Okay, Macker. I'm prepared to pass up on Con replacing one of his own boys with Abe. I'll talk with Seborjar. He hasn't the same scruples as Con. He wants something. If he's going to get it he'll have to give something away. Something additional to his promise that if federally he ever hits the top he'll have the penal clauses against unions withdrawn."

"Let's see if I have things straight, Chris." Kalley tapped with his right forefinger on the palm of his left hand. "You want a pledge from Con that he'll back your move with Seborjar to get penal clauses lifted from unions. Right?" "Right," said Tion. His heavy face was intent. "I'm prepared to trust Con on that one, Macker. I've no option. All I ask for is one public speech advocating the abolition of the penal clauses."

"Fair enough," said Kalley. "Then you want Con to do something about getting one hundred per cent closed shops for your union with all government contractors."

"Yes," said Tion. "I'll admit, Macker, I don't know how I can tie Con down on that one. He may make the promise and welsh later."

Kalley said, "Con doesn't welsh, Chris."

"He'd better not. He's going to need me later when Seborjar starts intriguing against him. As Seborjar's bound to do. He can't help intriguing. And if Con demonstrates that he's willing to play ball with me now I might be in a mood to continue playing ball with him. When Seborjar's gunning for him."

Kalley said, coolly, "Maybe it'll be you who'll be looking for someone to play ball with. Seborjar may decide that you're the one who should be cut down."

Tion smiled. His teeth were large, white and even. He said, "You forget, Macker, I'm not like Con. I don't draw my power from politics alone. Con does. I have the union. It's my strength. I can take political reverses and still survive. Con can't."

"Don't think you're indispensable, Chris. The graveyard is full of indispensables." Kalley got up and put his hat on.

Tion said quickly, "Is it a deal, Macker?"

"I'll phone you. I'll have to talk things over with Con. I've no authority from him to enter into any firm commitments. But I'd reckon it'll be okay. If Con agrees to your terms, your boys'll vote for Lilley?"

Tion said, dryly, "Con'll be getting his pay-off on the spot. My boys'll vote for Lilley. I'll have to wait for my pay-off."

Kalley said, "I'll be seeing you." Lomas followed him out of the office. As the door closed behind them Lomas said, "How about a drink, Macker?"

Kalley said, "Sure, Abe. Where'll we go?"

Lomas said, "There's a little bar across the street. I'll pick up my hat."

Lomas left Kalley standing in the outer office. The office was full of good looking girls. "Chris always had an eye for a decorative skirt," thought Kalley.

The bar was dim, intimate and warm. Lomas shambled past the long counter to a booth at the back. He was known. The barman inquired, "Whisky?" Lomas grunted. Kalley nodded. Lomas held up two fingers to the barman silently.

Kalley said, "Good luck, Abe." He swallowed the drink. Lomas sipped at his. Then he replaced it on the table.

"Where are things heading, Macker?"

"You ought to know, Abe. Chris knows what he wants."

"I'm not thinking of Chris, Macker. Or of us. I'm thinking of the Party."

Kalley shrugged. "Maybe Seborjar's taking over. Maybe Con is. What's it to us? We still get paid. Have another drink, Abe."

Lomas waited until the barman had brought him a fresh drink. He said, "The Party's changing, Macker."

"Everything changes," said Kalley.

"It's hard to get old, Macker. It's nice being young. You believe in things. Then suddenly you're old and there's nothing you can believe in."

"Things are different from when you were a boy, Abe." Kalley traced circles on the table with the wet bottom of his glass. "Men were closer to the basic things then. Hunger. Homelessness. Joblessness. You could touch 'em, smell 'em, taste 'em. And because you believed in them you believed in other things. Like the Party. But the Party has done much to wipe those things out. And when you lose your belief in them you go a long way towards losing your belief in the Party."

The old man said, wistfulness shading his harsh, dull voice, "I'd like to get out, Macker."

Kalley said, "Why don't you?"

"It's a job. Jobs aren't plentiful when you get to my age. I only know two things—politics and unionism. You don't learn new trades when you're old."

"How's Chris? Hard to take?"

"Sometimes," said the old man. "But mostly he's all right, not a bad fella, Chris." He looked at Kalley with weary eyes. "You know my history, Macker?"

Kalley knew, as everyone in the Party did, that Lomas had once been charged.

"Nobody in the Party'd touch me after my troubles." Lomas, then a strong, hotblooded man in his thirties had been arrested. Nothing could be proved against him. He was acquitted. "I'd worked for Lanny Bellin for years. He scrubbed me off. I was bad medicine politically."

Kalley could almost see the scene—Bellin, cold and incisive, unable to understand anyone getting into difficulties, other than those of the most temporary character, over a woman, telling Lomas to get the hell out of his sight and to stay out of it. "When Lanny died, Chris put me back on the payroll," Lomas said. "He was sorry for me, I guess. He ain't a bad fella, Macker."

"That's ancient history, Abe," said Kalley, softly.

"To you, maybe. To me it's yesterday. I don't like what Seborjar's going to do to the Party, Macker. I don't like what I think he's going to do to Chris."

"Chris can look after himself," said Kalley.

"Not against Seborjar," said Lomas. "Seborjar's too clever for him. Too devious. I'd like to see Con Fortune around to help him out."

"How could Con do that, Abe? Even if he wanted to—and I don't think he does. Chris doesn't like him. He doesn't trust him. They've nothing in common. Con doesn't like tough guys in politics. And Chris loves to act the tough guy. To belt over the skull with a blackjack anyone who opposes him."

The old man said, eagerly, "I can influence him, Macker. You know that."

Kalley nodded. "Sometimes, Abe. But only sometimes. Chris is a bull. When he breaks loose nothing'll hold him. And he breaks loose too often. That's his trouble. He's a good wrecker. But he can't build anything up in its place. Con has his weaknesses. But Con likes building things, more than he likes tearing 'em down."

When Kalley paid for the drinks he decided against going back to the office. He told the taxi driver to drop him at the bar opposite the Legislature building. The bar was frequented by the Party politicians from the Legislature, the more gregarious and convivial of the important players in the Party and their hangers-on and henchmen. It was a club rather than a bar. Politics were talked there as much as they were in the shabby, imposing building opposite.

Kalley knew most of the customers in the crowded bar.

They were almost without exception in politics or connected with them in some way. As Kalley paused at the entrance, several men waved to him. Kalley had no illusions. He had no personal popularity. But men usually wanted to talk to him. He had something they all wanted — precise knowledge of what was going on in at least a section of the Party's back alleys. He saw Lilley down at the far end of the bar. The fat man was surrounded by a circle of men. He was laughing and talking and gesturing expansively. Kalley nodded to the barman who served him a whisky without waiting for his order, and then crossed to an empty booth.

Kenny Serge sauntered across and, uninvited, took a seat opposite Kalley. Serge was a newspaperman. Short and fat, with thinning, colourless hair that had once been thick and blond. Kalley knew that he had neither depth nor perception. He collected news like a magpie collecting glittering objects, tirelessly, without being able to perceive the difference in value between a diamond and a piece of coloured glass.

Serge said, "What's news, Macker?" His eyes, deep-set in his plumpness, were quick and bright.

"I wouldn't know, Kenny. Nobody ever tells me anything. What do you hear?"

Serge was drinking beer in a long glass. He looked at it. "I hear that Con's dumped Bannion and is backing Lilley." His eyes went along the bar to the group around Lilley. "The fat boy's pleased enough for that to be right."

Kalley said, "You could be right, Kenny. I read about it in the papers. Under your byline."

"I never read newspapers, Macker. I only write 'em. What's the angle?"

"Have you talked with Bannion yet, Kenny?"

Serge said, "Yep. But he's pulling the stiff-lipped, ex-airforce officer stuff. Won't talk. Has no comment for the newspapers."

Kalley said, "Where do you stand, Kenny?"

"I stand with whoever is feeding me the news. That'll go for my paper, too. It's anti-Party. This is a Party fight. The paper won't care who's going to win. It'll merely be interested in the news."

Kalley said, "What's the angle being peddled to the newspapermen by Seborjar's crowd? Or Lilley's?"

Serge gulped at his beer. "They just claim that Con has switched to backing Lilley. When you ask 'em why, they don't seem able to give an answer. They just wisecrack that he's seen the light—that Fortune never backs a losing side and that Bannion has lost out."

"What do you think?" asked Kalley. "You've been in this racket a long time, Kenny. You ought to be able to come up with something."

"I don't know, Macker," Serge was troubled. "There's something phoney about this set-up. It's not like Con to dump an old friend like Bannion. Con doesn't like Seborjar. Lilley's a crook. Something smells, Macker."

He knew Serge was important. People took notice of and were influenced by what he wrote. But more importantly he influenced the other newspapermen all over the country.

Kalley said softly, "Con didn't dump Bannion. Bannion's his protégé. Con had great plans for him. He could visualise him some day becoming the Party Leader. Right at the top. Our Alex Pope. Why should Con want to dump the man he had created for big things?"

Serge was impressed. "Con really thought that, Macker? That Bannion could go all the way?"

"Yes. All the way." Kalley savoured his drink. "This isn't a fight between Bannion and Con. It's a fight between Domineco and Con. Domineco was close to taking over the Party. Very close. "Con?" He snapped his fingers. "Bannion?" He repeated the gesture. "They were both out. Finished." He looked at Serge. "Con hasn't dumped Bannion. Bannion dumped Con. To back Domineco.

"Why?" Serge's quick, bright eyes were alert.

Kalley shrugged. "Who knows? Bannion's like everyone else, I guess. Ambitious. Maybe he figures that he can get to the top quicker with Domineco. Maybe he figures that it's worthwhile compromising with a few principles to get to the top quickly. I wouldn't know."

Serge was suspicious. "It's a good story, Kalley. Hangs together, too. But how do I know that you're not just peddling Con's poison?"

Kalley said, gently, "Have I ever lied to you, Kenny."

The plump man smiled ruefully. "Not in the literal sense Macker. But when you tell things, you tell with your slant."

Kalley said, with good humour, "You wouldn't expect me to slant them against Con, would you, Kenny?"

"No," said the plump man. He rubbed his chin unhappily. "But I like Bannion. He seems sincere. The kind of fella who is prepared to make a few sacrifices for his beliefs. Your version doesn't fit in with Bannion."

"Suit yourself, Kenny," Kalley glanced round. They were being watched, not obviously, but carefully. But there was no-one in earshot. He lowered his voice. "How well do you know Franky Canover? Well enough to talk to him?" He remembered the fat, kindly ex-butcher's worried face, when he had told Bannion's group of Fortune's intentions. He felt sorry for the man. But he knew he could he used.

"I know Canover," said Serge cautiously.

"Don't quote me on this," said Kalley, in the same confidential tone. "Or publish it unless you can get Franky to confirm it. And don't even then name me as the intermediary. I went to Bannion's office the morning after Seborjar's meeting. Bannion's group were all there. I told 'em Con was with them. Every inch of the way. That he had no quarrel with them. That they were his friends. But that—in everybody's interest—Domineco's power had to be broken and that, as a tactical move, Con was backing Lilley for the chairmanship."

"How did they take that little packet of dynamite?" asked Serge curiously.

Kalley lit another cigarette. "They told me to go to hell. That they'd sooner throw in with Domineco against Con."

Serge considered. "That's not a bad line, Macker. From your viewpoint. It changes this from a brawl between Con and Bannion, whom everybody is inclined to like and admire, into a brawl between Con and Domineco, whom nobody likes." He got up. "I'll talk with Canover," he promised.

Kalley watched with bleak, expressionless eyes as the short, plump newspaperman walked away from the booth, "Jesus," he thought sombrely. "What is truth?" He had told Serge what had happened in Bannion's office. Not once had he lied. But his truths were tattered streamers blowing anywhere as the breeze dictated, whereas truth was a whole thing, like a seamless garment, that could not be divided without damage.

Kalley knew what would happen. Serge would go to Canover. The fat, kindly ex-butcher would be confused. Serge would question him. Canover would try to cover up loyally. Clumsily and stupidly, he would seek to prevent the breach between Fortune and Bannion from appearing as wide as it was. He would attempt to be noncommittal. But his attitude would confirm to Serge that what Kalley had said to him was broadly correct. Kalley thought, "I'm giving Con what he pays me for. I can't start questioning now whether I'm doing the right or the wrong thing."

A hand clapped Kalley lightly on the shoulder. Lilley asked jovially, "How'ya, Macker?" Bose Carlin was with Lilley. Carlin was long, lumpy, sour-faced, with blazing, humourless eyes under a shock of hair black as an Indian's. He was of immense physical strength. Nearly as broad as he was high, he had been on the fringe of the Party for years. He was selfless in his concept of patriotism; selfish in his determination to thrust his concept down others' throats. During the war he had been a brave and ferocious soldier who had risen from the ranks to a field command. After the war he had tried to establish a new political party, fanatically nationalist, with authoritarian overtones, tough, aggressive and militant. It had given promise of being successful. Carlin had gathered about him a group that he referred to as "my knuckle boys". They specialised in breaking up violently meetings of minor political groups, particularly the Communists. But the prosperity of the post-war period militated against them, as did the fact that Carlin had no real qualities for leadership. He knew only one form of persuasion—violence. When he and his followers ran into trouble with the police and the Party's State authorities, their decline was as abrupt as their rise.

Carlin drifted back into a queer association with the more unscrupulous Party Leaders. He had an instinct for scandal and the doggedness to track it down. It was rumoured that he had an extensive dossier on every prominent Party member. He had an unexpected flair for scurrilous journalism. In print he had a humour that he lacked in the flesh. He wrote a racy, vigorous style, amusing, pungent and devastating. His pen was for hire. But it was only his pen he sold. Not his independence in thought, action, or judgment. He was his own man. He was feared and hated.

Lilley said, "You know Bose, Macker?"

"Sure," said Kalley. "How'ya, Bose."

Lilley sat down. He waved Carlin into the seat alongside him.

The fat man's belly pushed against the table. He grumbled good-humouredly, "They don't build these booths for padded figures like mine. Only for the thin-gutted variety. Like you, Macker."

Kalley said, "You ought to take a few pounds off, Joe. You can afford it."

Lilley said ruefully, "That I could." He rubbed his hand over the expanse of his belly. "Tell me the secret, Macker."

Kalley said, "A virtuous life, Joe."

Lilley said, "That's no good for anyone, Macker. Too dull." He chuckled. " I just heard a good one." He threw back his head and laughed. "You know Jimmy Dancer? Stands for every post that falls vacant in the Party. And never wins."

"I know him," said Kalley.

"Well, I'm chewing the fat with a bunch of the boys down there at the end of the bar." His pudgy hand waved towards where he had been drinking. "Somebody mentions that the newspapers are carrying a story that the Pope is ill."

He wheezed with enjoyment. "One of the boys says, 'Jesus, I hope Jimmy Dancer doesn't get to hear about it. Or he'll stand for the job!'" He looked at Kalley from the corner of his eyes. "Not bad, Macker? Not bad, eh?"

"Not bad," Kalley agreed. He watched Carlin's face. The big man did not move a muscle.

"Talking of standing for jobs, Macker. What's the news?" Lilley's hard tiny eyes were intent.

"No news," said Kalley.

"No news?" said Lilley. He added, "You're cagey, Macker. That's good. But there's no need to be cagey with me. You're working for me now."

"You've got it wrong, Joe. I work for Con Fortune. Nobody else." He nodded at Carlin. "Who's Bose working for?"

Lilley said, "Well, he's working for me in a kind of way. Indirectly. And he's working for Seborjar."

Carlin said, "I'm working for myself, Macker." His voice was grating and unpleasant. But Kalley knew that he was a first-class mob orator. He had heard him.

Kalley said, pleasantly, "You two fellas ought to get together and make a decision about who's working for who."

Carlin said, "I'm not working for anyone. I'm working against someone. Domineco."

Kalley said, "Well, thank Christ we've got one supporter, Joe. What's put you over our side of the fence Bose?"

Carlin said, "I don't like Domineco. So when I heard that Seborjar's going to have a showdown with him I hotfooted to Seborjar. Told him I was willing to do anything to help." "Without pay?" said Kalley, lightly.

"Without pay." Carlin pulled a nail file from his pocket and started digging with it at his nails.

"What did Seborjar have to say to that?" asked Kalley.

"He made suitably grateful noises. Told me to see you. That you were doing the legwork."

Kalley said, "Sorry, Bose. I've nothing I can give you."

Carlin got up, a giant, grim figure, "Let me know if any time there is." There was resentment in his voice.

"Sure," said Kalley. He thought, "Bose doesn't like my quick brush-off." He watched Carlin return to the bar with his heavy, purposeful stride.

"Don't get offside with that baby, Macker," said Lilley softly. "You might live to regret it."

"I might," said Kalley. "What's his beef against Domineco? Political or personal?"

"Both," Lilley took a cigar from his vest pocket and lit it. "You remember a series of pamphlets against Domineco. They were dynamite. They accused Domineco of sexual aberrations, ballot rigging, fraud, wife beating, arson. The lot."

"I remember," said Kalley.

Smoke curled up from the fat man's cigar. "The pamphlets were unsigned, of course. Anonymous. They were given wide circulation." He chuckled. "Practically everyone who was anyone in the Party in this State got one through the mail."

"I saw one," said Kalley.

The fat man said, with enjoyment, "You must have wondered who the author was, Macker. The style was distinctive. Quite distinctive."

"I wondered," said Kalley.

"So did Domineco's wet nurse—Jasper Danke." The fat man ashed his cigar carefully and restored it to the corner of his narrow mouth. "Jasper not only wondered. He made a guess. He guessed Bose as the author. Jasper isn't like Domineco. He's a man of action. He didn't say anything to Domineco, who would have stopped him." He chuckled again. "Carr wouldn't like a nasty old sin staining his immortal soul. So Jasper went ahead under his own steam and had Bose followed. Bose lives in one of the new suburbs out in the Southern Hills districts. Those suburbs aren't thickly populated yet. It isn't far from the station to where Bose lives. But at night it can be very lonely." Lilley paused to puff at his cigar. "Jasper also found that when Bose got drunk he would leave his car in town and go home by train. He doesn't any more."

"What happened?" asked Kalley.

"Mind you, I've only heard Bose's version. It mightn't be objective. But he claims he's going home one night. Drunk. He gets in the train. He arrives at his station. He gets out of the train. He starts to walk home. One minute there isn't a soul about. Then bang. A team of thugs are roughing him up. Badly."

"How badly?"

Lilley shrugged. "Bose claims they would have killed him. I think he's exaggerating. But we'll never know. Bose has a quarter bottle of whisky in a brief bag that he's taking home. He gets in a couple lucky swings. He's as strong as an ox. When he's down they kick him around a bit. But they're rattled because they have casualties of their own. They left Bose lying there. Somebody trips over him. They shove him in an ambulance and he winds up in hospital for a couple of weeks."

Kalley said, "How does he know it was Jasper's arranging?"

"He doesn't. He just guesses it was. But he could be right. Jasper plays the hard way."

Kalley said, "Bose wouldn't like being roughed up."

Lilley said placidly, "That's right. After that he hated Domineco's guts. He went to Seborjar. Seborjar couldn't use him then. He was running with Domineco. But you know Seborjar. He tries to hang on to a tool that might be handy some day. He kept Bose on a string by feeding him bits of information. Then when he broke with Domineco, Bose was available." His false joviality suddenly faded. "You know Seborjar. Too cunning to use Bose openly himself, such a double-edged tool as Bose. So he says for Bose to see me. And you. In the hope that we'll have something we can employ Bose's undoubted talents on."

"What happens if we do use him?" asked Kalley.

Lilley puffed out a mouthful of smoke. "We do so at our own risk, Macker. If anything goes wrong Seborjar'll disown ever having had anything to do with him. It'll be us that'll get any backwash. But I thought I had better let you know he was available as Seborjar had sent him along."

"Thanks," said Kalley. "I'll let Con know."

Lilley looked at him, his small eyes cunning. "Will Con use him?"

Kalley said, "I don't think so, Joe. Will you?"

"I'm not in this fight for the good of my health, Macker. I will if I have to. And so will Con, if I'm any judge."

Kalley looked round the bar. Curious eyes were watching them. He thought, amused, "They'd give their ears to know what we were talking about." He could understand their interest. A lot of jobs were at stake. Some would lose out. But others would benefit. In Party upheavals there were always prospects of advancement for the courageous fishermen who were prepared to risk troubled waters. "But they've got to pick the right bait and be certain that they're in the boat that won't sink with all hands," he thought. Aloud he said, "What gives with Perry Nova and Max Steiner, Joe?"

Lilley said, cautiously, "What about 'em, Macker?"

"My orders are to leave 'em to you. How are they coming along?"

"They're coming, Macker. They're coming."

Kalley said, "What does that mean, Joe? Are they committed, or aren't they?"

Lilley said, blandly, "I'll let you know, Macker. In plenty of time. But stay away from 'em, as Seborjar says."

"Seborjar doesn't give me my orders, Joe. Con does. And you'll find working with Con that Con doesn't like loose ends. He likes a neat package. When he tells you that he wants the numbers that means that the numbers have to be there."

"I'll let you know when they are there."

Kalley knew that this deal is a bad one—from Con's viewpoint. That Con's put himself in Seborjar's power and that Seborjar'll gradually start to exert that power. Aloud he said, "Don't step on Con's toes. Joe. He mightn't like it."

Lilley said, reproachfully, "I wouldn't, Macker. You know that. We're allies!" There was a subtle note of mockery in his voice.

Kalley said, "I'll be seeing you, Joe." He left Lilley sitting at the booth, bland and inscrutable. He waved to Serge as he went out.

Fortune was alone in his office. Kalley told him Tion's terms. Fortune said, philosophically, "Those prices are not too high for two votes, Macker. In fact, they're reasonable." He chuckled. "Chris is getting some sense at last. He must have started listening to Lomas."

"Then it's a deal?" said Kalley.

"It's a deal," said Fortune. "You tell him, Macker. I find I can't talk to Chris. He's too much of a megalomaniac for me. You fix the details. Arrange with Chris that his boys show their votes to one of our boys before they go into the ballot box."

"Don't you trust Chris, Con?"

"I don't trust anyone. Particularly in a secret ballot."

Kalley said, "Con, I saw Lilley this morning. I called in at the Legislature bar."

Fortune said, casually, "Did he have anything?"

Kalley said, "He had Bose Carlin with him"

Fortune's voice was sharp. "That's a bad combination, Macker. What gives?"

Kalley said, "You wouldn't believe me. But it's as I said. Seborjar's been feeding out stuff to Carlin. Carlin claims he's anti Domineco. Lilley tells an interesting story that Bose was beaten up by some of Jasper Danke's boys. It could be right. Bose acts bitter enough for it to be right. Bose says he offered his services—without pay—to Seborjar against Domineco. Seborjar told him to see Lilley or me to find out if we had any use for him."

Fortune said, scornfully, "Without pay. That I find hard to believe."

"That's what the man said, Con. I told him we had no use for him. He didn't like it."

"Jesus, we couldn't use him," said Fortune. "You couldn't trust him, for one thing. He follows his own line. He doesn't give a damn for anyone else's views. And he's too dangerous. He'll invent anything. Do anything. He's like holding a packet of firecrackers in your hand with the fuse burning. He's liable to explode any time and blow your hand off. No, forget him, Macker. What else?"

"Con, couldn't you pull out of this deal altogether? You want to get Domineco. Okay. Get him on your own. Forget Seborjar."

Fortune said, impatiently, "We've argued this out before, Macker. Why do it again?"

Kalley said, "I don't like Lilley's attitude, Con. I asked him about Perry Nova and Max Steiner. He practically told me to go jump in a big, deep lake. You're not a partner in this deal Con. Not as Lilley sees it. He sees it the same way as I do. You're putting yourself in Seborjar's power. Seborjar's going to end up the Big Boss. With you as nobody."

Fortune said stubbornly. "I've told you before, Macker. We're in this to get Domineco. He's the important one. Not Seborjar. Let Lilley think what he likes. Until we get Domineco. Then we'll deal with Seborjar. And we'll trample over the top of Lilley as though he's a piece of dirt."

Kalley said, sombrely, "You're letting your dislike for Domineco warp your judgment, Con. That isn't wise."

"I'll decide the wisdom, Macker. And make the judgments." Then his long face lost its earnestness. "Jesus, Macker. The things you do to me. I was about to remind you who was boss round here."

"I know, Con," said Kalley, quietly. "You are boss."

"Nominally," said Fortune. "Very nominally. Don't think I'm not appreciative. I know you're worrying about my wellbeing. And that as you see it you're giving me the best advice you can." He walked round the desk patted Kalley on the shoulder. "But we see it differently,

Macker." His mouth was stern again. "Domineco's an evil man. Bad for the Party and bad for the country. I'm sure of it. Once he's out of the way we can start to rebuild. Without Seborjar and without Lilley. The old Party. As it was in its great days. Its pre-Domineco days."

"I hope you're right," said Kalley.

"I am right," said Fortune. "If I wasn't so sure, don't you think I would have some doubts."

"That's the trouble with bastards who rule, you never have any doubts." Kalley moved to the door.

"Thanks, anyway, Macker," said Fortune, absently.

"What for?" asked Kalley.

"What for?" asked Fortune. "Why the votes you fixed, you lunkhead."

Fortune was still smiling down at the pile of newspapers in front of him as Kalley shut the door.

CHAPTER 9

Con Fortune had the gift often possessed by politicians of being able to sleep almost at will and in the most uncomfortable of postures and surroundings. He dozed mostly, long legs twisted awkwardly under him, as the plane droned endlessly on, only waking fully when the air hostess served their meals. He was asleep when the note of the engines changed as the plane circled for landing. Sitting alongside him, Kalley nudged him.

"We're coming in, Con."

Fortune yawned and looked at his watch. "I don't like these long trips, Macker. They tire me. More than they used to."

"You're getting old, Con. We all are." Kalley leaned across Fortune to look out of the window. "We're almost down."

Fortune said, "Watch out for reporters at the airport, Macker."

"Someone is bound to know you, Con. That map of yours has been plastered for too many years to go unnoticed."

Fortune said, "So long as it is not newspapermen it won't matter. I don't want them camping on our trail to find out why we're visiting their State." The plane tilted steeply as it circled for the run in.

"Sarrett may talk or drop a hint to the newspapers. If it suits him to do so," Kalley said.

"No, I've known Sarrett for a long time," said Fortune. "I've sat with him on committees for years back before he became a Senator.

He's a conceited bull-headed bastard. Thinks he's a great idealist. He—
and he alone—knows the right answers. He'll do anything outrageous
if he thinks he's doing the right thing. But he plays it straight. He
doesn't go looking for the smart angles. I'll go straight through the
terminal and have a taxi waiting, Macker. You look after the luggage.
You're less likely to be recognised."

"I'll have 'em send our things to the hotel," said Kalley.

"Yes, we'll go straight out to see Sarrett." said Fortune.

The plane taxied to a stop. The door at the rear opened. The
passengers started to file out. The men rose and moved down the
centre aisle. The hostess smiled at them. Young, assured, smart, she
said, "I hope you enjoyed your trip, Mr Fortune."

She had recognised Fortune as he had come aboard.

"A very pleasant trip, my dear," said Fortune. "I hope I'll have
the pleasure of travelling with you again." Kalley saw the glint of
recognition in the face of the hostess at the foot of the step. She said,
"Hello, Mr Fortune."

Kalley said, "See what I mean?"

Fortune said, "The price of fame, Macker. I like it mostly. But it
has moments of disadvantage. Like now."

Fortune strode across the tarmac and through the air terminal
without looking right or left. Kalley paused to get their luggage.
Outside, Fortune was waiting in a taxi. "Bump into anyone?"

"No," said Kalley.

"Good," said Fortune who leaned forward and gave the driver an
address.

"I wonder why Sarrett asked us to see him at his home instead of
his office," Kalley said.

Fortune shrugged. "He's been sick. Maybe he's trying to keep away from his office as much as he can. Maybe he's like us, Macker. Maybe he'd prefer this visit to go unnoticed. Too many bastards in the Party add two and two together and make twenty-two instead of four. When the answer might be zero."

Sarrett's house was unimposingly small and old-fashioned, but bright with the freshness of new paint. It stood on an unexpectedly large area of ground out of proportion to its diminutive size. Waiting while Kalley paid the taxi driver, Fortune then pushed open a neat wicket gate. Together they crossed a smooth, well-tended lawn, up scrubbed steps onto a narrow cool verandah. Fortune pressed the bell.

The woman who opened the door was over sixty. In a starched apron, she had a soft, worn face, grey hair and a nervous mouth. Her eyes were red-rimmed. Kalley suspected that she'd been crying. She peered at Fortune short-sightedly. He said, "Hello, Mrs Sarrett. You've probably forgotten me. Con Fortune."

"Mr Fortune, you must excuse me. How are you? It's years since we met. And my eyes are not what they were. Do come in." She stood aside. The men entered a small hallway. Fortune introduced Kalley. He said, "Is the Senator in? I'm sorry to bother you at home. But he asked me to drop in as soon as I arrived."

"He's in, he's expecting you, though he wasn't sure whether you'd arrive today or tomorrow." There was worry in the tired face. "He's not been well. You won't excite him too much, will you, Mr Fortune? I do not want him upset." Kalley got the impression that the woman was on the verge of tears. He thought, his senses alert, "Sarrett's sicker than Con's been given to believe." He wondered how sick Sarrett was and whether his illness could be fitted into the pattern of Fortune's plans.

"We'll be careful, Mrs Sarrett." Fortune's face was expressionless but Kalley knew his mind was probing possible implications for himself and his cause if Sarrett was as ill as his wife's anxiety suggested.

The woman led them down the short hall to a door that opened onto a tiny garden surrounded by a high, carefully clipped screening hedge. "Raph'll be glad to see you. He hasn't had many visitors lately." She crossed to a summerhouse and opened the door. "Mr Fortune to see you, dear, and his friend, Mr Kalley."

The summerhouse was furnished as a study. Book-lined and littered with newspapers and magazines, but otherwise immaculately kept. The wooden floor scattered with rugs was highly polished, the shelves and window ledges gleaming as though dusted with minute attention. Framed photographs were everywhere. Sarrett was the central figure in all of them. There was Sarrett with the two anarchists he had defended successfully against arson charges back in World War I. There was Sarrett with Thonus, whose unconventional theories on co-education had led in the thirties to him facing an hysterical government-sponsored charge of corrupting the morals of the nation's youth. There was Sarrett with a procession of migrants, some prominent but others who had not mattered politically, whom he had saved from deportation on political grounds. There was Sarrett with the union leaders whose cases he had fought in the courts after the Dargin coal-field riots.

Elsewhere Sarrett surrounded by indigenes, their white teeth flashing as they smiled up at him in almost stylised attitudes of adoring admiration. The backgrounds and the other persons in the framed photographs changed but always in the centre was Sarrett, altering only in age. Almost always the occasion depicted was associated with some struggle in which Sarrett had been involved against what to him were the forces of tyranny and oppression.

"Vanity?" wondered Kalley. "Or the determination of a wise man aware of the corrupting influence of his environment to keep ever before him visual reminders of the ideals that he has tried to live up to?"

Sarrett had been writing behind a small desk in the corner. He put down his pen. Kalley knew that he was older than Fortune but he didn't look it. His face was square, forehead high and impressive. His hair was black, only lightly edged with silver. There was a touch of arrogance about his full-lipped mouth. A lawyer by profession though he had done only political work for years, defending without fee those he judged the victims of any kind of social injustice. He said, "Hello, Con. Hello, Macker."

"I'll leave you men alone," said Mrs Sarrett reluctantly. "You'll want to talk." She looked much older than he, though Kalley knew she was younger.

He had the impression that the couple were sharing some secret thought. Kalley again felt that she was on the verge of tears. Then wordlessly she turned away, closing the door behind her.

Sarrett said, "Sit down, Con. Sit down, Macker. So finally you've got round to seeing me. Things must be pretty desperate."

Kalley had a sense of amusement at the insinuation in Sarrett's comment. There was no real hostility between Sarrett and Fortune. There was no reason for any. Although both political animals, they lived in widely separated cages. Sarrett occupied an unusual position in the Party's structure. He was and had been for years in the Senate, elected and re-elected at election after election on the Party ticket. But he was an individual—not a machine man. Preoccupied with issues that were almost nebulous to Fortune—such as civil liberties and the rights of often unpopular minorities—Sarrett had no area of influence within the Party machine. He had no patronage to offer for support. In some ways remarkably unsophisticated despite a vast experience, he felt that the Party did not appreciate him sufficiently. He did not realise that there was any connection between the fact that he was disinterested in the sources of Party patronage and his ability to progress only so high in the Party and then advance no further. He was genuinely puzzled that he had been outstripped in the race for preferment by men who, he knew, were coarsely cynical and without his inflexibility of principle. At one stage early in his career he had been regarded as a potential Party Leader, but only for a brief period. Many apparatchiks regarded him as a bad team-player, obstinate and high-handed, who would pursue the course he believed was correct, irrespective of the consequences to himself or the Party. But he had a certain status with the voters. He had spent a lifetime fighting seemingly hopeless causes, and he often won them. It had become a habit in his State to elect him to the Senate. He had originally been appointed to the Party's Management Committee to fill a casual vacancy. His position as a Senator and the fact that he did not represent an active threat to any of the Party Leaders had kept him there.

Fortune said, good-humouredly, "Things aren't that desperate, Raph. But you're a vote on the Management Committee. I'd like all the votes I can get."

"Other people have the same idea," said Sarrett dryly.

Fortune said, "Tom Bannion been out to see you, Raph?"

Sarrett said with a smile, "As no doubt you are well aware, Bannion has flown out to see me several times. Domineco also. You're a little late, Con."

"We did not want to bother you while you were ill, Raph."

Sarrett said without rancour, "You're a liar, Con. A smooth one. But still a liar. You waited to see if you could be assured of Joe Lilley winning without my vote. If you could have been certain of being able to dispense with my vote you'd never come near me. Apparently you're not certain. Hence this visit. That's correct?"

Fortune said, "Could be, Raph. Could be." Kalley was examining Sarrett's thick hands. There was a yellow tinge about the knuckles and fingernails. "The man's really sick," Kalley thought. Illness was an important factor in politics, often deciding the outcome of events. Kalley decided that before he left he must notice how Sarrett's neck looked from the rear. Kalley had a theory. Voice, eyes and mouth could lie about the state of a man's health. But the back of the neck could not. Once it turned scraggy and scrawny it revealed that the person to whom it belonged had crossed the divide from energy and drive to declining faculties and mounting ill health.

Sarrett said, "What do you want, Con? You haven't travelled the distance merely to exchange pleasantries."

Fortune shrugged. "I'd like to know what you told Bannion. And where you stand in the present brawl."

"What I told Bannion?" Sarrett frowned thoughtfully. "I gave him to understand that, subject to being persuaded subsequently to a different viewpoint—and I told him I would inform him promptly if I underwent any change in outlook—he could rely upon my vote at the Management Committee going to him in preference to Joe Lilley. That's where I stand, Con. However, I'm open to persuasion."

Fortune lit a cigarette. "You've thought out all the implications in your decision?" he asked quietly.

"I think I have," said Sarrett. "But there may be angles I have missed. I'm prepared to listen to you expound them."

Kalley said, "You can't be happy with your decision, Raph. Domineco has lined up with Bannion. Domineco symbolises—and leads—the forces of reaction within the Party. Something against which you have struggled all your life. With varying success. But consistently. And honourably."

"I have also struggled against corruption, of which Joe Lilley is not only a symbol, but also probably the Party's most able practitioner."

Fortune said, "Lilley is unimportant in this fight, Raph. This isn't a struggle between Lilley and Bannion. It is a clash between the liberal school of thought in the Party—represented by Seborjar—which believes in the preservation of freedom for all, the betterment of their everyday lives, the brotherhood of all mankind and peace upon earth, not only in our time but for all time to come, and the catastrophic, gloomy Jeremiah-like Domineco who holds that men are in this world only to prepare for the next one, and are prepared to destroy mankind rather than retreat one inch from their fixed, narrow beliefs."

Sarrett smiled. "The voice is the voice of Con Fortune. But the phraseology, unless I am gravely mistaken, is Kaye Seborjar's. Do you believe anything Seborjar says, Con? Do you believe that he is ever capable of speaking the truth?"

"Yes," said Fortune, promptly. Kalley smiled inwardly at the firm certainty in his voice.

"Do you really believe that Seborjar is the Great Reformer?" Sarrett persisted.

"That's his record," said Fortune without expression.

Sarrett got up from behind his desk. His hands behind his back, he walked across the room. Kalley noted that though he was still straight and full-fleshed, his neck was thin and sunken.

"Jesus, Sarrett could be breaking up," he thought. "Really breaking up." Sarrett paused in front of a photograph. It showed him shaking hands with a little man whose face seemed exalted. Do you know who this is, Con?" He tapped the photograph with his finger.

"Yes," said Fortune. "I remember him. That's Twineham. He led some crackpot revolutionary movement during the war years. He was jailed. You defended him and got him out on the grounds that he was harmless."

Sarrett studied the photograph. "He was harmless. There was no group. He lived in a dream-world. The group which he was supposed to control existed only in that dream-world. He used to dream up plots to assassinate Presidents, Prime Ministers, and heads of State.

He would work out down to the last detail the organisation necessary to take over their governments. In his way he was a mad genius. His paperwork was brilliant. But it was only paperwork. It had no relationship to the world around him. His practice was to send out directives and copies of his plans to his non-existent followers. I know they said at his trial that he had followers. They even produced them. But most were government agent-provocateurs. Only a handful were genuine. And they were like Twineham himself. Harmless, eccentrics, living in the same dream world as him. Twineham may have been a minor embarrassment to a country preoccupied with war. But a very minor embarrassment. At worst he should have been sent to some quiet home for the mentally sick. Instead he was given a viciously severe sentence. After a trial that was nothing but a huge political parade designed to ballyhoo the political stocks of one man. You know who that man was?"

"Yes," said Fortune.

Sarrett turned away from the photograph. "The man was Seborjar."

"Seborjar made a mistake," said Fortune. "Twineham was a harmless eccentric. We know that now. But we did not know it then. Anyone can make a mistake. Especially in wartime!"

"Seborjar did not make a mistake," said Sarrett calmly. "He knew what he was doing. And why he was doing it. He knew Twineham was harmless. At least as well as I did. Probably better. In fact he knew Twineham personally. There was some association between them back in their younger days before Twineham's eccentricity dwarfed his other qualities, and while Twineham was still a member of the Party. He knew Twineham was harmless. But you'll remember it was a time when Seborjar's career was in the doldrums. He needed some spectacular publicity to bring himself forcibly into the public eye again. Some of Twineham's so-called instructions to his virtually non-existent followers had come into the authorities' hands. They had been shown to the newspapers. They created public hysteria. Seborjar fed that hysteria. It suited him to have Twineham jailed. Such decisive and brutal action gave Seborjar the aura—which he has never quite lost—of a national saviour prepared to act with promptness and firmness in a moment of crisis."

"You're too close to the trees to see the forest, Raph," said Fortune. "You were too deeply involved in the Twineham case to be impartial. You read too much into a mistake anyone could have made."

"A mistake?" There was contempt in Sarrett's voice. "Seborjar has fought for Communists wrongfully deprived of their civil rights. As I have fought for Communists wrongfully deprived of civil rights. But has he ever fought—as I have—for the rights of individuals and groups whose aims and outlook have been anathema to him? The Fascists? The strange little groups that exist in every democracy—and have the right to exist—and that preach against democracy? The eccentrics who preach racial superiority or some other doctrine equally as distasteful? Is it a mistake on his part, Con, that he has never fought for them—the politically unimportant? Does it not rather suggest that his causes are highly selective? That he operates only when it suits him politically?"

Fortune said, softly, "Not all men have had the strength to be as consistent in their political acts as you, Raph."

Sarrett smiled thinly. "Don't think to soften me with flattery. Not that I don't enjoy flattery. But I've been in politics a long time. I'm nearing the end of a long career. I look back now more than I look ahead." Kalley caught a suggestion of wistfulness. "And what do I see? A few minor successes on the personal level. No real achievement in the larger field of human endeavour."

"You can still achieve much," said Fortune.

"How? Time is running out on me," said Sarrett. He was merely stating something that he believed to be a fact.

"I'm prepared to make you an offer," said Fortune who drew his chair closer.

"What is the offer?" Sarrett asked.

"Despite what you say, Seborjar has the same dedicated interest in basic liberties as you have, Raph. Don't sneer. Not until you hear me out. He is prepared to do something which, as far as I can see, you have wanted done all your life. He believes that with Domineco and Bannion destroyed and his own position within the Party strengthened, he will be able to force the Party to devote more attention to some of the larger subjects that are so often lost to sight when the Party is preoccupied with internal rivalries. Seborjar is prepared to undertake that when he wins national power—as he is convinced he will at the next elections— he will have set up a Senate committee for the protection of civil liberties, with yourself as chairman."

Sarrett stared at Fortune through narrowed eyes. "You and Seborjar must be desperate. This offer. Is it direct from Seborjar?"

"Direct from Seborjar. Seborjar is prepared to give you his undertaking in writing. Here's your chance, Raph. For real achieve-ment. Something for which you'll be remembered long after you and I are dead."

"It's too late, Con." Sarrett said brusquely,

There was a moment of silence. Then Fortune said, "I don't get you, Raph. How can it be too late? You agreed to support Bannion only provisionally. Subject to persuasion from our side. I'm supplying the persuasion."

"It's still too late, Con," Sarrett was decisive. "Not because I have given a pledge to Bannion. But for a personal reason that is no concern of yours." He leaned back in his chair. "A short time ago your proposal might have won me over. But recently I found out something. About myself. Don't ask me what I found. I do not intend to inform you what it was. But as a result of my discovery I believe my thinking is clearer. I do not intend in my closing years to enact the role of Judas—to sell out the Party to such as Seborjar and Lilley."

"You're still selling out," Fortune insisted. "But to Domineco instead of Seborjar. Is Domineco any improvement on Seborjar? You can't seriously believe that, Raph. Not you. Not someone with your history of struggle against tyranny."

Sarrett said, "The alternative includes Bannion. I have some faith in him. I do not believe he will submit to domination by Domineco."

Fortune said, scornfully, "Domineco will eat Bannion. You know that as well as I do. Bannion's a babe-in-arms in this racket. Domineco will use him while it suits him to. And when he's finished with him he'll toss him away like a squeezed-out lemon. Bannion isn't part of your alternatives, Raph. It's between Domineco and us—Seborjar and me."

"You can't leave Lilley out of consideration, Con. I've nothing against you. But Lilley. And Seborjar. Is Domineco as evil as this pair? Domineco at least has beliefs. Mistaken beliefs possibly. But honest ones. What do Seborjar and Lilley believe in? Except themselves? And their own well-being?"

Fortune said, sharply, "Seborjar has faults—big faults. But don't let his faults blind you to Domineco's graver ones."

Sarrett said, "Why did Seborjar select Lilley as his nominee for the chairmanship, Con?"

"Oh, I dunno, Raph. Don't expect me to explain some of the inexplicable things that Seborjar does."

"But you still want me to vote for Lilley? Against Bannion?"

"That's what I want, Raph."

Sarrett shook his head. "I don't see how I possibly can, Con."

Recovering his poise, Fortune said calmly, "You can't take that attitude Raph. Not you. There's too much at stake—ideologically—

for you to make your decision on so simple a ground as Lilley being a crook. I know you've always been an idealist. But you've also been a practical politician. We deal with men. Not saints. So you believe that Seborjar is an opportunist and we both know Lilley's a racketeer. You may be right about Seborjar. You probably are. But there's more to this fight than that. There always is. That's part of living in a real live world with real live men. It's sad that things are the way they are. But that's the way they are. You can't live in any other world. There isn't any, Raph."

Sarrett said, "I am weary of compromising with evil. Of tolerating it."

Fortune said, "Your Senate job—and Party posts—depend upon practical things. Such practical things as not driving Seborjar and myself into a position where we will be compelled to take them from you. You're not a wealthy man. Whatever money you've earned you've spent. In defending people who could not afford to defend themselves. You can't afford to be jobless. Not at your age."

Sarrett said, "You're not threatening me, are you, Con?"

"Yes," said Fortune.

Sarrett's lips twisted in a smile in which Kalley felt there was genuine irony.

"I am beyond the reach of your threats, Con,"

"You're not beyond my reach. I admire you, Raph. You've fought some good fights. And won 'em. When the odds seemed hopelessly against you. But don't get in my way. Nor Seborjar's. We'll trample over the top of you. Ruthlessly. I won't like doing it, but I'll do it. So'll Seborjar. But he'll enjoy doing it. Play it shrewdly, Raph. You've only lasted this long in politics and in the Party because for all your idealism you've been practical. When the gale has been too fierce, you've bent before it and waited patiently for it to blow itself out. Keep bending, Raph or Seborjar and I will break you."

Kalley glanced sharply at Fortune. He thought, uneasily, "Christ, what's wrong with Con? Is he beginning to crack under the strain? He meant what he just said." Kalley wondered whether there was some factor that he had overlooked. Was Fortune engaging in a crusade, not a political manoeuvre? What was the basis for the passion that was now starting to show through the surface of his self-control? The galling knowledge of Bannion's defection? Seborjar's hypnotic influence? Dislike of Domineco? Or a combination of all three?

A vein twitched visibly in Sarrett's forehead. "I am open to persuasion, Con." He hammered down with his clenched fist on the desk top. "But not to threats."

Fortune said icily, "This is a war of extermination, Raph. You know Seborjar. He never forgets nor forgives. Mostly after a Party battle I'm a peacemaker. But this time I won't be. Line up with Domineco, and you're lining up against me. For all time. Whoever sides with Domineco in this fight is finished in the Party. Permanently. Both Seborjar and I are determined on that."

A vision of Tony's room in the Fortune's home, preserved as a shrine for the dead boy, the books and youthful possessions lovingly left exactly as Tony had last placed them, the Crucifix black against the wall over the *prie-dieu* came to Kalley. Mrs Fortune had showed it to him once while he had been waiting for Fortune to return from a meeting. Then he had been conscious only of the sorrow in the room. He had missed the hate. "Jesus," thought Kalley. "Have I been blind? Is Con fighting an ideological battle? Or is he seeking a personal vengeance that he is masking as a political struggle?"

The easy atmosphere of the earlier part of the interview had gone. There was passion in the room. Visibly making an effort at restraint, Sarrett said, "You're unbalanced, Con. You and Seborjar have delusions of grandeur. The Party will not stand for an orgy of destruction. A minor purge—yes. But not wholesale carnage. The Party has too much at stake. Its very existence."

With an effort, the intensity of which Kalley sensed, Fortune said quietly, "You've been warned, Raph."

"Not warned, Con—threatened." Sarrett stood up. "I can see no further point in continuing this discussion."

Fortune said, "Then you'll be voting for Bannion."

Sarrett nodded. "That is what I'll be doing."

"I won't wish you good luck, Raph. That would be hypocritical. But you're going to need plenty of it."

"That remains to be seen."

Sarrett made no attempt to shake hands with either Fortune or Kalley. Nor did he offer to phone for a taxi. He led them back through the house, pausing, undecided, in the hallway. Kalley thought he was going to call his wife to farewell them. But if that was his intention he changed his mind.

When they reached the footpath, Fortune glanced up and down the empty street. "There is a shopping block down this way. We'll probably get a taxi there." They walked in silence for a while. Then Fortune said, "Go on, Macker. Say that I handled that badly. But he wouldn't listen to persuasion. I had to threaten him."

"Where did that get you?"

"He wasn't going to vote for Lilley, anyway. So we've lost nothing."

"You slammed the door shut, Con," Kalley said softly. "For all time."

Long and loose-limbed, Fortune glanced down at the smaller man striding beside him. "What are you really thinking, Macker?"

Kalley said bleakly, "I'm thinking that I've been a sucker." Kalley broke his stride to put a match to the cigarette between his lips. "I thought that your opposition to Domineco was—basically—ideological. But that isn't the basis, is it, Con? It's personal."

"What does it matter? Ideological or personal. What's the difference? We're in a fight. We have to win it," Fortune said.

"But we're not going to win it the way you are going about it, Con. Since you've formed this alliance with Seborjar you've changed. You've become unbalanced. You aren't interested in winning any more. You're interested in extermination. The extermination of Domineco and everyone who has had the temerity to support him."

"That's part of what I'm aiming at, Macker" Fortune said. "The thing that'll hurt the poisonous little bastard most—the elimination from the Party of every vestige of his influence. He's a man who loves power. Like a miser loves his gold. When I'm finished with him he is going to be stripped bare. He's going to sit by in the next few years, tortured by the fear that the world and this country is slipping into the abyss of Godless Communism and helpless to do anything about it. But it's only part of what I'm aiming at. I'm aiming to clean up the Party. It's ideological, too. I'm against everything Domineco stands for."

Kalley said, "You're turning into a drunk. Your poison is hate, not alcohol. But the effect is the same. Your judgment is going, Con."

"Don't go psycho-analysing me, Macker," Fortune said angrily. "That's not your job. Your job is to do what I tell you to do. Not to probe my motives."

"You pay me, Con," said Kalley , "to do the best kind of job for you that I can. While you continue to pay me that's the job I'll do. Even if it involves me in questioning your motives and warning you against them."

Fortune faced the smaller man. His eyes narrowed, "I don't have to go on paying you, Macker. Not if I don't feel like it. Don't forget that. Don't ever forget it." His anger was immense.

"I won't forget it, Con." Kalley turned away. A taxi was passing. He whistled. Fortune joined Kalley in the back seat. Kalley gave the name of the hotel where he had sent the luggage. The men sat in silence as they drove toward the city.

At reception the clerk recognised Fortune. "It is a privilege to have you staying here, Mr Fortune." His tooth-brush moustache was quivering with his eagerness to be of service. "We have given you a very nice suite, Mr Fortune, If there is anything the hotel can do for you, Mr Fortune, let us know. Your luggage is already up."

Fortune and Kalley followed the bellboy. They went up in the lift without exchanging a word. Inside, Fortune said, curtly, "Get Lee Griers across for me. I want to see him." He opened doors leading off the sitting room, examined what was beyond them, and said, "I'll take this bedroom—my bag is in it." He went inside and closed the door.

Griers was Fortune's contact man in the local Party machine. Fortune had similar contact men in all States. Some were important in the local Party machines in their own right, and their alliance with Fortune was voluntary, based upon long association and the fact that, within his sphere, Fortune could do them favours just as they within the smaller areas of influence could do Fortune favours. But some were unimportant in their local machine except for the importance they derived from their association with Fortune. Griers was important in his own right in the State Party machine.

Kalley phoned Griers's office. Then Griers came on. "I've been expecting to hear from you, Macker. How did you get on with Sarrett?"

"Con'll tell you," Kalley said. "Can you get over here? Con wants to see you, pronto"

Kalley hung up. The door to Fortune's room remained shut. Kalley lit a cigarette. Lying back on an easy chair, Kalley smoked and stared at the wall in front of him.

He was still smoking when there was a knock at the door. Griers was plump, of middle height, bald except for tufts of woolly hair above small, well shaped ears. He had intelligent, quick eyes, a narrow slit for a mouth, and a disconcerting habit of breaking into a nervous, high-pitched laugh in the middle of a sentence. His suit was well cut; his tie smart but conservative. He looked mild, but Kalley knew he had an inner toughness.

"Where's Con?"

Kalley knocked at Fortune's door.

Fortune came out in his shirt sleeves, carrying a towel with which he was drying his hands. He looked at Kalley and hesitated. Then his face lit with a sudden smile. "Get drinks, will you, Macker?" he said. He crossed the room and shook hands with Griers. "Good to see you, Lee," he said.

Kalley poured drinks and handed them to the two men. Fortune looked at his, and then made a gesture that was half a toast to Kalley. "Thanks, Macker," Kalley sipped at his glass and felt a warmth that did not come from the drink.

"How did you get on with Sarrett, Con?" Griers asked.

"No good," said Fortune.

"I didn't think you would," said Griers. "Sarrett doesn't like racketeers like Lilley. And apart from that, Seborjar's backing Lilley. Sarrett distrusts Seborjar. He makes no secret of it." Looking down at his glass, he said abruptly, "Sarrett's dying, you know." He laughed a nervous high-pitched laugh that had no association with the words he was speaking.

"Dying?" Fortune's hand, half way to his mouth with a cigarette, halted.

"Yes," said Griers, "Dying." He again broke into his nervous laugh. "He's only a short time to live. The doctors told him so."

"Poor Mrs Sarrett," said Fortune softly. "Then that's why she looked—and behaved—as she did. How sure are you, Lee?" "As sure as it's possible to be," said Griers. "Sarrett told me. With his family doctor present."

Fortune said, "Well, what do you know? He told me that he was beyond the reach of any political threats. He was right. Any idea when it's likely to be, Lee? Before or after a vote is taken on the Management Committee?"

Griers said, "You're out of luck, Con." He laughed again.

"The doctor told me that he'll see out six months. So he'll be voting"

Fortune said, "What is it, Lee? Heart?"

"No, it's cancer. It's eating his stomach away," said Griers.

"In pain?"

"Not yet," said Griers. "But he knows it's coming."

"Christ!" said Fortune, "That's dreadful!"

There was another silence. Then Kalley asked, "How come he told you, Lee? Apparently he's keeping it pretty quiet. He didn't mention it to Con or to me."

Griers said, "He likes me, Macker. He knows I've always wanted to go into the Senate. I've been patient. Not trying to sabotage him so that I could take his place. I was willing to wait until he was ready to move out. Sarrett's got principles as well as guts. A lot of guts. When he found out he warned me. So that I would have everything organised so I'd be the Party's next Senator from this State. That's what I want to talk about to you, Con. I'm safe so long as the big boys from the national league don't interfere. If they know you're backing me they won't dare to. Even if their stooges in this State press them for support."

"You'll get my support, Lee. For what it's worth," Fortune said.

"It's worth a lot to me."

"It mightn't be. If the vote on the Management Committee goes against Joe Lilley, Seborjar and I'll be in real trouble."

Kalley said, "If Sarrett's too ill to attend the Management-Committee meeting, you're the alternative delegate from this State, aren't you, Lee?"

"Yes," said Griers, laughing nervously. "But Sarrett won't be too sick. At least his doctor says he won't be. And he'll get there if he's got to be carried on a stretcher!"

Fortune said, "A pity. Your vote'd be mighty useful, Lee."

Griers said, "I realise that, Con. But there's nothing we can do about it. I tried to talk Raph into voting for Lilley. Not that I want Lilley. But you did. That was good enough for me, Con. But Raph wouldn't listen to me."

Fortune said, "We've been friends for a long time, Lee. It's none of my business. But wouldn't it be better tactics from your personal viewpoint to delay publicising the fact that I'll support you to succeed Raph in the Senate? Until after the Management Committee vote for the Party chairmanship is over and done with? I'd hate to involve you in any possible setback I may suffer."

"No," said Griers. "I want to post as many warnings for trespassers to keep off my grass as early as possible. You have a habit, Con, of coming out on top in Party fights. That's what I'm counting on. Besides, you've been my friend for years. I don't run out on friends. Particularly when they're in a fight."

Kalley thought, "I can see why Sarrett wants Griers as his successor. In the small human things he has integrity. And courage." He wondered if Grier's integrity and courage embraced the larger issues. Aloud he said, "Con won't forget what you've just said, Lee. He's a bit gloomy at the moment. Our interview with Sarrett was depressing to say the least."

"Sarrett's a good bloke, but stubborn! Sometimes he's a little difficult to understand. I think he is making a mistake in backing Bannion who can only end as Domineco's captive. But he always acts with good intentions."

"The road to hell is paved with them," said Fortune.

"Sarrett is coming to the end of the road," said Griers. "You won't forget, Con? To see that everyone in your organisation gets instructed to support me? When I make my bid for Senate nomination?"

"I won't forget, Lee," Fortune promised. "And I won't forget the way you're sticking to me."

Griers said, "A man hasn't many friends in this racket. The way I look at it he must stick to 'em. Otherwise life isn't worth living. I'll see you both before you leave. If you want anything don't forget I'm at the end of a phone."

When the door closed behind Griers, Fortune said, "A likeable fellow Macker, plus Sarrett must like him. Death in politics," said Fortune. "It's different from death outside them. It hasn't the same dignity."

"How do you work that out?" said Kalley.

"Away from politics death leaves a gap that can never be filled. But politics continue. When a politician dies he doesn't matter. It is a gap that's important. It has to be filled. Sarrett isn't dead yet. But Griers, you and I are already trying to fill the gap." He paused. "Politics are lasting. They go on long after those who have supported them are vanished and forgotten."

"Men make the politics," said Kalley. "Don't forget that, Con."

"It's very sad, Macker. Particularly for Mrs Sarrett. She doesn't have any other family." Fortune stood up straight. "Our luck's out, too. I don't wish misfortune to any man. But if Sarrett has to go why couldn't it be just a bit sooner? We could use an extra vote for Lilley on the Management Committee."

"Inconsiderate of Sarrett, isn't it?" mocked Kalley.

"Don't be flippant," said Fortune, sharply. Then he softened. "I hope he doesn't suffer too much pain, the poor devil." The door closed behind him.

Kalley's mind kept coming back to Griers and to the difference a change in Griers's status would make to Fortune's influence over the local Party machine.

The door of Fortune's room reopened. Fortune's head protruded. "Come in here, Macker. I want to talk to you."

Fortune was brushing his hair in front of a mirror over a dressing table. He had the ability to give even an impersonal hotel bedroom the stamp of his personality. Always he carried with him framed photographs of his family. He made a shrine of them. They were standing now on the dressing table. There was Lottie, his wife, her face showing the gentle anxiety that Kalley always associated with her. The dead Tony. Michael, Fortune's surviving son. They were grouped about a small, ugly, upright Crucifix that Fortune invariably packed in his bag before leaving on a trip. In front of the Crucifix was a worn black leather purse. Kalley had never seen it opened. But he knew it contained Fortune's rosary beads.

Putting down the hairbrushes, Fortune said abruptly, "About what happened today, Macker. Forget it, will you, feller?"

Kalley said, "Sure, Con."

Fortune said, "I was worked up—angry. You and me, Macker. We've worked together a long time. As Lee just said, a man hasn't many friends in this racket—people he can trust. You know how I feel about you. That talk about I don't have to go on paying you." Fortune's forefinger worried at his long upper lip. "I'm prepared to go on paying you till the end of time. If you're prepared to go on taking it. What I'm trying to say, Macker, is, 'sorry'."

Kalley said, "Forget it, Con. I have already."

Fortune said, "Thanks, Macker." He brushed with his hands the lapels of his coat. "I'm going out for a while."

"Do you want me?" Kalley asked.

"No," Fortune said with an air of slight embarrassment, "It isn't politics, Macker. It's kind of personal. I won't be long."

When Fortune had gone, Kalley saw that the purse containing Fortune's rosary beads was no longer on the dressing table. Kalley smiled. Fortune never discussed his religion. It was part of his private, not his public, life. It was compartmentalised—something apart from politics. He had never tried, even when Kalley was a boy, to influence Kalley's religious outlook. But with the beads gone, Kalley knew where Fortune had gone. He had left, as he often did, to find a Catholic church. The almost childish furtiveness with which Fortune went on such occasions puzzled Kalley. Fortune did not thrust his religion upon others. But, equally, he did not seek to conceal it. It was part of him. He was proud of it. Yet, outside his home, he acted as though his attachment to the outward symbols of his religion was a weakness that he preferred to keep hidden from even his closest associates.

"Possibly it is not the fact that he is going to church that he wants to cover up," thought Kalley. "It might be the emotion that sends him there."

Kalley could picture Fortune, screened behind a pillar in the shadows at the rear of some nearby church, the beads slipping slowly through his fingers as he prayed for Sarrett and the short-sighted little woman who so obviously feared what was awaiting her dying husband. Fortune would be trying desperately to concentrate upon his prayers—to exclude from his thoughts what Sarrett's illness and death would mean to him politically.

"It's so pointless," thought Kalley bitterly. "Even if Con can close his mind temporarily to the political factors that arise out of Sarrett's impending death, when he comes out from that church, he can't close his mind.

What was it Fortune had said? Death in politics had no dignity. Con has something there." Kalley found himself thinking of the two Annes, wishing that now he was with them at home.

CHAPTER 10

The theatre was darkened and hushed. The music was loud and lively. On stage the dancer revolved dizzily, caught like a glittering moth in a shifting hoop of light. Kalley saw the flicker of a torch in the aisle. A dark form was alongside him. It whispered; "Mr Kalley, you're wanted on the phone. Urgently. In the foyer."

Kalley leaned across to Anne. Her hair was against his lips. "Someone's phoning me—I'll be back."

The phone was in a walled-in booth. "It is Mrs Belasco. Con wants you, Macker. He's had me chasing you all over town. I got this number from your child-minder." She put him through.

"Where are you, Macker?"

"At the ballet, Con."

"Christ, you're highbrow!" said Fortune. He chuckled. "We live and learn. I didn't know you liked ballet."

"Anne likes it," said Kalley.

"You'll have to leave it alone," said Fortune. "Seborjar phoned. He wants to see both of us urgently. At his place. Something's turned up. Seborjar didn't want to talk about it over the phone. Can Anne get home alone?"

"Yes," said Kalley.

"Good," said Fortune. "I'll pick you up in ten minutes in front of the theatre."

Kalley cradled the phone. He went back into the theatre. Low-voiced he told Anne that Fortune wanted him. "Don't wait up for me," he whispered. "I may be late." He brushed his lips against her cheek and went out. He stood in front of the theatre under the marquee. The traffic was heavy.

When Fortune stopped his car at the kerb, he slid into the passenger seat. "You drive, Macker," he said.

Kalley edged the car into the stream of traffic. "What's the score?"

Fortune's long legs were jack-knifed under him. "Dunno, Seborjar sounded excited. Very insistent. Do you know his place?"

"Yes, I've never visited. But it's been pointed out to me," Kalley said. "Big, rambling old mansion out on Waterview Drive."

"That's it," said Fortune. "Must cost him a packet to keep up."

Kalley had difficulty finding the driveway. Its entrance was hidden in a shadow of trees. Kalley peered at three parked cars. "Mark Payten, Joe Lilley and Kent Kerstey. Look's like the gang's all here."

Kalley rang the bell. Kerstey opened the door. "How are you, Con? How are you, Macker? The Leader's waiting for you. He's in the study." He led the way.

Leaning against the mantelpiece over a fireless grate, Seborjar looked tired and unkempt. The room was warm, stale with cigarette fumes. It was lined with books. Papers were strewn on a huge desk, and piled beside it on the floor. Payten and Lilley were sprawled in armchairs. Payten lifted an impish eyebrow in greeting. Lilley's drooping jowls gave him an appearance of mournfulness. But his tiny eyes were watchful and alert. "He's like a fat, cunning lapdog—waiting to snap up any dropped titbit," thought Kalley.

Seborjar said, "You were a long time getting here, Con."

"We came as fast as we could. Where's the fire?"

"Fire?" said Seborjar. "Fire he calls it." He addressed the room with gloomy violence. "Maybe he'll find it's a bomb, not a fire. A bomb that could blow me sky-high." He looked from Payten to Lilley, and on to Fortune. "You, too. All of you. Sky-high."

Fortune lit a cigarette. "Interesting, but hardly revelatory. Suppose you simmer down, Kaye, and start talking sense."

Kerstey said, "The Leader's upset, Con. As he's entitled to be."

"Okay, so the Leader's upset," said Fortune. He ignored the brooding figure at the fireplace. "But I don't know what's upsetting him. Or am I supposed to?"

Payten said, "Keep your hair on, Con. We already have one prima donna without you turning temperamental."

Unexpectedly Seborjar said, "You're quite right, Mark. I have been behaving like a prima donna." The petulance went from his face. He strode to the desk and picked up a roneoed document. Holding it between his thumb and forefinger as if he were trying to minimise contact with it, he said, "We have to deal with this piece of venom— this forgery—calmly and intelligently. Otherwise we shall fail to prove that it is the infamous document that it is."

Payten said, quickly, almost smirking, "Forgery, Kaye?"

"That's what I said. Forgery."

"How about telling me what it is all about," said Fortune. "Otherwise there's no point in me being here. Why am I here?"

Payten raised an eyebrow. "There mightn't be any point in you being here, Con. Originally you were summoned so that the Leader would have the benefit of your valued and experienced advice. But it seems that you have arrived too late." He nodded in the direction of Seborjar. "If I'm any judge, the decision has been taken. It is a forgery. Now all we can hope is that the voting public is sufficiently gullible to believe us."

Kerstey said, his voice shaking in earnestness, "Of course it is a forgery. The Leader has hit upon the truth. That is what it is. A forgery."

Payten grinned. "You're a loyalist, Kent. God bless you for that, my boy. The Leader'll reward you when he comes to power. If he ever does."

Seborjar was staring in front of himself." Of course it's a forgery," he said. "A wicked, diabolical forgery." His voice was slow, almost thoughtful. It was as though the other men were not there and he was talking aloud to himself. "A forgery that is the product of an obsessed, diseased mind with one aim. To drive me out of politics. Why? Because I side with the ordinary decent people against the crushing soullessness of monopoly capitalism." Seborjar flourished the paper. "And who is the evil, malevolent intriguer whose twisted brain spawned this clever, perverted fabrication?" He paused. He was awkward both in his speech and his movements. But his very awkwardness gave him an almost uncouth power.

"Jesus, he's practising a speech on us," thought Kalley who hadn't had previous close association with Seborjar in backroom discussions. He was used to dealing with men who deliberated over their problems, coldly, logically and without the histrionics they reserved for public platforms.

But Payten had witnessed such performances before. He breathed on his nails, polished them ostentatiously on the lapel of his coat, and with an exaggerated solemnity said, "I'll bite, Kaye. Who is this wicked man who concocted this diabolical, perverted forgery?" He winked at Fortune. "As if I didn't know."

Seborjar went on as though he had not heard him. "This is not the work of my official opponents. Not the work of the Prime Minister. Pope has merely been given a tool, by traitors within my own Party, to be used against me. He is playing politics. Playing them low. But he's opposed to me. And to the things I believe in. He's entitled to play politics as he wishes. But this . . ." Seborjar raised the document aloft. "This is not merely low. It is a supremely clever piece of evil—the product of a subtle, twisted, fanatical mind within my own Party. The insanely dedicated mind of Carr Domineco."

Kalley whispered to Payten, "What in Christ's name is he talking about?"

Behind his hand Payten said, "If you believe the rubbish he's talking you'll start hanging up your stocking again at Christmas time. Even at your age."

Kalley responded with a grin, "Are you insinuating that our revered Leader is mad?"

"None madder." Payten said. "But he's mad in the grand manner, old boy. In the grandest of manners."

Fortune said, stiffly, "Look, Kaye. I'm no office boy. I came here fast. At your invitation. You can't expect me to listen to a lot of incomprehensible double-talk."

"I'm sorry, Con," said Seborjar contritely. "Terribly sorry." He was suddenly relaxed and at ease. "Of course you don't know what it is all about. But just as you walked into the room I worked out the explanation for this distasteful document."

"Okay," said Fortune. "But what's it all about?"

"I'll tell you, Con," Seborjar leaned back in his chair, his eyes almost benevolent. "You know Alex Pope is out on the west coast? He made a speech out there tonight. He apparently regarded it as an important speech. His press secretary released it to the news agencies. In advance."

"So he made a speech," said Fortune, patiently. "And he thought it important. But then, the PM thinks all his speeches are important."

"This one was" said Seborjar with an engaging air of candour. "The agencies all asked me to comment on it." He lifted the document off the desk. "This was part of the speech. It purports to reproduce the minutes of a secret meeting of the national policy committee of the Communist Party. That committee—as you are well aware, Con—rules the Communist Party in this country."

Fortune's head jerked erect. He said, brusquely, "What does it say?"

"It deals with the present conflict within our Party. In effect, it sets out the tactics that the Communist Party is to pursue for the currency of that conflict. It says that the Communist Party of Australia must not embarrass me in my clash with the right-wing elements within our Party—that if I can succeed in having the right-wing elements driven out of the Party, our Party must inevitably move closer to Marxism. That what I—we—are doing could represent the most significant political advance the cause of Communism has made for years in this country."

"Christ!" exclaimed Fortune.

"That's what I said," said Lilley. There was an odd note of bravado in his voice, "Christ. In exactly that tone of shock and alarm."

"Yes," said Seborjar. "Joe was inclined to panic."

"Jesus," said Fortune. "So am I." He leaned across and took the document from between Seborjar's unresisting fingers. He glanced down at the document in his hand. "This is an atomic bomb, Kaye. How do you propose to handle it?"

Seborjar smiled. "I was going to ask you precisely that, Con. Then as you walked in it hit me."

"What did?" said Fortune.

"The answer," said Seborjar. His smile had vanished. His voice expressed unshakeable confidence and unconcealed arrogance.

His personality dominated the room. "Even Con scarcely registers alongside him," thought Kalley with reluctant admiration.

"What is the answer?" asked Fortune. Kalley could see him forcing himself to keep patient—to hold his temper in check.

"It's a fake," said Seborjar. There was deep conviction in his voice. "An obvious forgery."

"How do you work that out?" Fortune asked, sharply.

Seborjar shrugged. "It's quite simple, really, once you think round it."

He started to pace up and down the room. "Who would the Communists prefer to destroy? Us—the Party of reform—or Alex Pope's Party?" He paused to drive his clenched right fist into the palm of his open left hand. "Us, of course. We're the Party that stands between them and control of the workers of this country. We are the reason they have never been able to make any lasting political gains. Not Alex Pope and his mob."

The other men nodded in agreement. It was a familiar argument. It had been used from countless Party platforms for years to counter charges that the Party had Communist leanings. "But there's a flaw in that reasoning," thought Kalley. "As they all know, but won't admit, even to themselves. Pope is not a reactionary. At the worst he is a conservative—the defender of the status quo. More likely—as they also probably know but won't admit—he could be better described as a cautious reformer."

Seborjar had resumed his pacing. He was a restless, striding figure. "All right, then. We agree—and have established—that it would suit the Communists to circulate a document like that against us. A document ruinous to our Party's prospects at the next Federal elections. Possibly ruinous to the Party as a party for years to come. But there is a complication. If the Communists fed out this document themselves, or if it was put out anonymously and surreptitiously on their behalf, it would cause scarcely a ripple. Everyone—including the voters—would suspect its authenticity. The real threat to us and to the Party is not that the document exists. It is that it has been issued by Alex Pope, and gets from his sponsorship an authority that it would otherwise lack." The Leader threw back his head; "Why did Pope do this? Would he permit himself to be used as a catspaw by the Communists?" The growl of his voice deepened suddenly into a sneer. "Pope's anti-communist. That's about all he is. He's negative. Incapable of a positive thought of his own. But let us at least concede him sincerity in his anti-Communism."

"Indeed," said Fortune, softly. "Pope must believe that it is a genuine document. Otherwise he wouldn't have used it. He's an honourable man."

"He's a frightened man," corrected Seborjar. "He's frightened of me—of us. Of what we'll do in this country when we gain power. Of the reforms we'll achieve. Of the leadership we'll give the world. Of how we'll help lead mankind to peace—away from the atomic self-destruction towards which the human race is heading."

Kalley thought, "Jesus, he really believes in himself as a world figure. As a man of destiny."

In Kalley's ear Payten grumbled cheerfully, "Here we go again. Saving mankind. When we should be saving our own skins."

Fortune said coolly, "Whatever he is—honourable or frightened—Pope by using it has given this document an authority that we are going to find hard to counter."

Seborjar shook himself, like a dog after a swim. He became almost comically business-like. He said briskly, "The answer's obvious. Pope has been the victim of a confidence trick. He wouldn't accept this document from Communist sources. He'd suspect them. It wouldn't be manufactured in his own Party. Pope is as prudish as a chaplain in some ways. His code wouldn't let him condone such an act. No.

He got this document from somebody as bitterly and narrowly anti-Communist as himself. Someone in whose honesty — and fanaticism and dedication—he was prepared to trust."

"Domineco?" said Fortune.

"Yes," said Seborjar. "Domineco."

"It sounds plausible," said Fortune steadily. "But that's all. You haven't a shred of evidence to support it."

"The evidence is in the jargon. The phraseology. The clever innuendo. The subtle twists. That document provides its own internal evidence."

Fortune looked down unbelievingly at the document in his hand. Then he passed it to Kalley. "Read it, Macker. You know the Marxist vernacular. You've studied 'em."

Kalley could feel the eyes upon him. When he finished reading he handed the document to Fortune.

"What do you think?"

"It could be a forgery" Kalley said. "If it is, it's good. I know most of the top Communists. I know how they talk and how they write. It could easily be written by one of themselves."

Seborjar said placidly, "It's a forgery."

Fortune said, "I don't like it, Kaye."

Lilley said, uneasily, "Neither do I."

Payten said, silkily, "You got any better idea than Kaye's, Con?" He glanced at the clock on the mantelpiece. "It's ten-thirty. Kaye's statement'll have to go out to the newspaper offices before midnight. Otherwise the early editions won't carry it. They'll be carrying Pope's charges unchallenged."

Fortune said, "Let's think around it."

Seborjar was decisive. "I have thought around it. I know I'm right."

He took the document from Fortune's hand. "Domineco wrote this. He knows how the Communists think and talk. He knows better than Macker. He's studied them all his life. He fears them like he fears the Devil. Possibly more. To him they *are* devils. Devils who would steal men's souls. There can be no doubt about it. Domineco wrote it."

Kalley watched the faces around him. The men were thinking. Fortune's forefinger was rubbing worriedly across his smooth, long, upper lip. At last Payten said mockingly, "I'm still waiting for you to come up with a better idea, Con."

"I haven't one. Can you come up with anything, Macker?"

Kalley said, "I can come up with something. But nothing that would be acceptable in this company."

Lilley said, despairingly, "Any idea would be worth considering, Macker."

Payten said, with a sneer, "Not suffering from inhibitions, Macker?"

Kalley drew at his cigarette. "No," he said. "Discretion."

Fortune said, "Forget discretion, Macker."

Kalley looked at the others. "But first let me say that this is only how I see it." He glanced from Fortune to the figure of Seborjar, hunched in his chair behind his desk. "Con might not see it the same way."

"Okay, okay," said Payten, impatiently. "How do you see it?"

Kalley stubbed his cigarette in an ashtray. He said, "This document jams us two ways—as a Party and in the person of our Leader. We can separate them—the Leader from the Party—and deal with them as separate problems. If we do that we have a choice. A choice as to which we want to preserve—the Party or the Leader."

Seborjar's eyes swivelled slowly to fix on Kalley. Kerstey said, coarsely, "You are not suggesting that the Leader resign, Macker?"

"Something like that," said Kalley. His face was inscrutable. "You have to face it. A large section of the voters believe—mistakenly I'm sure"—there was no emotion in his voice—"that the Leader has pro-Communist sympathies. He says he hasn't. But the suspicion is there. It's been demonstrated by the number of times the Party—under his leadership—has failed to secure Federal power while the voters still continue to support the State Party Leaders who are not suspect—at State elections."

He gestured at the document. "Whatever else happens, some of the mud from this is going to stick. It could be made to stick to the Leader only, not to the Party. If the Party gets out from under quickly. It can get out by the Leader sacrificing himself for the general good of the Party. There are a number of ways in which he could do this. He could, for example, say that he believes the Party's Leader should be, like Caesar's wife, above suspicion. That there is no truth in the charges. But now that they have been made public he intends to resign, to prove the Party's *bona fides* to the voting public. The Party could then appoint a successor, somebody to whom these charges"—he gestured again with the document—"could not possibly apply."

Payten's eyes were slits. "Who would you pick, Macker? As the new Leader? Hoskin? That ruthless ex-tough? Carmont, a weak-kneed appeaser who'd join forces with Domineco tomorrow if it gave him a prospect of getting Alex Pope's job? Or Bannion? Fortune's friend, and yours." There was venom in his voice.

Kalley said, "You're the kingmakers. Not me. It is for you to decide who shall be the next Leader. In concert. Or in opposition to each other." His hand was steady as he lit a fresh cigarette. "But if you decide to put in a new Leader, this document will be a nine days' wonder. It will be forgotten within a matter of weeks. And"—his impersonal gaze swept over Seborjar—"it wouldn't surprise me if the Leader's gesture of renunciation did the Party a lot of good, possibly sufficient for it to win national power at the next elections."

Kerstey said with intense conviction, "You're a secret Domineco man. You're a traitor, Kalley."

"Act your age, son. It's about time you grew up. Con Fortune pays me. I don't work for Domineco. Or Kaye Seborjar." He shrugged. "I was asked to suggest a way out. I suggested one."

"An interesting suggestion, Macker," said Seborjar. He reasserted his supremacy by the force of his personality.

Payten said, "Interesting, Kaye. But crazy. If you step down at this point in the Party's history, it'll be the greatest victory Domineco has ever had. He's the strongest single influence there is in the Party today. Only a combination of you, Con, Hoskin, Chris Tion, Joe here and half a dozen others is beating him. If you bow out, we'll be finished. All of us." He jerked his thumb at Fortune. "Fortune, too. Domineco'll have complete control. That Fascist-minded fanatic. You can't sell out like that, Kaye. You'd be betraying the Party."

Kalley thought derisively, "You mean betraying Payten—not the party. If Seborjar sinks politically, you sink with him." But even as he thought it, he realised he was doing Payten an injustice. Payten's attitude was prompted by self-interest. But Payten also feared Domineco for ideological reasons that came from his own fundamental regard for the great traditions of unfettered speech and thought—traditions in which Payten believed, even though he did little to support them when they conflicted with his personal and political well-being.

Aloud, Kalley said calmly, "Domineco can be beaten. Even if Kaye is no longer Leader."

"How?" said Payten, scornfully. "By you and Con Fortune? Con's been trying to down him for years. By Gilly Hoskin? Who's been about as ineffective. By Chris Tion who changes his mind every five minutes? You've all been trying to down Domineco for years. And still he's with us. Stronger than ever."

Seborjar said quietly, but with his eyes pinpoints. "That's enough, Mark." They felt his authority. He was watching Fortune. "Where do you stand, Con?"

"Where do I stand, Kaye? I don't stand anywhere. But I can't force you to resign the leadership. I haven't the strength, even if I had the inclination. It's where you stand that matters, Kaye. It's your decision."

The suspicion went from Seborjar's face. "What should I do, Con? Get out? And almost certainly hand control of the Party over to Domineco and his henchmen for at least ten years—possibly longer? Or hang on? And fight? My every instinct tells me to do that."

There was tension in the room. It was the moment of decision. All eyes were fixed on Fortune's face, watching as his forefinger moved worriedly to and fro across his long upper lip.

Finally, Fortune said, "If I told you to pull back, Kaye, you wouldn't do it." For the first time in years Kalley sensed uncertainty in the familiar voice.

"No," said Seborjar. "I wouldn't." He reared to his feet. "I'll tell you why, Con. You and I hold a few simple beliefs in common. We don't talk about them much, except on the rare occasions when we are deeply moved. We believe that all men have the right to live without fear, with bellies that are full, and not aching with emptiness. We are part of the river of history. Progressive. Advancing slowly towards journey's end so that men can have a little bit of paradise in this world instead of an uncertain one in the next." There was about him an awkward grandeur. "But Domineco. He tries to stem the flow of history. He is not interested in men's mortal bodies. Only their immortal souls. He is a throw-back to the age of the thumbscrew. If in this atomic age he had to decide between the destruction of the entire human race and what he in his arrogance would regard as the loss of their immortal souls he would play God while claiming that he was merely acting as God's instrument. He would wipe out the human race. That is why Domineco here in this country—and his like all over the world—have to be—must be—eradicated as a political force."

Kalley interrupted, "Then why were you Domineco's running mate in the Party for so many years?"

Seborjar said harshly, "You have a capacity for cheap insolence, Macker. Like a guttersnipe."

"I work in a gutter, Kaye. In politics." Seborjar was sombre but Kalley could sense his fury. "I could ignore your question, Macker. I do not have to answer to you—or anyone—for any of my actions—past, present, or future. My responsibility is to the people of this country—and to the Party. But I won't ignore your impertinence, your pose of cheap scepticism. There are others here who are entitled to an explanation." He looked at Fortune. "I was associated with Domineco. That is true. But I was associated with him only while I was ignorant of his real purposes. When I found out that he was intriguing to pervert the Party—to use it for his own ends—I renounced him. As I renounce him now."

Payten said, hurriedly, "Look, Kaye. That's water under the bridge. We've all made our mistakes. Macker's made his share. Haven't you, Macker?"

"Indeed!" said Kalley.

"Well, for Christ's sake, let's forget post mortems," said Payten. "Let's have a drink. Before we settle down to write this statement. We are going to write it, aren't we? On the lines the Leader has suggested? You're in agreement, Con?"

Fortune nodded.

"How about you, Joe?" Seborjar asked Lilley.

Lilley said, "I'm one hundred per cent for it, Boss. It has been a privilege to be associated with you in the handling of this matter.

I have never heard a problem analysed, dealt with, and solved with such clarity and speed." The flattery was crude. Fortune turned an unenthusiastic, fish-like stare upon the fat man. Kalley saw the corners of Payten's humorous mouth twitch. Even Kerstey blinked and looked at Seborjar, wonderingly.

Seborjar said simply "Well, that's settled."

Payten bustled about busily. "Here. Kent, you pour the drinks. You know the run of this place better than anyone else." He chuckled. "Name your own poison, everyone. The Leader has a well-stocked cellar."

The men took their drinks. As he served Kalley, Kerstey, scowling, said, "I wish it were arsenic." Knowing how Kerstey hated to be patronised about his ageing youthfulness, he said, "Thanks, son."

As he gave Lilley his drink, Payten said in a low, sarcastic voice, "You ought to be ashamed of yourself, Joe. That drivel about 'I'm one hundred per cent for it, Leader,' "

The fat man smirked. "It worked, didn't it? The Big Man lapped it up. Like cream."

Payten said, "No-one else did."

"I'm not interested in anyone else. The Big Man's my meal ticket."

Fortune said, thoughtfully, "You face a technical problem, Kaye. With your statement, I mean. You can't charge Domineco straight out with having written the document. If you do, he'll slap a writ onto you immediately. Domineco's no fool. He'd be out to make you prove your charges in court. And you can't prove 'em."

Seborjar said, "Kent'll draft the statement. He's clever with words. Mark'll look after the legal side."

Payten said cheerfully, "Nothing like a legal training in your early youth to keep you out of jail."

"But," Fortune persisted, "that doesn't get you over the hurdle of how you're going to tie Domineco up with the forged document without the risk of a libel suit."

Payten said, "It's easily done, Con. We can't do it in one statement, I admit. Tonight's will have to be the first of a series." He was anxious to smooth away difficulties—to restore an atmosphere of harmony. "Tonight the Leader brands the document as forged, and declares that it has been forged by a traitor in his own Party. He goes on making similar statements for a week, or whatever he decides is the appropriate period."

"Not mentioning Domineco?" asked Fortune.

"Not mentioning Domineco," said Payten.

"Then at the end of a week—or whatever we deem to be suitable—the Leader puts out a statement saying—without giving any grounds — that Domineco is a traitor to the Party. Any connection between that statement and the Leader's previous statements is purely coincidental, and, more importantly, would never stand up in court."

"Not bad, Mark," said Lilley, approvingly. "Not bad at all."

"Not bad," said Payten, simulating a simper. "It is better than not bad. It has the hallmark of genius—simplicity."

"Then what?" asked Fortune.

Payten shrugged. "If we're lucky, Domineco'll panic. He will fit the cap to his own head. He'll deny that he wrote the document. Personally, I think he's too shrewd to fall for that one. He'll make no reference to the forged document, but will demand to know why the Leader is calling him a traitor. We'll reply with hints and insinuations." He waved airily. "Sooner or later it'll bust of its own accord. Somebody who is too unimportant for Domineco to sue will make the charge openly. He'll be forced to reply publicly. Once he does it'll be open season. The Leader'll be entitled to comment on his comment."

"That seems sound enough." Fortune glanced at the clock. "If our statement's got to be ready for midnight you had better make a start on it." He put down his empty glass and stood up. "I think Macker and I'll call it a night."

"Won't you want to see the finished production?" asked Payten.

"I'm satisfied with the outline. I'll read it in the morning papers."

Lilley said, "So'll I."

Fortune said, "Good night. Kaye." Seborjar came from behind his desk. He shook hands with Fortune and Lilley. "We three are in this together. I know we'll see it through together—to a successful conclusion."

Fortune said, "Sure, Kaye." He glanced over his shoulder at Kalley standing impassively near the door.

Seborjar hesitated as he ambled to the door. "You're a strange, unpredictable man, Macker."

Kalley wrestled against the temptation to comment that he knew at least one stranger and more unpredictable. "You think so, Leader?"

"Yes, you surprise me," said Seborjar. "I thought that you at least would have the perception to grasp the basic issues in this struggle. This isn't just a clash between Kaye Seborjar and Carr Domineco. It is part of the age-old struggle. The eternal conflict between the forces of good and evil."

Kalley thought, "You arrogant bastard. You place goodness upon your side and badness on the other. It's not like that. Men in politics do not have such a simple choice. They can select only between evils and if they are wise, select the lesser evils." Aloud he said, "I seem to have disappointed you, Leader."

"You have," said Seborjar, bluntly. "I expected more of you, Macker." His face suddenly lightened with charm. "But no hard feelings, Macker." There was an almost boyish eagerness in his voice. "I wouldn't like us to part tonight as bad friends. Will you shake hands, Macker?"

"Sure," said Kalley. He took the Leader's hand. The Leader did not release his grip. He kept pumping Kalley's hand as though he would never stop. . There was something theatrical about the two men standing there, their hands clasped for what seemed an interminable period while the others watched.

At last Seborjar stepped back.

"Goodnight, Leader," Kalley said.

Kerstey showed the departing men to the door. He was friendly with Fortune and Lilley; hostile and sullen with Kalley. Outside the night air was cool and fresh. Lilley paused as Fortune and Kalley got into their car. He leaned against the window on the driver's side and said across Kalley to Fortune, "What do you think, Con?"

Fortune lit a cigarette. He watched the match burn down until it was finally extinguished.

"It's a tight spot, Joe."

Lilley said, calmly, "I know. Can we get out of it, Con?" Fortune's cigarette end glowed.

"Maybe. Seborjar's fought his way out of some extraordinarily tight corners. Maybe he'll be able to fight out of this one."

"It'll make it harder for me to beat Bannion for the Party chairmanship."

"It won't make it any easier," said Fortune, curtly.

They left Lilley standing in the driveway, squat and shapeless in the darkness.

As their car emerged from the driveway and passed under a street light Kalley glanced at Fortune who was staring straight ahead.

Kalley said, "A bad break, Con."

Fortune said abruptly, "Why did you throw in that bombshell, Macker? Proposing Seborjar's resignation?"

"You wanted a suggestion. I made one."

"Jesus," said Fortune, grimly. "And now you know what a suspicious bastard he is. He'll never trust me again."

Kalley said, "Did he ever trust you or you him?"

"No," said Fortune grudgingly.

"Then what have you lost?"

Kalley drove slowly, watching him from the corner of his eyes in the occasional half-light. At last Fortune said, "You're a cold-blooded fish, Macker."

"I'm a realist, Con. You realise what you've done tonight?"

"Yes," said Fortune. "Agreed to Seborjar taking certain measures to patch up a boat which has suddenly sprung a bad, dangerous leak, and in which we are both trying to keep afloat." A horn sounded behind them. Kalley swerved closer to the kerb. A powerful car overtook them and passed, its tail lights receding into the gloom ahead. Kalley said, "You've done more than that, Con. You've saddled yourself with Seborjar. For as long as he stays in political life, he's your old Man of the Sea, Con. You might hate him. You might want to get rid of him. But you can't. Not any more. He's sitting up there on your shoulders now. And nothing you can do'll dislodge him."

Fortune said sharply, "You're mad."

"Am I, Con? Think it over. This started as a clash between Kaye Seborjar and Con Fortune—in partnership—and Carr Domineco. If anything you were slightly the senior partner. Your struggle against Domineco was a much older one. Seborjar was only a newcomer to that fight—a parvenu."

A traffic light glowed redly ahead. Kalley slid the car slowly to a stop. "Now what's happened? By agreeing to allow Seborjar to fasten, quite fancifully and without the slightest justification, authorship of that document upon Domineco you have enabled him, not you , at one stroke to become the symbol of anti-Dominecoism within the Party. He is the one who will be carrying the fight to Domineco, not you." The light turned green. The car moved forward.

"So what? What does it matter who leads the fight? So long as Domineco is defeated. Sooner or later Seborjar'll knock over Domineco. That'll free me—to move in against Seborjar."

"It's not going to work like that," said Kalley. "If Seborjar's wise—and if his mind works the way I think it does—he'll make a lifetime crusade out of anti-Dominecoism. He may knock over Domineco. But that won't be the end of it. There will be no Domineco. But there'll still be Dominecoism. You heard what he said tonight." He imitated Seborjar's voice. 'Domineco here in this country—and his like all over the world—have to be—must be—eradicated as a political force'. Seborjar's decided to try and survive as Leader despite this document of Pope's. He's going to make himself the symbol of anti-Dominecoism within the Party."

"Where's that going to get him?" retorted Fortune. "Even if he succeeds he's only replacing me. I've been that for years. And what's it got me? Except headaches? Domineco's no pushover. If anyone should know that, we should."

"Sure," said Kalley. "You've been anti-Domineco, Con. But you've had inhibitions and divided loyalties. You never thought your problem through to its logical conclusion."

"I thought I had," said Fortune, "or that you'd do it for me if I had overlooked anything. What's on your mind, Macker?"

"Look, Con, there are lots of things about Domineco that cannot stand the light of day. He fights fire with fire. He fights the Communists. He uses many of their techniques. His organisation operates an extensive intelligence service. It uses fear deliberately as an instrument of policy. Character assassination. Slander. Intimidation. If it judges that some non-Communist policy will assist—even indirectly—the Communist cause, it brands the supporters of that policy as Communists and hounds them out of public life. Or from the pulpit, the teaching profession or any other avocation in which his organisation can exercise an influence. It will resort to physical violence against an individual when it knows it is safe to use it. It wants a censorship that'll blanket not only Communist propaganda, but any thought that might—might, mind you—help the Communist cause."

Fortune said impatiently. "You're not telling me anything I don't know, Macker.

"You could have made Domineco one of the worst-hated men in this country, Con. By exposing publicly his mode of operation and his aims."

Fortune snorted. "That would have been like curing cancer by killing the patient. You know that. It couldn't be done. I wanted the patient—the Party—to live. The disease I felt was not incurable. It could be wiped out. I knew that, Macker. So did you. I couldn't expose Domineco publicly. Not completely. You know what would have happened. Every man in the Party with an enemy—and they all have them—would have accused that enemy of being a secret agent for Domineco. It would have split the Party from top to bottom. Wrecked it for years to come."

Kalley said, "That was your weakness, Con. Your love for the Party. Because of it you pulled your punches against Domineco. You hated all he stood for. But your love for the Party made you keep it a private hate instead of a public one."

"What more could I have done?" said Fortune. "I exposed Domineco publicly as much as I could both to the Party and the community—gave as much chapter and verse about what he was up to and his methods as I reasonably could. Could I help it if Seborjar's association with him gave him in the Party an aura of respectability?"

Kalley said, "Seborjar hasn't—as you had—loyalties divided between the Party and his hate. He has only one loyalty. To himself. He will try to make Domineco the most hated man in the country."

"How?"

"That I would not like to forecast. But he'll try."

Fortune said, "He'll have to be careful how he goes about it. He's disliked and distrusted himself. By men who have no tie-up with Domineco. A false move and he'll split the Party wide open."

Kalley said, gently derisive, "You think that'll worry Seborjar?"

"It should." There was a note of dryness in Fortune's voice. "He wants Alex Pope's job. And he can get that only if he's backed by a united Party."

Kalley said, "I think you're wrong, Con. Seborjar wants more than Alex Pope's job. He wants to be on top. That's what keeps him going. If it is a case of going under or sitting on top of a mass of ruins he'll sit on top of the ruins. Waiting for the turn of the political wheel to take him higher. But it's getting late. You'll want to get home, Con."

Fortune waited as Kalley opened the car door then slid across to the vacated driving seat. Through the open window in the dark he said, "What do you reckon are our chances, Macker? Of getting away with this fantasy of Seborjar's that Domineco forged the Pope document?"

"At least we are away to a flying start. Seborjar is thoroughly convinced."

"That's just an act. No man could convince himself that easily."

"Seborjar can. Therein lies some of his strength."

"I hope the voters are as easily convinced."

Kalley said, "If you keep on repeating things with conviction, as Seborjar will, often enough they'll believe you. Hitler showed that."

"Then you think there's a chance?"

Kalley said, "I wouldn't know, Con. I honestly wouldn't know."

He stood on the footpath for quite a while after the tail light of Fortune's car had faded into the blackness. Then he shrugged his shoulders and walked across the strip of grass to his front door. Deliberately, as was his custom, he tried as he put his key into the lock to dismiss all thoughts of politics from his mind. Upstairs Anne would he waiting for him, propped up in bed, reading. "I'm on my island," Kalley thought ruefully. "But sometimes it is hard to pull up the drawbridge."

CHAPTER 11

The funeral of a Party chieftain was viewed by members as a major event, as well as an excuse for a get-together. At an important funeral, practically everyone of any stature in the Party would be present, or would be represented by a trusted lieutenant. They would fly in from all over the country, horse trade, gossip, drink, negotiate and confer. In the case of men from distant States, involved in local rather than national politics, they were unlikely to see each other again until the next funeral or the Party's annual convention.

Fess Cabal's funeral was an important one. Cabal was a Party legend immensely gross in later years, his yellowed pate was hairless. A pair of blazing eyes was all that remained to remind men of the tall, slim figure with the thick mane of tawny hair that had dominated Party affairs for so many years. Still revered by the Party's rank and file, he represented a nostalgic era in which the Party achieved its greatest social reforms. Cabal had been a spellbinder, in front of an audience. He played upon its collective emotions expertly and with relish, speaking in a flat, ranting monotone, securing his effect from the seemingly accidental repetition, perfectly timed, of key phrases. His strength was that he could sense the vague aspirations and hopes of ordinary people and put them into words. Sometimes he honoured these promises.

His campaign slogan never varied. It was "Vote for Cabal, the Workers' Friend". Yet despite his boundless energy, Cabal exhibited a streak of sadism.

In his office Fortune read the tributes in the morning papers without emotion. Mrs Belasco, waiting until he put down the last paper said gently, "He was a great man, Con. The Party'll be poorer for his passing."

"I didn't know he was one of your heroes, Aggie."

"I never knew him. Only of him. He was before my time. You knew him, I suppose, Con? He must have been a genius."

"He was," said Fortune, dryly. "In his way. Where's Macker?"

"In his office. Do you want him?"

"Yes," said Fortune.

When Kalley came in, Fortune said, "I suppose you know Cabal's dead. When are they burying the old bastard?"

"Wednesday," said Kalley. "In his home town. The State boys over there are fixing up the funeral. It'll be a big show. You didn't like him, did you, Con?"

"He was one of the most vicious men I've known," said Fortune. "Not with the big boys, or anyone who could hit back. Only with helpless, defenceless little people. He wasn't a crook as far as I know. But he was greedy as a hog. Yet he could understand the mob. He knew what they wanted before they realised. And he knew how to go about giving it to them."

Kalley said, "I have given the papers your tribute. You'll read it in the afternoons."

"What did I say?" Fortune asked.

"Nothing sensational. You in common with the rest of the Party mourn the passing of its Grand Old Man. The period when he was at his political zenith produced some of the greatest social reforms in this country's history. His life was a model of public service. He blazed the trail. We have turned into a broad modern highway of widening progress. With the hint that if the voters have the good sense to get rid of Alex Pope and put us back into power we'll improve further and widen more that highway of progress. It's not inspired. But it'll do."

"Christ," said Fortune. "It galls me to say anything good about the old bastard. Even if he is dead. But I won't be going to the funeral. I'd vomit on the casket. Besides I can't get away. Wednesday's Michael's birthday. I've promised him I'll be home. You can represent me."

"Is that wise, Con? You'll be missed. Cabal stands for a lot in the Party."

"Wise or unwise I'm not going to pass up on Michael's birthday. You're it, Macker."

"What do you want me to do while I am visiting Mr Tenper's State?"

"See Tenper," said Fortune. "I thought I had his vote sewn up for Lilley. But now I'm not so sure. I've phoned him a few times since Pope unloaded that Communist minute on Seborjar. He's been evasive. He's a shifty customer, Macker. See if you can find out how his mind is running. And see Ferdie Lusk," said Fortune. "He's bound to be there. We want to know where we stand with both of 'em. Lusk originally agreed to support Lilley. But I have the impression that he's also gone cold on it since the PM produced his document."

Kalley said, "Seborjar, Lilley, Hoskin—the lot are certain to be there. How do I play it with Tenper and Lusk, if any of that group want to sit with me? Solo?"

Fortune said, "I'd prefer you did it solo, Macker. But I'll leave it to your discretion. "

"Wish Michael a happy birthday from me. But I thought you never let your private life interfere with your politics, Con."

"You've got it the wrong way round, Macker. I never let politics interfere with my private life. At least not when it gives me the excuse for not doing something in politics that I don't want to do."

Kalley and Payten were seated next to each other.

" Vote early and often, Macker," said Payten, playing on a stock Party jest that to be completely safe in a ballot a candidate had to see that his supporters voted as early and often as they could.

Kalley looked round the plane.

"Where are the others?"

"On later flights or coming in tomorrow," said Payten. "Where's Con?"

"He has an engagement that he can't break."

"Seborjar, Kerstey, Lilley and Hoskin are flying out tomorrow," Payten volunteered. "Going to see old Ten-per-cent, Macker?"

Theo Tenper had headed his Northern State government for years. Efficient, tough, hard-working and shrewd, he had given his State highly capable administration. The State was prosperous, progressive and expanding. The voters re-elected him at each election. But he ruled the most corrupt Party machine in the country. Even in corruption Tenper was business-like and methodical. It was rumoured that a fixed percentage of State expenditure found its way into the pockets of Tenper and his followers. Hence his nickname "Ten-per-cent Tenper".

"I'll probably see him," said Kalley, casually. "If I get a chance. How about you?"

"I'm just John the Baptist—the one who goes before," said Payten. "Teeing up interviews with him for Seborjar and Hoskin. And keeping an eye on Domineco and Bannion in case they're up to something."

"There'll be a few parties tonight, Macker. How about joining forces?"

"No," said Kalley. "I'll be turning in early at the worst hotel in town. But it's the Party hotel. So we all stay there."

"Tenper staying there, Macker?"

"Could be," Kalley said.

The hotel foyer was full of men they knew from politics, mostly men from local or neighbouring States as yet, but a few from the more distant places. There was a period of hand-shaking and back-slapping. Payten went off with a group to the bar, Kalley headed to his room.

A noisy party was already in progress on his floor. He said to the bellboy, "Mr Tenper's in the hotel, isn't he? I forgot to ask the clerk his room number."

The boy pointed. He said, "He has the suite at the end of the lobby, sir." He looked at Kalley. "Do you know him?"

"Yes," said Kalley.

The boy said, solemnly, "He's a great man, Mr Tenper. My father says he's done more for this State than any other politician."

"Your father could be right," said Kalley who tipped the boy. He washed his hands and face in the bathroom, before he went along the lobby and knocked at the door of Tenper's suite. Someone whose name he couldn't recall answered the door.

"Hello, Macker. Didn't expect to see you. Do you want to see the Chief? Ferdie Lusk is with him. I'll ask him when you can see him. Come in."

The room was crowded. Men were standing around in groups with glasses in their hands, talking and laughing.

There were no women. Tenper was indifferent to what his followers did away from his presence, so long as they didn't involve him in political embarrassment. But he lived an exemplary family life and preferred in politics to maintain an exclusively male entourage. Kalley went to an inner door, knocked and disappeared. Someone he knew pushed a beer into his hands.

"The boss'll see you, Macker." Kalley put down his untouched drink and followed him.

Tenper and Lusk were alone in the inner room. Tenper was a short, squat man with a chubby, kind face. He was, Kalley knew, clever and ruthless. He was in his shirt sleeves, with a glass in his hand. His waist bulged over his trouser band, he had small, twinkling eyes, a receding hairline, and a habit of punctuating his speech with grunting snuffles as he cleared his throat. Lusk, though younger, was thin and stooped. Kalley figured him as somewhere about his own age. He had a chalky pallor and eyes as cold and opaque as a dead fish. Kalley knew Lusk as an accomplished and hardy liar. At conferences under Lusk's chairmanship, he had heard a subject for hours and then minutes later outside the conference room had listened to Lusk deny with telling insistence to the newspapers or from the platform that the subject had ever been mentioned.

Tenper said, comfortably, "How are you, Macker. Good to see you. Come to help us bury old Fess?" He winked. "He's a great loss to the Party, boy. Though why he should be I wouldn't know."

Lusk said abruptly, "Con here yet, Macker?"

"He's not coming. He had an appointment he couldn't break."

Tenper said, "That was bad luck, Macker. I'd have liked to have seen the old Con. Good fella, Con. And he would have enjoyed burying Fess. He never liked him." He handed Kalley a bottle of whisky. "Help yourself, Macker. No-one else'll help you in this racket. There's ice and water on the table."

"Con wanted me to see you two fellas while I was here," Kalley said, pouring himself a drink.

Tenper said jovially, "Well, you're seeing us, Macker."

Lusk said, with a sneer, "Con worried, Macker?" Kalley knew that Lusk resented Fortune. In his relatively unimportant State, Lusk had lifted himself to supreme power in the Party. But he was insatiably ambitious. He wanted a wider stage. He hungered fiercely after the national power that Fortune had and of which he was jealous.

Kalley said, "Con's always worried until the numbers go up and his bets are paid off."

Tenper lit a cigar. He puffed at it thoughtfully, "That was an unlucky break for Seborjar and Con, Macker. Alex Pope getting his hands on that Communist Party minute."

Kalley said, straight-faced, "It's a forgery, Theo. It'll all blow over," he said.

"Maybe," said Tenper. "But while it's blowing over some people are likely to get blown down." He grunted again. "I wouldn't like to be standing anywhere near Seborjar when he crashes, Macker. He's big timber. A lot of people might get crushed when he falls."

"You won't be standing alongside Seborjar, Theo." Kalley said "You'll be standing alongside Con."

Tenper said, softly, "Con's standing alongside Seborjar, Macker. He'll continue to stand there while he persists in backing Lilley. I don't know that I want to be close to Con while he's close to Seborjar. It could be dangerous."

"What are you hinting at, Theo? Surely you're not considering switching to another horse at this late stage in the race? Don't tell me you'd fall for backing Bannion?"

"Why not?" asked Tenper who grunted softly, "Why not?"

"Bannion's tied in with Domineco," said Kalley. "You know that, Theo."

"So what? Domineco's a mad anti-Communist. But nobody's ever suggested I'm a pro-Communist. I own this State, Macker. To be quite frank with you, I enjoy owning it. And I'm not like Ferdie here. Ferdie only owns the Party in his State. He wants to be a big shot, nationally. I don't. All I ask is to be left alone to continue owning Queensland." He leered at Kalley. "As I'm not pro-Communist, Domineco wouldn't come interfering in this State."

Kalley sipped at his drink. He said, "Domineco hates Communism. But he hates corruption, too. It is easier for you to deal with Con, Theo. Con's more tolerant."

Tenper grinned at Kalley "I ought to object to that insinuation, Macker. But I won't. I'll take it that this is an academic discussion. Not an attack upon the purity of my administration."

"Take it any way you like, Theo. It won't matter much which way you take it. If Domineco decides to take it a different way, and goes after your scalp."

Tenper pretended to wince. "What good is my scalp to Domineco? Even if he could get it? Domineco can't take away my national power. I haven't any. And I don't want any. He can only get me in this State. And what's the position here?"

He looked at Lusk.

"I'm differently placed from Ferdie in Tasmania. He can't make any headway against the strong opposition he gets from the Party's opponents. But I'm in a much stronger position. The voters in my State are confronted with a problem that often crops up in a democracy. Who is it better to have? Somebody like me who gives Queensland a good and efficient if slightly dodgy administration—I know that some of my boys take a regular rake-off and I'm aware that it has been said that I do the same—but under which the State is prosperous, progressive and tranquil, a living proof that democracy is workable? I'm not an honest blockhead like my opponent from the other Party who won't let a dishonest penny stick to his fingers but whose incompetence is such that if he were running the State we'd probably wind up bankrupt within a very short period and provide an illustration for the Communists and Fascists to help prove that the democratic system will not work?"

Lusk said, abruptly, "You talk too much, Theo."

Tenper said, tolerantly, "I like the sound of my own voice, Ferdie.

I'd sooner listen to it than the voice you listen to. The voice of ambition."

Kalley said, "What are you trying to tell me, Theo? That you're switching? That you'll be voting for Bannion, not Lilley?"

"I am not *trying* to tell you anything, Macker. I'm voting for Bannion." He snorted softly. "Tell Con I'm sorry. I'd sooner deal with Con than Domineco any day. But when big trees like Seborjar start to fall I don't want to be under their branches. Pope's put the axe into Seborjar politically with this Communist minute. He must topple. He can't survive."

"Seborjar has a gift for survival," Kalley brooded for a moment. There was more in this than a cynical determination on Tenper's part to be on the winning side. He thought, "Tenper's pretending that the ideological aspect of the Pope minute has had nothing to do with his switch. But it's been a factor." He looked at Lusk. "How about you, Ferdie?"

"I don't know, Macker. I just don't know."

"Ferdie's situation is more complicated." There was malice in Tenper's tone. The two men controlled the Party machines in their respective States. Self-interest dictated that they should maintain a loose working arrangement whereby they assisted each other. But Kalley knew there was no love lost between them. Tenper professed to have few ideological beliefs. He held himself out to be merely a good administrator and a capable, practical politician. But Kalley knew Tenper had an instinctive distrust of fanatics whether they belonged to the Party's right wing or its left. In some ways he was like Fortune. Lusk on the other hand had an intensity that inclined him towards extremism. He shifted from the Right wing to the Left Wing and back again as political circumstances in the Party changed, constant only in that he always pursued his own advancement. He was psychologically incapable of ever linking up with a moderate, temperate section in the Party.

Lusk said angrily, "You're a self-satisfied bastard, Theo."

The fat little man chortled. "Why not? I've got what I want, Ferdie. You're still trying to get it. And you're jammed. You'd like to switch. You think like me, that Seborjar's had his chips. But a switch mightn't do you any good. Only harm. That's what you're worried about; Domineco. You've tried sucking up to him. He wouldn't have you. He probably thought you were too unstable politically. So instead you cultivated Seborjar, Hoskin, Kerstey and the rest of that Marxist crew. Domineco won't forget that, Ferdie. He likes about him those who want to be Gauleiters—not Commissars."

"Seborjar isn't Marxist, Theo."

Tenper chuckled. "Tell that to the voters, Macker."

"Neither am I Marxist," snapped Lusk. "I stand for the Party. Nothing else."

Tenper said , "You want to be a boss, Ferdie. A big one like Con. Or Hoskin. Or even Seborjar. You're the stuff out of which Commissars are made."

Kalley thought, "Tenper's up to something. Needling Lusk as though he'd prefer Lusk to vote for Lilley instead of joining him in backing Bannion. What's his angle? Does he want to involve Lusk in Lilley's—and Seborjar's—defeat? Would he like to see Lusk ruined politically? Has he someone lined up to take over Lusk's machine if Lusk can be pushed aside?" He filed the queries away in his mind for future investigation. Aloud he said, "Look, I don't want to be involved in any side wrangle between you two. Theo's declared himself, Ferdie. Can you?"

Lusk said, reluctantly, "I'm still with Con, Macker. I'll vote for Lilley. But Con—and Seborjar—'ll have to do something to take the heat off over this Communist minute that Pope's hollering about. It's frightened Theo to Bannion's side. It's frightening all the yellowbellies—those without guts."

Tenper winked,"I've got guts." He stroked his protruding belly.

"Not that kind of guts, Theo," said Lusk. "Real guts." He drained his glass. "You'll be around for a while, Macker?"

"Until after the funeral," said Kalley.

"I'll see you again," Lusk said. "I've a few things I want to discuss—privately."

He nodded at Tenper. "See you, Theo."

"See you, Ferdie," said Tenper. He waited until the door had closed behind Lusk and then he scoffed. "He wants to see you privately, Macker, you know what that means. He wants to see what's in it for him. If he can squeeze something out of Con and Seborjar for continuing to support Lilley. He wants to play in the big league." He poured himself another drink. For some reason he liked to give the impression that he was a hard drinker. But Kalley noted that the whisky barely covered the bottom of the glass and that he diluted it lavishly with water. "You don't have to give him anything, Macker. He has no alternative but to support Lilley. He can't throw in with Domineco. Domineco won't have him. If he's not a communist he's certainly a fellow traveller."

Kalley said, "You gunning for him, Theo?"

Tenper smirked. "Why should I be gunning for him, Macker?"

Kalley said, "Wouldn't have someone lined up in his State to take over his machine, would you?"

"I'm not that kind of a fella, Macker." Tenper dismissed Lusk with a contemptuous wave of his chubby hand. "What'll Con do, Macker? About me supporting Bannion?"

"What can he do, Theo? We can't knock you over in this State. It's your dunghill. You own it. Con's not going to like what you're doing. But he's a realist. There'll be other occasions when we'll be able to do business."

"I hope so," Tenper said. "I like Con. He's a professional. You can deal with him on a sensible basis. I hope he survives. But I don't think he's going to, Macker. The rank and file don't like this Communist minute. Or Seborjar's attitude towards the Coms. Con's crazy to get tied in with him. Seborjar's bad medicine. Big medicine but bad medicine. But he's in his death throes. I can sense the feeling against him. We're a weird collection in the Party, Macker. But we're reformers—not revolutionaries. Like the Communists."

"You're getting to be like Domineco, Theo. You're developing an obsession about the Reds."

Tenper grunted. "I know I'm only a small-time state politician, Macker. International affairs are supposed to be outside my range. But international politics work like local politics. What are the big boys like Seborjar doing all over the world? They're looking around at things. And what do they see? Communism winning everywhere. Authoritarianism once again on the up-grade under a different name. If they get on it they can ride a long, long way. To achieve power over their fellow men. That's what Seborjar and Lusk want. Power."

"Isn't that what you want—power?" Kalley asked.

"No," said Tenper, scornfully. "I want to stay the biggest fish in the small pool of my State. I want a bit of dough—an easy living. Politics is my trade, Macker. Not my dedication. Besides, I've a soft spot for Queensland. I like improving it, building up its industries, providing good roads, satisfactory health services, better school facilities and that kind of thing. I work at staying boss of my State. I'd cut a man's political throat to stay boss. But I wouldn't cut his physical throat. Seborjar and Lusk would. They're playing for bigger stakes. They've been bitten by the power bug. They want to be big men, Macker. They have no loyalty to State or country. Only to themselves."

Kalley said, "You're a shrewd bastard, Theo. I wish Con'd see it that way."

"He's playing with forces that are bigger than he, Macker. He'll find out just how much bigger they are if Lilley wins. Con's a democrat. There's an element of sport in the way he plays politics. His opponents—provided they are good or tough enough—have a chance of winning. But these boys like to deal from a loaded deck. They don't want there to be any opponents. Con and I know we're not always right—that often we do the wrong things. These boys are convinced they're always right."

Kalley sipped at his glass. Then he said, softly, "Not often you think in such broad terms, Theo."

"I think in 'em, Macker. It's just I seldom talk 'em. But someone'll have to do some thinking—and talking—soon. Otherwise the Party'll have had it. It'll degenerate into a front for authoritarians. Let Con know what I've said."

Kalley went through the crowded outer room.

The man who had first greeted Kalley broke away from a group. He said, "Okay?" He nodded in the direction of the room where Kalley had left Tenper.

"Okay," said Kalley.

The man said, "Would you like a few drinks and meet some of the boys?"

"Thanks," said Kalley. "But I've work to do."

Kalley walked along the lobby to his room. He closed the door behind him.

He sat on the side of the bed, taking off his coat and tie, and booked a telephone call to Fortune's home.

"How's it going, Macker?"

Kalley said, "Cabal's getting a good send-off. Parties everywhere."

Fortune said dryly, "You must be enjoying yourself."

"I'm not in an enjoying mood, Con. I've talked with Tenper and Lusk."

"What's the score, Macker?"

"Not good, Con. Tenper's switched. He reckons that after the Pope minute, Seborjar is on the way out. He's voting for Bannion. Told me to tell you that he's sorry. But he won't be with you. Lust is with us, Con. But only just. He's jittery. The minute's frightened him. Another bad break like that and he'll dump us."

Fortune said, "Any use me flying out to talk to them?"

"You could try it, Con. But I think you'd be wasting your time."

"What's the basis of Tenper's switch?"

"Ideological, Con."

Fortune's voice was irritated. "Ideological? Tenper thinks an ideology is something you plant in your garden."

"He opened up to me, Con. More than he's ever done before. He thinks Seborjar is washed up. That's primarily the reason he's switched. But there's an ideological basis to his switch. He thinks Seborjar, Hoskin, Kerstey—and Lusk—are Marxists."

"Someone's been wising him up. He always gave me the impression that he thought Karl was one of the Marx brothers."

"Con, Lusk wants to see me again. I think he wants to know the pay-off in sticking to you. What do I tell him? He's ambitious. He's desperate to get in the big time. He's looking for something in the national league."

"Promise him anything within reason, Macker. Things are getting sticky. We want every vote."

"Your boys playing up, Con?"

"Yes. They don't like this Communist minute any better than Tenper does. Imagine those mugs suffering from ideological twinges. If you mentioned the word in their hearing they'd think you were giving them a tip for a racehorse. But they're starting to look at me sideways."

Kalley said, "What do you want me to do?"

"Not much you can do, Macker. Sit tight. Placate Lusk. Have another crack at Tenper. Though I don't think you'll do much good. He's as pig-headed as he looks. If he's gone so far as to give you a message to pass on to me that he's voting for Bannion, we won't shift him. But keep on trying. We can't be worse off."

"Things out of hand, Con?"

"Not out of hand, Macker. Not yet. But they're getting that way. They're too big for me to handle alone. I'll phone Seborjar tonight. Where's he staying? At your hotel?"

"I think so," said Kalley. "Payten's staying here."

"Forget about things for a while, I'll phone you in the morning. It'll be too late to call you after I've talked with Seborjar. Have a couple of drinks. Give yourself a night off, Macker."

Kalley thought, "Jesus, I'm tired." He got into his pyjamas. He rummaged in his bag and took out a book. It was Evan Durban's *The Politics of Democratic Socialism*. Politically, Durban described himself as a militant moderate. Switching on the reading lamp, Kalley got into bed.

Someone rapped at his door. He glanced up.

"It's Payten, Macker. Open up."

Harassed and untidy, his suit was rumpled and his dark hair, usually smooth and well-brushed, was ruffled. "Seborjar wants to see you, Macker. In his suite."

Kalley, glanced at his watch. "Jesus, it's after one o'clock. I'm in pyjamas. Okay. I'll put on a pair of pants. What does he want?"

Payten said, "Jesus. Who ever knows what the Big Man wants? His suite's the next floor up."

"I thought you had a party on," said Kalley.

"I had, until Seborjar caught up with me. He got lonely. You know what he's like when he's away from home. He must have people round him. So he got Kerstey chasing round on the phone. Until he located Joe Lilley and me. He couldn't find Hoskin or Chris Tion. Lucky bastards." He sighed. "It had all the earmarks of developing into a good romp."

Kalley laughed. "Joe Lilley wouldn't like leaving a good party, Mark."

Payten said, with a touch of malice, "Joe likes the feeling of being in the big-time. It opens up all kinds of enthralling possibilities for him when Seborjar says he wants to consult with him. Not that Seborjar ever consults him. Every time Joe opens his mouth Seborjar shuts him up. But Joe's patient. He'll put up with insults. Contempt. Anything. If he can see a future pay-off."

Kalley put his coat over his pyjama jacket, "You're sure that you don't know what the Big Man wants to see me about?"

"Sure I'm sure. That's a secret between Seborjar and God. Even that's an assumption. Seborjar mightn't have let God know. You know what a secretive bastard he can be. All I know is that Con phoned a couple of hours ago. Ever since, Seborjar has been striding up and down, like Napoleon on the poop of the ship that took him to Elba. While Kerstey, Joe and I have sat there admiringly like three wise monkeys—hearing nothing, saying nothing and seeing only Seborjar." He grimaced. "And a singularly repulsive sight he is." He headed towards the elevators.

"Let's walk," suggested Kalley. "It's only one floor up."

"My doctor says a man mustn't pass either an elevator or a lavatory when he's more than forty. You'd never believe it from the youthfulness of my looks, but I'm over forty, Macker." The elevator was empty.

Seborjar was pacing up and down his sitting room, with Kerstey and Lilley sitting silently watching him. An unopened bottle of whisky was on a side table.

Seborjar stopped his stride.

"Why didn't you report to me, Macker? That Tenper was betraying us?"

"I don't know about Tenper betraying us. I told Con that he was voting for Bannion." Seborjar said sternly, "Isn't that the same thing?"

Kalley began to feel the sense of unreality that he so often had in Seborjar's presence. His eyes went to Kerstey who was watching the man with the hungry attention of a mongrel dog that knows where its next meal is most likely to come from.

Payten said, "How about a drink, Kaye? I'm as dry as a fire shovel." Seborjar waved him impatiently aside.

Kalley said, "Look, Kaye. I'm under no obligation to report to you. I report to Con. If he decides to tell you anything, that's his business."

Seborjar said, moodily, "Sometimes, Macker, I find myself doubting your loyalty in this struggle."

"I owe my loyalty to Con Fortune."

Seborjar said, "You also owe it to me, as I'm the one who is carrying most of the burden. If I fail, Fortune fails. You all do."

"The bastard's mad," thought Kalley, wearily. "Here we go again, arguing about something that doesn't matter." Aloud he said, "Let's not get involved in some side issues about my loyalties. Why did you pull me out of bed? What do you want?"

Seborjar scowled. "I don't like your attitude, Macker. You may regret it one day. I do not forget—or forgive—insolence easily. You told Con that Tenper is voting for Bannion. He must be persuaded back to his original intention of voting for Lilley. That's what I wanted you for. To tell you that."

Kalley said slowly, "I don't think it can be done."

"It can be done and it must be done." Seborjar was suddenly calm, unruffled and masterful. His assurance was impressive. "He must want something. Promise it to him." He was acting like a ruler distributing largesse.

"He doesn't want anything *you* can give him. He's got what he wants. He governs his State and he owns the Party machine in it."

"Then we must take the machine off him," he growled.

Kalley smiled thinly. "You can't take it off him, Kaye. His control is too tight. He's too well entrenched. His boys run the machine. Not yours. Nor Con's. Nor anyone else's. A threat to take the machine off him wouldn't bother him. Nobody knows the realities of the situation in his State better than him. He'd laugh at a threat of that kind."

Heavy jowls drooping, Lilley asked, "What's his beef?"

"He doesn't like the Communist minute that Pope produced. He believes that Kaye can't survive it—that his days as Leader of the Party are numbered."

Seborjar said, "They'll learn differently. Those who think I'm finished." He brooded for a moment. "But that's in the future. Right now, Macker, you'll have to work on him. We need him. Or rather we need his vote."

Kalley said, "You try working on him, Kaye. I'll certainly work on him. But I'm not going to do any good. I'm positive of that."

Payten said, his voice amused, "Kaye can't do anything. 'Ten-per-cent' refuses even to see him."

Kalley was surprised. "Christ, he must be confident that you're on the way out, Kaye. Tenper's not the kind to burn any boats he might have to use in an uncertain future. But that seems to confirm my diagnosis that he can't be persuaded or browbeaten out of voting for Bannion. Not as things stand at present."

Seborjar said, abruptly, "You told him the Pope document was forged, Macker?"

"Yes," said Kalley. "He laughed at me."

Seborjar responded, "He will pay dearly for that one day."

Kerstey said, angrily, "He's betraying you, Kaye. And laughing while he's doing so."

Payten said, an odd note of derision in his voice, "We seem to have lost another vote."

Seborjar said, with a theatrical grandeur, "Tenper has betrayed us to Domineco."

"I don't think Domineco got at him, Kaye," said Macker. "Domineco and he don't get along. Tenper's fingers are too sticky for Domineco's taste. He has them too often in the State cashbox to be acceptable to Domineco. I think this was his own decision. Not Domineco's."

Seborjar shook his head savagely. "Sometimes you are suspiciously naive, Macker. Tenper is venal. But Domineco is prepared to use against me any tool that is available. It matters not to him. The end at which he is aiming will justify whatever means he uses."

Payten crossed to the table and broke the seal on the whisky bottle. "Anyone else?"

Lilley glanced at the unheeding Seborjar. "Just a short one, Mark."

"How about you, Kaye?" asked Payten.

"No," said Seborjar. He resumed pacing up and down the room. . "How about you, Kent?" he asked Kerstey. "No, thanks," said Kerstey, not taking his eyes from the restless figure of Seborjar.

Kalley drank his whisky swiftly. "Anything else, Kaye? I'd like to get back to bed."

Payten winked at him. "See you in church, Macker."

Kalley paused outside the door. He heard the rumble of voices resuming the talk. He felt weary. He went back to his room. He stretched out on the bed with the light off. It was a long time before he fell asleep. The next day he saw members of the Party who had gathered for the funeral. They were cautious in their conversations with him. When they spoke about Seborjar he sensed a growing hostility to the Leader. "Pope's document has had an impact," he thought. "Con—and Seborjar—are going to be lucky if they win this one."

Patiently he tried to sift through what had been said. There was no deep feeling against Fortune. Only surprise—and some scorn—that he had become involved with Seborjar at a period when it looked as though Seborjar was washed up. "If Con can't win the chairmanship with Lilley he's going to lose a lot of prestige and power," thought Kalley. "But at least it looks as though he'll have some prospect of surviving. Which is more than Seborjar will." And survival was important. The man who could survive could fight his way back to the top, as Fortune had previously done after suffering a reverse.

On his way back to the hotel to dress for the funeral he met Louis Vittor. The professor was striding along the sidewalk, his long, thin arms and legs loose and flapping. He saw Kalley and stopped abruptly. "Hi, Macker."

"Hi, Louis."

"How about a cup of coffee?"

"Sure, Louis."

Vittor seemed angry, desperate and worried. He led the way into a small cafe. He hesitated and then strode to a booth at the rear.

Vittor waved the waitress away. "Just two coffees," he said, irritably.

Kalley said pleasantly, "How's it going, Louis?"

Vittor said, impatiently, "Where's it all going to end, Macker? Is the Party disintegrating? Are we finished as a social force?"

"That's a lot of questions to get out in one hit, Louis. Where's it going to end? I wouldn't know, Louis. Don't you? You're the professor of political science. Not me."

"This isn't just a Party faction fight, Macker. It's much deeper than that. I can sense it. Has the age of the reformer passed? Are we—you and I—out of date? I don't like it, Macker. The shape things are taking. This isn't the normal Party struggle. It's gone beyond that. It's a fight between two forms of authoritarianism. The men like myself who don't want authoritarianism in any form—the Party traditionalists—are being squeezed out. Why? What's gone wrong with us?"

Kalley's eyes were bleak. "The Party is feeling the impact of two things, Louis. Seborjar's immense personality. And world history. The world has become a very small place. Once Seborjar would have been content to limit his ambitions to his own country. Now he wants—must have—a world stage. His craving is to rule the world."

"You haven't studied your history sufficiently deeply, Macker." Vittor was suddenly a schoolmaster rebuking a backward student. "One man can't be responsible for fundamental changes—the type of change that is taking place in the Party today. This switch from defence of basic freedoms to authoritarianism. This is something more fundamental than the influence of a powerful personality."

"Maybe you're right, Louis. You've studied more history books than me. I've studied only men and events. But I believe that a single personality if large enough can—provided it is located in a key period of history—change the course of human destiny. Seborjar in my opinion is such a personality. But why should you be more frightened of Seborjar than Domineco? Domineco's your worry. He's the one you—and Bannion—are allied with." The waitress brought them their coffee. Vittor's intense face was withdrawn and anxious. As she moved away he said, "Domineco does worry me, Macker. It's not so much his politics. I don't like them. But he's utterly negative.

Where Seborjar is positive. Domineco wants to throw us back into medievalism. Spiritually, not physically. He wants to recreate the middle ages with modern plumbing. He won't get anywhere. He can't. But Seborjar wants to throw us centuries ahead into a brave new world. God knows what kind of world he wants. I doubt if he knows himself. Or cares. Provided that in that world he is the ruler. He frightens me, Macker."

"Forget Seborjar, Louis. There's nothing you can do about him. Except oppose him. And isn't that what you—and Domineco—are doing? What's your other beefs against Domineco?"

Vittor said, with a sudden flash of boyish candour, "I'm not a very good politician, am I, Macker? I shouldn't be crying on your shoulder. You're in the opposite camp."

"My shoulder is available as a wailing wall, Louis. It is a remarkably discreet shoulder. You know that."

Vittor thought for a moment.

"What do you think of Bannion, Macker? *Really* think?"

Kalley sipped his coffee. "As a person, I like Bannion. He's honest, stuffed to bursting with high ideals and he tries to practise what he preaches. Does that answer you, Louis?"

"Not at all," said Vittor. "You haven't said what you think of him politically."

Kalley lit a cigarette. Dropping his match slowly into his saucer, he said "I think Bannion is—and must continue to be—politically ineffective and unreliable. His ideals are dispersed over too wide a field. Theoretically, it is desirable that someone should hold tenaciously to the things that he believes in. But Bannion believes in too many things and is constantly acquiring new beliefs. He will march off into the desert in pursuit of some minor will-of-the- wisp and leave the citadel of his basic beliefs to be attacked in his absence. A man has only one lifetime. He must allot priorities even to his ideals. I like you, Louis, so

I give you this warning. The Bannions of this world are likeable. But don't place too much faith in them. You'll be disappointed.

"Bannion has fallen under Domineco's spell," said Vettor. "Bannion was prepared to have a guarded, temporary alliance with Domineco. That was the way it was to be. But Domineco charmed him. He's brilliant. You can't deny him that. Now he has Tom eating out of his hand—completely sold on the proposition that together they are saving the Party and this country from the rule of evil." There was an odd note of despair in his voice. "Are all men fools, Macker?"

"Yes," said Kalley. "Including you and me, Louis. But don't let it get you down. Tom's instability will ultimately cause him to break with Domineco. Sooner or later Tom'll want to go off after one of those will-of-the-wisps that dazzle him. Domineco, who is much more realistic, will refuse to follow him.

Then Bannion and Domineco'll part company. You watch and see."

Vittor said, "I don't want to wait that long, Macker. By the time that happens Domineco will have strengthened his grip on the Party. That is, if he and Bannion win this fight against Seborjar and Con."

"There's an easy way out of your difficulties, Louis. You can throw in with us. Give Domineco—and Bannion—away and tie up with Con."

Vittor said, angrily, "You make it sound simple, Macker. But if I tied up with Con I would he tying up with a hundred other people. I'd be allying myself with Seborjar and the forces—whatever they might be—Seborjar is allied with. It would be like climbing out of a snake pit into a tiger's den. No, Macker. I can't be with Seborjar. I'll admit that I thought about doing something like that. Until the PM produced that Communist minute. That finished me as far as Seborjar is concerned."

"Seborjar says the minute is forged."

"In a pig's eye it is, Macker. Domineco may be many things. A fanatic. An infernal, bigoted, intolerant little man. But he isn't a forger. Surely you don't accept Seborjar's claim that it is forged?"

Kalley said, a note of humour in his voice, "That's our story, Louis. And we're sticking to it. Until a better one is available. He glanced at his watch. "Time is moving on, Louis," he warned. "We'll have to get going if we're to make the funeral."

Vittor got up from the booth. He said, abruptly, "I don't know why I talk with you, Macker. You always succeed in making me more depressed than I was before."

"The truth is depressing. That is why with us truth is always one of the first things thrown overboard in a moment of crisis. Rulers and would-be rulers must preserve an atmosphere of optimism. Truth more often than not creates pessimism."

Vittor paid the bill. As they entered the hotel, he said with a burst of the uninhibited candour that Kalley liked in him, "Thanks for the talk, Macker. You've given me something to think about."

"If after you've done your thinking you decide to switch to Con's side, let me know."

Vittor smiled, "I won't." He waved to Kalley and went to the elevator. Kalley watched the elevator doors close behind him.

Kalley dressed carefully in a neat, dark suit. He wore a black tie. He joined those entering the church. As he produced his admittance card he thought, "Tenper's State boys have put on a good show."

The usher glanced at the card, "Mr Kalley, representing Mr Con Fortune. Will you come this way?" He led Kalley down the centre aisle. The church was already full. Familiar faces were on both sides. In the front pews Kalley saw the faces of Bannion, Hoskin and Chris Tion plus the back of Domineco's head bowed in prayer. The usher led Kalley to a pew at the right of the aisle. Payten pushed along to make room for him. He knelt. He could almost reach the coffin with the lighted candles at the foot and head. There was a strong scent from heaped wreaths. Payten whispered, "Here comes Seborjar. Hope the roof doesn't fall in."

Seborjar strode down the aisle, awkward but somehow dignified and impressive. His close-cropped hair had been sleeked down. He was wearing a new suit, which hung well on him. It was one of the few occasions when he looked well groomed and distinguished. He was shown into the pew just in front of Payten and Kalley. He bowed his head reverently.

The service started. The clergyman had a smooth, unctuous voice. It dripped like the wax down the candles beside the coffin.

Kalley followed the motions of the rest of the congregation. He knelt when they knelt, stood when they stood and sat when they sat. The drone of the clergyman's voice made him sleepy. After a while he made no attempt to catch the words.

Payten nudged him in the ribs. When they heard the clergyman say, "This great, good man who has gone from among us in the ripeness of years was a kindly man who gave himself to public service unstintingly, seeking only to serve his fellows, without thought of self, with charity, generosity and humanity."

"Christ," whispered Payten, "That can't be Fess Cabal he's talking about. We must be at the wrong funeral, Macker."

Kalley wondered how many in the congregation were thinking along similar lines.

CHAPTER 12

The large group of newspapermen standing outside the door to Seborjar's outer office parted to let the Leader through. He advanced in awkward, striding gait. Flashlight bulbs exploded in his face. He blinked resentfully. Many of the reporters were strangers. He believed he saw a sneering enjoyment in the faces about him. These men were part of the world he was trying to save from its own destructive madness. But they were incapable of gratitude. They were against him. "Bastards," he thought. He seldom swore, even to himself. "Bastards," he repeated, feeling a strange release in his mental use of the unaccustomed word. They were stupid. Like the voters who had preferred Alex Pope to him for so long. He wanted to help them—to lead them to the better life that he knew, given the opportunity, he could create for them. But they in their blind heedlessness were insensible to their true interests.

Kenny Serge stepped in front of Seborjar with the assurance of a journo who had status.

Seborjar distrusted Serge who had been critical of him in his paper. Seborjar suspected Serge was closer spiritually to Domineco, with his authoritarian outlook, than to the reformists.

"What do you want, Mr Serge?"

"Your comments, Mr Seborjar, on today's development."

Seborjar's head thrust forward angrily, surveying the eager faces of the listening newspapermen. "This is not a proper place to ask for that. I shall see the press in my office."

"When?" asked Serge, with a note of stubbornness in his voice. Seborjar sensed the guarded hostility in the group. They could not show their feelings openly. As Party Leader he wielded a power that even those who opposed him politically respected and feared. He had a habit of refusing contact with reporters for weeks at a time when he was involved in an issue on which his thoughts had not crystallised. Other politicians did the same. The newsmen pardoned the practice in others. "But not in me," thought Seborjar bitterly.

Aloud, he snapped, "I'll see you when I'm ready, Mr Serge."

"But when?" Serge persisted.

"Don't try to bully me, Mr Serge," Seborjar rumbled.

Serge lifted his eyebrows. "I am not trying to bully you, sir. I was merely hoping that you would set a time at which we could see you. Between us we represent every newspaper in the country."

"Very well, I'll see you at noon." He looked at his watch. "It is now 9.30. Noon. In my office." Seborjar closed the door behind him. Without looking to right or left he went through the outer office. He saw faces, but they did not register.

Hoskin, Payten, Lilley and Kerstey were in his inner office waiting for him. Hoskin was sitting quietly, reading a newspaper, a short, squat, composed man. Payten was smoking nervously, taking short puffs at his cigarette while his hand tapped restlessly on the side of his chair. Lilley sat hunched grossly, his fat hands plucking thoughtfully at his drooping jowls.

Kerstey's young-looking, handsome face was ravaged and grey. "Christ, chief, what a terrible break this is. What'll we do?" His face was twitching. It seemed as though he was on the verge of hysteria.

Seborjar strode to his desk. He took off his hat and dropped it on the floor beside him. He snapped, "What's known about this business? What do you know, Gilly?"

Kerstey started to speak excitedly. Seborjar curtly waved him into silence. "Your turn'll come; I asked Gilly what he knew."

Hoskin said, calmly, "Not much more than you can read in the newspapers. Paul Moray has defected from the Communist Party. Moray was in the Communists' inner group. Has been so for years. He's spilled some fascinating stuff on the Communists' methods and tactics in the unions and the way they have worked—with some success—to infiltrate our Party. He promises more interesting disclosures at some undisclosed future date. Presumably when he has tied up a lucrative contract with a newspaper or publisher for his memoirs." He looked down at his hands and spread his fingers fanwise. "None of that is very important to you or me, Kaye. What is important is that, when defecting he abstracted from the secret files of the Communist Party the original of the document Alex Pope recently produced against you." His eyes lifted suddenly to Seborjar's face. "Apparently the document wasn't forged—as you've been claiming. It was genuine. It was a faithful copy of a decision taken by the policy committee of the CPA that you were not to be embarrassed in your fight against Domineco, as your victory would represent the most significant advance the cause of Communism has ever made in this country."

"That all you know, Gilly?"

"Yes Boss. Except for one minor but revelatory fact. Domineco was with Moray when Moray saw the reporters last night. Jasper Danke is handling Moray's publicity. Domineco is the mastermind behind Moray's defection."

"Of course Domineco is masterminding it," said Seborjar. "Defections like this—with the blaze of publicity that this is getting —don't just happen. Months of planning have gone into it."

"It's a plot," said Kerstey, angrily. "Wicked and diabolical."

Hoskin gazed at him without expression. Seborjar said, "Be quiet, calm down Kent. What are you going to do, Gilly?"

"It depends on what you're going to do. My present intention is to bail out. There's no future in being associated with you. I intend to have a future." Hoskin shrugged, a hard, compact man with a hard, compact face. "But you may be able to come up with something. Though I doubt it."

Payten said, urgently, "You're in this too deeply, Gilly. You can't bail out."

"No?" said Hoskin. "You'll learn, Mark. I'm bailing out. Unless Kaye can convince me that he can manage things. Currently it's every man for himself and the devil take the hindmost. What happens if I don't bail out, Kaye? I am a dead duck, politically. Domineco's won this fight. You've had your chips. If I stay with you, I've had mine. But if I run away? I'm a bit weaker. Domineco's much stronger. But I live. That's the big thing. I live, Kaye. To fight another day. Maybe Domineco'll still get me. But I get a breathing space. Something might turn up. But if I stick with you, I'm finished. As of now. I'm sorry, Kaye. That's the way I see it. And that's the way Fortune'll see it."

Payten said, "Have you heard from Fortune, Kaye?"

"No," said Seborjar. He thought of how his phone had started to ring that morning. He had already read the papers. He had guessed that Fortune would be among the early callers. He did not want to speak to Fortune until he had collected his thoughts. "Tell everyone that I'm not here," he told his wife. "Particularly Fortune." When Fortune phoned he heard his wife tell him that her husband had been out of town overnight and was still away. "No," she said. "I haven't heard from him."

"Strange," said Payten, "that he hasn't been in touch with you by now. He must know what happened, even if he's out of the State. Moray's defection is on the front page of every newspaper in the country."

"Look," said Hoskin, wonderment in his voice. "There's no

mystery about what Fortune'll have to do. He's in a weaker position than me. It's an open secret that he's been having trouble forcing his boys to vote for Joe." He gestured with his thumb at the silent Lilley. "He could no more keep his boys in line after this one than fly. They're anti-Communist. They'd defy him in a showdown over this issue. Fortune has to bail out. He has no option."

Seborjar rasped, "There is no need for anyone"—he hesitated, grasping for a phrase,—"to bail out," he added angrily. "We will still win."

"How?" asked Hoskin.

Seborjar thought, "I can dominate the others with the sheer force of personality. But not Hoskin. He's a mixture of hooligan and intellectual. He has beliefs. But he is not prepared to hold to them at the price of political martyrdom. He's hard. He has faith in his judgment. He considers himself my equal mentally—possibly my superior. He's coldly practical. He has to be convinced. He can't be browbeaten." Aloud, he said, "We, as a group, have certain aims in common. We want the eradication from the public life of this country of Domineco—and his like. We seek the implementation of far-reaching social reforms which our enemies describe—wrongly— as Marxist-inspired. We have a determination that the world shall never know again the horror—the obscene indecency—of mass war. We believe we can—once we secure power in this country— provide mankind with the leadership that will preserve it from the destruction—perhaps extinction—for which it's now heading with frightening inevitability." He reared to his feet, his eyes glaring. "Are these great objectives to be thwarted by a public hysteria deliberately whipped up over a trifling forgery, unimportant in itself."

Hoskin said calmly, "What you say Kaye, is powerful. I agree with it. I'd like, however, to make one correction that makes all the difference in the political situation in which we find ourselves. The

Pope document is no longer a forgery. Paul Moray has produced the original."

Seborjar said, "How do we know it is the original? We have only Moray's word for it. The Communist Party will deny that it is genuine. They are not going to admit any document Moray has been able to get his hands on is genuine. They won't know what else he'll produce against them."

Payten said gloomily, "Somebody—probably Domineco—has guarded against anyone—including us—exploiting that angle, Kaye. Domineco's people have got hold of official letters, signed by the Communist Party's secretary. They've had experts comparing them with Moray's document. They were typed on the same typewriter as Moray's original. They even have the number of the machine. And a photostat of the records of the firm that sold the machine to the Communist Party. Showing the number, price, date of delivery—the lot. It's a pretty thorough job, Kaye—pretty thorough."

"What does that prove? Nothing," Serborjar said. "The document was typed on a typewriter that belonged to the Communist Party and presumably—as the machine was used for official correspondence signed by the secretary—typed on a machine to which there was only limited access. How limited was that access? Moray was a Communist in the inner councils. He was certain to have had access to this typewriter. What was there to stop him sitting down at this typewriter and writing this document himself?"

"Why should he do that?" said Hoskin, unbelievingly. "He's about to leave the Communist Party. It's been his life and livelihood for years.

"He wants every friend he can get. You're a big shot Kaye. You might even one day rule this country. If you don't, the Party certainly will. How silly do you think Moray is? To forge a document as explosive as this? Moray's not some ingenuous amateur who doesn't know the political score. He's a trained Communist. He knows the angles—the terrible risk he is taking if anything goes wrong and the document fails to destroy you politically. Think of what you could do to Moray. And the vengeance our Party would take if ever in his lifetime it was shown that the document he used to destroy you was a forgery. No, Kaye. It's thinner than your original proposition that the forgery was Domineco's work."

"Then why did he produce it?" Seborjar said, triumphantly. "On your argument, Gilly, it was in his interests to suppress it—even in the unbelievable event of it being genuine."

With almost agonised patience, Seborjar said "Can't you see, Gilly? I wasn't wrong when I said Domineco forged this document. I was only unaware of how he forged it." Seborjar felt very calm and sure of himself for the first time since he had opened his paper that morning and read the headline, "*Leading Communist Defects—Startling Disclosures—Others Promised*".

Almost forgetting Hoskin, Seborjar said, "Months of careful planning have gone into this defection. The fact that Moray, when he publicly dissociates himself from the Communist Party, is in open association with Domineco, with Jasper Danke acting as his political manager, proves that this is something which didn't just happen"— he snapped his fingers—"like that. Moray defected a long time ago. We only hear about it now because, at Domineco's bidding, he has decided to make it public. Why did he defect?"

He shrugged his shoulders. "He may have defected for any of a number of reasons. Perhaps he lost his Communist faith. Perhaps he felt he was getting old and tired and wanted to get out of a life that must at times get particularly hard for a man who no longer believes. When he was toying with the alluring thought of defection, with whom would he try to establish his first furtive, tentative contacts? With Domineco, of course." There was immense assurance in

Seborjar's grating voice. "Domineco, the archetype of blind, fanatical anti-Communism. Domineco, the tempter who would hold out to him the vision of money, an assured future, and protection in return for his treachery. Can't you see it? Domineco luring him to play traitor until at last he's irrevocably in Domineco's power?"

Seborjar's eyes swept round the listening men. But Hoskin knew that he was not seeing them. He was gazing into the limitless realm of imagination. "Then gradually, so gradually that the victim is almost unaware, the screws are tightened. I can almost hear Domineco telling him in that quiet, even voice of his, 'You must secure documents, Paul—to demonstrate the *bona fides* of your defection.' And Moray, caught in the trap of his own contriving, passing them across, shamefacedly at first; more confidently as he gets accustomed to his exciting role of betrayer. Then the disappointment."

Seborjar started to act grotesquely the parts of Domineco and Moray. " 'But there's nothing here, Paul, to discredit Seborjar.' 'There isn't anything, Mr Domineco.' 'But there must be, Paul. Isn't there, say, a minute outlining the Communist attitude to the present Party fight—suggesting that a victory for Seborjar over Domineco would represent the greatest advance ever made in this country by the Communist cause?' "

Seborjar reverted to his normal voice. His eyes were half-closed, contemplative. "Then comes the realisation on Moray's part of what is expected of him. The desperation. The mounting fear that unless he can deliver what is expected of him the promises of a well-paid, protected, secure future will never eventuate. The shocked awareness that he is implicated so deeply that there is for him no turning back from his path of betrayal. I can see him now, asking 'How do you think such a minute would go, Mr Domineco?' And Domineco, sitting there, poised and detached, replying in that gentle, mock-obsequious voice of his, 'Wouldn't it go something like this, Paul?' And then subtly warning Moray that he would expect such a document to be typed on the kind of paper and on the same machine and with the same care as all such minutes are produced."

Seborjar drew a deep breath. He again was conscious of those around him.

"A frightened man typed this forgery. Peering over his shoulder every second watching fearfully for someone coming. Moray typed this document. But Domineco is the real forger. He told Moray what he wanted—and forced the situation in which Moray had to give him what he wanted."

Hoskin released his pent-up breath. He said, an odd note of admiration in his voice, "Kaye. I realise the value of a diversionary move in a situation like this. But you can't use that one. Domineco'd ruin you financially as well as politically. He'd drag you through every court in the country. He'd make you prove every word. And you can't prove one. "

Seborjar said, defiantly, "The proof is there, in Domineco's obvious association with Moray, predating Moray's defection. In the fact that Moray is Domineco's puppet, with Danke commissioned to pull the strings."

Payten said, his monkey-like face mournful, "Gilly's right, Kaye. Your foundations are too shaky. You have a couple of suspicious facts. Domineco's obvious association with Moray which may—but equally may not—be of a longer duration than both have revealed. An inability to explain what motivated Moray to produce the original of the Pope document. Unless he was prompted by Domineco into manufacturing the original. Those are the foundations, Kaye. You can't build a skyscraper on them. One push and the whole structure collapses."

Hoskin's flat, fierce face was without pity. "As one old political campaigner to another, I can give you some advice, Kaye. You're looking for a diversion. You must have one. Otherwise you're finished.

You don't want a diversion that requires proof. That takes time. Time is running out on you, Kaye. You need a diversion that doesn't need proof. One that has a highly emotional content because when people are emotional they don't think—they react. Personally I don't think you can find a diversion big enough. If you do, let me know."

"What are you going to do, Gilly?" asked Payten.

"I'll tell you what I'm going to do, Mark. I'm going into hiding where the press—nobody—can find me. For twenty-four hours. At the end of twenty-four hours I'm coming out. If the situation is as it is at this moment, I'm announcing that I'm not supporting Lilley, never have supported him and never intended to. I'll announce that I'm backing Bannion and in fact have been backing him from the outset." He looked at Lilley. He did not try to hide his contempt. "I never did want you as Chairman, Joe."

Lilley snarled, his fat cheeks drooping, "No need to get nasty, Gilly."

Kerstey had panic in his voice. "Where do you stand as far as Kaye is concerned, Gilly?"

Hoskin looked at Seborjar, hunched massively behind the desk. "I won't be leading an attack on you to take the heat off myself, Kaye, if that's what you're afraid of. It doesn't suit me to have you emptied out of the leadership when I'm weak, as I will be after this debacle. But I'll be frank, Kaye. If the wolves go after you and I can't stay out of the hunt without risking my hide, I'll be there, right at the head of the pack."

Kerstey said, "You traitor! You vile traitor." Hoskin ignored him. He put on his hat and moved to the door. "I wish you success, gentlemen, in your deliberations."

The door closed behind him. There was a moment's silence. Then the phone on Seborjar's desk rang. Seborjar picked it up.

"Yes." He snapped into the mouthpiece, "Well, what did you tell him?"

He listened. "Well, tell him that I've gone out—that I rushed out before you could stop me when the conference broke up." He replaced the receiver.

Payten said, "Fortune?"

Seborjar said, "Yes. He's been phoning every few minutes. The girl told him I was in conference and refused to put him through. He just phoned again. You heard what I told her to tell him."

Payten said, "You'll have to talk to him."

Seborjar said petulantly, "I'll talk to him when I'm ready to talk to him."

Payten said, "What are you going to do, Kaye?"

Seborjar said, "I haven't decided—yet."

Payten said, "Don't you think we ought to decide on some line of action fairly promptly, Kaye?"

Seborjar said irritatedly, "I haven't thought it out fully yet. How can I? Surrounded by people. As I have been ever since I set foot in this office. You and Joe go away. Leave me alone. If you hear anything— anything—phone Kent immediately. I'll keep him here all day. All night, if necessary. But go away. I'll let you know my decision."

Payten said, reluctantly, "Okay, Kaye. But you won't dive in? With something impetuous? You'll consult us first? Joe and I have big stakes in this, you know."

"Yes, yes," said Seborjar, impatiently. "I'll consult with you before I do anything."

When the door closed behind Payten and Lilley, Kerstey said, "I'll leave you alone too, Kaye. I'll be in the outer office if you want me." He hesitated. "I'd just like to say . . ."—He made a gesture. "How

sick at heart it makes me, to see you the victim of such a foul plot—
hatched with devilish cleverness by that Papal Fascist Domineco."

When the words reached him, Seborjar's eyes narrowed. He saw
in his mind's eye Hoskin's flat, hard face and heard his unemotional
mocking voice saying, 'Time is running out on you, Kaye. You need
a diversion that doesn't need proof. One that has a highly emotional
content because when people are emotional they don't think—they
react.' He asked, "What did you just say, Kent?"

Kerstey said, wonderment in his voice. "I was just saying how
sorry I was. That they were doing this to you. The heart-breaking
rottenness of it."

"Not that," said Seborjar, impatiently. "How did you describe
Domineco?"

"As a Papal Fascist." His young-looking, drawn face convulsed
with hate. "That's what he is. You and I both know it."

"Yes, but who else knows it?" said Seborjar slowly. "

"Who else?" said Kerstey, bitterly. "Not many. A handful of clear-
sighted people only. If there were more do you think the Catholics
would have the immense power they have today in this country? It's a
power that grows daily. If Domineco wins this fight and control of the
Party it will be the dominant power. Yet this is a Protestant country.
Eighty per cent of the people are Protestant. Only twenty per cent are
Catholic. A Catholic minority ruling a Protestant majority. Preparing
the way for Papal Fascism. Why are people like you allowing it to
happen, Kaye?"

Seborjar said, almost mildly, "There is little Protestant feeling
against Roman Catholics in this country."

"Yes, there is, Kaye. Hoskin's Protestant. I've heard him say in
a rare unguarded moment that he has to work at maintaining his
dislike of Fascism and Communism. To him, the product of a long-
established democracy, they have a nebulous quality. They're not quite

real. They manifest themselves only faraway. They do not impinge on his every-day life. Whereas it's easy to maintain his dislike of Roman Catholicism. He imbibed it with his mother's milk. The feeling is there, Kaye. It's just that it has never been allowed to work its way to the surface."

Seborjar said, "Wait outside until I want you, Kent. And, Kent, no phone calls or visitors, however important they may seem. I do not want to be disturbed."

When he was alone he pushed his chair back against the wall. He slumped back, fixing his eyes on the ceiling. He thought, "I've been blind. It took a chance remark by Kent to open my eyes." He felt confidence surging back into him. The voters and the Party would support him when he revealed the peril to which the nation was exposed. They must. There were eight Protestant voters to every two Roman Catholic voters. The Catholic content of the Party might be greater. The Catholics, being a minority, had always, as seemed traditional with Roman Catholics in countries in which they were in a minority, tended to support the Party as the more radical of two major political groups. But though the Roman Catholic content might be higher in the Party than it was in the general community, it must on the simple arithmetic of the situation be so much less than fifty per cent of Party strength.

His mistake had been to view Domineco as an individual, an individual with authoritarian tendencies, but still an individual. As an individual, Domineco drew his strength from many sources, which viewed him merely as dedicatedly anti-Communist and consequently were in sympathy with him. While Domineco could maintain this pose as an individual, the conflict in the Party was only a clash between two warring personalities—Domineco and himself—and the opposed viewpoints they represented.

But Domineco was not really an individual. He was the

mouthpiece and the brain of an impersonal force—Papal Fascism. A Papal Fascism, probably without official Papal backing, possibly even disapproved by official Roman Catholicism, or existing unknown to it, but nevertheless Papal in some aspects of its aspirations, particularly the violence of its anti-Communism.

"Therein lies the explanation of the Alex Pope document," he thought triumphantly. "I found it difficult to convince people that the moral, high-principled Domineco forged the document to win power for himself within the Party. I can understand now why I was disbelieved. Domineco wasn't after power for himself. He was merely the instrument of this impersonal force. Pursuing a much larger aim. That aim was to capture complete control of the Party—to change it from the radical Party it is now into a Party dedicated to one aim— anti-Communism. Domineco would not forge the document for his own selfish purposes. But he would for that larger objective."

"Poor Moray," thought Seborjar. "The fanatic who can find a resting place only at the extremes. I wonder how long it will be before he is accepted into the Church as a convert from Communism to Roman Catholicism." So many of them went that way. Who was the English Communist who trod that much travelled road. Douglas Hyde? He'd written a book about it. Well written. Kindly sort of a book, too. The man had not vilified his former colleagues in the Communist Party. He had allowed them to emerge—as they must have been—decent men with honest but mistaken beliefs.

He felt almost benign. He smiled as he thought of what the afternoon headlines would be. *"Seborjar's Leadership under Threat"*. He told himself he must remember to have a look at them. "The newspapers'll have something different to think about tomorrow," he thought, almost contentedly.

Seborjar washed his hands. He leaned on the basin and stared at himself in the mirror. He studied the calmness of his face. "Stern serenity would be how a good reporter would describe it," he thought humorously. The mirrored face lit with the charm of his sudden smile. He winked at his image and shaped up to it, boyishly, like a boxer. "You're a long way yet from being down for the count, Kaye," he said admiringly. He went into the office and put on his hat.

His face composed, he walked into the outer office. Typists lifted their heads, glanced at him, and then resumed their work. Kerstey hurried to him.

"You look after things, Kent," Seborjar said. "I'm going home. But if anyone comes looking for me, you don't know where I am."

Kerstey said, low-voiced "Jesus, Kaye. Fortune's phoning every couple of minutes. He's furious. What'll I tell him?"

"Same as everyone else," said Seborjar, carelessly. "You don't know where I am."

Kerstey said, shocked reproach in his voice, "You can't go, Kaye. You're seeing the press at noon. What'll they say?"

Seborjar said, "Oh, yes. Our friends the press. I had forgotten them." He could see that Kerstey sensed that his mood had lightened but was baffled as to why it should. "You see them, Kent."

"Christ," said Kerstey, his voice rising. "What'll I tell 'em?"

"Apologise. Say I was unable to keep the appointment. Tell them . . ."—he hesitated. "Tell them to inform their editors that I shall make a statement tonight."

"They're not going to be pleased, Kaye and in the next few days you are going to need all the newspaper sympathy you can get. They've already started to pull you to pieces. We're already being flooded with demands that you resign the leadership." His voice faltered. "Some of them are signed by names big in the Party."

Seborjar said, suddenly angry, "See that every telegram is opened, Kent. Get more staff on the job if necessary. Give instructions that the name of every person of any consequence who signs a telegram against me is to go on a special list. I want to know every enemy in the Party. Some day—and it may be sooner than they expect—I shall deal with them. Every last one of them."

Kerstey said, diffidently, "Kaye, what are you planning to do?" Seborjar said, his little eyes guarded, "I'll let you know. Soon, I hope."

Kerstey asked, "How about Payten? And Lilley?"

Seborjar said, "Keep them away from me. My wife will answer the phone at home. I'll be out to everyone. Except you, Kent. Keep me informed on every development, however minor." He glanced round the office. "I'm going out through the side door. The newspapermen may be waiting outside the main door." Kerstey glanced up and down the empty corridor. "No-one there, Kaye." Seborjar marched swiftly down the corridor. The elevator was crowded. He felt curious eyes upon him. They knew who he was but their faces were unfamiliar. At the ground floor the other passengers hung back to allow him to go out first. His car was in a narrow lane beside the building. His driver, a thin, gaunt man with an unhealthy pallor and an aloof, disinterested manner, had driven him for years. Seborjar said, "Take me home, Jimmy." Nobody of any consequence seemed to have noticed his departure.

He settled down low in the rear seat, his hat pulled down over his face. They left the commercial section of the city behind. The car gathered speed. He felt a sense of escape. The car turned into the driveway of his big rambling home and stopped.

"Get back to the city, Jimmy. Report to Mr Kerstey. Stay at the end of a phone in the office. I may need you. If anyone asks you if you know where I am, you don't know." The driver nodded wordlessly.

Seborjar let himself in with his latchkey. Martha, his wife, emerged from a side room. She said, gravely, "What are you doing home, Kaye?

1 didn't expect to see you today. Until late. Very late." He bent and kissed her cheek. She was plain and matronly. Seborjar was grateful for the calm strength she offered him.

"How are things going, dear?"

"I think I have found the answer, Martha."

"I didn't have any doubt but that you would, Kaye." They never discussed the details of politics. But he knew that she was a large part of his capacity to endure. Her confidence in him and the correctness of his beliefs never wavered. On the rare occasions when he felt discouraged or beaten her quiet, inflexible assurance that he must inevitably triumph kept him from faltering and banished self-doubt.

He said, impulsively, "You're a very lovely woman, Martha." She smiled at him. "I'm an old woman, Kaye—quite an old woman. And I was never lovely. Except to your prejudiced eyes." There was an affectionate warmth in her voice. He thought, with the lack of inhibition that caused him, when he greeted her in public to forget the eyes that were ever upon him and to draw her hand through his arm with the engaging candour of a young lover, "I'm very fortunate to have had standing beside me throughout my life a woman like Martha."

He said, feeling suddenly relaxed and happy, "Just as well you're a respectable married woman, Martha. Or I'd be making advances to you. And your husband mightn't like that."

"I don't think he'd even notice. He's a politician. Seldom at home and always working. Remember?"

"I'll have to remember." His mood changed. "Martha, I want you to answer every phone call. I'm out—you don't know where I am—to everyone but Kent Kerstey. I'll speak to Kerstey. No-one else. Including Con Fortune. Even Mark Payten. I'm out. You have no idea where I am. You understand, dear?"

"I understand Kaye."

He paused with his hand on the rail of the stairway. "I'm fighting the greatest fight of my life. They think I'm finished—ended as a political force. Today every newspaper is writing my political obituary. But I haven't started to fight yet. When I start I'm going to go on fighting to the bitter, desperate end, if necessary. That's what you want me to do, isn't it?"

"Yes," Martha said. "Right to the end, Kaye. A man like you cannot flinch. You must go on until the world acknowledges that you are right and that those who are against you are wrong. That's your destiny, Kaye. You're a great man—very great"

"You give me the courage to go on. As you always have, my dear." He kissed her hand.

He turned and went up the stairs. He went into the bedroom he shared with his wife. It was a womanly room, soft and gracious. There were few signs that he shared the room with her. The desk that stood under the tall, old-fashioned window was small and delicate—a woman's desk. He lowered himself into the light, fragile chair that stood in front of it.

Fumbling in an inner pocket for his fountain pen he pulled a sheet of notepaper towards him, and sat motionless while the minutes passed.

Then slowly, with an abstracted air, he wrote in his angular script at the head of the page, "I accuse". He surrounded the two words with square old-fashioned brackets. Underneath he wrote, "I accuse a Fascist religious group of conspiring secretly to capture by infiltration, stealth and betrayal from within, the Party which I have the honour to lead."

Then he wrote, "Those belonging to this group have no sympathy with the Party's basic and traditional aim—the betterment of the economic lot of the ordinary people of this country." He paused and considered. He crossed out "of this country". In place he wrote "and the maintenance of the traditional, time-honoured liberties that our countrymen hold so dear".

His pen moved faster. "The sinister aim of this group is to use its control of the Party to force upon our community its alien, minority philosophy. The group is prepared to employ any means to gain its ultimate end, the promotion of hate between the politically differing sections of mankind out of which will come world war. World war, this group believes, will exterminate atheistical Communism. It contemplates fatalistically the other frightful prospect—that war in this atomic age will surely extinguish civilisation as we know it and possibly bring about the extermination of the human race."

He stared thoughtfully out of the window for a long while. Then he wrote, "This sinister group is Roman Catholic. But the evidence is that it exists unknown to that great Church which we Protestants respect for its major contributions to the social, cultural and economic life of the nation and to the great body of loyal Catholic citizens who support indomitably the traditional pattern of life in this democracy and in the Party." He paused and frowned, as he re-read what he had written. He scratched out "we Protestants" and substituted "the adherents of all creeds in our community".

Thoughts were crowding his mind. "This group is on the eve of its final triumph in the Party. Already it wields great power. Its secret agents—men who have no sympathy with the traditions and social programmes of the Party they profess to represent—have infiltrated deeply in the guise of loyal Party members. With the patience born of guile, using deception, intimidation, and fraud as deliberate instruments of policy, these agents have won key positions in the Party. They have used those positions to replace members who have held firm to the traditional beliefs of the Party and this nation, with their own creatures who are faithful only to the tenets of their own alien philosophy."

He stared unseeingly in front of him, his pen motionless in his small, neat hand.

"While I continue as Leader, their triumph is not assured—there is always the danger that I can take action to halt their increasing advance."

Seborjar felt a sense of exultation. They—he found himself thinking of them as "they", no longer as "Domineco and his organisation"—had destroyed everything before them in their march to power, like a horde of slow-moving locusts. "But they won't destroy me," he thought. "They will dash themselves to pieces against the cliff face of my determination." He wrote, "To enjoy the final triumph, this dedicated group of conspirators must replace me in the Party's leadership. So today I am subjected to the vilest political attack ever mounted against any political leader in the history of this country. They seek to brand me as sympathetic with Communists and with Communism. Behind the guise of being loyal supporters of the Party, they attack my honesty and disparage my motives. They flourish against me a document so palpably forged that they have to create a mass hysteria to secure its acceptance."

On he wrote, the words spilling out of him ever faster, giving him a sense of intoxication. Moray was a poor, weak creature—a frightened man defecting from a ruthless, pitiless organisation. He had been given money, protection, promises of a secure and guarded future. He had to give his protectors what they wanted. "They wanted something that could be used against me," he wrote. "It was not there. So Moray created it. One can sympathise with the plight of this weak traitor turning his back upon the allegiance of a lifetime. But we must not condone the act that was the outcome of his weakness."

Finally he put down his pen. He read through what he had written, nodding his head occasionally as his lips shaped the words. When Seborjar had finished, he sat for a long time staring alertly ahead.

At last he picked up his pen again. In his stiff, angular handwriting he wrote, "With the Grace of God, knowledge of this grave threat to the Party and the nation has come to me. I accuse Carr Domineco— traitor and intriguer—of being the brains and organising genius of this secret Roman Catholic group that seeks to impose upon the nation and the Party its alien and repellent philosophy that justifies tyranny and oppression."

He heard the faraway buzzing of the phone bell that had been continuous but had not penetrated his conscious mind while he was writing. The buzzing stopped. "Poor Martha," he thought. "She's having a busy day." The buzzing started and stopped again. He thought, "I'll rest—I've plenty of time to read again what I've written and to get Kerstey to arrange a press conference tonight so that I can release it."

Taking off his shoes, he walked over to the bed in his stockinged feet, and, fully clothed, stretched out on his back. He shut his eyes. He slept, his breathing deep and easy.

CHAPTER 13

Kalley expected Fortune to be angry at Seborjar's statement, perhaps even to exhibit a sense of panic. Fortune had frequently shown himself touchily and sometimes unreasonably sensitive about even relatively innocuous comments on Roman Catholicism and its influence on and the part it played in politics. Kalley knew that Seborjar had not consulted Fortune before issuing the statement. Fortune did not like being ignored. The statement was certain to split the Party into irreconcilable factions. Everything pointed to an explosion of wrath on Fortune's part.

Kalley was at breakfast with the two Annes when the phone rang. The morning papers were in an untidy heap on the floor beside his place at the table. *"Seborjar alleges secret Roman Catholic Conspiracy — Domineco named as arch-plotter—Defecting Communist Moray accused as R.C. tool"* the front-page headlines flared on the newspaper Kalley had propped up in front of him. Young Anne, crisp and well-brushed in her school uniform, raced to answer the phone. Kalley listened absently to her shrill, piping voice. She giggled and said, "He's not a lazy old fellow today, Mr Fortune—he's up and dressed and having breakfast."

Anne whispered importantly, "It's Mr Fortune, Daddy."

There was no rancour in Fortune's voice, only eagerness. He said, "Seen the papers yet?"

Kalley said, "I've certainly seen 'em, Con."

"Well, the Big Man's grasped the nettle, Macker. He had no alternative. He had to. If he was going to survive. He was licked. So were we. But if this thing's handled right, it's the end of Domineco."

Kalley said; "So we're backing Seborjar on this one, too?"

"Of course we're backing Seborjar."

"I thought you didn't want to bust the Party wide open, Con. This'll split it from top to bottom."

"It came to me after reading Seborjar's statement this morning. You can't cure cancer without cutting away the rotten flesh. The cancer of Domineco has been eating at the Party's bowels for a long time. The disease was gaining on us. It's doubtful whether we could have got Lilley elected as Chairman. Somebody had to use the surgeon's knife. I hesitated but now Seborjar's used it. If he had consulted me I would have advised him against the knife. But the knife's gone in now. I'm not sorry. I'm glad. Glad. This should be the end of Domineco and his gang. And even if the Party's weak and shaky after the cancer has been cut out, it'll be worth it. It'll be a cleaner, healthier Party. And in time a stronger Party."

"More than Domineco'll carry scars from this fight, Con. How do you feel about your Church being dragged into a political dogfight?"

Fortune paused. "It's sad, Macker. But the Church brought a lot of this on its own head. And there are some consoling aspects. It'll teach some of those cocky little parish priests who have been scuttling round drumming up support for Domineco to keep their prying noses out of politics."

"Has the thought hit you that Seborjar mightn't be using the surgeon's knife? He may be injecting into the Party's veins a sickness as deadly as the one he's professing to cure."

"I know what you're driving at, Macker. We are going to be embarrassed by the type of support we are going to get. I know that. We'll not only get the bigots. We'll get every Communist and every half-baked Communist in the country. And for a while we'll have to accept their support. We'll need 'em. Until the smoke of battle clears. Then their turn'll come. Just as Domineco's has."

Kalley said, dryly, "Ever read Lenin—and history—on the effectiveness of an organised, disciplined minority? It might be your turn instead, Con."

"Always the pessimist, Macker. But I'm keeping you away from your breakfast. I'll see you at the office. We'll go into it all more thoroughly then."

When Kalley returned to the table Anne said, absently, "What did Mr Fortune want this early?"

"Nothing really my love. He was excited over a statement Seborjar has made. He just wanted somebody to talk to, and to give me my riding orders for the day." He looked across at young Anne. "Don't you think you had better hurry, sweetheart? You'll be late for school."

"It's only a quarter past eight, Daddy. It only takes me ten minutes to walk to school, you know." She stood up, a square, chunky child, face shining. A smaller model of her mother. She sighed, "But I'm meeting Elizabeth this morning. At her place. So I suppose I had better get there a bit early. Elizabeth is always late."

Kalley said with a wink, "Not all the girls can be as perfect as you, sweetheart. Now can they?"

Young Anne said, "Daddy, you're teasing me again." She jauntily put on her beret and kissed her parents. "Bye Daddy. Bye Mum. Have a good day."

When the child had left, Kalley said, "She's a good kid."

"She's like all little girls, darling. Good in patches." Anne put down the newspaper. "I've just read Seborjar's statement. It can't be true, can it? It reads like a cheap novelette. Full of spies and traitors and secret organisations with sinister aims. How true is it?"

"It's like young Anne's goodness. Patchy. Part of it is probably true. Part of it is probably untrue. But nobody'll ever be able to prove the complete falsity of the untrue parts or the complete truth of the true parts."

Anne frowned at the paper in front of her. "Which parts are true, Macker? It all seems rather unbelievable to me."

"It's true that Domineco operates a secret type of organisation that he is using to try to capture the Party. It's also true that he has authoritarian tendencies. I suppose you could also say that it is true that he is Papal-minded. He is a devoted Catholic. His philosophical approach is strongly coloured by the devout regard he has for Rome and Papal authority."

Anne said, wryly, "That's a lot of big words, Macker. Are you trying to tell me that you agree with Seborjar that Domineco is—what do you call it?—a Papal Fascist? Whatever that may mean."

Kalley said slowly, "I suppose I do agree. To some degree at least."

"Is it true that Domineco's followers are—as Seborjar says—all Roman Catholics?"

Kalley said, thoughtfully, "That's not absolutely true. But yet again it is true in a way."

Anne said, "Darling, I can't even work out the puzzles that young Anne brings home. How do you expect me to understand ambiguous explanations like the one you've just given me?"

"It's rather difficult to explain my love. Domineco's supporters aren't *all* Roman Catholics. In fact, many of the more important ones haven't any sympathy with Catholicism. They're Protestants, atheists, agnostics. Some are ex-Communists who rarely believe in anything positive. They only know what they don't believe in—Communism. Domineco is supported by a very mixed lot."

Anne persisted, "Then it isn't true, as Seborjar says here, that they're Roman Catholics?"

"It isn't totally true." His face was thoughtful. "Yet it has more than a germ of truth. Domineco though is the driving force. He is Roman Catholic. He is an organising genius. He sets the tone for the anti-Communist organisation within the Party. And because he sets it, the tone is Roman Catholic. He possesses a weakness which he probably does not even know . He doesn't really trust anyone who doesn't belong to his Church. He'll use—or tolerate—a Protestant, an atheist, or an agnostic, as an anti-Communist front. But he never gives them real trust. He surrounds them with men of his own faith. His organisation draws its strength from these men whom he has placed in key positions. Therefore it is—basically—a Roman Catholic organisation."

Anne said demurely "I have no doubt that that is a very clever explanation, darling. But I don't understand what you're talking about. Remember my limited brain and just answer yes or no. Did Domineco and Moray between them forge this Communist minute as Seborjar says they did?"

Kalley said, "I can't answer that one. Probably no-one can, outside Domineco and Moray. Possibly even Domineco can't. Only Moray. And nobody is going to believe what he says. The Communist leaders could answer it, of course. But they're not going to. Unless one of them follows Moray's example and defects. And then he won't be believed because he'll have to say that it's a genuine document. It'll be in his interests to prove the *bona fides* of his defection to say so."

Anne wrinkled her nose at Kalley. "You're an exasperating man, darling. You never answer yes or no. Instead, you produce a complicated explanation that never seems to lead to a neat conclusion."

Kalley said, gravely, "Yes and no are black and white. There are no blacks and whites in politics, Anne. There's an infinite variety of shadings. But no absolutes." He stood up. "I'd better get moving. Con'll be early on the job this morning. The Party'll be excited." He gestured at the papers on the floor. "Now that Seborjar has thrown his hydrogen bomb."

"Will you be home for dinner, Macker?"

"I hope so," said Kalley who bent down and kissed the top of her head. "I love you very much."

Kalley drove to town with a warm feeling deep in his stomach. When he reached headquarters the place was simmering with excitement. He sensed the tension as he walked along the passage towards his office. He saw faces in the lobbies that he had not seen for years. "The crows are gathering," he thought. "They can smell the carcasses."

Kenny Serge was waiting outside Fortune's office. He eagerly grabbed Kalley's arm.

"What's doing, Macker?"

"You tell me. I've only arrived. But I've read Seborjar's statement."

"Isn't that enough? Seborjar's blown everything sky-high. It's on for young and old. Everyone's at each other's throats."

Kalley said, "Who, for example?"

Serge said, "Bannion for example. All hell's broken loose. He's made a public statement accusing Seborjar of launching a sectarian war to save his leadership. Accused him of deliberately stirring up religious hates—setting Protestant against Roman Catholic in what must be the most bitter and unrelenting religious strife that this country has ever seen." A thought struck him. "Bannion's Protestant, isn't he, Macker?" There was a note of puzzlement in his voice.

A man came rushing down the corridor. Kalley recognised him as a reporter who did legwork for Serge. He pushed a roneoed foolscap sheet into Serge's hand. Serge read it. Then he looked at Kalley.

"Apparently Seborjar says that Bannion's a secret Roman Catholic sympathiser. He's just issued a public statement saying so. This is it." He looked at the sheet again. He was uncertain. "How do we know it's true?"

Serge asked, "Are there many such sympathisers in the Party, Macker?"

Kalley said, "There will soon be, Kenny."

Serge said, "Vittor? Sarly Longac? Tenper? Sarrett? In fact every Protestant who happens to be voting against Lilley?"

Kalley responded, "Your guess is as good as mine, Kenny."

Serge said, "That's playing it hard, Macker. Mighty hard."

Kalley said, "Playtime's over. What's doing about Moray? What's the Big Man got to say about him?"

"Moray?" It was obvious that Serge was not interested in Moray, but was thinking over the implications in Kalley's earlier remarks. "Nobody's bothering about Moray. He's unimportant. These charges of Seborjar dwarf everything else. Nobody is going to worry much about Moray. Not while this fight between Seborjar and Domineco is on."

"Maybe Moray's a secret Catholic sympathiser, too," said Kalley.

In his excitement, Serge clutched at Kalley's arm again. "Do you know anything, Macker? Is he a secret Roman Catholic sympathiser? Is he going to be received into the Church? What have you heard?"

"Why don't you ask Seborjar?" Kalley suggested, his eyes hard, like a stone.

The newspaperman's hands dropped from Kalley's arms. He said, slowly, "I get what you mean." Almost defiantly, he added, "I might get round to asking Seborjar."

"Do that," said Kalley who turned away. But the plump little man detained him with a gesture in which there was an odd dignity. "You've already as good as told me, Macker. But where do Con and you stand in this brawl?"

"Con's backing Seborjar."

"Who are you backing, Macker?"

Kalley's hard, lined face showed a flicker of surprise. "I'm backing Con."

"And you reckon you'll win, Macker?"

"Don't you?"

Serge's plump, round face, was uncertain. "Seborjar could have miscalculated. The Roman Catholics are strong. There's a lot of them in the Party. Domineco's clever. One of the cleverest men I've met. A lot of people—and not just Roman Catholics—listen to him in the Party. Seborjar's on the skids. He's been on 'em for a long time. Maybe this diversion'll save him. But it's still only maybe."

Kalley said, "You're talking about yesterday, Kenny. Yesterday Seborjar was on the skids. He's no longer on 'em. Not any more. He's back on top. Right on top. Firmer than ever. Riding high, wide and handsome."

Serge said, slowly, "Bannion disagrees with you. He reckons Seborjar's destroyed himself."

Kalley smiled bleakly. "He's destroying a lot of things, Kenny. Maybe he'll even destroy the Party. But he's saving himself. At least for today. And that's how Seborjar lives politically. From day to day."

"Mostly I can follow you, Macker. But I can't see how you're working that out."

"It's mathematics," said Kalley, calmly. "This is a Protestant country, Kenny. There are eight Protestants to every two Catholics. The ratio supports us. But there must be many more Protestants in the Party than Roman Catholics. It is as simple as that. Seborjar can't lose. Not at this stage. Not until people get round to wondering whether he is really the champion of militant Protestantism against the secret manoeuvres of a sinister Roman Catholic group, or a conscienceless politician ruthlessly safeguarding his political hide by promoting a bitter sectarian war. It'll be a long time before anyone gets round to that kind of wondering."

Serge said, "You figure he must win, Macker?"

Kalley said, "He can't lose, Kenny. If you want to be on the winning side, back him."

Mrs Belasco was in the outer office. "Daryl Kandur waiting for you in your office, Macker. Mark Payten and Louis Vittor have been trying to get you. They want you to phone. And the Leader wants Con."

"Things are happening, Aggie. When did the Leader's office phone?"

Mrs Belasco said, "A few minutes ago. And it wasn't his office. It was Seborjar himself. As nice as pie. Was Mr Fortune there? Oh, well, it didn't matter. It was nothing urgent. It could wait until Mr Fortune came in. Would I mind telling Mr Fortune he had phoned? He'd like Mr Fortune to see him during the morning. If it was convenient to Mr Fortune, of course." She twisted her mouth into an expression of distaste. "I don't like that man, Macker. I don't trust him."

"You'd be a fool if you did," said Kalley, dryly. "I hope Con isn't mug enough to trust him too far. He's going to be very charming to our Con. He needs him. Con's a Roman Catholic and known to be a good one. Seborjar's got to salvage some Catholic votes from the wreckage, or he'll never rule this country. He'll try to use Con the way Domineco uses Protestants. As a front. To prove he's only against one kind of Catholic. Domineco's kind."

Mrs Belasco said, puzzled, "How many kinds are there, Macker?"

"Don't ask me, Aggie. I'm a babe-in-arms in these things."

Mrs Belasco said, "You're going to be very lonely in this fight."

Kalley's face lighted with sudden charm. "I'm probably the only genuine neutral in the Party, Aggie. I'm an atheist. One of the few atheists who doesn't make a religion out of atheism and become as partisan as any bigoted Christian. I know what I believe, but I'm not so positive that what I believe is correct that I want to push it down anyone else's throat."

Mrs Belasco said, "You're going to be very lonely in this fight, Macker?"

Kalley said, "Very lonely, Aggie." He paused at the door into his office. "I'll get Payten and Vittor later," he said. "I won't bother doing anything about Seborjar. Con ought to be in shortly."

Kandur was standing at the window in Kalley's office, looking out. His suit was dirty, ill-pressed, with dandruff embedded greasily on the shoulders. He turned and said, "How're you, Macker?"

Kalley sat at his desk, fished out a cigarette and lit it. He exhaled a lungful of smoke. He said, "What's the good news, Daryl?"

"I dunno whether it's good or bad," said Kandur. "You've seen Seborjar's statement? In the morning papers? I don't know where we stand, Macker. Con's a Catholic." He was suddenly self-conscious. "So am I. I'm not particularly good, Macker. But I'm Catholic. I didn't think much of that stuff of Seborjar's. Too . . ." he gestured ineffectually. "You know. Too . . . well, too sweeping, kinda."

Kalley's eyes narrowed. "Is that a general reaction on the waterfront, Daryl?"

Kandur's voice was apologetic. "Well, no, Macker. It ain't. Most of the men seemed to think it was about time somebody took on the Catholics. Bastards, some of 'em called 'em. There was quite a bit of excitement on the jobs. Most think Seborjar has done the right thing. Later, down at union headquarters some of the big boys got in a corner. I could tell they were talking about Seborjar's statement.

Macker, they froze me out. I've been friends with 'em for years. And they froze me out."

"Don't worry," consoled Kalley. "It'll probably blow over in a few days."

"I'm not so sure," said Kandur. "The Coms have come out of their burrows. They're racing round the jobs organising messages of congratulations to Seborjar. They're talking about holding stopwork meetings to pass resolutions supporting his stand. Men who yesterday wouldn't have anything to do with 'em are listening to 'em. This could snowball, Macker."

"Don't do anything, Daryl. Sit tight for a few days."

"Who are we supporting, Macker? Where do we stand?"

"We're supporting Seborjar, Daryl. See that all our boys on the waterfront know that. We are against Domineco."

Kandur said, "Jesus, we're going to have some peculiar running mates, Macker. I hope Con knows what he's doing."

Kalley said, "He does Daryl. Believe me."

After Kandur had left, Kalley phoned Payten's office.

Payten came on the phone. "Stirring days we live in, Macker. Can you meet me in ten minutes? In the Legislature bar?"

"What do you want, Mark?"

Payten said, "You're a suspicious bastard, Macker. I merely want to put a viewpoint."

Kalley said, "Seborjar's viewpoint? You acting on his orders?"

Payten said, amusement in his voice, "Yes, you suspicious bastard. Seborjar thinks your views'll influence Con. He wants you to know how he sees it."

Ten minutes later Kalley told Mrs Belasco, "I'll be at the Legislature bar. Payten wants to see me. Con can get me there on the phone. If he can stall on seeing Seborjar until I come back, I'll know what's in Seborjar's mind. And I'll know what's moving. Payten's sure to spill what he knows. He's indiscreet when he's excited."

There was only a handful of men in the bar. It was too early for the usual crowd. The barman signalled Kalley as he hesitated just outside the door. "Mr Payten's waiting for you in the back room, Mr Kalley."

Payten had sent out for coffee. He was drinking from his cup. He put it down and passed a cup to Kalley. "I thought you'd rather have coffee at this hour of the morning." His mobile, monkey face was alive and excited. He was wearing a dark red carnation in his buttonhole. He kept running his thumb up behind his lapel and sniffing at the flower.

Kalley said, "You seem on top of the world?"

"I am," said Payten. "You've got to hand it to the Boss. Yesterday? Down on the canvas. Battered. Almost out for the count. Today?" He kissed his fingers ecstatically. "The champ."

Kalley said, "The fight hasn't been won yet, Mark."

"Hasn't been won? You ought to have seen Seborjar's office this morning. The phones haven't stopped. They had to put extra girls on the switch within ten minutes of opening up. Pledges of support. From every State. From Party branch officials. From unions. From all kinds of associations. I tell you, this is big, Macker. It's going to get bigger. Churchmen all over the country are backing us. This issue's a bonanza. It's been there under our noses all the time and only Seborjar had the genius to recognise it. There's nothing like a bit of good old religious hatred to get people steamed up."

Kalley said, "You'll find that half the bastards who are supporting you have nothing to do with the Party. They'll vote for the PM and his crowd in an election. They're only exploiting the Party's troubles. As the Communists will."

"Do you think Seborjar doesn't know that?" said Payten scornfully. "But he's got the right attitude. He says we'll jump that hurdle when we come to it. And he's got another angle, Macker, that's worth considering. He thinks that for every Roman Catholic vote we lose to Alex Pope over this row we'll pick up at least two of Pope's Protestant votes."

"That's a long shot, Mark. A very long shot."

"By Jesus, I'm not so sure. I haven't had time to move round much today as yet. But everyone who's been in touch with me—and there's been plenty—have talked about nothing but Seborjar's statement. The swiftness of this reaction within the Party. I've never seen anything like it. There must have been hundreds of men who walked into offices and workshops and factories this morning and sent off a message of congratulation or support to Seborjar before they even thought of doing anything else."

A thought struck Kalley. "By the way, what religion are you, Mark?"

"I'm nothing, Macker. I belong to a long line of pagans. I'm not even sure that I was ever baptised. What are you?"

"The same as you. Nothing."

"Well, that qualifies both of us to participate in a religious war. At least neither of us should be inhibited by preconceptions."

Kalley said, "I still think Seborjar is playing with dynamite. He has unleashed forces that nobody—even he—can control."

Payten said, quickly, "But you must concede it puts the Boss in front. For the time being at least."

"Sure," said Kalley. "Hitler showed the value of bashing an unpopular minority. He bashed the Jews. You need a minority sufficiently numerous to at least give the appearance of being a threat to the majority. The Roman Catholics here have the necessary qualifications to fill the bill locally. Yes. I'd say that Seborjar has a winner. As far as the Party is concerned. I don't know about the electorate generally. The uncommitted voters aren't going to like the way we'll have to swing towards Marxism. And we'll have to swing that way."

"We don't have to," said Payten. But there was no conviction in his voice.

"Seborjar has to go left," said Kalley. "He can't help it. That's where he's going to get his support. And if he can hang on to the Party it'll follow him towards the left. And that'll be the natural tendency, anyway. If this fight is going to be as bitter as Seborjar obviously plans to make it, the Roman Catholics'll leave the Party in droves. They'll have to be replaced. Who'll replace them? The decent, ordinary man or woman won't want to be in as filthy a fight as this. The Party or Seborjar—those two names are going to become interchangeable—'ll have to recruit the bigots and the Marxists. The bigots'll run with whoever is most violently opposed to Rome." He shrugged. "Who's that? The Communists and their fellow travellers. The Party's going to change, Mark. And those who have a vested interest in staying in it will have to change with it. The only advice you can today give anyone in the Party interested in self-preservation, is, 'Go left, young man—go left.' "

"That's the advice you are going to give Con, Macker?"

Kalley said, with deliberate ambiguity, "Con's interested in self-preservation, Mark."

"Seborjar was fearful that you might overemphasise the dangers, Macker. That's why he told me to see you. The Roman Catholics don't have to get out. Only some of them."

"Those who put their religion ahead of their politics?"

Payten refused to notice the sardonic note in Kalley's voice. "That's right, Macker. Those who put their religion first. Domineco and his supporters. They'll have to go, of course. But Seborjar sees the dangers to the Party in a mass exodus. He told me to tell you that."

"Does Seborjar see the danger to the Party, Mark? Or does he see the danger to his ambitions if he estranges permanently and irrevocably practically the whole of the Roman Catholic vote? He'll never rule this country unless he can retain some Catholics."

Payten said, "What does it matter what Seborjar's motives are? The essential is that he wants to retain some of the Catholic vote. That puts Con in a key position."

Kalley said, "What's in it for Con if he comes up with public support for Seborjar?"

"Nothing concrete," said Payten, "except that he'd help to complete Domineco's ruin. And he'd get a great deal of personal satisfaction out of that. But in the abstract there's a lot, Macker. Con's anti-Communist. If he buys into this fight against Seborjar and gets himself expelled from the Party—as he inevitably must—a lot of Roman Catholics'll follow him out of the Party. The anti-Communist force in the Party'll be seriously weakened. There'll be a power vacuum. Power vacuums don't stay empty for long. The Communists'll fill it. That's how Seborjar sees it. And that's how he wants you—and Con—to see it."

Kalley said, "Who educated Seborjar? The Jesuits?"

Payten smiled, "Certainly not. As a matter of fact I think he could educate them in a thing or two."

"I'll see that Con gives consideration to those views," Kalley promised.

Payten said, "If he doesn't, Macker, he's a mug."

Kalley phoned the office from the telephone booth in the bar.

"Con there, Aggie?"

Mrs Belasco was apologetic. "He's seeing Seborjar. I gave him your message. But he wouldn't wait. He was too anxious to talk with him."

Kalley said, "It can't be helped, Aggie."

Mrs Belasco said, anxiously, "Was there anything important with Payten, Macker?"

"He wanted to put up a viewpoint which Con has already accepted."

Kalley cradled the phone. Then he picked it up again and dialled. He recognised Vittor's voice. "You wanted me to phone you, Louis."

Vittor said, urgently, "I want to talk with you, Macker. You say where to meet you and I'll come at once."

Kalley told him where to go. Then he hung up. The bar was getting crowded. Macker nodded to several of the members from the Legislature. He was stopped several times by those eager for news of the latest developments. There was the same atmosphere of excitement as there had been at Party headquarters. He saw Bose Carlin, huge, black-haired and scowling, towering in the middle of a group. He saw Kalley and thrust his way through the men toward him.

"What's the score, Macker?" he demanded.

"You know as much as I do, Bose."

Carlin said, "Seborjar's got guts. Somebody should have taken Domineco on years ago. Shown him up for the treacherous rat that he is. Where does Con stand? Or isn't he saying, until he finds out which way the wind is blowing?"

"It's no secret, Bose. Con is with Seborjar. But where do you stand, Bose?"

Carlin said, "I stand where I've always stood. Against traitors to this country. Whether they're Coms or Papal Fascists. Domineco is a traitor. The Coms'd sell out to Moscow. He'd sell out to Rome."

Kalley said, feeling oddly depressed, "How many battalions does the Pope command?"

Carlin said, "Not pro-Roman Catholic are you, Macker?"

"No," said Kalley, quietly. "Pro-commonsense."

He went out, down the wide square, past the old stately Legislature building set in its constricting area of narrow, well-tended gardens, towards the commercial centre of the city. A cool wind was blowing. The newsboys were calling the early editions of the afternoon papers. He paused to read them on the edge of the footpath. Follow-ups to Seborjar's statement still provided the front-page leads.

There were statements from most of the Party Leaders. With the exception of a statement from Domineco categorically denying all Seborjar's charges, and Bannion's angry condemnation of Seborjar's use of sectarianism as a political weapon, the papers reported the leaders as supporting Seborjar.

"They must support him," thought Kalley. "Even if they don't want to, they must. They can smell the breeze. They know that they can't survive unless they support him on this."

There was a statement from Theo Tenper from the North. "Seborjar has no loyalty to State or country," Tenper had previously said. "Only to himself." But now the test had come, Tenper was behaving like the political animal that he basically was. "I had intended to vote for Mr Domineco," he had told the newspapermen. "But only while I was unaware that he operated a secret organisation that aimed at capturing and perverting the great Party which I have the honour to lead in this State. Now that our National Leader has unmasked Mr Domineco and his followers, I stand solidly with our Leader and will fight beside him to the death to rid the Party of this malign and alien influence. My vote and the vote of those members of the Management Committee with whom I have influence, will go to Mr Lilley. Mr Seborjar is backing Mr Lilley. I hope that Mr Lilley can prevent Mr Bannion, whom Mr Domineco is supporting for the Party chairmanship, seizing what is the most important administrative post our Party has to offer. I pray that the honest men within the Party will follow my lead and give Mr Seborjar—through Mr Lilley—a resounding vote of confidence for his courage in exposing publicly this evil conspiracy." Tenper's statement was a hasty, scrappy one. But it was clear enough. Tenper did not intend to figure in any Party casualty list.

Kalley went through the papers, mentally noting the names of those who were hastily throwing in their lot with Seborjar. "It's a landslide," he thought. "Bannion couldn't win with a start. Lilley is as good as Chairman right now." He thrust the papers into a rubbish receptacle. There was no expression on his face as he entered the unpretentious restaurant where he had arranged to meet Vittor.

Vittor was seated anxiously at the table. "Macker. I'm glad you could see me. The whole thing has me baffled. I can't understand what's happening."

Kalley said, "Let's order." He passed a menu to Vittor, who looked at it uncomprehendingly. "I don't know that I feel like eating."

Kalley ordered two steaks. He waited until the waitress was out of earshot. Then he said, "How does it feel to be walking round with your head cut off, Louis?"

Vittor said, with an odd dignity, "Macker, we have always been friends. At least I always felt we were a friends. Surely this is too important for cheap, cynical witticisms?"

Kalley said, "You'll never really be a good politician, Louis. You take politics too seriously."

Vittor said, "They are serious things, Macker. You know that. The events that are taking place right now could have a most significant effect upon the lives of generations yet unborn."

"That's true, Louis. But history isn't shaped by wise men looking ahead. It's shaped by fools—and villains—trying to live through today and tomorrow. Perhaps even next year and the year after, but seldom the year after that, and never a generation from now. That's

why policies and ideologies—however fine and noble they are at the
start—get twisted and deformed as the years pass."

Vittor said, "I try to stick to what I believe is right. Not only for
this generation but the generations to come."

"And what does that make you, Louis? A rather kindly, conscientious
fellow, who's been able to get to a position of some influence within
a huge political organisation for a variety of reasons, of which the
main one is that the going has not been particularly tough and the
pressure hasn't been on. But now the going is getting tough and the
pressure is coming on. So you're going to be brushed aside by men
who are neither kindly nor conscientious. Just determined to survive
come hell or high water. Who know what they want and are going to
get it if they can."

Vittor, fingers playing restlessly with a fork, "So you think I'm
finished, Macker?"

"Yes," said Kalley. "As far as the Party is concerned. You and Tom
Bannion and the rest of the do-gooders like Bannion and yourself.
You're washed up."

Vittor said, quietly, "What about Domineco and Danke and that
crew?"

Kalley said, "They're washed up, too. But for a different reason.
They're not soft do-gooders like Bannion and yourself, who can see
both sides of an argument and consequently have inhibitions and self-
doubts. They are one-eyed. They know what they want and how to go
out to get it. They're tough and they're ruthless. But for the moment,
at least, they've been outsmarted by someone who is tougher and
more ruthless, and who has seized on their fatal weakness. They're
Roman Catholics in a Protestant country."

Vittor said, a note of disgust in his voice, "Once again you almost
persuade me to get out of politics."

"You might as well, Louis. You're getting out, anyway, whether you like it or not. You're going to get kicked out. Expelled from the Party."

Vittor said, "They can't expel me. I've always been opposed to Domineco and what he represented. I supported Bannion in preference to Lilley. I was entitled to do that. Lilley is corrupt. Everyone knows that. I've broken no Party rules."

"You think a small consideration like that will influence these boys? You don't know 'em, Louis."

"But why would they expel me, Macker? I haven't done anything."

Kalley said, "You opposed Lilley. You're pro-Roman Catholic."

"Pro-Roman Catholic?" Vittor was startled. "But I don't even *like* Roman Catholicism. I have spoken publicly from rationalist platforms *against* the Roman Catholic Church."

"Don't complicate the issue, Louis. You're against Seborjar. There is no reason to suppose that you will not continue to be against him. Ipso facto you are pro-Roman Catholic."

"Is that supposed to be humour, Macker?"

"No. It's not. It is the charge that from now on is going to be levelled against every man who opposes Seborjar. If he does not support Seborjar, he will qualify immediately as a Catholic sympathiser."

Vittor brooded for a moment. "Seborjar'll never get away with that, Macker"

Kalley said, "No? You watch and see, Louis."

The waitress brought their steaks. Kalley picked up his knife and fork. He ate steadily. He said, "This is a nice piece of meat, Louis."

Vittor looked down at his untouched plate. "I'm not hungry," he said.

"Life is but a brief passage between birth and the grave. Get through it as comfortably as you can, Louis. Eat, man. Today's tragedy is tomorrow's farce."

Vittor said, "You're right, Macker."

"Don't take my paperback philosophy too literally, Louis. It's suitable only for disillusioned cynics, and those who are ruled. Not those who would like to rule, as you would."

Vittor said, with a gesture of irritation, "I don't mean you're right on that. I mean you are right when you say Lilley is going to win."

Kalley said, "Lilley must win. There are eight Protestants to every two Catholics in this country."

Vittor wrinkled his eyes thoughtfully. "Of course," he said slowly. "I didn't even think of that. But that's the basic, isn't it, Macker?"

"What were you thinking of, Louis? That made you so positive that Lilley'll win."

Vittor said, "Perhaps I shouldn't tell you, Macker. But if I don't, you'll learn from other sources. We've already lost two votes, Franky Canover and Sarly Longac."

Kalley pursed his lips. "That was quick," he said quietly.

"Yes," nodded Vittor. "I think Franky only wanted an excuse. He hasn't been happy since Tom split with Con. He's been frightened that he was on the losing side. I don't suppose you can blame him. The only income he has he gets from politics. When he read Seborjar's statement this morning he phoned Tom. He said he couldn't support Tom after that. He was going to see Seborjar. To tell Seborjar that he would be voting for Lilley."

"And Longac?" asked Kalley.

Vittor said, "That was different. You know Sarly. As honest as they come. Decent. Courageous. Calm and dependable and strong." He shook his head slowly. "Sarly phoned me this morning. He had already phoned Tom. He said he had read Seborjar's statement. Until he read it he had not realised the issues that were involved. But after reading it he could not, despite his personal regard for Tom, continue to support him against Lilley. He asked Tom to pull out—not to run for the chairmanship. Tom refused. Sarly said that in all the circumstances he would not—could not—vote for Tom. Tom argued. I argued. But you know Sarly. He had made up his mind before he phoned. He was inflexible."

Kalley waved away the waitress. "Well, I'm off. Con'll be looking for me."

Vittor said, "Thanks for providing the shoulder for me to cry on."

"That's okay." said Kalley. As he paid the cashier, Kalley glanced back. Vittor was sitting at the table, gazing absently before him, his untouched plate still in front of him.

Mrs Belasco looked up as Kalley entered the office. "Con's waiting for you."

Fortune was behind his big desk, his long legs stretched out and his feet propped up on an opened drawer. An empty lunch tray was in front of him. He was smoking. He waved the cigarette at Kalley. "Where've you been, Macker?"

Kalley told him. He told him of the conversations with Payten and Vittor. Fortune was not particularly interested in what Payten had said. But he listened carefully while Kalley recounted his talk with Vittor.

"I didn't know Longac had switched," he said. "I knew about Franky. Franky was in this morning to make his peace with Seborjar."

"What's in the Big Man's mind, Con?"

Fortune said, "He's as excited as a small boy. There's been an extraordinary reaction to his statement. I've never seen anything like it before in the Party."

Kalley said, his face a mask, "The Roman Catholics aren't popular, Con. What are you going to do?"

"Firstly, I'm going to put out a statement. For publication tomorrow. Backing Seborjar in this fight. To the hilt."

Kalley said, "I'll work on it this afternoon, Con."

"You don't have to worry about it, Macker. Bose Carlin showed up while I was talking with Seborjar. Seborjar suggested I get him to help me. He's done a rough draft that I've okayed. He's polishing it now. He'll have it in here sometime this afternoon."

Kalley said, sharply, "I could have done it for you, Con."

Fortune said, "Seborjar thought that this was more Carlin's dish of poison than yours, Macker. He could be right. It needs the touch of someone who is convinced that Seborjar is a hero and Domineco a deadly evil. You don't, do you, Macker?"

"Do you?" asked Kalley.

"No," said Fortune, "I think that Domineco is evil. But I can't see Seborjar as a hero. Anyway, don't worry about it. Let one of Seborjar's stooges do a bit of the work for a change. You've done your share."

"Sure," said Kalley, quietly. "I'm not worried."

Fortune sat at his desk and pulled a pad towards himself. "I took some notes, Macker. These are broadly our plans. Lilley'll go in as Chairman. There seems no doubt about that now. Every swinging voter on the Management Committee—except Sarrett—has been in touch with Seborjar. They're voting the way he tells them to. We can afford to ignore Sarrett. He's on his way out, anyway. We know that. Franky Canover's okay. So, you tell me, is Longac." He looked at Kalley across the desk. "You're sure of Longac, Macker?"

"I'm sure," said Kalley. "Why should Vittor lie?"

"Okay," said Fortune. "Domineco'll be down to his closest supporters. And there may even be defections there. And Bannion and Vittor." Again he glanced at Kalley. "Or will Vittor weaken?"

"Vittor won't weaken," said Kalley. "Not now. He might have before Seborjar came in. But he won't run away now."

"Put it at its worst, we'll have a two to one majority. Probably better. We'll elect Lilley. Then we'll start moving."

"Expulsions?" said Kalley.

Fortune's face was stern. "Expulsions. We start at the top. Domineco and Danke. Bannion and Vittor. Every man who votes for Bannion on the Management Committee. Except Sarrett. No sense in providing Domineco with a ready-made martyr. Which he could turn Sarrett into. Then any of the Party big boys who come out publicly— or privately—in support of Domineco. They go, too. No kid gloves. We'll tell Lilley who we want expelled. He expels them."

Kalley said, "You'll wreck the Party, Con."

Fortune said, "Only temporarily. We'll rebuild. To our design. And without Domineco. The more ruthless we are now, the quicker we can clean up the mess."

Kalley said slowly, "The rank and file might not like it. Domineco has followers planted in every Party branch and every Party League."

Fortune said, "The slightest sign of revolt and we purge downwards. Seborjar and I agreed on that. It doesn't matter how insignificant they are. Anyone who speaks up for Domineco in the Party is out. Washed up. Finished."

"You'll be providing Domineco with material to form a new political Party."

Fortune said, scornfully, "What's the history of groups that break away or are forced out of the Party? We've had schisms before, Macker. Big ones. They don't last. The breakaway groups set up an organisation in opposition to the Party. They contest a few elections. They do no good. They wither away. Domineco's base is too narrow. It's purely Catholic. This, as you say, is a Protestant country. I forecast here and now that no organisation Domineco forms in opposition to the Party will last longer than one election. They'll be so disastrously routed that they'll not be able to endure."

Kalley said, "You know, there's a step pyramid in Egypt." He paused. "I wonder how many thousands of ancient Egyptians stood within that tomb and said, 'The name of the King that built this great monument will never be forgotten as long as men live'? But now no-one knows who built it."

"Christ," said Fortune. "You are not suggesting that the Party could disintegrate? It's too strong, too big, too well established."

There was a knock at the door. Mrs Belasco put her head round. She said, "Mr Carlin's here, Mr Fortune."

Fortune said, "Send him in, Aggie."

Carlin, big, black-browed, immense, stood quietly, looking from Fortune to Kalley. He had a file of papers clutched in his huge, paw-like hands.

Kalley said, quietly, "I've some things to do, Con. Do you want me any more?"

Fortune said, "No, I don't need you any more, Macker."

Mrs Belasco was biting her lower lip as Kalley walked past her. She watched Kalley go through the outer door. Behind in the room he had left, the heads of Fortune and Carlin were already bowed over the typewritten sheets that Carlin had spread out on the desk top.

Mrs Belasco closed the door behind her, shutting them off from her sight.

CHAPTER 14

The new office was spacious, with windows and colour tones adding to its size an air of luxury. The walls were adorned with murals depicting idealised toilers in heroic postures as they turned symbolical wheels of industry; or, naked to the waist in perpetual effort, performed untiringly mighty tasks. The carpet was thick, rich in colour and springy like turf. The desk was expansive, curving in boldly at the front, glass-topped, bare except for an array of silver telephones.

"Nice layout you have here, Macker," Carlin said. "Better than that gloomy coffin you had when you worked for Fortune."

"Much better," said Kalley from behind the desk.

"I'll bet the dough's better." Carlin paused. "I wouldn't mind working for Multicos myself, Macker. Not after seeing this layout."

Kalley said, "You looking for a job, Bose?"

"No, I'm not a nine-to-five man," said Carlin. "That's strictly for clerks. What do you do for your dough, Macker?"

Kalley said, "Why the questionnaire, Bose?"

"Just curious. I like to know how the other half of the world lives."

"I'm attached to Carter Garland. He's the Multicos big shot. If one of the subsidiaries runs into troubles with any of the unions he gets me to smooth things out."

Carlin said, "What unions do you have to deal with?"

Kalley told him.

"Jesus," sneered Carlin. "They're creampuff unions. Anyone could handle them."

"Sure," said Kalley. "Anyone who's reasonable can. I'm reasonable. So's Garland."

"That all you do, Macker."

Kalley traced circles idly on the glass in front of him. "Not quite. Whenever the subsidiaries run into any trouble that involves personnel, Garland sends me to the trouble spot."

"Still the tomahawk man, Macker?"

Kalley smiled. "Not quite, Bose. Nowadays I carry the pipe of peace more often than a tomahawk."

"Talking of tomahawk men," Carlin said, his eyes intent. "Do you see Fortune these days?"

"Only once in a while", said Kalley. "When you get out of politics you're quickly forgotten. Even by those who were closest to you. You'll find that out some day, Bose."

"I didn't forget you, Macker."

"It's nearly seven years since we saw each other, Bose. Remember our meeting in Fortune's office? When you wrote the statement for him to follow up Seborjar's historic outburst? We spoke together at the Legislature bar earlier that day. That's the last time we had a conversation."

Kalley opened a packet of cigarettes and pushed it across the desk. "You forgot me. Until today. And you didn't come now to pass the time of day with me. Why *did* you come, Bose?"

"You can help me, Macker." Carlin spread out massive hands deprecatingly. "You've heard that Seborjar and I no longer see eye to eye?"

"I read about it," said Kalley. "The newspapers gave it lots of cover."

"I couldn't stomach the set-up any longer. Seborjar reckoned we had to go carefully with the left wing. That we needed their support. It got so that I was expected to bow three times every time a Com or near-Com came within bowing distance. It sickened me."

"So Seborjar told Joe Lilley to expel you and Joe fixed it that you were expelled?"

"That's right, Macker." The big man lit his cigarette with expressionless eyes. "They expelled me for disruption."

"They couldn't have picked a better word to describe your activities over the past twenty years," Kalley said calmly.

"They didn't expel me for that, Macker. They expelled me because the Coms wanted me expelled. Because I was stating publicly that I didn't help get rid of Domineco and his gang so that the Party could be infiltrated by the Reds. That's what's happened, Macker. The Communists have given away any thought of gaining control of this country through their own political organisation. They put their boys into the Party in the hope that some day they'll own it, and through it, this country."

"They're pipe dreaming," said Kalley scornfully.

"It was a pipe dream when they sent Lenin to the Finland station," said Carlin. "But the dream materialised."

Kalley looked round the luxurious, expensively furnished office. "It can't happen here," he thought. He then wondered.

Remembering the multitude of strings that he could pull from his old office alongside Fortune's in the shabby headquarters building. Far stronger and more effective strings than he could operate from this suave, spacious room even though it was set in the giant office building of one of the country's largest corporations. "You're not alone, Bose. The Party's been expelling them in droves for years."

Carlin said, "That's where the Coms are running into trouble. They can't capture control of the Party unless the expulsions continue. But, the more expulsions, the weaker it makes the Party and the harder it becomes for the Party to win national power."

"It's deadlock," said Kalley.

"Deadlocks don't last," said Carlin impassively. "They're always broken. Sooner or later."

Kalley said, "You're talking the big stuff, Bose. The stuff I'm finished with."

Carlin said, "But I'm not."

Kalley gazed at him thoughtfully. "Maybe not, Bose. How can I help you?"

Carlin said, "You have no reason to love Seborjar?"

Kalley responded, crisply, "I have no reason to hate him, either, Bose."

Carlin said, "I figure it differently. You know why Con got rid of you. Seborjar told him to. Not in so many words. Seborjar doesn't work that way. He just kept nagging at Con. Telling him that they could never operate in double harness. Not while you were around the place. Con finally saw that there was no profit in sticking to you. You were a load round his neck. So he dumped you."

Kalley leaned back, hands behind his head.

"Just for the record, Bose. Con didn't dump me. He arranged for me to get this job. He and Garland knew each other. I was prepared to stay with Con. But he said, 'No. The dough's too good. You can't afford to pass up on this opportunity.' "

Carlin said, brutally, "Con dumped you. He had sufficient of a conscience to fix a job for you before he did. But he dumped you, Macker. At Seborjar's insistence."

Kalley shrugged. "Okay. You say he dumped me. I say he didn't.

Let it go at that. If he did dump me it was into a pleasant featherbed." He waved a hand around his office. "You must admit that, Bose."

"Okay," said Carlin. "So you hold no grudge against Con. But you must where Seborjar's concerned. That's where you can help me."

"How?" asked Kalley, impassively.

"I'm gathering some dirt on him, Macker."

Kalley's eyes were narrow. "Who are you working for, Bose?"

Carlin gave a rumble of laughter in which there was no mirth. "I'm not working for anyone, Macker. This is pleasure. I'm doing it in my own time."

"Why?" said Kalley.

"Because Seborjar's a bloody traitor, Macker." The big man's eyes blazed with anger. "Seborjar drove Domineco out of the Party because he was a traitor. But Seborjar's a traitor too. I tell you, the Party's riddled with Coms and fellow travellers. They persecute anyone who isn't a Marxist. They persecuted me. They got me expelled. And Seborjar didn't lift a finger to help me. Me. Who did his dirty work against Domineco and his gang when the going was really tough and Domineco was fighting back."

Kalley said, "You've the same unbalanced obsession about Coms as Domineco."

Carlin said, curtly, "I don't like Coms. But for a different reason. They're a lot of crooks."

"You're wrong, Comrade. Some of them are crooks. But most of them are like Seborjar. Or Domineco. Or yourself. They've convinced themselves they're right. To prove that—and to get to rule—or to keep on ruling—they'll go to any lengths. Just as your mob would if you ever had the chance. The Communists have better, more scientific techniques. They sell their line of goods without being under an obligation to adopt a moral attitude, however hypocritical, towards the customers. They don't have to seek to satisfy. They have only to make a sale. Under their system, the sale's the important thing. Once they've made it, the customer is too frightened to complain. It's easier to make a sale than to satisfy. That's one reason you don't like 'em. You envy them their freedom from the restraints that operate in a democracy. It's professional jealousy, Bose."

"You don't like me, Macker? You think I'm Fascist?"

"I think that given the opportunity you'd behave like one."

"You're wrong, Macker."

"Maybe. But I wouldn't like to see the circumstances created in this country that would test you, Bose."

"You only think that, Macker, because I'd be merciless where Coms are concerned."

"Anyone who disagreed with you would be a Com, Comrade."

"They're crooks, Macker. They've nothing to sell. Except pie in the sky and statistics to prove that if you pull your belt tighter and let some fat-arsed shyster kick you around to his heart's delight, someday, somewhere, as a result, all men'll be better off."

Kalley said, "They're dishonest. Just as all you bastards who rule or want to rule are dishonest. They tell the ruled that they are leading them along the road to human perfection. They close their eyes. They deceive themselves more passionately than they do those they rule. If they didn't, they would know that the road goes on endlessly, and with innumerable sidetracks. There's not much difference between your kind of ruler and them, Bose. They have rediscovered an old secret. That the ordinary, decent little people—the ruled—'ll suffer more patiently under the authority of religion than under anything else. They'll applaud cruelty, approve ruthlessness and accept repression without complaint. So long as it has religious justification. So they've made a religion out of the goods they sell. As they did in Germany with Nazism. In Italy with Fascism. As they're doing in Russia today.

They've made a god out of the doctrine of inevitability. With a Book of Common Prayer composed of magical symbols to prove men are inevitably happier than they were and are to become inevitably happier still." Kalley gazed in front of him. When he spoke again there was a note of mockery in his voice, "The Coms are fronting better than your team, Bose. They're fronting for a religion."

Carlin crushed his cigarette in the ashtray on the desk between them. He said contemptuously, "You know all the answers, don't you Macker? You talk big. Impressively. I bet Multicos thinks a lot of you. But what are your answers? Words. Have you ever tried to find the answers that come out of sweat? From trying to do things because you feel that they're the right things? Have you ever done anything in your life without first unloading onto someone else the responsibility for deciding what you should do and how you should do it? You worked it that way with Fortune. I bet you work it that way with Garland. You're weak, Macker. Weak as piss."

"I'm one of the ruled," said Kalley, quietly.

Carlin sneered. "That's just another way of saying you're scared. Scared of facing up to decisions that have to be made. You'd sooner sit back and pretend to greater holiness than those who have to make them and have the guts to make them—right or wrong. You need to have over you somebody to make all the decisions. In the final analysis, you're lily-livered."

Kalley drew thoughtfully at his cigarette. He was not offended and he knew Carlin did not expect him to be. It was the type of chess game that he had often played in politics with the pieces men's vanity, or fear, or pride; and the moves their reactions to their opponents' provocation. "Carlin's trying to goad me into recklessness," he thought. "And he's not a bad psychologist at that." Aloud he said, "Well, I'll hand it to you that you're not lily-livered, Bose. Not if you're willing to tangle with Seborjar. He'll run you clean out of politics. You're fighting out of your class."

"He doesn't scare me," Carlin said. "And I don't accept that anyone is out of my class. Seborjar or anyone."

"Seborjar's too big for you, Bose. Is anyone backing you?"

"Chris Tion feels as I do."

Kalley said, "You make a beautiful pair of wreckers. You and Tion. But Seborjar's bigger than both of you. Because he can build. Even if only for himself. You haven't a hope against Seborjar. You're two pygmies. Trying to knock over a giant."

"Maybe," said Carlin, coolly. "But he'll know he's been in a fight before he's finished. And you can help me, Macker."

"With some of the dirt?"

"With some of the dirt."

Kalley said, "You've come to the wrong place. Domineco is the man you should go to."

"Domineco?" The big man shook his head. "I wouldn't be found dead within smelling distance of that bastard. He hates my guts. And I hate his."

Kalley said, "Men who hate each other's guts have been known before to collaborate politically."

Carlin said, "Maybe. But we couldn't collaborate even if we were both willing. Domineco's trying to build a new party out of the people who have been expelled from the Party. He's keeping any dirt he has against Seborjar for himself, pumping it out when it suits him. He's not giving away dirt. He's collecting it."

"How about Bannion or Vittor or some of those who were expelled from the Party but didn't go with Domineco?"

"Be your age Macker. Bannion and Vittor were amateurs. You saw how quickly they dropped out of sight once they were expelled from the Party. They're small lads lost in a big world. They didn't even have sufficient brains to link up with Papa Domineco. Whatever else you might be, you and Con are professionals. But you were on the inside of everything that happened in the Party for years. I'll bet you kept a lot of stuff, Macker. You must have garbage can on garbage can full of dirt on Seborjar. And there must be some you can drop without involving yourself. Or Fortune, if you're still fool enough to want to protect him."

"Why don't you go to Con direct? Or to Hoskin? Neither has any love for Seborjar."

The big man sneered. "Hoskin's not ready to destroy Seborjar yet. He's always on the verge but something always stops him. Domineco might even now make a comeback in the Party if Seborjar's destroyed. Somebody other than Hoskin might grab the leadership. Or there's some other reason why the time is not right. Hoskin's a permanent bridesmaid. He'll never be the bride."

Kalley said, softly, "And Con?"

Carlin was brutal. "Fortune's a shell. Seborjar's allowed him to keep the trappings of power. But none of his own. He used to control a slice of votes on the Management Committee. None of them bother about him now. He's laughable. He parades round, going through all the motions. Phoning people and telling them what line the Party should be taking. Standing round at conferences and meetings, and pretending to pull strings and tell people what to do. He may have himself convinced differently. But it's make-believe. It has no connection with reality." His thick lips twisted in derision. "Con's had it, Macker. He's a has-been."

Kalley said, "Don't underestimate Con, Bose. He'll make a comeback."

Carlin said, "You've a blind spot where Con is concerned. He's punch drunk. He's seen the Party fall to pieces round his ears. He's seen Seborjar kick to fragments everything he ever believed in and yet hang on to control of the Party. Con's punchy, Macker. He's too uncertain of himself to take an independent line of his own. He's too uncertain of himself. Seborjar has them all hypnotised. Or buffaloed. Con more than anyone."

Kalley said, "The Coms gunning for him, Bose?"

"Why should they?" Carlin said impatiently. "He doesn't count any more. And while he's there he gives an air of credibility to the claim that there are no Coms in the Party. These days he's Seborjar's captive. And theirs."

Kalley was silent.

After a pause, his eyes curious and probing. Carlin asked "Doesn't he talk politics with you nowadays, Macker?"

"No," said Kalley. "We haven't really spoken for years."

Carlin said, almost idly, "I often used to wonder how much of Fortune was Fortune and how much of him was you."

"Fortune was a big man."

"You're using the correct tense, Macker. He was."

Kalley said, "He knows plenty about Seborjar. He's the man you should try for your dirt."

Carlin said, softly, "I've tried, Macker. He won't deal. But how about you?"

"Sorry, Bose. I'm out of politics. I'm staying out. I've nothing for you."

Carlin said, "You're a mug, Macker. I'm offering you a chance to get your revenge. You know I could make good use of any material you supply."

Kalley said, "Yes, I know the use you'd make of it. But my decision is final."

With reluctance Carlin got to his feet. Immense and powerful, he said, "If you change your mind get in touch with me."

Kalley said, "I won't be changing my mind." He rose and came from behind the desk. "How about a drink?"

"Thanks," Carlin nodded in agreement. Kalley pressed a button on the desk. Part of the wall swivelled open. There was a small bar inside.

"Something to be said for capitalism, Macker. You didn't have one of these gadgets in your old office." Carlin took the proffered glass of whisky and swallowed it. His Indian-black hair flopped loosely as he threw back his head.

"Has Seborjar any chance of knocking over Alex Pope, Bose? Becoming No 1 in this country?"

Carlin revolved the glass, tiny in his giant hand. "I wouldn't say so. Would you?"

Kalley's face was inscrutable. "I wouldn't know."

"I wouldn't know," mimicked Carlin. "Christ, come off it, chum. You don't have to be careful any more. You don't matter any longer. You're just an outsider looking in."

Kalley thought, "He's right. I don't have to be careful any more."

"Okay, Bose. If you want to know, I think I'll tell you." He poured drinks while he marshalled his thoughts. "Seborjar won the fight in the Party. No-one can deny that. But his victory carries within it the seeds of future defeat. He won in the narrow sense that he defeated Domineco and his other enemies within the Party. But in the wider sense he's lost. That's how I see it."

"That's doubletalk, Macker. I say he can't beat Alex Pope. But that doesn't mean he's lost. He won't have lost until he's out of the leadership. Flat on the floor, with his face kicked in."

"He's actually lost, Bose. That's if your judgment that he can never get to the top—never take the PM's job—is correct. And I think it is correct." The bottom of his glass was wet. Aimlessly Kalley made circles with it on the top of the highly polished desk. "What were his ambitions? Were they ideological?" He smiled without mirth. "Seborjar had no deep ideological convictions, Bose. You and I know that. No convictions. Only a preference for what he believed would look well in the history books. But his ambitions were almost wholly personal. I don't think he has ever been particularly interested in the Party. To him it was merely a stepping stone. To bigger things. He wanted to rule nationally, and through this rule achieve a position of power and influence in world affairs. That was his real ambition, Bose."

"You're using the past tense, Macker. Why?"

"That's how you have to consider Seborjar now. In the past tense. Time has run out on him. The Party dogs—yourself included, Bose—are quarrelling over a bone that has no meat. While the Party has Seborjar as Leader there'll be no meat on the bone. Take a look at his record since the blowup. In seven years, he's led the Party to electoral disaster after electoral disaster. It's weaker now than it's ever been. State after State that we had held for years has thrown Party administrations out on the street. Alex Pope's followers have the meat — the nice, fat jobs. The Party is like a pack of starving animals. It's living on internal cannibalism. And a pack, however big, can feed itself that way only for a limited period. In short, the pack just wont exist any more. Seborjar can't carry on much longer."

Carlin reached across for the bottle. He filled his glass.

"You're losing your punch, Macker. You're contradicting yourself. A few minutes ago you told me Chris and I hadn't a hope against Seborjar. He was the giant. We were pygmies. Now you say Seborjar is on the way out."

Kalley stared at his glass: "All men are on the way out. From the day they're born."

Carlin sneered. "Don't give me philosophical rubbish."

"Okay, Bose. But it won't be Chris or you who'll down Seborjar. It'll be events. If I'm any judge he's still big and clever and ruthless enough to beat you two or any combination that can be built up against him within the Party. All he has to do is keep the dogs quarrelling over the meatless bone. While they're quarrelling he's safe. He's shrewd enough to see that. And to be able to keep 'em quarrelling for quite a bit yet. If it suits him." He paused deliberately to give his next words extra emphasis. "But it mightn't suit him to keep 'em fighting. Have you thought of that?

Bose's huge hand, carrying the glass to his mouth, stopped in mid air. He put down the glass and lit a cigarette.

"You're not suggesting that he'd get out voluntarily. I know the rumour that's current in the Party. That a group of the big boys in the Party have put their heads together. That they've persuaded one of the States which the Party still controls to put Seborjar up for some prestigious international appointment. That to get him out of the way they're prepared to finangle him into some big-shot position that gives him a chance of going down in history. That's what Seborjar lives for—his name in the history books. And Seborjar's prepared to move out if they get it for him." He thrust his big head forward almost aggressively. "Don't tell me you believe that crap, Macker."

Kalley said, "I know nothing. But it could be true."

Carlin said, "You've lost more than your punch, Macker. You've gone soft in the head. You get plum jobs on the way up. When you're a threat to someone higher up. Not when you're on the way down."

Kalley said, maliciously, "I can see why you'll never go high in the Party, Bose. You think in black and white. Hasn't it occurred to you that you get plums when powerful men who want you out of the way, but who are not strong enough to push you out immediately, are prepared to pay a price to get you out of the way quickly?"

Carlin's eyes turned thoughtful. "Men like who, Macker?"

Kalley was enjoying himself as he hadn't done for years. "Men like Tenper who by some miracle of survival still rules his State. Tenper survived the last elections in his State only by the skin of his teeth. He knows the voters weren't against him. They weren't even against the Party. They were against Seborjar."

Kalley sipped at his glass. "Even Tenper—good as he is—can't keep in power forever. No. Seborjar is the National Leader. I'll bet Tenper would pay a steep price to get rid of Seborjar. Even if the price is to help finangle a man whom he hates and distrusts into some plum job."

Carlin sat silent for a while, nursing his drink. "I agree that that northern slug'd do anything to save his political hide. But I can't see Seborjar getting out voluntarily. His vanity wouldn't let him. He knows what people would say. That Alex Pope and Domineco between them had run him out of politics. He couldn't take that. His pride wouldn't let him."

Kalley said, "Do you believe he cares anything about what you or others think? He's interested only in what history will say about him. He's gambling. Just as he did when he split the Party. If he keeps on in his present job, events or age or death'll beat him. He'll be out and his public record'll show that he went out without ever getting the things he wanted. Alex Pope's job. World stature. But if he shifts from politics into another, international sphere, history may accept him as a success. It may look that way to the historians. He won't have been forced out of the leadership. It could appear as though he got what he wanted."

"Nobody thinks that way," said Carlin.

"Big men like Seborjar do," said Kalley. "His horizons are limitless. If circumstances and his own doggedness had ever given him the opportunity, he would have left his mark on world history. He thinks he's a great man, Bose—very great."

"Great", said Carlin, curtly. "He's mad."

Kalley laughed. "In politics, greatness and madness are not mutually exclusive."

Carlin said, impatiently, "Forget that nonsense about Seborjar going out voluntarily. It won't happen. He's trapped this time, Macker. In a net of his own making. He can't beat Alex Pope unless he's backed by a united Party. The Party's disunited. Has been since the blowup. He can't suborn Domineco's followers. He's tried that. They're unforgiving. And he can't make peace with Domineco over their heads. His own left wing backers'd break with him if he did."

Kalley said, "He's been in traps before. And got out of them. I'll be interested to see whether you can spring it, Bose. Personally, I don't think you're big enough."

Carlin poured another drink. He said contemptuously, "You always had a weakness for the bastard, Macker."

Kalley felt the warmth of the whisky within him. "You wouldn't understand, Bose. You're small time."

Carlin said with genuine amusement, "Are you trying to insult me, Macker? Or is that the liquor talking? The fact is, your hero's on the skids, Macker."

Kalley said, "He's not my hero. Never was. But I've seen him on the skids before. And he's still there, Bose. On his feet. And on top."

Carlin said, "He can't last forever."

Kalley shook his head. "You're wrong, Bose." There was no flippancy in his voice, only gravity. "He's immortal, unconquerable. Indestructible. As long as there are men with passions to be fed, hates to be fanned and hopes to be exploited. Seborjar's immortal in the sense that there are always Seborjars. There always will be. Only the names differ. I'll admit you rarely see them as good as this one. Most have some weakness. They drink. Or have a mistress other than politics. Or they worry about what their fellow men think about them. Or the verdict of history. Instead of striving like Seborjar for a place in history whatever the verdict. They may even have a few friends whom they like and whose trust they want to keep. Or they may occasionally have doubts about their infallibility. Or have the remnants of a conscience that keeps them awake once in a while worrying in the dark hours of the night about what they are doing. Few politicians have Kaye's qualities.

Seborjar's big-time, Bose. If Machiavelli were alive today he'd rewrite *The Prince* with Seborjar as his model of the man of limitless ambition with the qualities to achieve anything."

"You're a contradictory bastard, Macker. Sometimes I'm convinced that you somehow love the Big Man. And sometimes I think you loathe him."

Kalley picked up the bottle and poured fresh drinks. "If ever you find out which is correct, Bose, let me know. I'd be interested to find out myself."

Carlin said, "He's a mug. A lucky mug. If he hadn't been lucky, he'd never have become Party Leader. How did he get there?"

"By tenacity, energy and determination. And because of his unshakeable belief that he is a man of destiny. That's how he got to be Party Leader. But how does he hold on to the leadership, Bose? That task alone would have killed any ordinary man. Anyone else would have died with a broken heart. Perhaps he hasn't got a heart. Maybe it's like his conscience—mostly missing."

"Most men don't really want to get into the big-time," continued Kalley. "They want to be comfortable. Well-fed, well-housed, and not overworked. But after that, they want to live happily with their wives and their kids and their gardens. They are not under some inner compulsion to crack the whip over their fellows' backs. They're prepared to leave it to others to rule. They don't particularly want to."

"Give 'em the chance and they'd leap at it," Carlin Replied.

"I was given the chance and I didn't leap at it," said Kalley.

"You're a sucker," said Carlin who poured more whisky.

Kalley said, "I'm getting a glow up, Bose. You shrink with each drink we have. A couple more and I'll reckon you're a dwarf. Don't antagonise me."

Carlin said, "I'll tell you why you didn't go into the big-time. You didn't have the guts. And because Seborjar has the guts—and I don't deny that he had to go out after the things he wanted—you are in awe of him. But I'm not."

"That's because you're spiritually closer to him than I am, Bose. You're a ruler—a would-be one."

Carlin said stubbornly, "He's not so terribly big, Macker. There's been others."

"That's your jealousy speaking, Bose. Not your judgment." He refilled his glass.

"I've often thought that jealousy—if Stalin hadn't intrigued Trotsky out of the Party he'd never have had supreme power—and Stalin knowing it was the real driving force, then that simple act of jealousy changed the entire course of the Russian Revolution. And yet we persist with the myth that it is always impersonal forces, not the personality of men, which shape great events."

"What are you proving, Macker?"

"I'm not proving anything. I'm just thinking aloud."

"You're drunk."

"I'm not drunk," said Kalley. He extended his hand. "Steady as a rock," he said. "I'm just happy to see you, Bose. And I don't even like you. Just as you don't like me."

Carlin said, "We ought to drink to that, Macker."

Kalley said, "Not to that, Bose. It's too hackneyed. There are no friends in politics. Only associates and acquaintances." He poured out fresh drinks. "Let's drink to something unique. To Seborjar. The biggest of them all."

Carlin said, "All right. To the biggest bastard of them all. Kaye Seborjar. A prince among bastards." He emptied his glass in a swallow. He said without conviction, "I suppose I ought to get moving."

Kalley said, "Not yet, Bose. Just one more drink."

Carlin said with a fatalistic gesture. "Okay. One more."

Kalley found that he was anxious that Carlin should not leave. He was avid for the news that did not appear in the newspapers or learned publications but was whispered about in the back alleyways of politics. The men stayed, drinking or talking for a long time. Occasionally Kalley's phone rang and he answered it. But each time he gestured for Carlin to stay. When his secretary came in with letters he signed them hastily and told her that she could leave.

It was nearly dark when Carlin drained his glass with an air of finality and said, "I'll have to get going, Macker."

"I suppose so, Bose."

With a perception that Kalley had not expected he said, "You miss it, don't you, Macker?"

Kalley said, "It's a virus, Bose."

Carlin said, "It's a living, Macker. That's all."

Kalley said sharply, "It's a way of life, Bose. An exciting way of life. It's rotten and corrupting. There is no friendship in it and little loyalty. You learn to lie to yourself more easily than you do to others. You revile it and tell yourself you hate it. But, when you're out of it, you miss it. Those who have once drunk deeply of its muddy waters don't forget it. They remember the taste. They never find anything else to give them the same kick."

Carlin said, slyly, despite the huge amount of alcohol he had consumed, "You can still get the kick, Macker. By giving me what dirt you have on Seborjar."

Kalley said, "I swore I'd never play God. That I'd leave that to the Seborjars, the Fortunes, the Dominecos and the rest. I'm not going back on that, Bose."

After Carlin had gone, Kalley leaned back and closed his eyes.

He thought of Seborjar, human, with all the imperfections, defects and shortcomings that living men possessed. Did Seborjar himself know what he was thinking? Or was he living from hour to hour, rationalising the happenings about him to fit into a larger pattern?

He thought of Fortune and the politician he had been. Assured and in control. Which was Fortune? That man? Or the one Carlin described playing like a child with imagined toys—the power he had lost, the influence that he no longer had, and the strings that he could no longer pull.

"Well, I'm out of it now," Kalley thought, with some sadness.

He stood up and clicked the switch. The lights went out behind him.

It was dark outside. Across the street a newspaper poster beckoned. A street light illuminated the bold lettering. It read *'Political bombshell: Seborjar accepts new post.'*

Kalley bought a paper. What did this mean? For Domineco who had built his life around two hates—hatred of Communism and of Seborjar? For Fortune, play-acting, pretending to wield power that was broken and lost? For Lilley the corrupter, who wanted to be more than to be a rich man? For Hoskin, passionate but self-contained, who lived only to fill the shoes now vacant? For Payten? For Tenper? For Tion? For the host of others, venal, honest, corrupt, and decent, who collectively made up the Party? What did it mean for the Party itself?

Kalley thought, "I'll phone Con." He walked back across the street. At Multicos' huge entrance he stopped and lit another cigarette.

Then he abruptly turned away. He strode out into the anonymous darkness and into the loneliness that he knew comes to all men with imagination who have been part of politics and no longer are—a loneliness that even the two Annes would never completely fill. Kalley knew deep inside that, for such as he, politics had the eternal fascination of problems that are never really solved.

THE END

Postscript

by Laurie Oakes

When Alan Reid retired in 1985 after nearly 50 years in the Federal Parliamentary Press Gallery, MPs interrupted Question Time to give him a standing ovation. It was an acknowledgement that the wily pressman, nicknamed the Red Fox, was as much part of the story of Australian politics as the politicians he had covered. No other political journalist has exercised such influence.

Reid was a newsbreaker *extraordinaire*, noted particularly for the detail and accuracy of information leaked to him from within the Labor Party. It was Reid, for example, who lifted the lid on what he termed the "Svengali-like" role of B. A. Santamaria, starting the process that led to the great Labor split of the mid-1950s. His devastating 1963 portrayal of Labor's Parliamentary leaders waiting outside a Canberra hotel late at night for instructions from the "faceless men" of the national conference drove Gough Whitlam's push for party reform.

Reid's heavy focus on Labor affairs undoubtedly served a proprietorial agenda, but also reflected his belief that Labor was "the dynamic of Australian politics" and therefore more interesting than the Liberal Party. When he felt the urge, however, he had the contacts to expose intrigue and dirty deeds on the Coalition side as well, as he showed in his books and articles on the Liberal Party leadership drama following Harold Holt's death and the subsequent destruction of John Gorton's prime ministership.

The picture of politics and politicians that emerges from *The Bandar-Log: A Labor Story of the 1950s* is extraordinarily bleak. There is no room for principle. The whole business is irredeemably filthy and disgusting—a sewer. As Reid sees it, people involved in politics cannot help but be corrupt. Even those who begin with high principles are inevitably corroded and eaten away.

Reid used to pretend to be aloof from this world. He would tell young journalists arriving in Canberra: "Just because you work in the zoo doesn't mean you have to get close to the animals." But in fact he was one of the animals himself. He was not just an observer and a chronicler but, at times, also a behind-the-scenes participant in the events that were the subject of his journalism.

Les Carlyon has written that Reid's life "reminds us that journalism can be as morally hazardous as politics". This is what makes him such a fascinating, controversial and—yes—important figure in our political and media history. That is why the publication of Alan Reid's hitherto suppressed novel is so welcome.

Laurie Oakes, Award-winning, long-serving Canberra-based political journalist.

Here are the main characters

in Alan Reid's hitherto unpublished novel

A Labor Story of the 1950s: The Bandar Log.

1. Kaye Seborjar ("Cesare Borgia") = Dr H. V. Evatt
2. Carr Domineco = B. A. (Bob) Santamaria
3. Con Fortune = A. A. (Arthur) Calwell (with traces of Victorian Senator P. J. Kennelly)
4. Kent Kerstey = Dr J. W. (John) Burton
5. Gilly Hoskin = NSW federal Labor firebrand E. J. (Eddie) Ward
6. Alex Pope = R. G. Menzies
7. Tom Bannion = In part based on a young Gough Whitlam
8. Macker Kalley ("Machiavelli") = Alan Reid (the author)

Professor Ross Fitzgerald AM writes a regular column for the *Weekend Australian*, reviews for the *Sydney Morning Herald* and the *Weekend Australian* and regularly appears on ABC Radio, the Alan Jones Show, ABCTV, Sky News and Channel 7.

Emeritus Professor of History and Politics at Griffith University, Professor Fitzgerald has published 37 books, spanning fiction and non-fiction, including his memoir *My Name is Ross: An Alcoholic's Journey*, which is available as an e-Book and a Talking Book with Vision Australia. Professor Fitzgerald is the co-author, with Stephen Holt, of *Alan ('The Red Fox') Reid*, published in 2010 by NewSouth Books, Sydney, which was shortlisted for the 2011 National Biography Award.

* * * * *

Alan Reid (1914-1987) was one of the most influential political journalists in twentieth century Australia. Working for most of his long career as Canberra correspondent for the *Daily Telegraph*, Reid not only reported key events in Australian politics, but from time to time actively participated in them. Apart from his hitherto suppressed novel *The Bandar Log: A Labor Story of the 1950s* Alan Reid also wrote three major works of non-fiction: *The Power Struggle*, published in 1969, *The Gorton Experiment*, published in 1971 and *The Whitlam Venture*, published in 1976.